STEPHANIE FAZIO

THE FORSAKEN'S CHOICE

The Fount Book 2

Syafant Press

Syafant Press

New York, New York

Cover designed by Keith Tarrier

This book is a work of fiction. Names, characters, places, and incidents either are the product of the author's imagination or are used fictionally, and any resemblance to actual persons, living or dead, business establishments, events, or locales is entirely coincidental.

Stephanie Fazio

Visit www.StephanieFazio.com

Printed in the United States of America
First Printing: April 2020

Library of Congress Control Number: 2020905329

ISBN 978-1-951572-01-3

To Mom, for always being my champion

PROLOGUE

2000 YEARS EARLIER

On a cold mountaintop, with the gods as their only witnesses, they fought.

Her weapon was her mind. His was his fists. Both were evenly matched and equally ferocious.

The Celestial and the Supernal—neither god nor human—battled for their people and for themselves.

No blood was spilled, since the beings' veins ran with something far more powerful: pure Source. It was part of their essence, just like it was part of the world they were made to guard and protect. As they rained down blows on each other, Source leaked from their wounds. The mountainside was already slick with it.

"Your Chosen are weak of body," the Supernal snarled. "They are greedy, taking whatever they can just to taste power."

A crack of thunder echoed his words.

"And yours are weak of spirit." The Celestial pushed back her opponent with another slice from the talons of her mind. "They seek only to dominate. They are barbarians."

The Supernal's fist, tougher than any metal and pulsing with magic, slammed into the Celestial.

A wheeze of air made it out of her before she collapsed in a drift of snow.

The Supernal circled the other being.

He towered over her. His long, golden hair was tinged with the blue of his magic. His black eyes, rimmed with gold, fixed on the Celestial.

"The gods care nothing for your beloved Chosen," the Supernal taunted. "I will banish them from existence. There will be none to mourn their passing."

"The Chosen are mine protect," the Celestial hissed. She rose to her feet. "Mine to defend." An unnatural glow took hold of her ebony skin. Her eyes became pools of pure silver light. "Mine to love."

Both beings were lifted off the mountain's summit by the force of her fury. They hung above the clouds, suspended, as their ages-long battle raged.

The Supernal struck out. His fist met nothing but frosty air.

The Celestial was illuminated as silver flames spilled from her very being. They didn't burn her. They were of her.

The air rippled, and the flames winked out of existence as the Celestial gathered her strength. The Supernal raised his fists, but it was too late.

A tremendous burst of power shot toward him.

The Supernal staggered back.

The Celestial raised her hands to the heavens, and raw magic flooded her system. When she spoke, her voice cut through the wind and thunderclaps.

"Your people will be bereft of guidance. There will be no one to deliver their pleas to the gods. They will be Forsaken."

The Supernal tried to retaliate, but the Celestial showed him no mercy. She hurled another wave of power at him. He cried out.

The Supernal, one of the two strongest beings in all the worlds, fell back to the mountain's summit on his knees. The blue light illuminating his fists began to dim.

"Surrender!" the Celestial shrieked. She was filled to the brim with the gods' strength.

"My people will avenge me," the Supernal choked.

The Celestial laughed. The sound was beautiful and terrible. Her voice was louder than the howling wind when she called, "Your people are leaderless."

The air crackled with the electric heat of magic. Both beings were silent and unmoving, but their struggle continued. The battle was fought in their minds, with power so old and terrible none but the gods could comprehend it.

Their screams came in unison—the Supernal's of defeat, and the Celestial's of victory.

A ball of light and power, brighter and hotter than any sun, hovered just above the Supernal's head. He looked up and saw it. Then, he collapsed in an unconscious heap.

Still gasping for breath, and with rivulets of Source leaching from her body, the Celestial pulled out the obsidian stone she had carried for millennia in anticipation of this moment. Trembling from exhaustion and the amount of strength needed to complete the task, the Celestial steadied her hand. She squeezed her eyes shut.

The ball of power hovering over the Supernal was sucked into the obsidian stone. It glowed bright blue before settling back to its original color.

The stone scorched the Celestial's palm and tore through her insides. She could not survive contact with the enemy's power for long.

"You have been defeated," the Celestial told the unconscious Supernal in a hoarse voice. "I banish you to the mortal world. You will live for an eternity, devoid of your strength and your people."

With her remaining strength, the Celestial opened a portal between the two worlds.

A swirling vortex dropped down from the sky. An unnatural wind swept the Celestial's black locks across her face. She shielded her face from the flying bits of ice and rock as she watched the Supernal's body lift into the air.

His limp body hovered. The only part of him that moved was his long, golden hair as it whipped in the wind. His eyes cracked open just before the edge of the vortex made contact with his body.

The Supernal's shriek of pain and fury was dampened by the effect of the portal. He writhed and reached for a power that was no longer a part of him.

The Celestial stood on the mountain's summit, with the obsidian stone still burning a hole through her hand, as the Supernal cursed her name. She watched until he was swallowed up into the void.

CHAPTER 1

ADDY

The Texas heat smacked Addy in the face the moment she stepped off the plane. Her T-shirt fused to her sweaty skin. The air even smelled hot, like she was entering a furnace. As she walked down the stairs of Tol's plane and onto the tarmac at the Corpus Christi Airport, she tried to shield her face from the brutal Texas sun. Her hair was red enough. There was no need to add lobster-burned skin to complete the look, thank you very much.

Private planes got private airstrips and a welcoming committee, apparently. Airport people wearing those orange-and-yellow reflective vests were milling around and doing whatever airport people did when a private plane arrived. Addy ignored all of them. She raced to the edge of the tarmac where Aunt Meredith was waiting.

Addy threw herself into her aunt's waiting arms. The force of her hug sent Aunt Meredith's cowboy hat flying off her head. Despite being in her late fifties, Aunt Meredith squeezed Addy until her ribs compressed.

Aunt Meredith's tanned, sun-wrinkled face wavered in and out of focus as Addy blinked through her tears. She had thought she was all cried out, but the sight of her aunt, who looked so much like her mom, brought the water works right back to life.

Aunt Meredith's arms fell away from Addy, but it was only to make room for Livy. Addy wrapped one of her arms around her twin and the other around her aunt. They were all crying and enveloping each other in a three-way hug.

"Oh, my girls," Aunt Meredith said when they finally broke apart. "Welcome home."

It wasn't home, but it was the closest Addy and Livy had after what had happened to the rest of their family. Addy and Livy had been babies when their parents moved away from Texas. Neither one of them remembered any home aside from their upstate New York corn farm.

Addy had only recently learned about the reason for her parents' paranoia and the sheltered life she and her sisters had led. She had discovered Sue and Gary Deerborn weren't her birth parents, and that she was the Forsaken general's daughter.

A familiar anger tightened Addy's chest. If only her parents had told her the truth. If only she had known, maybe she could have prevented….

"Are you going to introduce us, Addy?"

Tol's black velvet voice banished her bitter thoughts. Addy stepped back, making room for the others to join their little circle.

"Aunt Meredith, this is—"

The prince of a magical race from another world. The love of my life.
The man destined to blood marry my sister.

"—Tol."

Raising an eyebrow at her, like he understood all the thoughts racing through her head, Tol stepped forward and took Aunt Meredith's hand.

"It's a pleasure to finally meet you," Tol said.

His English accent made his polite words downright swoon-worthy. Not that Addy was the swooning type…but for Tol, she could make an exception.

"Aren't ya'll the most beautiful men I've ever seen." Aunt Meredith's gaze moved from Tol, to Erikir, to Gerth. She took in their bronze skin, black hair, and dark eyes. Aunt Meredith couldn't even see the golden Haze surrounding all of them, which only added to their unearthly good looks.

"I don't know about my associates, but I prefer suave and debonair," Gerth said, grinning as he shook Aunt Meredith's hand.

Gerth's black hair was falling out of its messy pony tail. His shirt had come untucked on one side of his baggy jeans. He was a foot shorter than Tol and Addy, and he had to tip his head up to meet their gazes. Unlike Erikir, Gerth's dark eyes shone with mischief and good humor.

Gerth had been Tol's best friend since they were kids, and it had taken Addy about two seconds to understand why. Brilliant didn't even begin to describe Gerth. He was also funny and one of the most loyal people Addy had ever met. She was grateful he was with them now.

Erikir scowled at Gerth before giving Aunt Meredith's hand a quick shake. He crossed his arms and stepped back, looking stiff and uncomfortable. His mouth was pressed in a disapproving line.

Addy wasn't sure if Erikir's bad mood was something that she brought out, or if it was just a state of being for Tol's cousin. Addy suspected the latter.

To say Addy wasn't a fan of Erikir would be the understatement of the century. In the limited time she'd known him, Erikir had mocked Tol's prosthetic arm, claimed he would make a better prince of the Chosen, and scoffed at Addy's Forsaken fighting abilities. In turn, Addy had dangled Erikir over a cliff and threatened to drop him.

"Hiya, sweet boy," Aunt Meredith said to Fred.

It was hard to tell which one of them was the bear in their bear hug, since they both somehow managed to engulf the other.

Addy felt a sharp pang of guilt at the thought of everything her best friend was giving up to be here now.

With Mr. Brown's health failing from Multiple Sclerosis, Fred had taken over the lion's share of the farm work. He also ran a side business of building furniture and fixing any piece of machinery the residents of Nowell, New York could dig out of their garages. Both parts of Fred's business were suffering because he was here to help her.

"Come on, ya'll." Aunt Meredith looped one arm through Addy's and the other through Livy's. "Let's get into the air conditioning before you fry up like green tomatoes."

She directed the guys to a cab after shoving a wad of cash into Fred's unwilling hand. She steered Addy and Livy to her beat-up old truck. The engine had barely roared to life before Aunt Meredith said, "Alright, girls. Tell me what in the Sam Hill is going on."

Addy and Livy had a brief, silent exchange. Livy put a finger on her nose, which meant *not it*. Addy stuck her tongue out in an act of petty revenge.

"We need to get some supplies together in the next couple of days," Addy began. "Then, Livy's going to re-open the portal between the two worlds so we can go searching for the Celestial—she's this godlike being who gave all her powers to Livy—and try and get her to shift those powers to me. Then, Tol and I are going to use those powers together in a…um, ritual…to give his people back their immortality and save their ruined world."

Then, she gave her aunt a quick summary of the Chosen and Forsaken. When she was finished, Addy sat back against the seat and fanned herself.

Aunt Meredith scruffed her short, brown-and-gray hair. It stuck straight up before she replaced her cowboy hat. She let out a long, whistling breath.

"That was a good summary," Livy said from the backseat. "You get an A for conciseness. Maybe a C- for clarity."

Addy turned and grinned at her twin sister.

Livy had been quiet for most of the plane ride from London to Texas, and Addy could only imagine how crazy all of this must be for her. It had only been four days since they'd rescued Livy from the Forsaken who had imprisoned her in an Alaskan Air Force Base. After they broke her out, they'd discovered that Livy, and not Addy, was the Fount whose abilities made her the savior of Tol's race.

Still, Livy was just as calm, cool, and collected as ever. She even looked put together, with her beautiful brown curls swept back in a neat ponytail. There wasn't so much as a hint of sweat on her flawless skin. Addy, on the other hand, was daydreaming about a cold shower and another round of deodorant.

"Two worlds? Celestial?" Aunt Meredith gave Addy a suspicious look before turning her attention back on the road. "Don't tell me you girls have been getting into that liberal propaganda again."

Addy and Livy exchanged an eye roll.

"*The New York Times* isn't liberal propaganda," Livy told Aunt Meredith patiently.

"And everything I just told you is real," Addy added.

Aunt Meredith opened and closed her mouth twice. She looked a little like a fish.

"I know, right?" Addy laughed a little. "I thought I was going crazy at first when Tol told me everything."

"I didn't believe your parents." Aunt Meredith's voice came out choked, and Addy realized it was because her aunt was crying.

"Aunt Mer—"

"Maybe if I'd listened, I could have done something. Maybe I could have saved them."

"Don't," Addy and Livy said at the same time.

Her aunt's guilt tore at Addy's heart, because it was the same guilt she lived with every single day. She didn't want anyone else she loved to feel that kind of pain.

"It's the Forsaken general's fault for ordering their deaths," Addy said, using the argument Tol gave her every time she started blaming herself. "And I'm going to make sure she pays."

They all sat in silence for a few minutes, lost in their own thoughts.

Aunt Meredith dabbed her eyes with her sleeve. "Well, you bet your bottom dollar I have a few questions, but we can talk about everything more once you've eaten and gotten some shut-eye. But there is one thing I'd like cleared up now." She took her eyes off the road long enough to glance at Addy. She raised one graying eyebrow.

"What?" Addy asked.

"Pray tell, what kind of ritual involves having six carats' worth of precious stones on your ring finger, hmm?"

"Oh."

Addy was still having trouble wrapping her head around the idea of being married by her nineteenth birthday. Not just married, she reminded herself. *Blood married.*

If it was with anyone except Tol, she would have run screaming in the opposite direction. Or sliced the man up with her trusty garden shears. Into tiny pieces.

Addy patted the side pocket of her duffel, comforted by the outline of her weapon. She knew most people would have preferred a sword or gun, but—the logistics of obtaining those kinds of weapons aside—Addy trusted her garden shears. They didn't glow blue like the Forsaken weapons that had been forged on Vitaquias, but it didn't matter. Addy had Source in her blood. That strength made her shears plenty lethal. They'd never failed to protect her.

Plus, there would be a poetic kind of justice in killing her family's murderers with an object that had belonged to them.

"Addy and Tol are perfect for each other," Livy said, coming to the rescue. "And he's crazy about Addy."

"Well, he's better looking than any man I've ever seen, I'll give him that," Aunt Meredith said. "But why the rush, pumpkin?"

So, Addy gave her aunt the abridged explanation of the blood marriage. She explained how it would telepathically link her and Tol for eternity and generate the power needed to restore an entire world.

Addy couldn't let herself think about what would happen if they failed…if Livy remained the Fount and the only way for Tol to save his race was through blood marrying her instead of Addy….

They couldn't fail. That's all there was to it.

Aunt Meredith frowned. "That's a whole lotta pressure for two young people."

"Don't I know it." Addy wiped sweat off her forehead with the hem of her T-shirt.

"That's why you have all of us," Livy reminded her, reaching forward and giving Addy's arm a comforting squeeze. "We'll help you in any way we can."

Addy's heart swelled with gratitude. Growing up, Livy had always known exactly what to say to make Addy feel better. It was no different now.

Addy didn't care what anyone said or how much she looked like the Forsaken general. Livy was her twin in every way that mattered.

They passed the rest of the drive with easy chit chat, just like they used to when Aunt Meredith came to New York to visit. No one talked about how everything was different now, even though Addy knew it was what they were all thinking.

Aunt Meredith turned off the empty road and onto a long, gravel driveway. Cows on either side of the wooden fence snuffed the dusty ground for hidden morsels of grass. Addy stared out at the flat landscape. She took in the longhorn cattle and prickly pear cacti as she waited for some sense of familiarity. It didn't come.

She hadn't been here since she was a baby, but some part of her had been hoping she would remember it. Addy could tell from the expression on her twin's face that Livy didn't have any memory of this place, either.

Aunt Meredith parked the truck under a beautiful old oak tree next to the wooden ranch-style house. In the open front yard, which was brown and desert-looking compared to the lush New York grass she'd grown up with, there was a fire pit and a picnic table. Addy thought she caught the smell of an old campfire in the air. Tiny mason jar lights had been strung across the scrubby trees that bordered the front yard. Addy could only imagine how cool this place would look at night.

The taxi had beaten them to the house, and the guys were waiting in the shade underneath the oak tree. All of them except Tol had stripped down to their undershirts. Even though it was sweltering, Tol kept his long-sleeved shirt in place. Addy knew it was because of his prosthesis that, even among friends and family, he wouldn't want to show more than he had to. It infuriated Addy that people had made him ashamed of something that, as far as she was concerned, was totally badass.

She caught Tol's eye and managed a wink before Aunt Meredith put one arm around Addy's waist and the other around Livy's and led them to the house. The front porch was long and shaded, and the breeze passing through it made the Texas heat bearable. There was a swinging bench on one side of the porch and four wicker chairs on the other. Addy could picture her aunt sitting out here with a sweating glass of iced tea and one of her crossword puzzles as she watched the cattle graze.

The inside was rustic and inviting. Everything was wood—exposed wood beams, polished wood floors, and wood walls. The open family room had two comfy-looking leather couches, end tables covered with framed photographs of the Deerborns, ornate lamps, and bowls overflowing with candy. Basil, chives, and rosemary grew in wooden planters perched on the window sills. The whole place smelled like wood polish and leather. It wasn't her home, and yet, Addy felt right at home.

Tol picked up a framed photograph on the mantle and grinned.

"What?" Addy asked.

In answer, he held it up.

Toddler-Addy was sitting in a high chair, diapered, shirtless, and with her wispy red hair askew. Something green and sticky-looking was smeared all over her face.

"Addy and Livy's first birthday," Aunt Meredith said, smiling at the photo. "Their favorite color was green, so that was the theme of the whole birthday. Sue had stirred green food coloring into the icing of their cake, and she even had the idea of dying the kiddie pool green—"

Aunt Meredith stopped. Her smile faded. Addy knew exactly what was going through her aunt's mind, because it was the same thing going through Addy's.

Her mom, Aunt Meredith's sister, was dead.

It still seemed so impossible. A hundred times a day, Addy caught herself thinking about what her parents and younger sisters would say about what she was doing, before remembering they were gone.

The Forsaken had killed them in their search for Addy, and they'd done it under the orders of Addy's birth mother—the Forsaken general.

Tol put the photo down and came to stand next to Addy. He rested his hand on the small of her back. His silent presence was a comfort, and Addy leaned into his touch.

Aunt Meredith busied herself in the kitchen. A few minutes later, they were all sitting in the family room with mason jar glasses full of homemade lemonade. For a few minutes, the only sounds were the clinking of ice cubes in their glasses and the wind chimes hanging on the front porch. Addy let the comfy couch swallow her up as she tilted her head from side to side, letting the air conditioning work its magic on the back of her neck.

Tol was the first to speak.

"Meredith, there's something you need to know." He glanced at Addy before continuing. "There are people from my world hunting us. We'll do everything we can to keep you safe, but—"

Aunt Meredith pffed and waved away his concern. "Being the town weirdo isn't as fulfilling as it used to be. I'm ready for a new adventure."

"Yeah, if you call an adventure babysitting a lovesick prince who's going to get us all killed," Erikir muttered.

"Don't be a git," Gerth said, causing the other boy's scowl to turn into a death glare. If they could use their Source to Influence each other, Addy was sure the two of them would be going at it by now.

"I'm not sure you understand," Tol said to Aunt Meredith. "These people are warriors. It's all they know, and they're very good at what they do."

Fred glanced up at the ceiling and around the open floor plan. Addy knew that look. It was the look he got whenever some especially challenging repair was dropped off at his garage under the "We Fix Everything" sign. For Fred, challenging meant that it might take him a whole five minutes to figure out the problem and how to repair it.

"If you've got some tools, I can rig you up some booby traps," Fred told Aunt Meredith. "At least that'll slow down anyone tryin' to get in here."

"Tools are in the shed," Aunt Meredith said with a shrug. "But I don't think any of that's necessary. I have my shotgun if any of these folks start getting too frisky."

Tol shook his head. "A shotgun won't help against these people."

Aunt Meredith took a long swig of her lemonade. "That's what they'll think, too. Right before I blow a hole in their chests."

CHAPTER 2

TOL

The girls were in town gathering the supplies Gerth had listed out. Fred was hard at work with a nail gun and a drill. The rest of them gathered around the coffee table and planned.

Gerth had brought every map of Vitaquias the Chosen had, which turned out to be a lot. He also had dusty tomes full of information about the Celestial. As their self-proclaimed master strategist, Gerth had lists, spreadsheets, and diagrams that documented everything from where the portal would deposit them on Vitaquias, to the most likely place they'd find the Celestial…if she was even still alive.

Gran, who claimed to talk to her dead husband and was suspected of insanity by most of the Chosen, had been the one to suggest that the Celestial might be able to help. Tol had been desperate enough to cling to this one piece of hope, since it was his last chance at spending eternity with the woman he loved…rather than her sister. But the closer it came to actually attempting this mad plan, the more Tol thought he was just kidding himself.

Still, he had to try.

While Gerth and Erikir argued about the time difference between Earth and Vitaquias, Tol slipped into one of the guest bedrooms and shut the door. He pulled out the high-security, encrypted cell phone he'd gotten to replace his old one and dialed his father's number. When it went to voicemail, he tried his mum's.

No answer.

He'd left each of his parents half a dozen messages, but neither of them had called him back. *Were they screening his calls? Were they in trouble?* Tol raked a hand through his hair as guilt gnawed at his insides.

He'd left the manor a week ago. It had been on fire, and there'd been an angry mob coming for him and Addy. In a jealous rage, Nira had told everyone that Tol had found the Fount but wasn't going through with the blood marriage. Then, Tol and his parents had disappeared to go rescue Addy's sister.

Now, his parents were sorting out the disaster he'd created. And he had no idea what was going on.

"No luck, mate?" Gerth asked when Tol came out of the bedroom.

It didn't surprise Tol that Gerth knew exactly who he'd been calling. Not only was Gerth the most brilliant among a race known for the power of their minds, he knew Tol better than just about anyone alive.

Tol shook his head.

Erikir looked up from the books spread out on the coffee table.

"Can you blame them for ignoring you?" he asked Tol.

"Shove off," Gerth said without looking up from the list he was making.

"No." Tol stood to his full height and glared down at Erikir. "Go on. Say what you have to say."

Erikir got to his feet. "If you just did what needed to be done, we wouldn't be going on this suicide mission. And the rest of our people wouldn't be on death's door."

Tol didn't respond, because he knew Erikir was right.

"We've been through this," Gerth said, coming to Tol's defense.

"If I was prince of the Chosen," Erikir continued, "I wouldn't put my own happiness above the survival of the rest of our people."

"I'm not going to let any of our people die." The words sounded hollow even to Tol. "And you're not our bloody prince. I am."

"If your girlfriend's barbarian of a mother hadn't murdered my father, I'd be prince right now instead of you."

That was also true, but Tol wouldn't give his cousin the satisfaction of hearing him say so.

Tol picked up a framed photograph on one of the end tables. He tapped the glass. "This is Addy's family. And the general killed them, too. Addy's as much a victim as any of us."

"Tell me this." Erikir crossed his arms. "If you had to pick between Addy and our people, who would it be?"

"Shut your mouth, Erikir," Gerth said, slamming his book closed.

Words stuck in Tol's throat. He knew the answer he was supposed to give—the one he'd have to give if it ever came down to it. He just hoped to the gods it wouldn't.

"See? There." Erikir pointed an accusing finger at Tol. "You're worthless as a prince, and you'll be even worse as a king. Anyone who puts one girl, and the daughter of our enemy no less, above his own people isn't a king worth following."

Tol had reached the limits of his patience. It was worse because everything Erikir was saying was true. He had no room for insults on top of the mountain of grief and guilt he was already carrying. Tol snapped. He lunged at Erikir.

They went down in a heap of limbs and shouts.

The Chosen fought others with Influence rather than fists, but since their people weren't susceptible to Influence, Tol improvised. He'd seen the way Addy fought, and he tried to channel some of her moves. He got in a good punch to his cousin's face before Erikir hit him in the stomach. The blow drove the air from his lungs.

Erikir's next punch went wide and glanced off Tol's prosthesis. A lamp tipped over, and the bulb shattered before Tol got his cousin in a headlock.

Gerth sat on top of Erikir's legs, which were scrabbling across the wood floor. Fred stood over all of them with his nail gun clutched in his hand. His eyes darted around, like he was trying to decide what to do.

"What. The. Hell?" a feminine voice demanded.

Addy.

They all looked up. Tol's anger turned to shame in the space of an instant. Addy, Olivia, and their Aunt Meredith were standing in the open doorway, their arms full of supplies.

Meredith looked amused. Olivia looked concerned. Addy was pissed.

Tol let go of Erikir and got to his feet.

"I'm sorry," Tol said to Meredith, bending down to right the fallen lamp. "This won't happen again."

They were guests here, and they were mauling each other like a pack of ravenous wolves. Or Forsaken.

Addy marched over to Erikir and whispered something that made Erikir's face blanch. From the look on Addy's face, Tol knew now wouldn't be the right time to tell her how sexy she was when she was angry.

"Well, now that that's settled, how about some dinner?" Meredith asked cheerily.

* * *

The sky was dark by the time they'd unloaded all of the travel supplies from the truck bed. While Meredith and Fred got the fire going outside, the rest of them made trips back and forth out to the picnic table carrying packages of hot dogs, bags of BBQ crisps, and all the fixings for s'mores.

Tol and Olivia both reached for a stack of paper plates on the kitchen counter. When their fingers brushed, power washed over Tol. His Haze flared a blinding gold. Tol's vision flickered as his perspective changed from his own to Olivia's.

Grimacing, he wrenched his hand away.

Confusion and hurt flashed across Olivia's face, which only made Tol feel worse. He considered apologizing, but instead, he grabbed the plates and headed for the porch.

"Give it a rest, Tol." Gerth jabbed him in the side as soon as they were out of earshot. "Don't you think the poor girl's been through enough?"

Tol knew Gerth was right. Still, he had no idea how to behave around the Fount. She was the one he was destined for, and every time he was near her, he felt the incessant pull of the connection between them.

An involuntary shudder went through Tol.

He didn't want to feel that link with Olivia. He didn't want to feel the tug of her emotions or sense the corner of his mind that lit up whenever she was within arm's reach. That spot in his mind belonged to Addy.

Tol felt like he was swimming against a tide that was constantly and inevitably drawing him closer to Olivia.

"At least be polite," Gerth said. "Don't forget that she's going to be your sister-in-law."

"Right." Tol nodded. "My sister-in-law."

Tol just hoped that was all she'd ever be.

Outside, they settled themselves around the fire. Tol leaned against the trunk of a tree, and Addy sat with her back propped against his legs. Her nearness made some of his tension fade.

As they roasted hot dogs on sticks—a first for Tol, Gerth, and Erikir—Tol asked Meredith about what Addy had been like as a kid. He wanted to know everything about her. He wanted to know about the family he wished he could have met before they became mangled corpses on a kitchen floor.

Olivia and Fred jumped in to add their two cents. Afterward, Gerth regaled them with the story about Gran's first encounter on Earth with a whistling tea kettle. By the time he was finished, everyone was clutching their sides from laughing. Even Erikir's scowl slipped before he remembered to put it back in place.

"Well, in your grandmother's defense," Meredith said, "I can't imagine moving to a whole other world. Your people must have needed to learn a whole new language…a whole new…*everything*." She waved her cowboy hat around as she spoke.

"Our people are born with the ability to pick up any language after hearing it spoken," Tol explained to Meredith.

"I didn't know that," Addy said, her eyes full of awe.

He gave her wink.

"We couldn't let the mortals find out about us," Gerth added. "Our only option was to assimilate…and fast."

While they talked and roasted marshmallows, Tol lets his fingers glide through the strands of Addy's hair. He loved that he could pick out her piña colada scent even amid the stronger smells of campfire and burnt marshmallow.

For the first time in days, he felt himself relax.

As his eyes drifted shut, the ground beneath Tol lurched. His eyes flew open.

Tol and Addy were both on their feet in a second. Tol had his vial of Source open, and Addy gripped her garden shears. The earth heaved. Particles of dirt jumped in the air. The glasses on the picnic table clattered up and down before smashing to the ground. The oak tree groaned in protest at the movement.

"What the—" Fred put out his arms, like he was a surfer trying to balance on the unsteady ground.

As quickly as it began, the shaking stopped.

Tol looked around for some sign of the Forsaken, but he saw no glowing blue weapons or golden Haze aside from that of his own people. He didn't see anything that was cause for concern except for a thin crack that cut straight across the front yard.

"Spread out," Erikir hissed. "They could be anywhere."

"This has nothing to do with the Forsaken," Gerth said, his voice uncharacteristically subdued.

"That's been happening on and off for the past year." Meredith's eyebrows pulled down. "No one else in town ever seems to feel it, though."

Tol's heart was racing.

Gerth peered down at the crack that had formed across the yard. He strode to the house, measuring his steps and counting out loud as he went. Gerth returned, his face pinched in thoughtful concentration.

"This crack is on the exact location of the portal," Gerth announced. In response to Meredith, Olivia, and Fred's confused expressions, he explained. "The Celestial used the last burst of her magic to create a link between the two worlds. Right here." He pointed at the fissure.

Tol and Gerth exchanged a look.

As Olivia's nineteenth birthday neared, Vitaquias must be growing less stable. Some of that volatility was seeping through the portal to the mortal world.

"Should we go right now?" Olivia asked, looking petrified at the thought.

Tol opened his mouth, but Gerth spoke first.

"Let's wait until morning," Gerth said. "We're all jetlagged, and if my calculations are right, it's nighttime on Vitaquias right now. I'd rather arrive when it's light out."

Tol agreed.

Addy stepped back until she was leaning against Tol. He wrapped his arm around her as they stared down at the crack in the earth.

They were running out of time.

He didn't need this fissure in the ground to remind him of it, and yet, here it was.

What if Erikir was right? What if this was just a fool's mission that would get all of them killed and destroy his people's last hope?

The hot dogs he'd eaten earlier turned to rocks in his stomach.

"I understand you need to go to this other world," Meredith said, "but I need you to promise me you'll all come back in one piece."

She looked at Tol.

Tol held Addy tighter, like he could keep her safe with the force of his grip.

"I won't let anything happen to them," he said. Even as he said the words, he knew it was a promise he might not be able to keep.

"Psh, *I'll* make sure we all come back in one piece," Gerth said.

In spite of himself, Tol managed a grin. If anyone could keep them from a horrible, fiery death, it was his best mate.

"Alright," Gerth announced. "Time for bed. I want everyone refreshed and ready for whatever meets us at the other end of that portal tomorrow."

Gerth jabbed a finger at Tol and Addy. "You two especially. I won't have you being anything less than your full strength tomorrow because you spent all night making gaga eyes at each other."

"But I'm not tired, *Mum*," Tol complained, trying for the lightness they'd had a few moments ago.

"Let's just hope that's all they're doing," Erikir said, his perpetual frown deepening to a look of pure disgust.

"In my house, it will be." Meredith pointed an accusing finger at Addy. "I swear I heard your mother shouting at me on the wind when I said you and Tol could share a bedroom."

"We'll behave," Tol promised. "We appreciate you, er, giving us space to be together." And then, thinking about how she might misinterpret his words, he tried to clarify. "I meant together as in just be near each other. We won't do anything. Except sleep."

Addy smacked a palm to her forehead. Gerth snickered.

Tol wished the crack in the ground would widen enough to swallow him up. He was usually good with words, but he was on unfamiliar ground at the moment…both literally and figuratively.

Meredith tilted her head in thought. "As far as I'm concerned, if you're old enough to save a whole world, then you're old enough to share a bed with whomever you choose."

"Anyone?" Addy teased her aunt. "What about a Democrat?"

Meredith looked at Tol the same way she'd looked at the roach that had been unfortunate enough to climb onto the picnic table during dessert. Remembering the way she'd squashed the thing without mercy, Tol put up his hands in surrender and backed away from Addy.

"My people don't have political parties," he hurriedly explained. "We're a monarchy."

"I think it's disrespectful to sleep together before you're married," Fred grumbled into his can of orange soda.

If Tol hadn't been trying to be civil to Fred for Addy's sake, he might question whether Fred's morals would still hold up if the farmer was the one sharing Addy's bed. Tol didn't bother explaining that he and Addy really couldn't do much more together than sleep until the blood marriage.

The farmer could keep his assumptions.

"The last one in bed will have to play me in chess and suffer the consequences," Gerth warned.

"Right then," Tol said. "I'm off."

Gerth was downright insufferable when he played chess, or really any game for that matter. Or maybe it was just the fact that Gerth never lost that was so insufferable.

They all helped to clean up and put out the fire. In spite of Gerth's threat, Tol let the others file into the house ahead of him. He stared down at the crevice in the ground.

What would they find when they got to the other world?

Did it even still exist?

There was a very real possibility that when Olivia opened the portal, they'd be shot into some kind of black hole because Vitaquias had ceased to exist.

"Hey, you okay?" Addy asked.

He nodded, shaking his head to clear his mind. They'd find out what was happening on Vitaquias soon enough. There was no point in wondering and worrying now.

He was further distracted from his worries as Addy headed for the porch ahead of him. She was wearing shorts that bared her long legs, and Tol couldn't stop himself from thinking about those legs wrapped around his waist.

"Guess I'm losing at chess later," Tol muttered.

"Huh?" Addy turned around to look at him.

He didn't give her time to react before hauling her around the side of the house. He pressed her against the wall and kissed her.

If she was surprised, she didn't show it. She curled her hands into his shirt and dragged him closer as she kissed him back.

She tasted like marshmallow and chocolate. The way she sighed and sunk deeper into the kiss made him lose track of everything except for her. The buzzing of the cicadas was drowned out by their thundering pulses. Their hearts beat in time against each other's chests.

There was nothing gentle about the kiss. It was all heat and desire, and beneath that, desperation. They both knew that, depending on what happened tomorrow, this kiss might be their last.

The thought made him hold her tighter, press closer.

I won't let you go, he thought, even though he knew he might not have a choice. He had responsibilities. He'd made promises he couldn't break.

He wouldn't think about that. Not now. Not yet.

"Tol, Ad-dy! Quit snogging and get in here," Gerth called from inside.

They broke their kiss on a gasp. They were hidden in shadows, but Gerth didn't need to see them to know what they were up to. Sometimes, Tol really hated what a know-it-all Gerth was.

The porch light flickered on and off.

Sighing, Tol stepped back.

"I've been waiting all night to do that," he confessed with an unapologetic grin.

Addy smiled at him. The unguarded love in her expression was enough to leave him breathless.

"I'm going to spend eternity with you," Tol said, reaching up to touch her face.

Addy let out a soft sigh. "I keep forgetting about the whole living forever thing. I guess with the Source inside me, I never needed the blood marriage to become immortal."

A complicated range of emotions passed through her green eyes.

"Forever won't be long enough for a lifetime with you," Tol said, leaning in for another kiss.

"Don't make me send Freddo and his nail gun out there," Gerth called from inside.

Shaking his head in an attempt to clear it, Tol offered Addy his hand. She took it, and together, they went into the house.

CHAPTER 3

OLIVIA

Olivia startled out of a restless sleep. There was a crash, followed by a yelp.

Addy.

Olivia raced down the hall, her heart in her throat. Fred and Tol reached the bathroom first, where more thuds and curses were coming from inside.

Fred practically tore the bathroom door off its hinges as the guys stormed inside. Olivia followed, caught between terror at whatever was inside and a desperation to help her twin however she could. If anything happened to Addy—

Olivia peered around Fred.

Addy, wrapped in a towel and standing on the toilet seat, held an electric toothbrush in her hand like a weapon.

"What's going on?" Tol demanded, his golden light flaring as they all stared around for the threat.

Olivia jumped as Addy bashed the toothbrush down on the counter. There was a flicker of movement as a small scorpion scuttled out of the way just in time.

"I'll save you, Ads!" Fred announced, trying to flatten the poor insect with the palm of his hand. He missed by a hair.

"Wanker," Tol muttered under his breath.

It took Olivia a few more seconds for her panicked brain to understand that there was no emergency.

"Stop!" she cried as Addy brought the toothbrush down again.

Everyone went still.

Squeezing past Tol, Olivia grabbed a hand towel off the rack and approached the counter. The tiny creature faced her, its pincers opening and closing in warning.

As the creature eyed her, Olivia had the fleeting wish that she possessed a small fraction of the scorpion's bravery.

"Smash it, Livy," Addy said, climbing off the toilet and adjusting her grip on the toothbrush.

"She's scared," Olivia said as she tried to coax the scorpion onto the towel. "I'll just bring her outside where she belongs."

"How do you know it's a *she*?" Tol asked.

"It's definitely a dude scorpion," Addy declared. "The thing was creeping on me while I showered."

"Never thought I'd be jealous of a scorpion," Tol said pensively.

Olivia tried not to notice the heated gazes Addy and Tol were exchanging as she swept the scorpion into the towel and hurried it outside.

When she came back into the house, Olivia heard Addy speaking to Tol through the closed door of their bedroom.

"...wouldn't hurt a fly...always called her Sweet Livy."

Olivia turned away before she eavesdropped any more.

Surrounded by people with superhuman abilities, kindness didn't seem like a useful contribution. Olivia doubted her penchant for saving helpless insects would translate into the skills needed to rescue an alien race.

If only she was more like Addy—who fearlessly charged into mischief and mayhem at every opportunity—instead of the twin who was afraid of her own shadow.

Olivia stood in the quiet hallway, not quite sure what to do with herself. She needed to get some sleep before tomorrow, but she was too restless.

On warm nights when she was back at home, she and Addy used to sneak out after the rest of their family was asleep. They'd lie between the corn stalks and stare up at the stars as they told each other ghost stories.

A raw pain went through Olivia's chest at the memory of the life she'd loved and lost. She dug her nails into her palms, focusing on the half-moon indentations to keep her mind from spiraling out of control with grief and loss.

Olivia forced out a calming breath. And then another.

She headed for the porch, thinking the night air might help calm her thoughts. She wished she had one of her books from home. *The Chronicles of Narnia* would be an appropriate choice given her own upcoming journey. Then again, reading about people who walked into another world was becoming less of a bedtime story and more of a promise for her future.

But of course, Olivia didn't have her beloved book collection with her. The monsters who killed her family hadn't exactly let her pack a bag before they kidnapped her.

Olivia swallowed the lump in her throat at the thought of her parents and younger sisters. That crushing wave of guilt and all those *what ifs* would drown her if she let them. Right now, she had to keep herself together so she'd be able to help Addy. Afterward, when her twin became the Fount and Olivia was just Olivia again, she'd give herself permission to fall to pieces.

She reached for the handle of the door. Everything in front of her disappeared as a black veil slid over her vision. All she had time to think was, *not now*, before her knees gave way.

The moments before the darkness took her were always the worst. Terror swept through her, along with the sense that she had no control over her own mind. She always had just enough presence of mind to wonder if this would be the time the darkness refused to let her go.

It felt like a nightmare that might never end.

Olivia's body thudded to the wood floor. She heard male voices and felt cool fingertips on her cheek. She heard someone say, "Get Tol."

After that, she was aware of nothing except for flashes of images that moved too fast for her to see any of them clearly. It was like someone was flipping through a picture book at lightning speed. It made her head ache.

Someone took her hand, and her vision immediately sharpened. The blackness turned to a bright white that should have blinded her. Instead, it transformed the chaos of her mind into calmness and clarity.

She saw Tol standing beside her. His golden Haze lit up the front yard where the crack in the earth had opened earlier in the night.

Tol inclined his head, and when she followed the direction of his gaze, she saw they weren't alone. A heavyset man in overalls and muck boots was walking the line of the fissure in the lawn.

What're you up to, witch? the man muttered to himself. *What're you up to?*

He knelt on the ground and reached into the fissure.

The man screamed and wrenched his hand back. His entire arm was blackened and smoking.

Run, Olivia thought, her heart fluttering in panic. A dark shadow crept out of the fissure and rose behind the man.

In one swift move, the shadow dragged the man into darkness. Then, it returned for Tol and Olivia. Tentacle-like shadow arms snaked around them. Olivia fought, but it was useless. They were dragged into a blackness as complete as it was endless.

Olivia tried to scream, but no sound came out. She felt the heat of blood pouring from her lips. The taste of copper filled her throat as she choked.

She turned to the side and saw that Tol was as broken as she was. Bones jutted out of torn flesh. Blood streamed from his ears, nose, eyes….

Tol's body dissipated into blue smoke. That was all. One moment he'd been there and alive. The next, he was wisping away into the depths of a waterless black sea.

The vision shattered.

With a gasp, Olivia opened her eyes. She was back in Aunt Meredith's house. Tol was kneeling beside her, his hand still clasped in hers. His olive skin had blanched, but unlike in her vision, he was very much alive.

"Livy? Tol?"

At the sound of Addy's voice, Tol dropped Olivia's hand like it was covered in molten lava. Olivia felt confused, and more than a little overwhelmed.

She added embarrassment to the list when she realized everyone in the house was awake and crowded around her.

"Here you go, sweet pea." Aunt Meredith handed her a cold washcloth.

Olivia gave her aunt a grateful smile as she pressed it to her aching forehead.

Her embarrassment deepened when she realized Erikir, the angry boy who had touched her cheek and called for Tol, was still hovering over her. They were close enough that the silky ends of his black hair brushed against her cheek. He seemed to realize their proximity at the same moment she did, and with a scowl, he retreated to the edge of their circle.

"Did you see that?" Olivia asked Tol, her voice coming out breathy, like she'd just run a mile.

Tol gave a slow shake of his head. "I saw you standing in your aunt's yard." His gaze slid to Addy. He looked…ashamed, like he'd done something wrong by being inside Olivia's vision. It made Olivia feel guilty, even though she still didn't understand what had happened.

Tol continued, "I felt your fear, and I knew you were seeing something terrible just out of my line of sight. And then," he paused, and Olivia saw a shiver go through him. "I saw you die."

"What?!" Addy demanded.

Olivia swallowed. With her voice trembling only a little, she recounted what she had seen. When she was finished, she expected to see skepticism written across everyone's faces. Maybe even derision. After all, she'd just had a vision that made no sense.

Instead, Tol and Gerth exchanged a look that was full of meaning. And then the two of them got to their feet and hurried for the door. Olivia stood on unsteady legs. Addy wrapped her arm around Olivia's waist as they followed the others out into the yard.

A choked sound escaped Olivia's lips as Aunt Meredith flipped on the porch light. There was a man in overalls and work boots standing on the lawn. It was the same man from her vision.

"Anthony Fowler, what in the Sam Hill are you doing on my property?" Aunt Meredith stalked across the yard in her bathrobe and cowboy boots.

Addy, Tol, Erikir, and Gerth's Hazes flared to life. Aunt Meredith and Fred, standing with their arms crossed, looked almost as lethal.

"Aunt Meredith, who is this guy?" Addy asked, gripping her garden shears.

"A nosy neighbor who needs to learn to respect property lines, that's who," their aunt replied, still glaring at the man—Anthony Fowler.

"We got laws 'gainst blowin' shit up," Fowler said. He took a toothpick out of his pocket and stuck it between his teeth.

"I haven't been blowing anything up, and I'll thank you to watch your mouth," Aunt Meredith replied. "I don't want my nieces and their friends to think *all* of my neighbors are lowbrows."

Fred and Gerth snickered.

Fowler squinted at all of them. "You gonna claim there was *another* earthquake that only hit *yer* land?"

"I'm not claiming anything," Aunt Meredith said coolly.

"You upset my cows," Fowler persisted.

"You give your cows too much credit," Aunt Meredith replied. "I imagine if the sight of you doesn't put them off their feed, then neither will a little earthquake."

Olivia clapped a hand over her mouth to keep from laughing out loud. All of her mirth transformed to horror in a heartbeat as Fowler knelt down next to the crack in the ground.

Everything, from the positioning of his body to the way Tol's light illuminated his profile, was the same as it had been in her vision.

"Don't!" Olivia shouted.

Fowler ignored her. He bent down to poke at the crack in the earth.

The man's scream reverberated in her ears.

When he pulled his arm out of the crack, it was blackened and smoking. An awful, burning flesh smell assailed her nose.

"Oh my Lord!" Aunt Meredith shouted.

Olivia watched in muted horror as her vision came to life before them.

"Tol, what's happening?" Addy demanded.

Tol shook his head.

"This is exactly what I saw in my vision," Olivia said, her insides cringing at the sight of the man's arm shriveling and shrinking. The farmer let out an agonized howl.

"What do we do?" Fred demanded.

Olivia exchanged a look with Tol. Her nerves tingled a second before she saw something black creep up from the earth's crevice.

"Watch out!" Olivia yelled as that oozing black shadow began spilling out of the crack in the ground.

It was too late. The shadow grabbed hold of the screeching man's foot. It was already sucking him into its depths. Everything was happening exactly the same way it had in her vision, and she was powerless to help the man.

"Grab my hand," Tol ordered Fowler.

Panic unfurled in Olivia's stomach.

"No," she gasped. "You can't."

Olivia knew that if any of them touched that black shadow, they'd be sucked into its depths and killed, just like she and Tol were in her vision.

She ran forward. Olivia grabbed Tol's arm and wrenched him back just before his fingers reached into the pool of shadows. He stumbled into her, and both of them fell back into Addy. They collapsed in a heap on the ground just as Fowler and the black shadow were sucked into the fissure. The crack in the earth was only a few inches wide, and yet, it somehow swallowed up the entire man.

Fowler's desperate cries cue off. All that was left was silence.

"Oh, Lord. Oh, Lord. Oh, Lord!" Aunt Meredith clutched Olivia with a grip tight enough to bruise.

"What the hell happened?" Fred asked.

Gerth, Tol, and Erikir looked as confused as the rest of them. Their uncertainty scared Olivia even more than the fact that she'd just seen a man die before her eyes.

"We have to call the police," Aunt Meredith said. "Then, we're going out to buy more guns. Whatever's happening, we need to be able to defend ourselves. I'll need to call Anthony's wife, and—"

Aunt Meredith stopped pacing back and forth. She pinned Olivia and Addy with the stern gaze their mother only used when nothing else would suffice.

"You are *not* going into that other world. No, madams. You're all the family I have left, and I'm not letting you get burned up or swallowed whole or whatever else just happened to that man. Do you hear me?!"

Olivia looked at her twin.

Addy bit her lip. She looked at Tol.

"Tell me if you want me to do it," he murmured.

Cold shivered through Olivia in spite of the warm air. She'd seen Tol and the rest of his people use their mind control before, and she understood this was what Tol was offering to do to their aunt now.

"Don't you dare." Fred stomped over and pointed a finger in Tol's face. "Don't you even think about using your freaky mind control on Meredith. I won't let you."

"How do you plan to stop me, Farmer Fred?" Tol asked, before sliding a guilty glance in Addy's direction. In a more subdued tone, he told Addy, "I won't Influence her unless you want me to."

Aunt Meredith was still pacing and talking to herself, completely oblivious to the argument that was going on about her.

"What should we do?" Addy asked Olivia.

All eyes turned to her.

Why are you asking me?! she wanted to shout.

Instead, she took a few deep breaths. She tried to assess their problem and potential solutions, the way she'd seen Gerth do these last few days.

Olivia knew the answer she needed to give. She couldn't bear to put her aunt in any more danger. She'd already lost the rest of her family.

She turned to Tol, her throat burning with emotion.

"Do it," she told him. "Just…don't take away her memories any more than you have to."

"You people are unbelievable," Fred accused.

Addy looped her arm through Olivia's. Olivia was grateful for her sister's presence as Tol went to Aunt Meredith and said, "Look at me."

When their aunt's eyes glazed over and her frown turned to a sleepy smile, a sick feeling twisted in Olivia's gut.

But what else could we have done? she argued with herself. *It's the only way to keep her safe.*

"I'm off to bed," Aunt Meredith announced a few moments later. Her eyes were a little unfocused, but other than that, she seemed completely normal. "Make sure ya'll have a good breakfast before you head out for your little vacation."

Aunt Meredith pulled Olivia and Addy into a hug. Olivia clung to her aunt, wishing she didn't have to let go.

"Do you have any idea how messed up that was?" Fred demanded when Aunt Meredith was out of earshot.

Olivia chewed on her bottom lip. She knew Fred was right.

"It was the best of bad options," she said, not quite sure whether she was trying to convince Fred or herself. "At least here, your booby traps will help keep her safe."

Addy nodded, but her face mirrored Olivia's regret.

"There was nothing else to be done," Tol said. "Any mortal who knows about our world is a threat to us and themselves."

"I know everythin' and I'm not a threat," Fred argued.

"The only reason you aren't bumbling around with no memory is out of respect for Addy." Tol gave Fred a pointed glare. "But don't think for one second I'll hesitate to Influence you if your involvement in our affairs endangers any of my people."

"Are you threatenin' me?" Fred snarled.

"Look, what my less-than-diplomatic mate is trying to say," Gerth offered, holding out his hands in a conciliatory way, "is that we're doing our best to stay under the radar. If mortals discovered another race was living among them, using other-worldly gifts to control their governments and militaries, they'd be hells-bent on eradicating us."

"That wouldn't happen," Fred said weakly.

Erikir scoffed. "We know your planet's history and what happens to those who are different."

"Oh yeah," Fred retorted. "Because your planet sounds like a regular paradise."

"This is all a little bit irrelevant at the moment," Gerth interrupted before Fred and Erikir came to blows. "Everyone get your things. "We're out of here in ten."

* * *

Aunt Meredith's rooster wall clock told Olivia it took everyone exactly eight minutes to get dressed and finish packing the huge bags now strapped to their backs. When they went outside, the sky was just beginning to lighten. Normally, Olivia would think the gray-blue color of the sky was beautiful. After the vision she'd just had, everything seemed painted in different shades of *ominous*.

By silent agreement, they all made their way to the fissure that had swallowed up Aunt Meredith's neighbor only a short while ago. Olivia was still trembling from watching her vision play out in real life before her eyes.

The closer she got to the crack in the earth, the more Olivia felt a strange tug inside her. It was like there was an invisible string connecting her to the site of the portal. The closer she got, the more taut the string became. Her feet brought her closer and closer, even though her brain told her to run away…to go back into the farmhouse and crawl into bed with Aunt Meredith.

Olivia stood next to Addy, trying to calm her hummingbird-quick pulse, and waited. She expected Tol, Gerth, and Erikir to drink from those vials around their necks and do something magical. When nothing happened, she looked around.

Everyone was staring at her.

"We need your blood to open the portal," Gerth explained to Olivia, who imagined she was looking very much like a deer in the headlights. "Just don't get too close to that crack in the ground until the portal opens."

Olivia shivered at the memory of the shadow that had dragged a full-grown man into the narrow fissure. She took a step back.

"Just a second," Addy said, squinting at the guys in suspicion. "How much blood are we talking?"

"Not much," Gerth replied, giving Olivia a kind smile.

Olivia wasn't afraid of blood. Minor injuries came with the job when one worked with farm equipment and the Cluckers—their family's five hens. Still, it felt different to cause her body harm on purpose.

Addy wrapped an arm over Olivia's shoulders in a protective gesture that made Olivia feel like she was the younger sister instead of Addy's twin.

"It's okay," Olivia heard herself say.

Do it for Addy, she reminded herself.

Olivia used Addy's garden shears to prick her finger. Blood immediately beaded up along the cut.

"Drip your blood right onto the ground near the crack," Gerth told her.

She did as she was told. As soon as her first drop of blood fell, the ground beneath their feet began to shake. If it hadn't been for Addy's arm wrapped around her, Olivia would have lost her footing.

My blood, Olivia thought dazedly. *My blood is causing an earthquake.*

The wind picked up. Olivia's loose curls whipped across her face as a spiraling cyclone of dust and debris formed in the place where her blood had fallen.

Something inside Olivia—like energy or molten fire—began to churn. Normally, she'd default to *terrified* right about now. But there was no room for fear.

She felt strong, although strong enough to do what, she couldn't say. Something old and ancient that she didn't understand stirred inside her. It was a part of her and also separate from her. It made no sense, but she didn't have time to question it.

Olivia felt the vortex of swirling dust dragging at her. Her feet slid forward an inch.

Without warning, a tremendous boom rippled the air around them. The sky bent and warped. There was the sound of nails on a chalkboard, or maybe the pages of a giant book being ripped out. It was like the sky was tearing apart at its seam.

Her stomach dropped. Her breath snagged in her lungs. She wanted to run…hide…scream…. But she was frozen.

Through the rip in the sky, Olivia saw colors and movement. Everything blurred together until all she could see was a shimmery film.

Olivia had never been so desperate to run toward and away from something at the same time.

The color rippled again. Olivia thought she caught sight of mountains and a castle on a cliff. When she blinked, the image disappeared.

The temperature in the air was dropping…fast. Wind and dust and energy swirled around Olivia until she could barely think…could barely breathe.

"Go!" Gerth shouted from behind them.

Addy tugged Olivia's arm. Together, they stepped closer to the seam in front of them. A faint light began to pulse at its center. It looked like a tornado made out of color. It was beautiful and terrible all at once.

That was Olivia's last thought before she was swallowed into the portal's swirling depths.

CHAPTER 4

TOL

Tol watched Addy and Olivia disappear into the portal. If he'd thought about it for a second, he would have told Olivia to go last, in case the portal closed up before everyone was through.

Too late.

Wind churned and billowed around them. A harsh scraping sound of metal on metal was coming from inside the portal. It was deafening.

"Get moving," he yelled to Fred and Erikir.

They disappeared into the churning clouds, and then it was just him and Gerth.

"Ready, mate?" Gerth called, the portal making his voice echo.

Nodding, Tol strode forward. A moment before his body was absorbed into the whirling mass, someone grabbed his arm and pulled him back.

Tol turned to see bright red nails digging into the sleeve of his shirt. He followed the hand to a slender arm, to the last face he ever expected to see here.

"Nira?"

Tol hadn't seen his ex-friend-with-benefits since the night he'd watched the manor burn.

Since the night she'd *told everyone about the Fount.*

If it hadn't been for Nira, none of the Chosen would have known Tol was intentionally postponing the blood marriage. If it hadn't been for Nira, his family's monarchy would still be intact.

Nira's eyes were wide as she stared at the open portal.

Do you have any idea what you started? he wanted to shout at her.

"What in the two hells are you doing here?" Gerth demanded, since Tol was too shell-shocked to ask the question himself.

"Tol, the manor's a mess," Nira said, tearing her gaze away from the portal to look at him. She had to shout to be heard over the roar of the wind.

Tol's blood went cold. His growing anger retreated just enough to make way for true alarm. His parents and Gran were back there. All of Tol's people were back there.

What was happening?

He glanced at the portal—was it just his imagination or was it getting smaller?—before turning his attention back on Nira.

"What's happened?"

"The rebels are trying to force your parents to abdicate, and our elders are on the brink of death. Everyone's panicking."

"Tol, come on," Gerth yelled.

This time, when Tol looked, there was no doubt the portal was shrinking.

Tol hesitated. He had to hear what Nira needed to tell him. But he wasn't going to let the portal close with him on the wrong side. In a second, his decision was made.

"What are you doing?" Nira demanded as Tol grabbed her arm and dragged her along with him.

"You burned down my manor and put my family at risk, all for the sake of petty jealousy," he growled.

He could tell from the bewildered look on Nira's face she hadn't heard a word over the shattering glass sound coming from inside the portal.

Nira's eyes were wide with terror. Tol felt badly for what he was about to do. And then he remembered what she'd done. He remembered what she'd caused.

"Addy won't be pleased," Gerth said.

That was the last thing Tol heard before he was sucked into the vortex.

All of the air was ripped from his lungs. Nira and Gerth were beside him when he stepped into the portal, but they were all torn apart by the violent gale.

Tol shot through the air. He was weightless and had the distinct sense his insides were being pulled right out through his skin. His sight blurred from the force of the wind that blasted him through space. A harsh whistling sound filled his ears.

Aside from the silver smoke that Tol cut through like a missile, he was aware of nothing.

He should be afraid, but there was no time. Terror was frozen along with every other emotion he'd felt before stepping into the portal.

On and on he flew.

The journey was both instantaneous and eternal.

Tol still hadn't taken a single breath. At least, he didn't think he had. Everything in this in-between place was scrambled.

Including his brain, most likely.

The vortex released him. Tol fell.

Gravity took over. He was pulled down, down, down. When he tried to look, all he saw was an expanse of white nothingness. It didn't matter what was at the bottom of this abyss. No person—mortal or immortal—could survive it.

Oh gods. Had he sent all of the others to their deaths?

Without warning, his momentum slowed. It was like the air around him had thickened. He was still falling, but it was a gentle descent. He sucked in a breath as his heart threatened to beat out of his chest.

He tasted ash on the air. The gray particles floated down and coated his hair…his clothes…even his eyelashes. The air had a charred scent similar to the one that had filled the air after that man's arm had burned.

The true foolishness of what he was doing hadn't occurred to him until this moment. He'd brought the most important people in his life to a ruined world without having a clue about what they would face when they arrived.

What in the hells had he been thinking?

Tol hit the ground with the gentleness of a parent placing a child on his feet. Except in Tol's case, his legs had turned to jelly. His whole body crumpled.

"Tol," Addy gasped, moving on hands and knees until she was close enough to touch.

"Are you okay?" he managed, scanning her for injuries. Aside from the ash coating her hair and clothes, she looked unhurt.

She nodded, her eyes searching him in the same way he'd done to her. Tol glanced around, making sure everyone else was in one piece.

Alive. Every one of them was alive. Cool, sweet relief rushed through him.

Olivia was trembling, and Fred was vomiting onto the ground. Erikir was already on his feet. Gerth was untangling himself from the straps of his pack, and Nira was…well, Nira was Nira. She was wearing a tiny lace dress that covered less of her than it revealed. Somehow, she had managed to fall all the way down without getting a speck of ash on herself. She was sitting on the ground in a way that showed off her legs all the way to her upper thigh. She was frowning at one of her nails, which as far as Tol could tell, looked as perfectly lethal as ever.

"What's *she* doing here?" Addy glared at Nira before unconsciously reaching for her garden shears with one hand and brushing ash out of her hair with the other.

Tol opened his mouth to explain, but he didn't get the chance.

Nira glanced at Addy with far less interest than she'd shown her nail. "Don't be jealous, Red. Play your cards right, and I'll even give you some pointers so you're not *too* much of a disappointment after me."

"Shut up, Nira," Tol said, feeling embarrassment creep up his neck. "You're here for one reason, and it isn't to torment my fiancé."

Addy and Gerth knew about what he and Nira had been, but Tol didn't fancy the others knowing his business. He certainly didn't appreciate the judgmental look Fred was giving him.

Tol wanted to tell the farmer that he had vomit on his shirt, but he reminded himself of his oath to be polite for Addy's sake. He shut his mouth.

"We need to find shelter," Tol said, his voice sounding loud now that the wind had died down a fraction.

"No worries." Gerth squinted into the distance as he pulled a compass out of his pocket. He studied the needle, oblivious to the rain streaming down his face, and started to walk.

The others fell into step around him.

The rain was like icy pinpricks against Tol's face. After the adrenaline rush of the portal wore off, only the wet and cold remained. He found himself longing for the suffocating Texas heat.

The ground was covered with brittle, black rocks that crumbled to ash underfoot. The powder caked onto his wet sneakers, weighing down his every step.

Tol couldn't see anything beyond the cliff because of the rain. He turned his attention up, where a churning mass of purple and silver clouds moved across the sky with more speed than any clouds in the mortal world.

Angry clouds, Tol thought. He didn't need to be a meteorologist to know a storm was in their future.

There was a thickness to the air here. It made his every breath feel waterlogged and demanded more energy than breathing should require.

"Phew, who's been cookin' rotting eggs?" Fred asked, pinching his nose.

"I'm never going to get this sulfur smell out of my hair," Nira complained, her high heels wobbling on the uneven ground.

"I'm pretty sure I've swallowed a gallon of liquid ash," Addy said.

Tol's own tongue felt thick, like it was coated in the stuff.

Without warning, a change came over Tol. He couldn't pinpoint what was happening, except that the freezing rain no longer bothered him. A few seconds later, he felt warm even though everyone else was shivering.

Maybe he had a fever. He didn't feel feverish, though. Quite the opposite. He felt...*good*.

Heat and light and energy surged through him.

Golden light spilled from him like he was made of it. The strength of it repelled the rain, sending the droplets ricocheting back into the sky before they could reach his skin.

The rain blasted away as Tol's Haze exploded.

"I think Tol's on fire, or something," Fred commented, not sounding overly concerned.

"Gods, you're gorgeous," Nira breathed.

Tol was having trouble seeing any of them through the brightness of his Haze. Everything else ceased to matter when his left shoulder began to prickle. It wasn't the dull ache where his flesh rubbed against the prosthesis, which he'd felt for his entire life. This was something else.

Something nudged against the place where his prosthesis met his shoulder.

What the—

He yanked off his shirt and unbuckled the clasp at his sternum. Normally, he wouldn't let anyone except Addy and Gerth see him like this, but some compulsion was driving him that was too powerful to resist. He let the prosthesis fall to the ground.

His heart began to race in anticipation of…something.

Golden light danced and shimmered in the air beneath his left shoulder. He watched, mesmerized, as the light particles gathered and rearranged themselves until the shape they were forming was obvious. It was an arm…made out of golden light.

Tol's breath caught. This couldn't be happening. It wasn't possible. *Had he hit his head? Was it possible he was just imagining all of this?*

Someone gasped.

"Holy shite," Gerth said. And then, again, "Holy shite."

Tol couldn't look away as the prickling sensation traveled from his shoulder downward.

This was impossible. And yet, the sensations were too real to be mistaken for a dream or a vision.

One-Arm. Skinny Terminator. Metal Boy.

The taunts of his childhood raced through his mind and then washed away on the rain. A choked laugh escaped his throat.

Tol could feel his left arm. Emotion welled up from somewhere deep inside him.

His arm was translucent and made of golden light, but it felt like flesh and bone. He lifted his arm. It obeyed, just like a normal limb would. He pressed his new hand to his cheek. He felt the warmth of his skin against his palm, felt the brush of stubble along his jaw. It was no different from the sensations he got from his right hand.

"Tol." Addy was looking at him, her face full of wonder.

"Addy," he choked.

The others moved aside as he went to her.

He reached up with his left arm, letting his fingers comb through the wet strands of her hair. *It was real.* His arm was real. Somehow, the gods had given him back what they'd taken when his parents brought him away from this world.

Swallowing against the tightness in his throat, he took Addy's face in both of his hands—two hands that didn't just obey commands, but *felt.*

"I never thought," he began, and stopped. He didn't have the words.

He brushed away the tear sliding down her cheek. Addy wasn't looking at his arm, though. Her gaze was fixed on his face and whatever emotions were written in his eyes.

He slid his left hand experimentally around to cup the back of her neck.

"Does it feel…different?" he asked, his voice scratchy.

"No." Addy was crying and laughing at the same time. "It feels like you, Tol."

He pulled her face to his—with both hands—and kissed her.

"Jeez, get a room," Fred muttered.

When they broke the kiss, Tol's Haze was even brighter. Addy stepped back, shielding her eyes.

As his light grew, his view of the world around him changed. Instead of the rain, fog, and crumbling stones beneath his feet, Tol saw a glistening lake full of Source. He saw a castle glittering on a hill, and the crown that belonged to him. Instead of the ruined world he knew was actually surrounding him, he saw eternal possibilities.

Tol's heart lifted. His blood pumped faster through his veins, filling him with a sense of purpose greater than any he'd ever known.

He was strength, wisdom, and everything else that would be required of the greatest king his people had ever known. He was—

"Um, Tol?"

It was Olivia who had spoken. He turned toward her and saw that her expression was uncertain. Her Haze was bright, but not like his. His was blinding.

Somehow, Olivia had sensed the change that had come over him, and it was scaring her. He could feel her fear.

"Right," he muttered, shaking himself.

Those thoughts had come from somewhere outside himself. That voice in his head had not been his own. He was drunk on emotions and this new world that recognized him as a part of it.

Power, that voice called out. *Strength.*

He took Addy's hands in both of his. It was something he never thought he'd be able to do, and he used that miraculous sensation to bring him back to reality. His Haze receded. It was still brighter than ever before, and the pulsing golden outline of his arm hadn't changed, but he felt like himself again.

"Blimey." Gerth blinked, like he was seeing spots from looking at Tol. "If anyone had any question about whether Tol is the true prince of the Chosen, I think the gods just answered it."

Erikir scowled. A trickle of cold sweat slid down Tol's back.

He'd been on Vitaquias for two minutes. Was it possible he was already falling prey to his people's greatest weakness?

He'd felt that power and sense of limitless possibility. He'd felt the same ambition that had caused this world's destruction in the first place. And instead of rejecting it…of fighting its seductive pull, he'd leaned in.

He'd sworn he would never lead his people to ruin again…that he'd never allow them to succumb to their endless appetite for more.

A shiver that had nothing to do with the icy rain sluicing down his skin took hold of him.

And yet, when he looked down at the way his two hands were still clasped with Addy's, he couldn't help but wonder about the gods' strength. If they could give him back his arm, what else might be possible in this world?

"We need to keep going," Gerth said, squinting through the rain. "We still have a long way to go."

Gerth offered Tol the shirt he'd abandoned, which was covered in mud.

"I'm not cold," Tol said, feeling downright giddy.

"Sure, 'cause all of us just want to stare at you naked for the rest of the walk," Fred grumbled.

"Don't be so prude," Nira told Fred. "It's not like I have anything better to look at right now."

"Stop checking out my man," Addy snapped at her.

Tol tuned out the others as they continued to argue. He couldn't stop staring at the golden outline of his left arm.

Gerth didn't say anything about the shirt, but he did pick up Tol's abandoned prosthesis and stuff it into his already-stuffed bag. Tol wanted to tell Gerth to leave it in the mud.

✳ ✳ ✳

The rain slowed to a drizzle, and the wind calmed. That pervasive sulfur smell was stronger, but at least the air wasn't coated with ash anymore.

They were walking across a wasteland. Everything was varying shades of brown and gray. Burned, blackened stubs were all that remained of what must have once been mighty trees. Dips in the ground slicked with luminescent slime indicated where there had once been running water.

Steam hissed out of pockets in the ground, expelling green, sulfuric puffs of air into the storm-purple sky. A puddle of something gray and gelatinous bubbled and slurped. When a drop of the liquid landed on one of the rocks beside the puddle, the rock disintegrated in a sizzle of smoke.

"Stay away from those puddles," Tol warned the others.

"Ya think?" Fred replied.

Tol didn't have the heart to reply. After everything he'd read about the beauty of this place, to see what it had become....

Tol was glad his parents and Gran weren't here to see this. He was glad none of his people who remembered what Vitaquias had been were here to see it now.

When they reached the remains of a village, Tol's mouth went dry. His every muscle tensed at the sight before him. Addy, Olivia, and Fred hung back as the four Chosen entered the ruins.

Tol stopped, his feet forgetting how to move. He stared.

"Gods," Erikir whispered. He sunk to his knees and bowed his head.

Gerth, who always had a joke and a smile ready, stared straight ahead. Silent tears ran down his cheeks.

Tol couldn't form a single word. He couldn't breathe.

Partial walls and charred foundations marked the places where homes had once stood, but that wasn't what held Tol's attention. It was the corpses.

They were splayed out on the ground, encased in solid black ash. Their eyes were gone. The black holes and exposed, blackened teeth made the corpses look like something out of a horror film.

"Ash suffocation. Maybe heat surges," Gerth said in a whisper-thin voice.

Tol's feet carried him to a pair of the dead. Their skeletons were curled in on themselves, and their mouths were parted like they'd died mid-scream. The bodies were small and shrunken.

The sickening realization hit Tol all at once.

They were children.

Tol had read the accounts. He knew the number of Chosen who had perished by heart. None of those written records had prepared him for what he was witnessing now.

My people. The words repeated in his mind over and over again. These were his people, and he'd failed them. It didn't matter that he'd been an infant when this happened.

Gerth and Nira's parents had died. Thousands of others had died. And for what? So his people could become even more powerful than they already were?

Tol was sick at the thought of it.

A sob cut through the silence. Nira, who never showed weakness of any kind, was shaking as choked, tortured sounds poured from her throat.

Tol wanted to go to her. He was desperate to ease this crushing burden that had settled on all of them. But guilt kept him fixed in place, even as Nira and Gerth held onto each other as their shoulders shook.

Tol's parents had made it out alive. Nira's parents, and so many others, had died to protect his family. They had died so he could live.

"I'm so sorry." His words rasped out. He wasn't even sure who he was talking to—the dead encased in solid ash, or Gerth and Nira.

As their prince…as a friend…he should say something. It was up to him to make this better. It was up to him to fix this.

But if there were any words that could make the ache of all of this less raw, Tol didn't know them.

"Do you understand now?" Erikir asked in a quiet voice that, for once, was free of malice. "You have to do the blood marriage for them." His voice broke on that last word. "Otherwise, they'll have died for nothing."

Tol looked at his cousin. Erikir's expression held a sense of urgency that Tol felt beating alongside his own pulse.

Erikir was right. The knowledge squeezed against Tol's chest until he could barely breathe.

For eighteen years, Tol had been unable to save his people because he couldn't find the Fount. Now, that was no longer the case. He had everything he needed to save his people. He was just choosing not to.

That made everything so much worse.

He looked at Addy. She was standing, arm-in-arm with her sister, as they stared at the ruins. Olivia turned and looked straight at Tol, like she could sense his thoughts.

"We need to keep moving," Gerth said, saving Tol from having to respond to his cousin. "I want to make it to the castle, or whatever's left of it, before dark."

CHAPTER 5

ADDY

Addy trudged along, taking in the horrible landscape that surrounded them. It looked like the setting of an apocalypse movie, except without the burned-out cars and zombies.

Addy wished she could scrub that village of mummified people from her brain. She remembered reading about Pompeii in one of her history books, and it had reminded her of that. The only difference was that Pompeii had happened two-thousand years ago to people who didn't matter to Addy. This had happened in her lifetime…to Tol's people.

To her own, too, she supposed. Addy was trying not think about how the Forsaken had perished on this world, as well as the Chosen. She didn't want to think about how she just as easily could have become one of the corpses left behind.

Still, her connection to the Forsaken was an abstract one, and one she didn't care to dwell on. For Tol and his friends, this was personal.

Addy knew there was no way she, Livy, or Fred could understand what the others were going through. She also knew Tol was finding some way to blame himself for all of this. She wanted to take away his hurt and make all of this somehow less awful. She just didn't know how.

"Ads!"

Fred threw his arms around her and hauled her back.

"Wha—"

The ground right where Addy had been about to step gave way. Dirt and rocks were dragged underground as a giant sinkhole formed. It was so deep she couldn't see the bottom.

"Holy crap," Addy said. "That was close."

"Everyone back up," Fred commanded.

He didn't need to tell them twice.

Holding out his hand for the rest of them to stay back, Fred shuffled forward, testing the ground in front of him. Addy tensed, ready to grab him if he hit an unstable patch.

"How did you know about the sinkhole?" Gerth asked, after Fred had cleared the path ahead and waved them forward.

"I noticed that the land here seems to dip," Fred replied.

Addy looked and, sure enough, there was a circular depression. She hadn't even noticed she'd been walking downhill.

"Also, look at how the dirt is all cracked around here." Fred pointed. The ground looked like a turtle's shell.

Fred turned to Addy.

"'Member that Labor Day storm when we were kids?" he asked.

"Vaguely," Addy replied.

"There was a lot of floodin', and after, it made a sinkhole open up on the road into Nowell. The pavement around it looked just like that."

"Well, I'll be damned," Gerth said. "Freddo, you're a peach."

"Freddo?" Fred demanded.

Gerth gave him an easy smile. "Would you prefer *Farmer Fred?*"

Fred glowered. Addy gave his arm a sympathetic pat.

"I ain't as useless as some people might think," Fred huffed, aiming his glare at Tol.

"If we thought you were useless, you wouldn't be here," Gerth told him.

Tol, who was lost in his own thoughts, didn't even seem to be aware of the conversation. Addy wanted to talk to him, but she had no idea what she could say to ease the naked pain in his eyes.

For the time being, she left Tol alone with his thoughts and quickened her pace to catch up with Fred.

She draped an arm around Fred's shoulders as they walked. "I'm glad you're here," she told him.

"Not just 'cause I saved your life?" Fred asked, squeezing her arm.

She grinned down at him. "Mostly that."

"I'm worried about you, Ads." Fred's smile disappeared, and his brow furrowed. "You don't belong with these people. Come home with Livy and me."

If those words had come from anyone else, Addy would have been angry. But Fred was her best friend, and she knew he was only talking out of concern for her.

"You should be with someone who'll keep you safe, not lead you straight into danger," he continued. "You should be with someone who'll take care of you."

Addy tamped down her irritation before she said something she wouldn't be able to take back.

He's worried, she reminded herself.

Addy wasn't sure what to say to Fred. She knew what it would do to him if she told him the truth…that she belonged in this world of magic in a way she had never belonged in her life at Deerborn Family Farm. She couldn't tell Fred that the thought of living without Tol was the same as someone ripping out her heart and stomping on it.

She glanced at Tol, who was walking between Gerth and Nira with his head bowed. Fred, who read Addy's mind from the direction of her gaze, made a sound of disgust.

"Why him?" Fred demanded in a harsh whisper. "Is it because he's a prince and I'm a farmer?"

"Do you really think I'm that shallow?" Addy retorted, feeling her temper begin to unravel.

"Then tell me why, Ads. You know I would have treated you right."

Addy stopped walking to give Fred her full attention. "You're acting like I was just hanging around and waiting for the highest bidder," she accused.

"I ain't. I'm just tryin' to say we belonged together, like your parents did. It woulda been easy. Not like this." He scowled around at the boiling lava and churning purple storm clouds.

"Here's the part you never understood," Addy said, trying to keep a leash on her temper. "I don't want to be like my parents."

Guilt flashed through Addy as she said the words, but it didn't make them any less true. Her parents had loved her, and in a way, she was dishonoring their memory by distancing herself from the life they'd wanted for her.

"So, is this just some teenage rebellion thing? You know, pick the bad boy alien instead of me 'cause I'm the one your parents woulda wanted you to end up with?"

Addy swallowed her furious retort. She could tell from the look on Fred's face that he was trying to hide all the pain he was feeling.

"It's not like that," she told him, trying to gentle her voice.

"Then what is it like?" Fred clenched and unclenched his fists as he grew more agitated.

"I—" Addy stopped walking. "I'm in love with him, Fred. I won't live without him. Not if I can help it."

Addy could see the way her words sliced through Fred's heart like a razor.

"I'm sorry," she told him. She hated the hurt expression on his face and the fact that she'd been the one to put it there. "You know I love you. Just not like that. You're my best friend in the world—in any of the worlds— and I don't want things between us to change."

But things had changed, and they both knew it. The deeper she fell into the world of Chosen and Forsaken, the farther she was drawn from Fred. And from Livy.

"If anythin' happens to you because of *him*, you know I'll kill him, right?"

Addy felt her lips twitch, but she didn't let her smile show.

"Don't worry," she told Fred. "With my ninja skills, the only people you have to worry about are the ones whose asses I'm kicking."

CHAPTER 6

OLIVIA

The sun, which had been covered by a thick layer of clouds all day, appeared just as it was setting. It lit everything in reds and oranges. It should have been pretty. Instead, it made Olivia think of all the blood that had been spilled in this world.

There was something about this sad, abandoned place that called her. When no one else had been paying attention, she'd squatted down and pressed her palm against the ground. Some fanciful part of her mind had thought that, maybe, she could heal this broken place with whatever abilities were inside her.

Of course, the exercise had had no effect, except to make her feel ridiculous.

As far as she could tell, the sun traveled the same path in the sky as the one on Earth, although she knew they weren't in the same solar system. Olivia wondered if they were even in the same galaxy. She hadn't had any concept of distance or direction when she'd been in that portal, and she still couldn't quite wrap her head around the fact that she was on another planet right now.

Olivia was working up the courage to ask Gerth, who seemed the most likely to have all the answers about this world, when she noticed a corner of the sky that had been leached of the bloody sunset. At first, she thought it was a dark cloud moving across the sky.

The hairs on her arms rose. A warning prickled at the back of her mind.

It looked like the shadow that had consumed Aunt Meredith's neighbor. And it was heading toward them.

"Do you guys see that?" she asked.

No one had spoken in hours, and the sound of her own voice startled her.

"That can't be good," Fred noted, following her gaze.

The shadow was oozing nearer. It looked like a giant pot of ink had spilled across the sky. A giant, *sinister* pot of ink.

"It seems like it's coming for us," Addy said, taking an involuntary step back, away from the darkness.

Olivia's skin crawled. Half of her mind was screaming at her to run. The other half knew there was no escaping this evil. It was moving too fast.

"I know what that is," Gerth said, squinting into the distance. "I wasn't sure when we saw it on the mortal world before, but I read accounts of it from the Crossing.

"It appeared when the Source was drained. The scholars called it the Nyxar, but nothing else was known about it."

For several, heart-rending seconds, they all just stared.

There was a tightening all around them, like all the air had been sucked out. Olivia's ears popped. Then, the Nyxar was on them.

Run! Olivia thought.

But there was nowhere to go. The pooling darkness lowered from the sky, undulating back and forth like a giant flag. Too frightened to move, Olivia watched as the shadowy mass began to take shape. Something like a bulbous head formed at the top, with dozens of tentacle-like shadow arms extending out from its core.

"What do we do?" Nira asked, the whites of her eyes growing larger in her panic.

Addy moved first, leaping at the Nyxar. She slashed at one of its smoky arms with her garden shears. The weapon went right through the shadow the way it would pass through smoke. Addy screamed as the darkness enveloped her.

"Addy!"

Olivia staggered on the uneven ground, and Erikir grabbed her arm to keep her from going sprawling.

Tol, his golden light blazing around him, charged. The Nyxar retreated from him, rippling and hissing as it yanked its inky tendrils back.

"Source!" Tol yelled. "Fight it with Source!"

On either side of her, Erikir, Gerth, and Nira were drinking from their vials and running for the shadow. Addy shouted, but her words were torn away by the Nyxar.

Move! Olivia shouted at herself. *Help them!*

She felt the icy cold…the utter wrongness of the shadow creature. The Nyxar carried a rotting smell that was so strong it made her eyes water. Olivia was doused with a feeling of utter hopelessness.

A shadowy tentacle lashed out at her, but stopped just short of her skin. Its darkness hissed and curled away from her. Unsure of what to do next, Olivia backed away from the Nyxar.

The shadow bowled over Tol, knocking him to the ground. Olivia watched in horror as his head struck a stone. His body went limp.

"Tol!" Addy screamed.

Erikir, who was closest, grabbed Tol's arm and tried to yank him back. Nira and Gerth began pulling on him, too. But the Nyxar had latched on to Tol's unconscious form and was dragging him into its boundless depths.

"More Source!" Erikir shouted from somewhere nearby, his silhouette wreathed in shadow.

"I'm out," Nira gasped.

"Me too," Gerth called.

The Nyxar unfurled and stretched. It sensed their weakness.

Olivia could almost feel the shadow's hunger and anticipation as it readied itself to swallow them whole.

"What are you doing?" Olivia cried as Addy slashed one of the blades of her shears across her palm.

"There's Source in my blood," Addy shouted back, striding fearlessly into the shadow with her bleeding palm held outward.

The Nyxar recoiled from her blood, the way a person might suck in their stomach to avoid a knife digging into their skin. When Addy pressed her hand directly on the shadow, the blackness began to smoke and steam.

"It's working!" Addy called, digging the point of her shears into her other palm. She shoved at the Nyxar with both hands.

The shadow retreated. It was moving away, but it was dragging Tol, and everyone who was trying to pull him out of its inky clutches, with it.

Olivia knew her sister well enough to know Addy would bleed herself dry before she gave up on Tol. She had to do something.

As a corner of the shadowy void billowed toward her, Olivia put a hand up on instinct to keep it from swallowing her. It didn't grab her the way it had Tol. Instead, Olivia found that *she* could grasp *it*. It felt like holding onto an oil-slicked blanket.

Fear made her knees wobble and her teeth chatter, but Olivia wasn't going to let her twin face this evil alone. She wrapped both hands around the corner and pulled.

She yelped in surprise when she found she could drag the Nyxar away from Addy and the others. It took all of her energy to move the shadow even a little, but it was possible.

Olivia and Addy pushed the darkness back, allowing the others to yank Tol further out. Olivia gathered more of the shadowy fabric into her arms.

The weaker Addy's blood made the shadow, the easier it became for Olivia to move it.

Tol's unconscious form tumbled out of the blackness.

"Push, Addy!" Olivia yelled.

Understanding, her twin used her bloodied hands to drive the Nyxar toward Olivia. Using the black hole's own momentum, Olivia dragged it farther away.

"Just like…the time…the Benz…ran out of gas," Addy huffed as she shoved at the blackness.

In spite of their current situation, Olivia couldn't help but grin. She fondly remembered their family tractor, which Addy had dubbed *the Benz*.

Instead of facing their parents' wrath when Addy forgot to fill up the tank, Olivia had helped Addy tow the out-of-commission tractor all the way to Fred's house. Aside from the fact that they were on a different planet and dealing with a human-eating shadow instead of a tractor, it was kind of the same.

Addy pushed; Olivia pulled. Together, they slowly dragged the dark shadow away from their friends.

As Olivia gathered more of the Nyxar into her arms, she heard something. It wasn't a spoken voice, but more of a feeling radiating off the shadow creature. Olivia felt its hunger and strength. She sensed its need to destroy.

"I think…we should throw it," Olivia gasped out.

"On three." Addy's red hair was dark with sweat.

Olivia tightened her grip. "One."

"Two," Addy huffed.

"Three!" they yelled together.

Olivia dragged. Addy shoved. The Nyxar was thrust up and into the blood-red sunset.

The two girls collapsed on the ground. They were both shaking from the strain of what they'd just done. Olivia watched through spotty vision as the black shadow flew away from them and winked out of existence.

"We did it," Olivia murmured before flopping back onto the ground.

For the first time in as long as she could remember, Olivia felt like herself. She hadn't just been dead weight on someone else's adventure. She'd been useful.

"Addy, Olivia are you alright?" Tol, who had a nasty gash on his forehead, limped over.

The rest of their group congregated around them. Fred pulled Olivia into a crushing hug before dragging Addy into his arms with them.

"Can't…breathe," Olivia managed.

"Oh, sorry." Fred grinned before releasing them.

"We'd all be dead if it wasn't for your quick thinking," Erikir said.

Olivia startled to find that he was looking at her as he spoke those words.

"I don't believe it." Gerth stared at Erikir in stunned amazement. "Did you actually say something *nice*?"

Erikir's scowl returned. He gave Gerth the finger.

"You both earned your keep today," Gerth told Olivia and Addy.

"What can I say?" Olivia said with a shaky laugh. "The Deerborn twins are unstoppable."

"We certainly are." Grinning, Addy offered Olivia a bloody, dirty hand.

Giving her sister a tired smile, Olivia took her sister's hand and got to her feet.

CHAPTER 7

TOL

In the distance, Tol saw the castle built into the side of a cliff. *His castle.* His breath caught.

"Welcome to the Magnantius' humble abode," Gerth announced.

Tol had seen countless artistic renditions and written accounts, but none of them could compare to seeing it in reality. It didn't matter that Tol could see the crumbling stones and partially-missing roof from here. It was hauntingly beautiful in a way that made Tol's chest compress.

He had no memory of this castle or anything on this planet, and yet, it called to him. It felt like coming home in a way returning to the manor never had. It was closer to the way he felt when he held Addy in his arms. It was a sense of rightness…of belonging.

After less than an hour of steady climbing, they reached the castle.

Tol knew from paintings that there had once been ornate doors in the entrance. Now, it was just a yawning open space with nothing but blackness beyond. It was more than a little eerie. When the wind howled through the open rooms, Tol could swear he heard the cries of all the dead.

Their Hazes and the torches they'd brought along illuminated the grand foyer, which was now just a dark, open space. It was cold, musty, and smelled like rain rot. There wasn't even the skitter of insects along the stone floor. The silence set Tol's nerves on edge. From the way Addy was clutching her garden shears and everyone else seemed to be holding their breath, he knew he wasn't the only one feeling unsettled.

"Alright," Gerth said, slinging down his bag. "First thing's first. We need to find someplace dry to sleep." He pulled a mesh bag full of walkie talkies out of his backpack and handed them around. "We stay in groups of twos. No one wanders off alone."

Tol felt a wave of gratitude for his best mate, and not just for his planning and organization skills. Gerth was the one who got all of them moving when it would have been easier to sit down and contemplate the pointlessness of it all.

The longer Tol spent on this planet, the more certain he became that nothing could have survived the devastation. He would search this whole planet from top to bottom, but logic told him there was no way the Celestial was still alive.

Tol had known this was a fool's errand with a negligible chance of success, but he'd still hoped. Now that he was here, that hope was fading faster than the weak sunset.

"Addy needs her hands bandaged, first," Tol said, pocketing the walkie talkie Gerth handed him.

"Oh." Addy looked down at her bloody palms. "I'm fine."

"No way we're taking chances with that," Gerth said before Addy could argue. He plunged his arm back into his bag and came out with a first aid kit.

"Give it to me." Nira held out her hand in a way that made it clear she didn't expect to be questioned.

"Nira's in her surgical residency," Tol said, anticipating Addy's protest before she opened her mouth.

"Graduated from med school in two years," Gerth added. It was the only thing Gerth had ever approved of when it came to Nira. "It's probably good you brought her along, Tol."

"I wasn't brought here. I was kidnapped." Nira glared at Tol. "And thanks *so* much for that glowing endorsement."

Nira's medical skills were not what had been on Tol's mind when he dragged her into the portal. He was torn between wanting to apologize for putting her in danger she hadn't asked for and shouting at her for all the trouble she'd caused back at the manor. He was still undecided, so he said nothing at all.

Nira tossed her head, reminding Tol of one those women from a hair commercial. She certainly didn't look like she'd just lived through the portal, hurricane-force winds, and freezing rain they'd actually been in.

"Sit down," Nira said in a haughty voice.

Addy looked ready to bite Nira's head off.

Tol gave her a pleading look. Addy muttered something about *evil beauty queen*, but she huffed out a sigh and sat.

"Remind me why you're here again," Addy said to Nira, the slightest hint of bitterness tinging her words.

Tol opened his mouth to explain.

Sensing that things were about to get awkward, Gerth announced, "The rest of us will explore the castle. Erikir, go with Fred. Olivia, you're with me."

Tol held out his vial of Source to Gerth, trying to hide his worry that Gerth and Nira's were now completely empty. Gerth made no move to take the vial.

Tol lowered his voice, using what Gerth referred to as *the king voice*. "Don't make me order you," he said. "What if the shadow…the Nyxar…comes back?"

"Then you'll need your Source even more," Gerth replied calmly.

"Don't you dare," Tol began, getting to his feet in preparation of *making* Gerth take it, when Addy interrupted him.

"I've been thinking." She gave Tol a look that immediately set him on guard. "You know how I helped make the shadow creature go away because my blood has Source in it?"

Tol didn't say anything. He had a bad feeling about what Addy was about to suggest, and he didn't even want her to speak the words.

"Yeah?" Gerth asked.

"I know it's super gross, but maybe you could…you know…," her gaze slid to Tol again before she said, "get Source from my blood."

"Absolutely not," Tol snarled.

At the same time, Fred demanded, "Are you out of your goddamn mind, Ads?"

"Just hear me out." Addy gave Tol a look that made his jaw click shut. "My blood regenerates, so you wouldn't be taking something that I wouldn't be able to get back."

"That does make sense," Gerth said, pursing his lips as his mind churned with possibilities. "Her blood isn't pure Source, but something's gotta be better than nothing, right?"

"Wrong," Tol snapped.

For the first time in his life, he wanted to strike his best mate.

"Tol, be reasonable," Addy said. "I don't see any waterfalls of Source around here, so unless you want everyone to be defenseless, this is the only option."

"You ain't bleedin' yourself like some kind of vampire," Fred told her.

For once, Tol was in complete agreement with Fred.

"Vampires are the ones who drink the blood, not the ones who give it," Nira informed Fred. She gave Addy a wide smile. "I think bleeding you is a brilliant idea. Here, give me those shears. I'll do it—"

Tol put himself in between Addy and the rest of their group.

"It's not happening," he ground out.

First, Addy would give her blood to Gerth and Nira. Then, Erikir would need some when his Source ran out. After that, every one of the Chosen would be wanting some. At first, it would be just enough to stave off the end of their immortality. But then….

Tol knew his people. He knew of their insatiable ambition and what happened when they got a taste of power.

Addy wasn't some tool to be used by his people.

"This is stupid," Addy said. "Tol, it's not your decision to make." She dug the point of her shears into the smooth skin of her forearm.

Fury made Tol's tongue swell until he couldn't manage a single word. He watched as Nira and Gerth handed over their necklaces. He watched Addy's blood collect in the vials.

"You're letting your emotions get the better of you," Gerth said quietly.

Tol clenched and unclenched his newly remade fist, unable to speak.

"I made an oath to protect her…to protect you both," Gerth continued in that same low voice that no one else except Tol could hear. "Give me more credit."

Tol knew Gerth was right, but it didn't stop his overwhelming terror from clawing its way up his throat.

Gerth held up his vial, now filled with Addy's blood, and inspected it. "Are you going to be the guinea pig or am I?" he asked Nira.

"After you." She waved an imperious hand.

Gerth unstopped his vial and poured a single drop of Addy's blood onto his finger. Grimacing, he put the blood in his mouth.

Gerth's Haze reacted even more quickly than it would with regular Source. And it was doubly bright. Tol had to shield his eyes.

"What do you think?" Nira asked. "Are you about to keel over?"

"Not a chance." Gerth flashed a grin at Addy. "Tastes like blood, but gods it's *powerful*."

"Why, thank you," Addy replied.

Tol ground his teeth.

"Not sure why that would be," Gerth continued, "but I can sense my Influence is stronger, and will last longer, with your blood."

"I'll take your word on that." Nira gave her vial a distasteful look.

"Well, now that that's done," Addy said in a falsely cheerful voice, "we can bandage me up and go about our business."

"We'll, uh, go check things out," Gerth said, with an uncertain glance at Tol.

Tol continued to fume in silence.

"Be careful," Addy told them, looking straight at her sister.

Olivia nodded before disappearing with Gerth. Erikir and Fred went in a different direction. Tol turned all of his attention on Addy's wounds.

"Do her hands need stitches?" he asked, worry churning in his gut as fresh blood oozed from one of her palms.

"Tol, if you want to be useful, get your blinding Haze out of my face," Nira told him.

Tol decided to keep his mouth shut while Nira was armed with tweezers and rubbing alcohol.

Acid surged into Tol's throat when Nira plunged in the tweezers. Except for a slight wince, Addy didn't react.

"Just a little more gravel stuck in there." Nira smiled sweetly as she dug the tweezers back in.

Addy sucked in a breath.

"Be gentle," Tol snapped.

"She's just a big baby," Nira huffed, but her prodding got a little gentler after that.

"Tell me what's going on at the manor," Tol ordered Nira as soon as Addy's hands were clean and bandaged.

With everything else that had happened since the portal deposited them in this world, more pressing matters had captured his attention. Now, all of the urgency Tol had felt when he yanked Nira into the portal returned.

"I don't want to talk about this in front of *her.*" Nira inclined her head at Addy.

Tol stared at Nira, unblinking, and waited.

"Fine." She sighed. "But I really don't see why our business is any of her business."

"Addy is our future queen." Tol let a cold warning enter his voice. "Whatever is happening at the manor is very much her business."

He saw Addy's pale skin go colorless at the mention of her becoming the Chosen queen. He knew it was an inordinate amount of pressure for her to shoulder. She had become so completely enmeshed in his life it was difficult to remember that, two months ago, she hadn't even known his world existed.

He reached out his left hand—the one made of golden light and the gods' power—and brushed his thumb across Addy's cheek.

You're going to be a brilliant queen, he tried to tell her through his touch.

She leaned into him like she understood.

Tol turned his attention back on Nira. "Start talking," he ordered.

"The rebellion is getting worse." Nira carefully replaced the cap on the antibiotic ointment. As she did so, her hand shook. The movement was slight enough that, if Tol hadn't been carefully observing her every move, he would have missed it.

"The Jesul family gives speeches every day about how your parents are incompetent rulers, and that you'll be the king to bring about our final demise. They're making moves to dethrone your parents before you can complete the blood marriage."

Tol swore. He wanted to shout at Nira. As he parted his lips to do just that, he stopped himself. Nira might have been the fire that lit the powder keg, but it was his decisions that had made this whole shite storm possible. He was the one who had postponed the blood marriage. He was the one who was putting the Chosen in a desperate position.

"Who are these Jesul people?" Addy asked, inspecting the new bandages wound around her palms.

Tol drew in a shuddering breath as he tried to take hold of his emotions.

"Lord and Lady Jesul are the last descendants of the oldest Chosen family on record," he explained. "They still resent that, a thousand years ago, the Celestial named my family as the Chosen rulers instead of theirs. They've never gotten over the slight."

"Tol." Nira clicked her nails against the stone floor. "They're planning to execute you."

Tol laughed at that. "Let them try."

Addy closed her newly-bandaged hand around her garden shears, looking like she wanted to attack the Jesuls here and now.

"This isn't something to joke about," Nira told him.

"The only reason they have any power at all is because you told them I wasn't doing the blood marriage," Tol accused.

It wasn't completely fair or accurate, but Tol was angry, and Nira was the easiest target.

Nira flushed. "I was... upset." She looked away from Tol. When she spoke again, her voice was softer. "I didn't realize how far it was all going to go."

If Tol didn't know better, he'd think Nira was apologizing. In eighteen years, he'd never heard Nira apologize to anyone.

"I tried to stop them from burning down the manor," Nira continued when he didn't say anything. "I just wanted to piss you off. I never wanted to put anyone's lives in danger." Tears glittered on her lashes. "If I could go back in time and do it all over again, I would."

Tol sighed, all of his irritation seeping out of him. "I know. I don't blame you."

Nira had lost everyone who had ever mattered to her. Her parents were killed during the Crossing, and like most of the Chosen, she had no siblings. Her only remaining family were her two-hundred-year-old aunts, and they were both almost out of Source. Even Tol had abandoned her after he met Addy.

If he'd been in Nira's position, he would have been angry enough to want to hurt him, too.

"You're my prince," Nira said, her voice devoid of its usual sharpness. "I know I messed up, and that I can't change what's happened. That's why I came to warn you."

"How did you even know where to find us?" Addy asked.

Nira stared at Addy the same way she might regard a piece of gum stuck to her shoe. At the look Tol gave her, Nira sighed.

"I overheard the king and queen discussing your," Nira twirled her finger through the air in front of Addy's face, "little problem. I was able to fill in the rest, and with the little crush the Magnantius' pilot has on me, it didn't take much to figure out where he'd brought you." She gave Addy a saccharine smile. "It's going to suck for you when this whole plan fails miserably and Tol ends up blood marrying your sister."

A wave of sickness passed through Tol at the mere mention of it.

"Shut it about the blood marriage," Tol warned her. "Tell me more about the manor."

Nira looked up at him, and Tol saw her expression shift to genuine worry. "There are rumors Lord and Lady Jesul bought Forsaken weapons. And our people are angry. Everyone thinks you and the Fount abandoned them. Your parents haven't said where you went or why."

Tol raked a hand through his hair. "I thought everyone would calm down when my parents distributed the Source reserves."

Nira arched an eyebrow. "You parents haven't said anything about distributing the reserves."

"What?" Tol demanded.

"They haven't. They're just telling everyone to keep calm until you get back, but they haven't said anything more specific than that."

"You're not making all of this up, are you?" Addy asked.

"Why would I do that?" Nira shot back. "You think I was desperate enough for a free vacation that I wanted to tag along with you lot?"

Addy crossed her arms but didn't say anything else.

"Listen to me, Tol." Nira turned her attention back on him. "If you don't do something, the Jesuls are going to take the throne."

Any amusement Tol might have felt before at the Jesuls' desire to kill him vanished. His parents hadn't distributed the reserves.

Why? What did that mean?

He thought of his parents and Gran, returning to a burned-down manor and subjects clambering for a blood marriage that wasn't happening.

What had he forced his family to walk back into?

And here he was, a world away, with nothing to show for putting everyone's lives at risk.

"As soon as we leave here, we'll go straight to the manor," Addy said, breaking into Tol's endless loop of regret and self-scorn. "I'm sure once you talk to everyone—"

"Gods, you really are a naïve little thing, aren't you?" Nira asked.

Addy ignored her. "Tol, you're their prince. They'll listen to you."

Before he could respond, the walkie talkie in his pocket crackled to life.

"Mates?" Gerth's voice cut through the static. "You are not going to believe what we just found."

CHAPTER 8

ADDY

Addy's Haze flared to life as she raced through the dilapidated rooms and hallways, her shears clutched in her hand. Tol and Nira were right behind her.

They met up with the rest of their group on the far end of the castle. The others were lined up along the edge of a crumbling stone floor and looking out.

"What's going—" Addy broke off as she caught sight of what had captured their attention.

There was a small courtyard in the middle of the castle walls. Unlike every other part of this world they'd seen so far, this little patch of land wasn't barren and ugly. Instead, there was some kind of crop growing in neat little rows up and down the space.

Addy knew a well-tended garden when she saw one, and it was obvious this wasn't some leftover remnant from eighteen years ago. And that meant there was someone else here.

"T-Tolumus?"

They all whipped around.

A tall man with olive skin and long, white hair was looking back at them. His beard grew down to his stomach, but it was neatly combed and there wasn't a hair out of place. His clothes were threadbare, but they were clean. The man didn't look like an apocalypse survivor. His spine was straight, and Addy could see pride and dignity in the way he held himself. On the whole, the man looked a lot more put together than Addy felt. He wore a vial around his neck that looked like it only had a drop or two left at the bottom.

It was the man's eyes that made Addy loosen her grip on her garden shears. He had kind eyes.

"Walidir Magnantius?" Gerth asked, at the same time Tol choked out, "Grandfather?"

Addy gaped. This was Getyl Magnantius' husband—the man everyone assumed was dead, but Tol's gran talked to like he was standing right beside her.

"The last time I held you, you were an infant." Walidir's eyes shone with emotion as he stared at Tol. "I thought Getyl was just pulling my chain when she said you'd become a man."

Addy held her breath as Walidir and Tol moved toward each other.

Walidir reached up to touch the ends of Tol's hair. "Your grandmother never stops complaining about how short you keep this." He laughed softly. "She said you're as willful as your parents."

"I—" Tol swallowed. "I thought—"

The men wrapped their arms around each other in a fierce embrace.

Addy felt her throat burn as she watched Tol hold the grandfather he had believed to be dead.

Erikir took careful steps forward, like he was afraid he might not be welcome. With a start, Addy remembered this man was Erikir's grandfather, too. Walidir gave a little cry at the sight of him.

"Erikir!" Walidir wiped a tear from his eye and beamed at Tol's cousin.

"Grandfather," Erikir whispered. His face had drained of color. He looked like he was rooted to the spot.

Walidir wiped away another tear. "Come here, my boy."

The contained, sullen boy Addy was familiar with transformed. Erikir ran to his grandfather. He hugged Walidir with as much vigor as Tol had.

Walidir cupped Tol and Erikir's faces and stared at them through tear-bright eyes. He murmured, "I never thought I'd get to see you. Getyl said you were coming, but—"

"You actually talk to Gran?" Tol asked, his mouth falling slightly ajar.

"What did you think, that she was conversing with empty air?" Walidir peered at Tol. "How do you think I survived all this time without losing my gods-damned mind? Her voice in my head kept me going day after day."

"But that's not possible," Erikir said.

"You weren't even blood married," Tol added.

"My boys, blood marriage isn't a necessity for the deepest kind of bond between two people. Only true love is needed for that, and that's something your gran and I have in spades."

Tol caught Erikir's gaze. It was the first time Addy had seen them look at each other with an expression besides loathing.

"How does it work?" Erikir asked. "With Gran, I mean."

"It's not the kind of talking we're doing right now, of course," Walidir said, still staring at his grandsons in loving disbelief. "It's more pictures and feelings than actual words. Although I find myself conversing with her at all hours of the day as though she really were here with me."

Tol laughed. "Gran does the same with you."

Walidir beamed.

Addy had been wondering how Walidir could speak flawless English since he'd never left Vitaquias. He must have somehow absorbed the knowledge from Tol's grandmother.

The power of their connection was staggering.

"There's someone I want you to meet," Tol said, turning to motion Addy forward.

Walidir looked up, and his joyous expression turned dark. The kindness in his eyes transformed to something hard and unyielding. His lip curled, like it wanted to pull back into a snarl.

Addy felt her stomach drop out.

"You." Walidir pointed an accusing finger at Addy. "You murdered my firstborn."

"Addy is Lezha Bloodsong's daughter," Tol said hurriedly, "but she's no more Forsaken than the rest of us."

Addy almost couldn't process the meaning of those words. *Lezha Bloodsong's daughter* sounded like someone else. Addy was the daughter of corn farmers…not the woman responsible for murdering her entire family and hundreds of Tol's people.

Addy put a tight leash on her rage before it could take anything away from this beautiful reunion.

"My name is Adelyne Deerborn," Addy said, her voice coming out stronger than she felt. "Sue and Gary Deerborn were my parents."

She looked at Livy, and her twin gave her a smile and nod of encouragement.

"Addy is my fiancé," Tol explained to his grandfather, whose wariness had turned to confusion.

Tol turned to her. Addy's nerves gave a pleasant jolt of warmth at the way he was looking at her.

"She's going to be our queen as soon as we're blood married," Tol continued.

Addy's anxiety spiked at that reminder.

She wasn't wise or well-spoken or any of the things she knew a monarch needed to be. Somehow, *excellent killing record with garden shears* didn't seem like the necessary resumé point for the Chosen queen.

"Getyl didn't mention anything about her," Walidir said, more to himself.

Addy hesitated by Tol's side, not knowing what to say or do.

"But—" Walidir's wrinkled face became even more pinched as he drew his fluffy white eyebrows together. "I thought the Fount was to be a mortal?"

"Right, well, that's a bit of a longer story." Tol wrapped an arm around Addy's waist, as though he could sense her discomfort. "But Addy is the woman I'm going to blood marry."

Hearing those words from Tol's lips, and the certainty with which he spoke them, quieted the nervous fluttering in Addy's stomach.

"This is the real Fount," Erikir said, his ugly sneer back in place as he pointed to Livy.

"And I'd also like you to meet my best mate," Tol said, giving Erikir a warning look. "Gerth was just a baby when we left but—"

"Gerth." Walidir took Gerth's hands in both of his. "I knew your parents well. They were the best sort of people."

It was the only time Addy had ever seen Gerth without a reply on the tip of his tongue. Gerth swallowed several times. When he spoke, his voice was barely audible. "I don't suppose—"

Addy felt like someone had plunged their hand into her chest and grabbed hold of her heart. Gerth was always so happy and put together, it was easy to forget he'd lost his family just like Addy.

Walidir shook his head. "I'm so very sorry, my boy. I am the only one left."

There was such a sense of loss in the way Walidir spoke those words. It made Addy think about what it would mean to survive in this place for eighteen years…alone.

She would have lost her mind.

"How is it possible that you're here?" Erikir asked, his eyes still wide with disbelief.

"Your grandmother and I believe our connection kept me alive. Your gran and I always had a way of making each other stronger. I believe that because she was alive and well in the mortal world, it was enough to get me through the worst of the storms here."

Walidir let tears fall unabashedly down his cheeks.

"Surviving has been both a blessing and a curse."

Tol looked at Gerth, apology and guilt written over his features. Gerth gave him a short shake of his head and turned away.

Addy knew how Gerth was feeling. The loss of her own parents and sisters was fresh in her mind—an ever-present wound that shrunk and expanded but would never fully heal. She wished there was something she could say to Gerth to ease his pain.

Livy, who was standing next to Gerth, put a hand on his forearm and said something to him. Her words were too quiet to overhear, but Addy knew her twin was saying exactly what Addy would have said if she could find the right words.

Sweet Livy. Their family's childhood nickname for Addy's twin was as accurate as Addy's nickname of *Firecracker Addy.*

Addy caught Livy's eye and smiled her thanks.

"Ah, and let me guess." Walidir held out his hands to Nira. "Meline and Elios's daughter, I presume?"

"Yes," Nira whispered, stepping forward.

"You look just like your mother." Walidir took Nira's hand and raised it to his lips. "Every Chosen man on Vitaquias was in love with her. Getyl never let me go visit because she said the puddles of drool I left were embarrassing."

Nira let out a choked laugh. In spite of herself, Addy felt something for this girl she never thought she would: understanding. The whole thing made Nira human in a way she had never been before.

Walidir let go of Nira's hand. "Come here, Fount. Let me have a look at you."

Livy looked to Addy, and then she came to stand before Walidir.

"I'm Olivia Deerborn," Livy said, her voice full of the gentle confidence that was just so Livy.

Addy felt a fierce pride for her sister. Livy had only known the truth about these other people…this other world…for less than a week. And yet, Livy was handling it the way she handled everything, with grace and poise.

"Now, explain to me why you don't wish to blood marry the Fount," Walidir said to Tol without taking his eyes off Livy. "This lovely young lady radiates goodness."

Addy's heart lurched.

Tol answered without hesitation. "Because I can't live without Addy."

Addy moved closer to Tol. She expected Walidir to start listing the reasons why Livy was the better choice for Tol than Addy. Instead, he nodded like he understood.

"You love your Adelyne the way I love my Getyl," he said, like it all made perfect sense.

Addy didn't trust herself to say anything.

Walidir raised his chin in Addy's direction. "As my grandson's eternal love, you are every bit a part of my family."

Addy hesitated only a moment before taking the hand the old man offered to her.

As soon as their skin touched, something like a static shock went through her ring finger. Piercing rays of sapphire light shot out from the three stones in her engagement ring.

"Oh." Walidir let out a startled gasp. "The Celestial's ring."

Addy stared in wonder at the stones. She had felt the power hidden inside them from the moment Tol put the ring on her finger, but they had never actually done anything before. Now, instead of the blue-black color she was used to, the stones had turned more sapphire. Addy could see light swirling and pulsing in their depths. She felt their magic.

"What's happening?" she asked, pulling her hand back from Walidir's before the power in her ring lifted her off the ground. Or exploded.

"I was the first one to ever wear that ring," Walidir said. "I believe it recognizes me."

Normally, Addy would think it strange for someone to be talking about a ring like an old friend. But even in the short time she'd been wearing it, she felt a connection to its power.

"You know, the ring feeds off the inherent strength of its wearer," Walidir continued. "For me, it made every drop of Source I consumed as potent as ten drops. For Getyl, it provided light whenever she was in need of it. For you, it will behave differently."

When Tol first gave Addy the ring, he'd told her the Celestial had infused a part of herself into these gemstones, and that they would reveal their abilities at a time of their choosing.

With a sinking feeling, Addy wondered if being a Forsaken by blood would make the ring not work for her.

The thought made her stomach flip-flop.

Walidir said, "I gave the ring to Getyl on our five-hundredth anniversary. There are centuries of love bound up in those stones." Walidir took Addy's hand again, and the swirling mass of light and color flared back to life.

"Gran gave the ring to me when I told her about Addy," Tol explained.

Addy was afraid Walidir would be offended that his wife had given away something so precious, but he only nodded.

"This ring is one of a kind and priceless," Walidir said.

"Just like the woman wearing it." Tol grinned at her.

Gerth made a gagging sound. Addy shook her head, but she could feel her own smile curving her lips.

"I wonder," Walidir said, almost to himself. "The stones seem to react to both of us. I wonder if we can combine our strength to bring them to life."

Walidir closed his hands around Addy's left one. Immediately, she felt the stones' power begin to churn. Someone gasped as a pulsing blue glow seeped out from her clenched fingers.

Ropy wisps of smoke emanated from the stones. They swirled and thickened, until they formed a kind of lasso made out of light and smoke. Addy felt it tugging on her, like a magnetic pull. When she looked into the lasso's center, she caught a faint glimpse of Aunt Meredith's farmhouse.

She tore her hand free from Walidir's, somehow knowing that if she didn't, whatever this ring's magic was doing to her would expand out of her control.

As soon as her skin was free from Walidir's, the blue light faded. The gemstones' magic settled down.

Addy was breathless.

"My gods," Walidir said, his voice hoarse. "Did you see that?"

"My aunt's house," Addy managed, still winded from whatever had just happened. "Back on Earth."

Walidir shook his head, looking as amazed as she felt.

"Incredible," he said. "I believe this power will allow you to create portals."

They were all silent for several seconds while they processed that.

Walidir continued, "The ring is bound to you now. No one else can remove it."

"Will it only work for Addy, or could someone else latch on for a ride?" Gerth asked. "Say, for instance, that Addy's very dear friend was hankering for a vacation in the south of France. Could she bring him there? Hypothetically?"

"That's a region in the mortal world," Tol explained at his grandfather's puzzled look.

Chuckling, Walidir nodded. "I expect she could."

"Excellent." Gerth rubbed his hands together. "Don't make any big plans for after the blood marriage," he told Addy.

"Yeah, because I definitely want to spend my honeymoon with you," she teased him.

"Speaking of the blood marriage," Tol said. "We need to speak with the Celestial." He paused, like he was afraid to ask the question that was burning a hole through Addy's brain. "Is she…alive?"

CHAPTER 9

ADDY

Addy held her breath. All of their hopes hinged on the answer to this question.

Is the Celestial alive?

"Yes," Walidir said. Addy's heart leapt. "But—"

Whatever else he was about to say ended on a wheeze. Walidir began to cough. And cough. The fit seemed to grow worse by the second. Tol put a hand on his grandfather's back, while Gerth dug in his bag for a bottle of water.

Walidir grasped the vial around his neck with a trembling hand.

Once the drop of Source made it between his lips, Walidir stopped coughing. He sighed and thumped himself on the chest.

"Grandfather?" Erikir asked, his brow knitted in worry.

"Ageing is a hairy old bitch, if you'll pardon the expression," Walidir said, waving away his grandsons' concern.

Tol and Erikir looked at each other, and then at the nearly-empty vial around their grandfather's neck. They seemed to have the same idea as they both reached for the chain around their necks.

"No." Walidir backed away from them.

Addy felt tension thicken in the air around them. She saw Tol's expression harden in determined stubbornness.

"Grandfather," he began, but Walidir interrupted.

"I will not take your Source." His voice was surprisingly firm. "I will not take so much as a drop from you young people. Do you hear me?"

Addy heard genuine anger in his voice, and beneath that, fear.

"But Grandfather—"

"No! Not a drop. You are young, and you have your whole lives ahead of you. I've had my time."

"Um." Addy didn't look at Tol, not wanting to see the fury she knew would light his gaze as soon as she suggested using her blood.

"Adelyne Deerborn, don't even think about it," Fred said, crossing his arms over his chest.

Addy glared at him before turning her attention on Tol's grandfather.

"My blood has Source. It's kind of a long story about why, but it'll give you what you need without having to take any from Erikir or Tol."

"Addy, no," Tol said through gritted teeth.

Addy stopped herself from rolling her eyes. She understood that Tol wanted to protect her, but she didn't understand why spilling a little blood to help his grandfather should even be a conversation. To her, it was a total no-brainer.

"I am not drinking your blood," Walidir said, looking offended.

"By all means, let's bleed her some more," Nira said cheerfully.

Addy didn't appreciate how eager the other girl seemed at the thought of sucking out her blood.

"Here." Gerth reached into his own bag. "If we mix it with this, I bet you won't even be able to taste the blood." He pulled out a bottle of Coke.

"What is that?" Walidir asked, flinching back as Gerth unscrewed the cap and the carbonation hissed through the broken seal.

"It's a mortal drink," Gerth explained. "You'll love it."

"I imagine it will taste better than rotcumbers at any rate," Walidir said, still looking skeptical.

"Rotcumbers?" Fred asked.

"Nastiest things on the planet." Walidir wrinkled his nose. "Only things I can get to grow." He flicked his hand in the direction of the garden.

Perking up, Fred carefully made his way among the rows of plants.

"Can I?" Fred asked, bending down to study the green leaves and tubers that were poking up from the soil.

"Be my guest," Walidir replied. "They've kept me alive all these years, but I won't pretend to be grateful for their flavor." He sniffed in distaste. His scorn turned to one of interest when he asked no one in particular, "By the way, what is that mortal drink your gran is so fond of?"

Tol and Erikir both smiled.

"Tea," they said at the same time.

Fred inspected the shriveled, brown, hairy tuber he'd just pulled out of the ground. After wiping the dirt off on his shirt, he took a tentative bite. He gagged and immediately spit it back out.

"That is nasty. Here." He passed the tuber to Livy. "Try it."

Livy crossed her arms and gave Fred an affronted look. "Why would I want to try something that was too gross for you to swallow?"

Livy had a point, but Addy had to admit she was curious. When would she have another chance to try food from a different planet? It was like the time their mom had bought freeze-dried astronaut ice cream from the grocery store when she was teaching Addy and Livy about the solar system. Except this was so much cooler.

Fred was now waving the hairy vegetable in Livy's face. Livy was ducking behind Gerth and making threats they all knew she'd never have the heart to follow through on.

Addy was about to request her own taste of alien food when Tol moved in front of her, like he was shielding her.

"Taking Addy's blood isn't a good idea," he said to the group before turning to his grandfather. "But I insist that you take some of my Source."

"It's just some blood." Addy pushed him aside and rolled up her sleeve.

She knew how precious every drop of Tol's Source was. She wasn't going to make him use it if he didn't have to.

Using her garden shears, she made a small cut along the forearm that wasn't already bandaged from giving some of her blood to Nira and Gerth. She took Walidir's nearly-empty vial and let her blood drip into it.

"Is this enough?" she asked after the vial was mostly full.

"The more the better," Nira said. "Maybe you ought to just keep going." She gave Addy that sugar-sweet smile.

Addy resisted giving her the finger, because she wanted to make a good impression on Tol's grandfather.

"That's enough," Tol said, sounding both kingly and angry.

"Bandage her up," he snapped at Nira. "Now."

Addy didn't see what he was so upset about. It wasn't like she was about to faint or anything.

Gerth took the vial with Addy's blood, poured a few drops into the Coke, and swirled it around.

"Bottoms up," he said cheerily as he handed the bottle to Walidir.

Walidir took it but made no move to raise it to his lips.

"Do it for Gran," Erikir said, his voice softer than Addy had ever heard it.

Grimacing, Walidir lifted the bottle to his lips. He made a soft sound of surprise as the bubbles hit his tongue. Then, he guzzled down half the bottle.

Walidir let out a loud belch and then laughed. Addy felt her own grin spread over her face at the old man's delight.

"Plenty more where that came from," Gerth said. At the death glare Tol gave him, he clarified, "Coke, I mean. Sheesh."

Addy blinked. Was Walidir's face less wrinkled than it had been a second ago?

A few more moments passed, leaving no question. His arthritic fingers were straightening. His too-pale skin was turning a deep bronze like the rest of the Chosen. His cloudy eyes brightened. His hair turned from white to salt-and-pepper.

Addy's blood had made Walidir age in reverse.

Weird.

"I—" Walidir looked down at himself. "Thank you, Adelyne." He let out a choked laugh. "I never thought I'd survive long enough to see the return of my people to this world. You have given me a gift beyond words."

"It's no problem," Addy said, feeling awkward that someone should have this kind of a reaction to drinking her blood.

Walidir dabbed at his eyes with his ragged sleeve. "You best make sure you don't do that for Tolumus, otherwise he'll never be able to blood marry."

Addy turned to look at Tol, who nodded like he already knew this.

"It would contaminate my blood, which needs to be pure for a blood marriage to work," Tol explained. He gave her a small smile. "Fortunately, I have no intentions of drinking your blood, so I think we'll be fine."

"Just don't forget there are other ways of invalidating the blood marriage." Walidir nudged Tol in the ribs and winked at Addy.

"Oh gods." Tol rolled his eyes skyward. "You're as bad as Gran."

Gerth snickered.

Addy's cheeks burned. She knew what Tol's grandfather was referring to, and she was more than a little uncomfortable with discussing her and Tol's sex life…or lack thereof…in front of his grandfather.

"Aww, don't look so glum, sweetie," Nira said in that honeyed voice that made Addy want to punch her. "He's worth the wait. I taught him everything he knows."

"Shut it, Nira," Tol said, looking as flustered as Addy felt.

Gerth cleared his throat. "Anyway, about the Celestial…."

Walidir's mischievous expression turned serious. "Before we talk about that, I got the sense from your gran that our people are nearly out of Source." He licked his lips. "Is it true?"

Addy watched Tol's embarrassment turn to that look of heavy responsibility he got whenever he thought about his people's future. He gave his grandfather a grim nod.

"What I don't understand," Erikir said, stabbing an accusing finger at Tol, "is why, if you knew Addy's blood had Source in it, you didn't start giving out her blood when you brought her to the manor the last time? She could have—"

One second, Tol was standing next to Addy. The next, he had Erikir pinned against the wall. His golden hand was wrapped around Erikir's throat.

"Say it again," Tol growled. "Suggest bleeding Addy. See if you live to finish your sentence."

Erikir glared at Tol, but didn't say anything. He must have seen the same thing Addy did—Tol was serious.

As soon as Tol released him, Erikir shoved Tol.

"You care more about your precious Forsaken girlfriend getting a little anemic than you care about our entire race's survival."

For once, Addy didn't completely disagree.

"I really don't mind," Addy began, but then Tol turned his fury on her.

"They wouldn't just take a few drops. They'd bleed you to death." His face had paled, and Addy could tell he had already given this some thought.

"You have a low opinion of your own people if you think anyone would do that," Erikir said, but there was a hint of uncertainty on his sullen face.

"Look around you," Tol said. "How do you think this happened? Do you think our people intended to drain the Source?"

"No," Tol answered his own question when no one spoke. "They told themselves they only needed a few more drops. And then a few more. Don't you get it? They never stopped needing just a little more."

Tol was breathing heavily now. Addy was overwhelmed by the depth of his feeling. On the one hand, she felt like if her blood could save some of his people, it was her responsibility to give them what they needed. On the other, the thought of being sucked dry by hundreds of people with an insatiable appetite for Source was less than appealing.

"At the very least, our scientists would want to pick her apart like a lab rat," Gerth acknowledged.

Addy didn't like the sound of that, either.

"Let me make myself perfectly clear." Tol stared around at the others, his dark gaze fixing on Nira and Erikir. "If *anyone* outside of this group finds out about Addy's blood, I swear to the gods it will be the last thing you ever do."

"If it comes down to Addy spilling a few drops of blood or one of our people dying, then I'm going to choose the former," Erikir said.

Either he didn't notice the promise of death in Tol's eyes or he didn't care.

Tol strode up to Erikir. The other boy didn't step back, although he looked like he wanted to.

"Look at me," Tol commanded.

Erikir did, and to Addy's surprise, she saw his eyes glaze over. Nira squeaked in surprise. Gerth murmured, "This is a new development."

Tol was Influencing Erikir, Addy realized.

The Chosen weren't susceptible to Influence, or at least, they weren't supposed to be. Addy remembered how Tol had once told her he was the most powerful of his people. She looked at him with new eyes now. There was no denying that Tol was something altogether different, even from the other Chosen.

"Tol?" Addy asked.

He didn't even seem to hear her.

"Give me your word that you will not reveal the secret of Addy's blood to anyone."

"I give you my word," Erikir replied immediately in a tone that was devoid of all emotion.

"Tol, you're crossing a line," Nira said, looking nervous. "He's your cousin."

Tol's gaze was locked with Erikir's. Addy didn't think either of them were aware of anything that was going on outside of their connection.

"Tol, come back," Livy said in a quiet voice.

Tol reacted, wrenching his gaze from Erikir's and pulling his Haze back inside himself. Erikir slumped to the ground. He gave Tol a death glare, but he looked too weak to manage anything more.

Addy knew Livy had done the right thing, but she wasn't quite sure how to feel about the fact that her sister had been the one to draw Tol out of whatever trance he'd fallen into.

"None of our people are going to die," Tol said, breaking their stunned silence.

He turned his attention on Walidir. "It's time you told us about the Celestial."

CHAPTER 10

OLIVIA

Olivia couldn't begin to process all of the bizarre, terrible, and wonderful things she'd seen since they were sucked into the portal and deposited onto this entirely different planet. It wasn't that she hadn't believed all of it existed. She'd seen too much strangeness since she'd been imprisoned by the Forsaken in an Alaskan army base to have any other explanation. It was just that being here made everything she'd been told about more real than it had been before. It was like the difference between reading a book and being dropped into the world described on the pages.

She'd seen Tol's missing arm essentially grow back. She'd witnessed an old man age in reverse. And she'd listened as Tol and Erikir's grandfather explained that the Celestial—the one who had transferred all of her power to Olivia—was still alive.

They were on their way to try to talk to the Celestial now, although they didn't have high hopes of finding her. In eighteen years of searching for her, Walidir had only glimpsed her once. He hadn't seen hide or hair of her again.

They would begin their search at the place where Walidir had seen her before.

Olivia tried not to get her hopes up, since Walidir wasn't even sure himself if he'd seen the Celestial or if she'd been a figment of his imagination. Olivia couldn't blame the man if he'd hallucinated after everything he'd been through.

Olivia noticed Erikir was lagging behind the others. He hadn't looked well since Tol took over his mind, although it didn't seem like anyone else had noticed. She slowed her steps until he caught up.

"Are you alright?" she asked.

"Why do you care?" Erikir shot back.

Olivia knew his foul mood wasn't really directed at her. She didn't say anything, but she kept her pace slow enough so he wasn't walking alone.

"I'm sorry," Erikir said after a few moments. "You're not the one I'm angry with."

"I know." She offered him a small smile. "And apology accepted."

For a few seconds, they walked in companionable silence.

"Is it Livy or Olivia?" he asked.

"What?" she turned to face him.

"Your sister and the farmer call you Livy, but you always introduce yourself as Olivia. So, which do you prefer?"

No one had ever asked her that before.

"O-Olivia," she stammered, taken aback. "I always liked it better."

"Okay. Olivia, then." He didn't smile, but he wasn't scowling anymore, either.

"Oh my God."

The panicked cry came from Addy. The others had disappeared around a path skirting the edge of the cliff so Olivia couldn't see what Addy saw, but she didn't have to. There was only one thing that could terrify her sister that much.

Olivia ran.

She glanced over the side of the cliff, confirming what she already suspected. There was a lake at the bottom.

The lake was polluted and all but dry, and yet Olivia recognized it from the way Addy had described her dreams. There was the rocky shore, and the burned, leafless remains of the trees that encircled the lake. The sunken pit that must have once been full of clear Source was now no more than an oily, black puddle. But Olivia knew that wouldn't ease Addy's panic after what had happened to her there.

Addy had been terrified of drowning ever since they were little kids. It was only a few days ago when Addy learned that her birth mother had nearly drowned Addy in the lake of Source to make her immortal even on the mortal world.

Olivia hurried to her sister, but Tol was already there.

He wrapped his arms around her, turning them both so his body blocked her view over the cliff. Addy was shaking, but whatever Tol was murmuring in her ear was calming her.

"Tol, what's the problem?" Gerth asked, looking around for some sign of whatever had caused Addy's reaction.

Tol said something to Gerth, and then he turned all of his attention back on Addy.

Addy was still pale as a ghost, but her lips moved as she responded to whatever Tol had said to her. She was coherent and standing on her own two feet. It was better than Olivia had seen her on more than a few occasions when her twin woke up from the dream. During the worst times, nothing Olivia said could make her feel better.

"Wonderful. Tol's found himself a cowardly Forsaken," Nira said, flicking an invisible piece of dust from her dress. "How boringly ironic."

Olivia turned to the other girl, ready to defend her twin, when she saw the look on Nira's face. There was naked pain and longing, and the whole of Nira's gaze was fixed on Tol. Fred was looking at Addy in the same way.

Tol and Addy were oblivious to everyone except each other.

Olivia felt a strange protectiveness over Nira at the sight of her pain. It made no sense. She'd just met the other girl, and Nira had made it abundantly clear she had no interest in befriending Olivia.

It was the same way she had felt toward Erikir after Tol hurt him, and how she'd felt toward Gerth after Walidir told him his parents were dead. She couldn't explain why. She just felt a deep desire to know and protect these people.

Olivia watched as Addy's heaving breaths became steadier, and she no longer looked like she was about to pass out.

Olivia tried to ignore the tiny, painful hole that had opened up inside her.

It wasn't that she was jealous that her sister's heart belonged so completely to Tol. It was just that Olivia no longer knew where she fit into her sister's life. These people…this world…belonged to Addy.

Realizing that she was intruding on a private moment between Tol and Addy, Olivia turned her attention back on the ruined lake at the bottom of the cliff. The sight of it filled her with a crippling sadness that she didn't understand. Her chest ached almost as much as when she thought about her parents and sisters.

Her reaction made no sense. How could she grieve for a lake?

But when she looked around, she saw Gerth and Erikir staring at the lake with the same kind of endless sadness she felt.

"Are they just going to stay like that all day?" Nira complained loud enough that they could all hear.

Olivia took a deep breath, and then she walked over to where Tol and Addy were still huddled together.

"I can't," Addy said, her voice muffled from where it was pressed against Tol's chest. "I just can't."

"I'll stay with you," Tol replied, his voice low and quiet.

"No." She lifted her head. "You and Livy have to go. I'll just slow you down."

"I'm not leaving you like this," Tol said.

For just a moment, Olivia wondered what it would be like to be loved like that. She had always felt loved by her parents and sisters, of course, but this love was entirely different. It was also different from the partnership she had imagined with her future husband. She had imagined respect, appreciation, and a deep affection toward each other. Maybe in her most fanciful moments, she'd daydreamed about a relationship like Jane Bennet and Charles Bingley from *Pride and Prejudice*—one based on mutual attraction and cheerful dispositions. She hadn't known such passion and devotion were even possible. It made her heart hurt with longing for something she hadn't even realized she craved.

When Addy first told her about the blood marriage, it had sounded violent and terrible. Now, Olivia wasn't so sure. The idea of being inextricably linked to someone and to know his every thought…. To have him in her mind and heart for eternity…to never be alone….

It sounded beautiful.

"Freddo and I can take Addy back to the castle," Gerth said, seeming to have no compunctions about interrupting the couple's private conversation. "Besides, maybe it'll be easier for you and Olivia to sense the Celestial if the rest of us aren't hanging around."

"What do you think?" Tol asked Addy.

She gave him a shaky nod. Tol wrapped his golden arm all the way around her and pulled her in for a kiss.

When he let her go, he turned his attention on Gerth. "Olivia and I will meet you back at the castle."

Tol caught the walkie-talkie Gerth tossed to him.

"If you need us, give us a ring," Gerth said, draping a friendly arm around Addy's shoulders and steering her away from the view of the polluted lake.

"Erikir and Nira, go with them," Tol said. "Olivia and I can take care of this."

"What if you run into trouble?" Nira asked, crossing her arms.

In answer, Tol let his Haze flare blinding white.

"We'll be fine," Tol said. "Watch each other's backs."

"You want me to come with you, Liv?" Fred asked, throwing Tol a distrustful glance.

She shook her head and smiled, grateful for his concern. Fred was the brother she'd never had, and his presence among all these strangers made her feel less unbalanced…less alone.

"We'll be fine. Take care of Addy," she told Fred.

Fred nodded at her, glared at Tol, and went to follow the others.

Tol watched Addy go. Then, he turned and started down the hill without so much as glancing at Olivia. She hurried after him.

CHAPTER 11

TOL

Tol and Olivia stopped when they reached the edge of the oily, dark lake. It was where Tol's grandfather said he'd once glimpsed the Celestial before losing sight of her forever.

Tol looked at the contaminated puddle of Source. There were countless paintings of the lake's beauty, and to see it like this made his throat constrict.

"Any ideas?" Tol asked. He didn't look at Olivia, but he could feel her sadness mirroring his own.

"I can almost sense her," Olivia said, frowning in concentration. "She's close by."

She hesitated, and Tol could sense her discomfort.

"What is it?" He turned to face her.

Olivia chewed on her lip. "I, um, think we're going to need to combine our strength to find her."

Tol understood. The connection between them wasn't emotional, but there was something intimate about the linking of their minds that felt wrong.

Tol didn't want to touch Olivia. He didn't want to feel his power grow and see into her mind. Because, if he did, it would be like admitting fate had won and that he had no future with Addy. It would be like giving in.

We came here for a reason, he reminded himself. Addy would understand.

He tried and failed not to flinch as he took Olivia's small hand in his. The moment their fingers touched, Tol's vision transformed.

The lake was no longer dark and polluted. It was filled to the brim with crystal-clear Source. Rays of sunlight cut through the water, making the smooth black stones on the bottom gleam metallic.

Instead of the jagged volcanic rocks littering the beach, pure white sand cushioned Tol's feet. The lake was rimmed with impossibly tall, green trees. A cloudless blue sky stretched out overhead.

When Tol looked down at himself, he sucked in a breath. His entire body had turned as golden and radiant as only his left arm had been before. Olivia was just as bright. It was like staring at the sun, except it didn't hurt his eyes.

It wasn't just Olivia's physical presence he could see. He knew her emotions, too.

His cold aloofness was hurting her. He saw it as plain as day, and it filled him with self-loathing.

"Olivia, I'm sorry," he began, knowing she deserved an explanation. "It's just—"

"You don't have to say it," she said quickly. "And there's nothing to be sorry about. I want to be rid of this magic as much as you want it to belong to Addy."

Tol nodded, not sure what else there was to say.

He knew Olivia could see into his emotions the same way he saw into hers. What was she seeing?

Tol curled his fists by his sides. Olivia was a nice person, but Tol wasn't keen on her knowing his mind almost as well as he did.

Olivia wasn't looking at him. All of her attention was fixed on the lake in front of them. She didn't have to explain the pulse of connection she felt with the being beneath the lake. Tol could sense it through her.

The image before them flickered between the beautiful lake, which existed only in their minds, and the oily puddle that was their reality. He matched his steps to Olivia's so they reached the puddle at the same moment. He felt the oily muck seep through his sneaker.

A tremendous force yanked him down.

Tol screamed. At least, he tried to. No sound escaped his parted lips. Maybe he did scream, but it was drowned out by the ripping sound that exploded in his eardrums.

Tol was being torn out of his own body.

There was no other way to describe it. It was painful, although not as agonizing as it should have been given what was happening to him. The pain was nothing compared to the strangeness of what he was seeing.

His physical body was still standing in the oily puddle. His consciousness was sucked beneath the earth.

Tol didn't have time to be afraid as he fell through darkness.

He hit the bottom of…something. It was confusing because he hadn't thought there could be anything below the bottom of the Source lake, and yet, here they were.

He felt nothing, although he could see and hear. It was like he'd become an apparition.

"Are you okay?" he gasped out to Olivia.

"I think so," she replied, sounding as winded as he felt.

He looked at Olivia. She was beside him, not so much standing as hovering. She was still radiating golden light, but she was translucent now instead of solid. She looked like a golden hologram.

"This is bizarre," Tol said.

At least his voice sounded normal.

He glanced around. They were in a cave, which was empty and small enough to cross in ten steps. He wondered how he was breathing in this airless place before he realized he had no need for breath. If there was any smell or temperature down here, he couldn't sense either.

Bloody bizarre.

Before either of them could say anything else, they both sensed another presence. Tol turned and saw…a ghost.

The woman floated through the air. Her tattered, white dress flowed behind her like jellyfish tentacles. Her waist-length white hair rippled in a breeze Tol couldn't feel. Everything about her was haunting. It wasn't just her ghostly physique. There was something utterly different about this…being.

"Celestial," he whispered.

She was here. She was alive…sort of.

Not real, his brain said. *Impossible.*

And yet, as he stared at this ghostly figure hovering before him, he believed anything was possible. For the first time, his desperate wishes gave way to something even more dangerous: hope.

"Welcome home, Prince Tolumus." The Celestial's voice was such a thin whisper Tol shouldn't have been able to hear her at all. Yet, it was like the words were echoing inside him.

"And welcome to you, Fount." The Celestial's ghostly fingers tilted Olivia's chin up so their eyes met.

Olivia's body moved with all the fluid grace of something that wasn't burdened by the limitations of gravity or bones.

"Are we dead?" Olivia asked.

The Celestial's breathy laugh filled the cave.

"No. Your physical bodies are alive and well. I can feel the beat of your hearts from here. It is only your spirits that are with me now." She frowned. "Although, if you had completed the blood marriage, you would be powerful enough to draw your corporeal selves down here, too."

"We aren't blood married," Tol said quickly. "That's why we're here."

Olivia was the one who telepathically explained their situation to the Celestial. When Olivia had finished, the Celestial turned to Tol.

"You gave your heart to a Forsaken? And not just any Forsaken, but Lezha Bloodsong's daughter?!"

Her voice hammered against the cave walls. Her fury filled Tol's mind…compressed it…burned it. He felt like he was being squeezed into pulp and ripped apart at the same time.

"Celestial, please," he began.

"The Forsaken are godless. Leaderless," the Celestial thundered. "They are barbarians!"

The walls of the cave shuddered. Bits of dirt and stone rained down around them.

Silver flames burned in the Celestial's eyes.

Would she kill them? Could she kill them?

Enough, Tol thought.

The Celestial was the reason why Tol had spent his life tracking down the Fount, all the while fearing he'd be too late to save his people. The Celestial was the reason why he was fated to spend eternity with the sister of the woman he loved. And she was tossing blame around at him?

I don't think so.

Tol met the Celestial's gaze with a righteous anger of his own.

"Addy is no more Forsaken than the Fount. She was raised by mortals, and her loyalty is to the Chosen."

Tol was getting sick of having to explain this. He didn't like anyone questioning Addy's motives or goodness.

"It's true," Olivia added, her own voice coming out timid compared to Tol's. "She's my sister, and she loves Tol with all of her heart. She'd never do anything to hurt his people."

"I've already chosen her," Tol said, his voice firm and leaving no room for interpretation. "We just need you to give her the Fount's powers."

He mentally kicked himself when a flash of Olivia's emotions passed through him. He'd referred to her as *the Fount*, not even giving her the courtesy of calling her by name. Like she was more of a thing than a person.

Stop being a prick, he told himself.

Realizing Olivia could probably sense the thoughts going through his mind, he just felt weird.

"Please, Celestial," Tol said, his anger evaporating as a great weariness settled on his ghostly shoulders. "She's the right woman to be our queen. She's…everything."

The shuddering walls and raining dirt stopped as the Celestial's emotions calmed. While she considered him, Tol held his breath…metaphorically.

"Even if I wished to do what you are asking, I could not," the Celestial said. "All of my abilities are now embodied by the Fount. I have given all I had to her."

Before Tol could put words to any of the arguments or questions rising in his mind, the Celestial continued.

"I did not select the mortal who would become the Fount. My magic chose her." The Celestial pointed a ghostly finger at Olivia. "It is not just about the strength she embodies, but her innate spirit. This girl is the one who possesses the ability to temper the Chosen people's ambition."

Olivia shook her head. "Addy has always been the strong one in our family."

"It is not physical strength of which I speak," the Celestial replied. To Tol, she said, "Patience, empathy, mercy. These are the traits that are your perfect balance. The one you love is not the right counterpoint to your power."

Tol started to argue, but the Celestial said, "You have a fierce need to protect your people. This need will drive you to expand, rather than temper, your strength. I've seen it before."

The Celestial sent fragmented images through Tol's mind.

Fire. Earthquakes. Blood. Devastation.

If Tol had been in his physical body, his legs would have given out.

Did the Celestial know this was his greatest fear? Was she just trying to scare him in the hopes that it would make him choose to blood marry Olivia instead of Addy?

The Celestial continued, "With the Forsaken girl by your side, there will be no one to stop your ambition from consuming you and all those you've sworn to lead." Her whisper-thin voice got even quieter. "If the Chosen destroy themselves again, there will be no second chance for redemption."

"Then, I'll just have to do better." A dangerous edge entered Tol's voice. "It's my weakness to overcome, not my wife's."

Even as he spoke the words, a nagging doubt crept into his mind.

He thought about how it felt to have an arm made out of the gods' power. Then, he remembered how he'd lost track of everything else when he was angry with Erikir. He'd heard the others pleading with him to stop; he just hadn't cared. Only Olivia's voice had been loud enough to bring him back.

My problem, Tol thought with a savage fierceness. *My weakness.*

It was a weakness he'd overcome or die trying. He wouldn't fail his people.

The Celestial inclined her head toward Tol, like she was listening to his silent thoughts.

"The one you love is not meant to be the Chosen queen," the Celestial said.

"Addy is brave and loyal, and she'd do anything for the people she cares about," Tol argued. "She's the one I want to rule our people by my side."

"Perhaps you are not the future king of the Chosen I hoped you would be," the Celestial said, her tone full of regret.

Tol's temper flared as an old anger sprang to life.

"You have dictated every aspect of my life since the day I was born," Tol accused the Celestial. "I have never made a single choice that wasn't in some way connected to the future you set out for me." His entire apparitional form was blazing with light and heat. "Let me make my own choice this one time. Please."

The Celestial hung her head.

"I regret all of the responsibility that has burdened you," she whispered.

"I don't want apologies. I want you to make Addy the Fount."

"I no longer have any power left to me." The Celestial motioned to her translucent self. "I cannot undo the magic that has already been set in motion."

Olivia let out a defeated sound, but Tol wasn't ready to give up.

"Olivia has your abilities now, so shouldn't she be able to do what you can't?" he persisted.

"Fate is a vast ocean. The tides are powerful and unyielding, and they have brought you and the Fount together."

"To hells with fate," Tol said. "There must be another way."

A single, translucent tear slid down the Celestial's cheek. "Yes," she agreed reluctantly. "There is a way."

CHAPTER 12

OLIVIA

What you are asking for is possible.

The words echoed inside Olivia's mind, and she could tell the Celestial was speaking only to her. It was strange enough to have a ghost—or whatever the Celestial was—talking inside her head. It was even weirder when she realized the Celestial's words weren't in English. She was speaking some other language Olivia didn't recognize, and yet, Olivia understood every word.

"How?" Olivia asked out loud. "How can I make my sister the Fount?"

You can choose to transfer your powers to her.

Hope and fear surged in Olivia's chest in equal measures, but the Celestial wasn't finished.

But it will require a great sacrifice.

The way the Celestial said those words, *great sacrifice*, had warning prickles dancing along her skin. She ignored them.

"How do I do it?" Olivia asked.

Tol gave her a strange look, probably because he was only hearing her half of the conversation.

First, you must first fully realize and embrace your powers. Then, at your time of greatest need, you must choose to give them away.

Olivia's mind swam. "Time of greatest need? How will I know?"

"Olivia—" Tol began, but she held up a hand to stop him.

You'll know the moment when it comes. Then, you will need to relinquish your powers. The chance will only come once. If, instead of giving your power away you choose to use it, you will remain the Fount forever.

The Celestial was staring at her, waiting for her to understand.

"Olivia," Tol began, but she shook her head. She needed to think.

The Celestial's warning about a great sacrifice came back to her.

"Oh."

There was only one possibility that made sense. Her time of greatest need would come when her life was at risk, and only magic could save her.

For Addy to become the Fount, Olivia would have to let herself die.

The thought sent a shudder through her incorporeal body. The Celestial had a mournful expression in her eyes.

Even as Olivia tried to come to terms with the sacrifice she'd need to make, there was one truth she knew beyond any doubt. When the time came, she'd gladly give her life in exchange for Addy's eternity of happiness.

The blood marriage requires two people to selflessly give themselves to each other, which is an enormous sacrifice, the Celestial's voice said inside Olivia's head. *I sacrificed everything to give my powers to you, and if you choose, you will need to selflessly give of yourself to make the transfer.*

"Olivia, tell me what's going on," Tol demanded. "What's she telling you?"

"She—she says I need to embrace my powers and then choose to give them to Addy after I've realized my full strength," Olivia said, her voice coming out almost as whispery as the Celestial's.

Olivia didn't tell him the other part. She understood Tol's mind enough to know her life was a price he wouldn't be willing to pay. And if Addy found out, she'd never let Olivia go through with the choice she'd already made.

"How do you realize your powers?" Tol asked.

Olivia looked at the Celestial.

You must want to use them. You must accept that they are a part of you. You must abandon your fear.

"I don't—" Olivia began, but she stopped herself.

Olivia didn't know what to think about any of what the Celestial was telling her.

"You must go," the Celestial said, glancing at the cave's ceiling. "There is a storm coming, and your physical bodies are vulnerable."

"Tell me how to access my abilities," Olivia begged, hearing the anxiety in her voice.

This was what she needed to do for Addy. She just had no idea how to go about it.

It's all inside you, the Celestial told her. *It will be more difficult in the mortal world. Here, all you must do is reach out and take hold.*

It seemed to Olivia that the Celestial was seriously overestimating her abilities. If all she had to do was reach out and grab this power, she would have done so by now. She gave the Celestial an uncertain look, hoping for some clue.

The Celestial just waited.

Olivia wished her sister was here. Addy would know what to do.

I'm not cut out for this, she thought, as her desperation began to mount. *Your powers made a mistake when they picked me.*

Neither Tol nor the Celestial was offering her any help. Olivia was on her own.

She tried to sense the churning power that had been making her feel unbalanced ever since she set foot on this world. She closed her eyes, but in her current state of unrealness, she could still see. She tried to let her gaze go unfocused.

It worked.

She was sucked out of the cave, away from Tol and the Celestial.

Her first thought was that she was flying. Her second was that she wished Addy was with her, because there was simply no way to describe the starlit galaxies and swaths of darkness that flashed by. It was beautiful and endless, comforting and frightening.

Olivia had no concept of time or distance. She was surrounded by shadowy worlds that formed and dissipated before she could grasp for them. She was weightless. She was alone. She was free.

Sometimes, when she got lost in a good book, Olivia felt like she was being pulled into another realm. That was nothing compared to what she was experiencing now. It was exhilarating and terrifying. She had never before wanted to cower in fear and whoop with joy at the same time.

The blurring images slowed when a tiny planet came into focus. She immediately recognized it from countless images, textbook covers, and movies she'd seen throughout her life: Earth. She plunged into the atmosphere, unbothered by the heat or a need to breathe. She kept flying until blue sky and clouds surrounded her and the pinprick of skyscrapers, tiny at this distance, appeared below.

That was when she saw the first explosion.

In an instant, Olivia's elation was replaced by horror as she took in the city below. It was on fire.

She gasped as another city went up in flames. And then another.

Help them, Olivia! a voice shouted in her head. She clawed at the air, trying to get closer to the people down below who were being incinerated. She tried to call out…to warn them…to do *something*.

No matter how hard she tried, she couldn't get any closer. She couldn't speak to them.

Do something. Do something. Do something!

As she flew back and forth, she realized she wasn't the only being hovering amid the clouds.

There was someone else flying through the air. The only difference was that he wasn't translucent like she was. He was flesh and bones. Balls of blue fire were materializing on his bare hands, and he was hurling them at the cities below. He was laughing.

"Stop!" Olivia screamed. "Please!"

No matter how much she cried and begged, the man didn't stop. He didn't so much as glance at her as he continued to hurl his fire balls at the defenseless people below. When Olivia tried to grab him, her wispy hands passed right through his flesh without the man so much as noticing her.

Olivia's mind filled with the cries of the people on the ground. She saw and heard the terror of every individual person. Her focus narrowed on an infant in a stroller. The baby was crying, its tiny fingers reaching out for something on the ground. When Olivia adjusted her view, she saw the charred corpse beside the stroller.

Olivia screamed until her throat was raw.

One by one, more cities around the globe exploded into flames. All the while, the man hovering beside her laughed.

The awful scene dissolved.

The next thing she knew, Olivia was back in the cave with Tol and the Celestial. She was gasping for air, which seemed to be more of a reaction to the horrible scene she'd just witnessed rather than a physical need to breathe.

"Why did you show me that?" Olivia asked, her voice stilted and too high.

"That was your own vision, generated by your own power," the Celestial said, her ghostly cheeks somehow even paler than they'd been before. The Celestial seemed as stunned by the images that had gone through Olivia's mind as Olivia felt.

"What happened?" Tol asked. "What did you see?"

"There was a man." Her voice cracked. "He was burning the world." She sucked in another breath. "The mortal world," she clarified.

Tol's eyes widened. They both turned their attention on the Celestial.

"It is my fault," the Celestial whispered. "And now, my Chosen ones will all be killed along with all of the mortals."

"When is this going to happen?" Tol demanded. "How do we stop it?"

"There is one other like me," the Celestial said, ignoring Tol's questions. "He watched over the Forsaken, just as I watched over the Chosen. They called him the Supernal."

The walls of the cave began to tremble and pulse again as the Celestial's anger grew.

"The Supernal wished to see the Chosen annihilated," she continued. "Two-thousand years ago, the Supernal and I fought. It was violent and terrible, but in the end, I triumphed.

"I contained his strength within a Vitaquias-forged stone and banished him to the mortal world."

The Celestial turned her fierce gaze on them.

"There was no one left to advocate for the Supernal's people. That was when they became known as the Forsaken.

"You must understand that I thought I was doing right by the Chosen people. It was only centuries later when I came to understand that by eliminating the Supernal, I had upset the gods' balance in our world."

Olivia and Tol exchanged a puzzled look.

"The Supernal and I were meant to balance each other, just as the Forsaken and Chosen were meant to be halves of a single whole," the Celestial explained. "But without the Forsaken's direct connection to the gods, they became weaker, and the Chosen grew stronger. It was because of this imbalance that the Chosen were able to extend their power, unchecked, until they drained the Source."

Tol started to say something, but the Celestial wasn't finished.

"Everything began to fall apart after that. The Source on Vitaquias didn't just provide power. It restrained a malevolent spirit, which was released without the Source's protection."

"The Nyxar," Olivia said, putting the pieces together.

The Celestial nodded.

"We destroyed it," Tol said, looking from Olivia to the Celestial. "It's gone now."

"The Nyxar cannot be destroyed now that it has been released," the Celestial replied. "It thrives on absorbing people's consciousnesses. The more it consumes, the more powerful it becomes. It wishes only to destroy."

Olivia remembered feeling the shadow creature's hunger and desire to bring ruin on them all. Now, it made sense.

"When I realized Vitaquias was on the brink of destruction," the Celestial continued, "I tried to undo the balance by bringing the Supernal back to Vitaquias." Her expression turned stormy. "He...took advantage of that gift and did something terrible to one of his own. I was forced to banish him to the mortal world once again."

"What does any of this have to do with the mortal world exploding?" Tol asked, clearly unimpressed by the Celestial's long-winded explanation.

Olivia gave him a meaningful look. She shared all of his urgency, but she didn't think it would be a good idea to turn the Celestial's ire on the two of them.

"Once the Supernal is reunited with the stone containing his strength, he will be as powerful as I once was," the Celestial explained. "The Fount's vision has shown what will happen after that."

"Then, we have to make sure he never gets the stone," Olivia said.

"Or kill him before he gets it," Tol said.

"If the Supernal regains his abilities, he'll make the Forsaken stronger than you can possibly imagine," the Celestial said. Her words sounded even more dire with the way they echoed off the low ceiling. "Neither the Chosen nor the mortals will be able to stand against him."

They'd all die.

Olivia's vision had left no room for interpretation.

"You must find a way to kill the Supernal. Only then will you be able to destroy the magic contained in the stone," the Celestial said. "But even in his weakened form, it will be no easy task."

It was no longer just Tol's people who hovered on the brink of ruin. If they didn't find a way to keep this future from happening, Olivia's entire world would be destroyed, just like this one had been.

"You must go now," the Celestial said, her worried glance going to the ceiling overhead once again. "The storm—"

"Where is the stone that contains the Supernal's powers?" Tol asked.

The Celestial's chin wobbled. "When our world began to tear apart, I feared the stone would be caught up in the destruction and shatter, and then that strength would be released back to the Supernal. So, I gave the stone away to someone who wouldn't be tempted by the power it held. He was killed in the Crossing, and now, I have no idea who possesses it. But there is one thing the Fount's vision has made clear."

"Which is?" Tol prompted.

The Celestial looked from Tol to Olivia.

"The stone is on Earth."

CHAPTER 13

TOL

Tol's mind was so full of everything he'd just learned, that he barely noticed the strange reverse journey that reunited his ghostly spirit with his physical body. That alone should have been enough to make his brain go haywire. But as soon as his mind and body were back together again, he realized he and Olivia had bigger problems.

He had no idea how much time had passed while they were in the cave, but the storm the Celestial mentioned was now a full-on hurricane. His skin hurt from dozens of little cuts and scrapes. The wind screeched, and Tol could barely see through the torrential rain.

"Come on!" he shouted, grabbing Olivia's arm. He was afraid the wind might actually be strong enough to pick her up and sweep her away.

Once their skin was touching, their combined Hazes blasted a path through the rain and swirling winds. As much as he wanted to reject this connection with Olivia, he couldn't deny its usefulness.

He flexed his left arm, watching the way the golden particles of light moved in time with the motion.

If he could somehow manipulate this power…harness a small fraction of it…he might be able to save his people without having to eternally shackle himself to Olivia. If he could grow back a limb, maybe he could give his people what they needed even without Source. He could stop all the killing and death between the Chosen and Forsaken. He could save the mortals from the Supernal.

Would that really be so bad?

Tol shook his head, trying to banish this unfamiliar hunger. It alarmed and intoxicated him at the same time. The Celestial had said he needed a queen who could temper his ambition.

Tol had spent his whole life comprehending the greed that had led his people to destroy Vitaquias. He'd vowed to be better when it was his turn to rule. Now that he was here, he trusted himself less and less by the minute.

The clouds changed from bruise-purple to black. The more exhausted he and Olivia became, the less their combined Hazes protected them from the elements. Freezing rain pummeled them from every angle. By the time they made it to the top of the cliff, they were both soaked and bleeding. He could feel her whole body shaking from the cold. She didn't complain, though. If anything, it was her voice in his head pushing both of them on.

Tol expected to get some relief from the storm once they were inside the castle. Instead, the hollow rooms created a wind tunnel that made it as cold and wet in here as it was outside. The mostly-missing roof didn't help matters.

The others were huddled in a small, dry section of what Tol thought might have once been a bedroom.

"Tol, Livy!" Addy ran to them.

"Mate, we need to get the hells out of here," Gerth called above the howling wind.

"It's only going to get worse," Walidir said, his voice barely audible. "The storms have been getting more powerful over the past months. The last one—"

Whatever he was going to say was cut off as a whole section of the wall blew out. Tol heard the rumble of stone on stone as the chunks of wall toppled down the cliff.

"I think it's working!" Addy called, drawing all of their attention to her ring, which had started to glow.

Tol, move!" Fred shouted.

He did, moments before a section of ceiling came crashing down. It missed him by centimeters.

Erikir swore. Gerth pushed everyone further away from the still-crumbling ceiling.

Blue smoke exploded from Addy's ring. It billowed and whirled, until a funnel began to form in front of her. Addy had to brace herself to keep from being sucked inside.

"Hurry!" she called.

Olivia let the portal drag her in first. Nira and Fred were next.

"Move," Addy yelled, her voice hoarse as she struggled to hold the portal open.

Tol grabbed his grandfather's arm and pulled him toward the open portal.

As soon as the tendrils of sapphire-blue light touched Walidir, his skin began to smoke. Tol's grandfather screamed and drew back his hand, which was covered in a nasty burn.

The rest of his grandfather had changed, too. He'd aged in the span of seconds.

"What's happening?" Tol demanded, having to shout to be heard over the roaring winds.

"I have too much of the gods' power in me," Walidir said with a small smile. "They won't let me go." He touched his fingertips to Tol's golden arm.

Tol's mind was in chaos. The gods wouldn't let his grandfather leave…just like they'd ripped Tol's arm away as they fought to keep him eighteen years ago.

Fury lanced through Tol. He didn't give a damn what the gods wanted. He had promised Gran he'd bring her husband back, and Tol had every intention of doing just that.

"Go on, now," Walidir insisted. "I'll be fine."

Like hells he would.

"I'm not leaving here without you!" Tol planted his feet.

"I've survived storms like this one before," Walidir said, as calm as Tol was frantic. "The castle will protect me from anything out there."

"Tol, I can't hold it," Addy gasped.

He glanced at the portal, which was smaller than it had been a moment ago.

"Try again," he begged his grandfather.

"Tol, he can't go through," Gerth shouted. "He'll die."

No. There had to be another way. He just had to figure it out…just had to find a way….

"We have to go," Erikir said, the expression on his face saying he was as horrified by the idea of leaving their grandfather as Tol. "You and the Fount are the priority."

"I'm not leaving anyone behind," Tol snarled.

His mind raced.

"Gerth," he began. If there was anyone who could solve an unsolvable problem, it was his best mate. "There has to be something we can do."

"It's no use, Tolumus," his grandfather said. "You need to go. Now."

Tol wasn't going back and telling Gran that they'd abandoned the man she'd been waiting eighteen years to be reunited with. Either they all left together, or—

A ragged scream tore out of Addy's throat. Her left hand shook, and the ropy tendrils of the portal wobbled.

Another chunk of wall broke off. It cracked against the floor and sent debris skittering toward them.

Walidir said something to Erikir that was lost in the wind. Tol saw his cousin's face pale and harden. He and Gerth exchanged a glance. And then, they came at him.

Gerth bear-hugged Tol from behind, while Erikir pinned his legs.

"Get off!" Tol writhed and swore as they dragged him to the portal.

"Tell your gran I love her," Walidir called above the wailing wind and Tol's shouts. "And tell her I'll be waiting here for her."

No. They couldn't leave him.

"Grandfather, please. Walidir!"

The storm would rip this place to pieces, and with it, Tol's grandfather. He'd be alone and defenseless.

They had to get him out…had to get him away from here. Tol couldn't go back to the mortal world and tell Gran he'd abandoned her beloved husband.

Addy mouthed *I'm sorry*. Then, she closed her left hand into a fist. The blue rings of the portal brightened.

Gerth and Erikir dragged him forward. He writhed and fought for all he was worth. Fred joined the others who were shoving Tol toward the blue rings of the portal. Tol opened his mouth to shout again, but his voice was torn away.

He was sucked into the portal.

CHAPTER 14

ADDY

Addy's back thudded into the ground hard enough to make a depression. If she'd had any air in her lungs, it would have been knocked out of her. As it was, Addy was pretty sure she hadn't taken a breath since she entered the portal.

How long had it had taken to get from Vitaquias to here?

She was more than a little concerned about her brain going so long without oxygen. Or at least, she would have been more concerned about that if she didn't have more pressing issues. Like the fact that her insides were in extreme danger of coming up her throat.

Addy felt like her body had been torn apart and put back together again about as effectively as Humpty Dumpty.

The oppressive Texas heat should have been a relief after the biting hail and winds on Vitaquias. Instead, it was just making her queasier. Someone was lying on top of her. It made the contents of her stomach rebel even more.

"Sorry," Livy gasped, looking as green as Addy felt.

Her sister wriggled off Addy. Someone—Fred, maybe—was throwing up.

"Oh Lord, Livy!"

Addy heard Aunt Meredith's voice, but she didn't turn her head for fear the small motion would have her puking next to Fred.

"We're okay," Livy said in a dazed voice.

"Like heck you are, you're covered in blood!"

That snapped Addy out of her nauseous fog. She looked up at her twin. *How had she not noticed before?*

Livy's face and arms were covered in scratches. Tol looked even worse. His torso was still bare from when he'd taken off his prosthesis, and his chest and back were covered in shallow scrapes. Several of them were still bleeding.

"Let me see," Nira said, putting a hand on Tol's right, non-golden arm.

He shrugged her off and stood up.

"Take me back," he told Addy. He was a little unsteady on his feet, but there was raw determination in his eyes.

Addy shook her head, hating herself a little. "I'm so sorry, Tol."

It had gone against her every instinct to leave Walidir in that storm, but she'd had no choice. Walidir couldn't enter the portal without being killed, and they couldn't stay.

Addy understood that going back to Vitaquias before the blood marriage was a risk Tol's people couldn't afford. Tol and Livy were the two missing halves to the Chosen people's salvation. Their safety was the highest priority. Not to mention the fact that they were the two people Addy loved most in all the worlds.

"Addy," Tol said, and the soft pleading in his voice cut her deeper than any blade.

"I can't," she whispered.

"No one's going anywhere until we get you and Livy bandaged up," Aunt Meredith scolded in her no-nonsense voice. "Let's get you folks inside."

Tol's gaze hardened. He turned on Erikir and Gerth, who looked like they'd been bracing themselves for his fury.

"You know he's probably dead, right?"

"Walidir would have died if we brought him through the portal," Gerth said, his voice calm and reasonable.

"So, we just abandon people, now?"

"It's not like that, mate," Gerth said.

"We made the hard decision because you wouldn't," Erikir said. "Because some of us understand responsibility, unlike you."

Tol's Haze flared. Addy had never seen him this angry. It reminded her of that dark, ugly thing inside her. It scared her a little.

Tol grabbed Erikir, his movements faster than they should have been.

"Don't Influence him." Gerth hurried over. "Tol, he's one of ours."

Addy knew Gerth had no love for Erikir. The concern on Gerth's face was all for Tol.

Addy was trying to decide if she should force Tol to let go of his cousin, when the golden Haze around Tol started to retreat. It was still brighter than anyone else's, but it was no longer blinding.

The particles of light making up his left arm started to fade, too. Tol let go of Erikir and stepped back. They all looked at his arm.

"Oh my," Aunt Meredith whispered, her eyes bulging as she stared at Tol.

The strands of gold that made up his arm began to vibrate. It was like a many-layered necklace, and one of the thin strands had been cut. Tiny golden beads were slipping away one by one. There was a soft burst of light, and then Tol's arm disappeared. It was like it had never even been there.

The expression on Tol's face tore through Addy's heart. She searched for something to say, but there was nothing.

Gerth rummaged through his bag and pulled out Tol's prosthetic arm. Without a word, he passed it to Tol.

Tol strode away from them to strap it on.

"He'll want a shirt too," Addy said, her voice barely more than a whisper.

Gerth already had one out, which he threw to Tol. Tol caught it without looking at any of them.

When he came back, Tol's Haze was its normal brightness. His eyes were so full of emotion Addy couldn't begin to decipher everything he was thinking. For several seconds, no one spoke.

"I'm sorry," Tol said to his cousin. "I was out of line."

Erikir looked at him with loathing.

Tol took a steadying breath. "I couldn't Influence you now even if I wanted to. I don't have that ability here."

"Lucky me," Erikir muttered.

"I don't know why I did that to you before. I…wasn't myself. It won't happen again."

"All of that power must have made you a little drunk," Gerth said. "I've never felt anything like it, and it must have been a thousand times stronger for you."

Tol nodded.

So, what happens now?" Fred asked. From the look on his face, Addy could tell he was praying it wouldn't involve another portal.

Not that she could blame him.

"You have to go back and deal with the manor," Nira said to Tol, looking nervous. "You have to calm everyone down before our people start killing each other."

Tol rubbed his jaw. "How am I supposed to tell Gran we abandoned her husband?" he asked, his voice breaking.

"When Walidir told me to get you out of there," Erikir said in a subdued voice, "he said Gran would understand."

"This wasn't on you, Tol," Addy insisted.

He nodded, but Addy could tell he didn't feel any better about what had happened. Neither did she. If there had been any other way, she would have taken it.

"Can we switch directions for a minute and talk about what you learned from the Celestial?" Gerth asked.

Addy looked at Tol and Livy expectantly. With the storm and everything that came after, she hadn't had a chance to ask the question that had sent all of them to Vitaquias in the first place.

Tol and Livy exchanged a glance. It made a strange, unpleasant pulse go through Addy's chest.

A sharp whistle cut through the air. Aunt Meredith, fists on her hips, glared at all of them.

"Inside, all of you," she ordered. "You're hurt, and we don't need to add third-degree sunburns to all of this madness."

"Watch the booby traps," Fred reminded them, grabbing Nira before she stepped on one of his homemade land mines.

"Once you're all cleaned up, someone's going to tell me what the Sam Hill's going on," Aunt Meredith said, following after them. "And if any of ya'll try to tell me you were hanging out at the beach, I'm liable to have a cow."

If Addy had been in the mood, she would have made a joke about Aunt Meredith already having lots of cows. At the moment, she couldn't imagine joking about anything ever again.

They all filed inside the air-conditioned living room.

That's when Addy felt them. It was a whisper inside her, which she ignored at first because she was distracted by the way Nira was holding Tol's cheek as she wiped away the blood on his neck. But then, one whisper turned into three…and then into fifteen.

"They're here," Addy said, shaking off the last of the nausea from the portal and pulling her garden shears from her back pocket. "The Forsaken are here."

CHAPTER 15

ADDY

A crash came from somewhere in the yard, followed by several screams.

"My booby traps," Fred said, starting for the door. "Someone's set them off."

"There's fifteen Forsaken," Addy called, outpacing Fred. "More are coming."

The golden light of Addy's Haze seeped out of her body until she was surrounded by a warm glow.

She threw open the front door and stopped dead in her tracks.

Two Forsaken were floundering in what looked like an old fishing net. They were hacking at the fibers and swearing at each other as they tried to get free. One of the Forsaken was screaming from the bottom of a stake pit Fred had dug and camouflaged. Addy ducked back into the house as something exploded. Three Forsaken were thrown off their feet.

Way to go, Fred!

One of the Forsaken spied Addy and barreled toward her.

A little to the left…a little more….

The man shrieked as the buckets rigged to the porch's rafters overturned. Black motor oil spilled down onto the man's head before he reached the second step.

Addy watched in bemusement as the Forsaken man spit and gagged.

Her satisfaction turned to anger at the thought of what would have happened if the Forsaken showed up ten minutes earlier. Aunt Meredith would have been home alone.

The dark, angry thing inside Addy roared to life.

She leapt off the porch like a cat, avoiding the oil-slicked floor. Her garden shears found the back of a Forsaken's neck before the man even knew she was behind him.

He transformed from a young man in the peak of his strength to one who was bent and haggard in the space of a few seconds. With a puff of blue smoke, the man was gone altogether.

Addy had seen people from the other world die before. She'd seen the blue smoke and pile of clothes that were all that was left of them. Still, it was rattling to see a person just disappear.

She recovered quickly.

Addy's rage was like a coiled-up cobra inside her that was just waiting for its opportunity to pounce. The only way to tame the beast was by feeding it the blood of her enemies. So, that's what did.

She jumped over the stake pit and launched herself at a warrior who was in the process of swallowing a drop of Source.

Her weight drove them to the ground, with her opponent taking the brunt of the force. He had a dagger, which was glowing blue from the Source that strengthened it. Addy didn't give the man a chance to raise it.

She slashed the open blades of her garden shears across his throat. This time, she didn't wait to see him disappear.

Addy heard Tol's command of *Look at me* behind her, and knew one of the enemy warriors was under his Influence. She didn't look back, knowing Tol could hold his own. She raced forward to kill two more Forsaken. She felt the spray of blood across her T-shirt. The warmth and coppery scent fed her frenzy. Her garden shears moved so fast she couldn't keep track of her own hand.

Nira, Gerth, and Erikir were outside. Addy's enhanced senses picked up Nira gagging as she ingested a drop of Addy's own blood. She saw Hazes flare.

Nira's complaining was muted by a different, more important sound.

Army trucks.

They were coming from the back of the house. And there were a lot of them.

"Take care of the rest of these," Addy shouted to Tol.

She sprinted around the side of the house, leaping over one of Fred's tripwires.

Instinct had her ducking before she knew why. A glowing blue hatchet went whistling past her ear. Addy looked up to see the Forsaken soldier who had thrown it—a giant woman with her white-blonde hair gelled into spikes.

The hatchet stopped in mid-air. It defied gravity to fly back at Addy's face.

Instead of trying to avoid it, Addy stabbed the point of her garden shears into the other weapon.

The hatchet was bigger, but she was stronger than the other Forsaken. The glowing blue weapon shattered.

The Forsaken woman's eyes bulged as the pieces of her weapon fell to the ground. She bared her teeth at Addy. Then, she uncorked her vial and drained it in a single sip.

Bring it on, Addy thought.

She ran for the soldier. Addy stabbed with her garden shears. The Forsaken woman ducked. They spun and crashed against the side of the house.

The woman's Haze flared to life as Addy raised her shears to strike again. The Forsaken soldier's fist connected with Addy's stomach.

Addy went down. Hard.

She choked. She gasped. She sucked in a searing wisp of air through lungs that had forgotten how to work.

That was all the time Addy had to recover.

The Forsaken woman might be weaponless, but her Source-infused blood made her as strong and fast as Addy. And the woman clearly had combat training that Addy didn't.

The warrior threw punch after punch. Addy blocked a vicious kick with one of her own. The other woman didn't so much as hesitate, even though Addy heard the crunch of bone.

That was another thing about Forsaken hopped up on Source. They didn't feel pain. At least, that's what it seemed like to Addy as the woman continued to advance on her. The Forsaken woman was bleeding from countless wounds, but she didn't even seem to notice them.

In a desperate effort to put the woman down quickly, Addy ducked around the side of the house and stuck her foot out.

She couldn't stop her surprised guffaw when the Forsaken warrior tripped right over her foot. The other woman went sprawling.

"I can't believe that actually worked," Addy exclaimed.

Addy didn't let the other woman regain control of the fight. She dealt a punishing kick to the Forsaken soldier's back. While the woman was still trying to regain her balance, Addy brought her garden shears down. The warrior's body jerked. Then, it turned to blue smoke.

The beast inside Addy roared in approval.

Addy sucked in breath after breath. When she stood up, wiping blood and blue dust from her skin, she heard the thrum of an engine.

Engines.

Seven army jeeps and three Hummers were bumping their way across the cattle pasture toward the house. The vehicles blasted right through the wooden fence without slowing. Forsaken warriors poured out before the jeeps had even come to a stop.

Eight…ten…twenty…. They kept coming. It was like the deadliest bunch of clown cars of all time.

Addy readied her garden shears.

"Gerth, get the Fount out of here!" Tol yelled.

Addy spun around, looking for her twin. Her heart dropped out of her stomach. Livy was standing with her back to the wall of the house. She was staring wide-eyed at the motor oil and blood streaked across the grass. There were five Forsaken moving toward Livy, but Addy could tell from their defensive movements they were under Tol's Influence.

The roar of a shotgun got Addy's attention back on the Forsaken swarming toward her.

"Take that, trespassers!"

Aunt Meredith reloaded her shotgun and fired again.

The Forsaken man Aunt Meredith had been aiming for didn't fall. Instead, his Haze brightened. Addy saw his golden Haze warp as the bullets tried to penetrate it. It was like the bullets were moving in slow motion. The particles of golden light bent, absorbed the bullets, and shot them back.

"Duck!" Addy shouted.

Aunt Meredith flattened herself.

"No mortal weapons!" Gerth shouted. "They won't work against the Forsaken."

"Coulda told us sooner," Fred grumbled. He was gripping a nail gun.

Addy stabbed her garden shears into the Forsaken man before he could retaliate. When he disappeared into a cloud of blue smoke, Aunt Meredith and Fred both shouted in surprise.

"I'll explain later," Addy told them. "Now, go back to the house."

The Forsaken getting out of the jeeps were all drinking from their vials. Things were about to become a lot more complicated.

While Addy appreciated Fred and Aunt Meredith's courage more than words could say, their human weapons couldn't hurt this enemy. But Addy could. With a feral cry, she raced to meet them.

A wicked, curved blade cut through the air. It was followed by two glowing blue arrows fired in quick succession.

Addy was so busy making sure none of the weapons found their intended targets, she stopped paying attention to everything else around her. It was her mistake. She didn't notice the man rushing straight for her like some kind of sumo wrestler until he'd tackled her.

Addy hit the ground. She heard her skull crack against the hard-packed dirt. Her vision went dark.

There was someone on top of her. If she didn't move, she'd suffocate. She couldn't force her limbs to obey her brain. Her skull felt like someone had taken a hammer to the back of it.

All at once, the weight on top of her vanished.

Two of the Forsaken, their eyes glazed over from Influence, dragged their comrade off Addy. Two brutal strokes of their swords turned the one who had pinned Addy into smoke.

Fred's blurred face appeared as he hauled her to her feet.

"You okay? he demanded.

"Fine," Addy replied, still a little stunned.

She could feel an egg-sized lump forming at the back of her head.

"Watch out!" someone yelled.

Fred pushed Addy behind his back as a Forsaken man advanced. Just as abruptly, the warrior turned around so his back was to them. His movements were jerky as he raised his crossbow and aimed it at the last jeep full of Forsaken.

Nira followed behind the man, barking commands and motioning with her hands like she was some kind of puppeteer.

Aunt Meredith shouted a warning somewhere behind her. The sound jolted Addy out of her pain-induced fog.

Addy vaulted into the air.

As she moved from one Forsaken to the next, a sense of rightness came over her that she hadn't felt in…well, since the last time she used her fighting skills. Addy didn't feel helpless or like she was at the whim of forces she couldn't control.

She felt like herself.

Addy spun around, searching for her next opponent. That's when she realized the only Forsaken still on their feet had glazed-over expressions in their eyes and were standing protectively around Livy, Fred, and Aunt Meredith.

Tol and Gerth were back-to-back, both looking like they would fall down if they weren't supporting each other. Nira and Erikir were in the same pose and looked just as exhausted.

Addy had seen Tol control close to twenty Forsaken before. But after what they'd been through on Vitaquias, Addy was surprised any of them had strength left to do anything.

There was a quiet lull in the pandemonium now that there was no one left to fight. Tol's cold command rang out through the yard.

"Kill yourselves."

Aunt Meredith let out a strangled scream as, one by one, the Forsaken did as they were told.

Most of the bodies disappeared into clouds of blue smoke. The few that remained fell to the ground like any dead mortal would. Addy knew the reason was because their age hadn't yet exceeded the span of a mortal life.

As much as Addy had enjoyed the battle, she took no pleasure in this execution. The Forsaken were powerless to fight against Tol's Influence, and that seemed wrong. Addy knew their enemies would take an unfair advantage if they had it, but she still felt dirty.

There was nothing to be done. There wasn't time to take on all of these people in single combat, and Addy was too tired to fight all of them at once.

The final man left standing raised his dagger. He was standing close enough to Addy that she could hear his hoarse whisper.

"He said you would help us."

"What?" Addy asked, too caught off guard to manage anything else.

"You were our only chance." The man's throat came up against the blade of his dagger. His gray eyes flicked to the blood-covered lawn.

"Tol, wait," Addy said.

The man's arm went rigid.

"How did you find us?" Addy asked.

The Forsaken man's glazed-over eyes hardened in resentment.

"Answer her," Tol growled.

The Forsaken man winced. He said, "Jaxon could sense you. He was going to come himself, but his commander called him back to base."

Addy had no idea what this man was talking about, or who this mysterious Jaxon person was.

"Who else knows where to find us?" Tol asked.

"We were the only ones besides Jaxon."

The Forsaken soldier's mournful gaze went to the bloodstained grass once again. Addy felt the vaguest sense of unease before she caught herself. She knew from experience the Forsaken didn't hesitate to cut down anyone who stood in their path. If Addy hadn't killed all of his people, they would have done the same to everyone she cared about.

"Do you have anything else of use to tell us?" Tol asked.

Addy could tell from the sound of his voice that he was reaching the limits of his strength. He'd pushed himself too hard already, and Addy could see his fatigue in the way he leaned against Gerth.

Instead of looking at Tol, the Forsaken man spoke to Addy.

"You murdered your own," he accused. "You are no leader of mine."

Addy decided something about Tol's Influence must be messing with this man's brain. Nothing he said made any sense.

"Kill him, Addy," Tol said.

Addy felt a strange reluctance inside her. Before she could make sense of the feeling, it was replaced with something far more familiar. The ravenous cobra inside her sprang to life. She whipped her shears across the man's throat.

Hot blood sprayed through the air.

CHAPTER 16

TOL

Tol felt the weight of his mind ease a fraction as the Forsaken man's body wisped into blue smoke.

"What do we do now?" Fred asked. He was still holding his nail gun. Tol resisted the urge to remind him that it wasn't an actual gun.

The poor farmer was staring slack-jawed at the blue cloud, which was already dissipating on the breeze. It was the only reminder of the man who had existed moments before. Well, that, and the blood covering Addy's face and clothes.

She looked slightly feral. As she sliced that Forsaken's throat, Tol could have sworn her eyes changed from green to pure gold for a fraction of a second. He was probably imagining things. Still, in that brief instant, she hadn't looked human.

"So, what do we do about her?" Erikir asked.

Tol followed the direction of his cousin's gaze and bristled.

"If by *her*, you mean my fiancé, then the answer is nothing different than we already planned."

"Did you somehow forget the forty Forsaken who just tracked her here?" Erikir looked incredulous. "Wake up, Tolumus. What'll it take for you to recognize that Addy is going to get all of us killed, one way or another?"

"Do you think I called them up and invited them over?" Addy fisted her hands on her hips. "Although, if I was the traitor you're implying, I can't imagine why I would have killed all of them and left *you* standing."

For all the anger in Addy's words, Tol knew that Erikir's comment had struck her in a way she'd never admit.

The one you love is not meant to be the Chosen queen. The Celestial's words came back to him, making Tol's blood boil in rage.

"What's happening to our people isn't Addy's fault," Tol said.

"You're always going to choose her, aren't you?" Erikir asked, his face reddening in his growing rage.

Tol didn't say anything. He was getting bloody tired of his cousin's judgment.

Erikir nodded to himself, like he'd reached some kind of decision. With a huff, he stalked away and disappeared around the side of the house. Probably to sulk.

Tol turned to Addy, poised to tell her that Erikir was a git and she shouldn't give his words another thought. He saw the shame and regret on Addy's face, but he didn't have a chance to say a word.

Nira let out a choked scream. She was standing stock-still. A Forsaken's glowing blue sword was pressed against the back of her neck.

ADDY

"You need to listen," the Forsaken woman said to Addy.

"Let my friend go first," Addy countered.

Friend might be a stretch, but time was short.

"So you can kill me like you did the rest?" The woman let out a harsh bark of laughter. "I think not."

Nira whimpered as the blade pressed into her neck.

Addy might fantasize about killing Nira, but she didn't actually want anything to happen to the other girl. Nira was one of Tol's people, which meant she was Addy's, too.

The angry cobra inside her hissed in protest, but she ignored it as she let her garden shears drop onto the ground.

"Now, let her go," Addy ordered.

The woman opened her mouth, but instead of speaking, her eyes glazed over and her jaw went slack.

Erikir, who must have snuck up behind her, was gripping the warrior's wrist.

"Drop your weapon," Erikir commanded.

Without a moment's hesitation, the Forsaken soldier did as she was told.

Nira picked up the glowing blue sword, looking awkward and tiny as she hefted the large weapon.

"I get to kill her," Nira said, her voice trembling from fear and rage.

"No, I have a better idea," Erikir said. "I'll Influence her into thinking she found us somewhere else."

Addy exchanged a look with Tol.

"It's not the worst idea," Gerth admitted.

Erikir didn't wait for permission. With a look of grim determination, he ordered the Forsaken woman to get into one of the abandoned jeeps.

"I'll go with her to the edge of the property and make sure my Influence holds," Erikir called over his shoulder as he got into the passenger seat.

The jeep's engine revved. The Forsaken woman hit the gas, and the vehicle sped off. Everyone heaved a sigh of relief.

Addy took a quick inventory to make sure everyone else was more or less in one piece. That's when she caught sight of her twin.

Livy was standing with her back to the wall of the house. Her eyes were saucer-round. She was staring at the blood staining the grass.

All Addy saw were the remnants of their vanquished enemies, but when she thought about what Livy must be seeing—blood, gore, and violence perpetrated by her own sister—Addy felt a deep shame.

The fight had made Addy feel alive in ways no normal person should ever feel. Her anger and bloodlust weren't new emotions, but they still scared her. Whenever that sleeping cobra roared to life, part of Addy wondered if she'd be able to put it away again.

Maybe she needed anger management classes.

Deep down, she knew it was more complicated than that.

Addy went to her sister.

"I'm so sorry," she began, reaching for Livy before remembering her hands were covered in blood.

Livy let out a shuddering breath. "You have nothing to apologize for." She swallowed hard, and then she stepped forward to pull Addy into a tight hug.

Arms came around both of them, and Addy knew it was Aunt Meredith.

"Your parents told me about these people, but I just didn't believe," Aunt Meredith said, her words choked with tears. "I should have…I should have—"

"No," Livy told their aunt. "There was nothing you could have done."

"You fought like a *boss*," Addy reassured her aunt, her voice a little muffled from where it was pressed into her aunt's shirt.

Aunt Meredith pulled back to raise an eyebrow at Addy and Livy. "You folks didn't spend the weekend at the beach, did you?"

Addy exchanged a guilty look with her twin.

"No, we didn't," Addy admitted, at the same time that Livy said, "I'm so sorry, Aunt Meredith."

Aunt Meredith humphed. "Well, let's get you inside and clean that blood off you before the flies come."

"Who in the two hells is this Jaxon guy, and why is he after *her*?" Nira asked, giving a disdainful sniff in Addy's direction.

It was a valid question, although Addy would never admit that to Nira. The other girl's near death had done nothing to soften Addy's feelings toward her. Especially with the way Nira swooned and batted her eyes at Tol for asking if she was alright.

Gerth dug something out of his pocket and tossed it to Fred. It was the bracelet Fred had given Addy right before her family was murdered.

"You said you were able to follow Addy with this," Gerth said to Fred. "How?"

Fred scowled at Gerth. "I dunno. Just when I held it, I got this feelin' about where I should go to find her, and she was there."

"Could it be the Source in my blood?" Addy asked. Her anger stirred to life at the thought of how the Forsaken general had almost drowned her in the lake of Source to make her immortal. She hadn't even begun to wrap her mind around the fact that she would live forever.

"If I were to mix Source with my blood, no one would be able to use it to find me," Gerth said, frowning in thought. "There must be something else about you."

With a sinking feeling, Addy thought she knew. The Forsaken had somehow sensed her the same way she could feel them.

Because she was one of them.

For as often as Tol said she belonged with his people instead of the Forsaken, she fought like the enemy. Her strength was the same as theirs. And she was the spitting image of the general.

"I can theorize about why the Forsaken can find Addy, but what I can't figure out is how Freddo could track her down with just a drop of her blood," Gerth continued.

Addy felt her anxiety spike as the others continued to debate the freakish properties of her blood. She left Fred, Livy, and Aunt Meredith and walked over to Tol, who had finally managed to free himself from Evil Beauty Queen.

"I'm sorry," Addy began. She wasn't quite sure what she was sorry for—the Forsaken somehow using her blood to track all of them…the fact that her love for Tol was endangering his whole race…the way she fought like Tol's enemies—

"Don't be sorry." Tol pulled her against his chest. He didn't seem to care that she was covered in blood.

"My warrior goddess," he said into her ear before pressing a gentle kiss to her forehead.

Addy's limbs, which had gone cold in the aftermath of the battle, flooded with warmth at Tol's touch. She was about to kiss him, when he gasped and let go of her. He staggered back and would have fallen if Addy hadn't grabbed him.

"What happened? Tol, what's wrong?"

Tol half-stumbled, half-ran to Livy, who was standing motionless against the side of the house with her eyes closed. She hadn't collapsed from one of her visions the way she usually did, so Addy hadn't even noticed anything was wrong. Tol had, though.

The two of them were connected in a way that defied normal senses. Without opening her eyes, Livy held out a hand, and Tol took it. As their fingers met, both of the Hazes flared to life.

A strange, unpleasant sensation flooded Addy. With the golden light surrounding them, Tol and Livy looked like angels. She looked down at her bloodstained clothes.

Addy knew better than to question Tol's love, but when she thought about Tol's people, her certainty wavered. Didn't they deserve a queen like Livy, whose heart was pure gold, rather than the blood-splattered daughter of their enemy?

Tol and Livy opened their eyes at the same time and dropped their hands.

"What did you see?" Tol demanded. "I felt pain, and then…nothing."

Livy licked her lips. "There was a beautiful house, and people sitting in a garden. There was a woman with black hair, but I couldn't see her face." She looked at Tol. "A glowing blue axe was heading straight toward her."

Tol and Gerth exchanged a look.

"I have to get back to the manor. Now." Tol's chest rose and fell with all of the emotions he was holding in check.

"That's what I've been trying to tell you," Nira grumbled.

"We can use my ring," Addy said. "It'll get us there in seconds."

I think, she wanted to add. The ring's power seemed within her reach now that she'd used it once, but she couldn't be sure until she tried it again. The idea that something that had worked like a glorified flashlight for Tol's grandmother should create portals for her was…strange.

Tol gave her a grateful look.

"Now just a Texas second," Aunt Meredith said, raising a finger. "You aren't going anywhere with those maniacs on the loose."

Livy and Fred each leaned closer to Aunt Meredith, murmuring comforting words to her. Addy was grateful to them, even as guilt for keeping her aunt so much in the dark crawled up her spine.

She promised herself then and there that, as soon as she and Tol got back from the manor, she'd tell her aunt everything.

"You should wait for Erikir to get back," Gerth said to Tol. "If the two of you present a united front, it'll make the Jesuls weaker."

"We can't wait," Tol said. "There's no time."

Addy felt the same restlessness she saw in Tol's every movement. The storm that was raging on Vitaquias had made it more than obvious they didn't have time to linger. Walidir said that the storms had been getting worse over the last several months. If they waited much longer, Tol's people wouldn't have a world to go back to.

Hold on, Walidir, she thought.

"I'll come with you," Nira said.

Before Addy could open her mouth to protest, Tol said, "I need you to stay here and help protect the mortals."

"I don't know which *mortals* you're referring to," Aunt Meredith said, irritated now, "but I'm perfectly capable of protecting my nieces and their friends." She pointed an accusing finger at Addy. "And you aren't going anywhere, missy."

Before Addy had to ask Tol to Influence her aunt again, Livy interceded.

"We're sorry we've kept you in the dark about everything. Once Addy's gone, I'll answer all of your questions. I promise."

Aunt Meredith grumbled out something, but she didn't try to argue anymore. Addy threw her twin a grateful look.

"Do you want me to come with you?" Gerth asked Tol.

Tol shook his head. "Addy and I will handle it. I need the rest of you to help Olivia figure out her powers."

"Mate." Gerth looked uncomfortable. "You should bring the Fount with you. Our people—"

"Want to see their future queen," Tol finished. "And they will." He threaded his fingers through Addy's.

Another wave of guilt passed through Addy, but it didn't stop her from curling her fingers around Tol's. Addy wasn't used to needing someone to defend her, but when it came to this, there was no foe she could plunge her garden shears into.

Gerth sighed. Addy could tell he had plenty more to say on the topic, but he knew there was no point.

"You need to figure out how to control your visions without my help," Tol snapped at Livy. "We need to find that Supernal and his magic stone, and we need to make Addy the Fount before I lose my people and our world. It all depends on you."

"*Tol.*" Addy couldn't believe the way he was ordering Livy around. He never talked to anyone like that, except for maybe Erikir.

Tol looked remorseful, but he didn't take back any of what he'd said. Addy knew it was desperation and a growing sense of helplessness that were making him talk like that. She understood what he was feeling.

Walidir was stuck on Vitaquias in the middle of a maelstrom. A being with the strength to destroy all of Earth was on the loose, and someone was apparently about to kill one of Tol's people.

"No, Tol's right." Livy shook her head, looking a little dazed. "I have to do this." She gave Addy a weak smile.

"I'm so sorry," Addy told her sister again, pulling her twin close for a hug. Addy did the same with Aunt Meredith and Fred.

"Don't worry, Ads." Fred wrapped Addy in his big bear arms. "I'll make sure no one hurts Livy or Aunt Meredith."

"Thank you," she whispered, feeling awful she'd dragged Fred away from his life and into her mess.

Addy would gladly take on a hundred Forsaken, but this feeling of helpless in the face of problems she'd caused was unbearable.

"Ready?" Tol asked her.

Addy curled her left hand into a fist. She closed her eyes and pictured the manor. She forced other thoughts from her mind, focusing on every small detail she could remember…the beautiful tree-lined driveway, the cliff overlooking the sea where Tol had kissed her…the cottage where Tol had given her the ring.

She felt the wind pick up as light spilled from her ring.

"Tol," she called without opening her eyes.

She felt his arm come around her. Then, she was lifted off the ground as they were sucked inside the swirling vortex.

CHAPTER 17

OLIVIA

When Addy and Tol had gone, the rest of them looked at each other.

Aunt Meredith was pinching herself and saying something about *Harry Potter*. Under different circumstances, Livy would have smiled at the literary reference. Right now, though, her mind was too full of everything that had happened to make space for anything else.

Olivia felt breathless, even though she was the only one who hadn't done any fighting.

She had wanted to help, but those huge men and women had looked so much like the ones who had killed her family. She'd just frozen.

Addy hadn't, which was even more proof that she deserved to be the Fount instead of Olivia.

"Okie dokes." Gerth rubbed his hands together. "We need to find somewhere else to stay."

Aunt Meredith frowned. "Do you know how many people have tried to drive me off my land for one reason or another over the last eighteen years? If these people are going to get rid of me, they're going to have to try a lot harder, thank you very much."

"But—"

"Let's get this place tidied up," Aunt Meredith said in that no-nonsense way of hers. "After that, I'll rustle us up some grub and you folks can fill me in on everything." She gave Olivia a hard look. "And I do mean *everything*."

Olivia gulped, but she gave her aunt a nod. She knew Aunt Meredith deserved an explanation after everything they'd put her through.

Olivia had a minor heart attack when one of those army jeeps rolled up to the front of the house. When it was only Erikir who got out, she relaxed again.

"Any problems?" Gerth asked.

Erikir shook his head. "I took her to the airport and Influenced her to tell any other Forsaken who ask that we're hiding out in New York. That should buy us some time."

Time. The one thing that seemed to shrink as the number of tasks they needed to accomplish expanded.

"Come on, pumpkin," Aunt Meredith said, squeezing Olivia's shoulders. "Let's get this place cleaned up, and then we can talk about whatever's put that look on your face."

Even though Aunt Meredith didn't understand what they were all up against, Olivia was grateful for her aunt's steady presence.

They all trooped back into the house to don rubber gloves and arm themselves with sponges.

"Tol's going to get himself killed," Nira muttered to herself as she scrubbed blood off one of the window panes. "Bringing his Forsaken girlfriend back to the manor in the middle of a rebellion? *Really?*"

"Have you already forgotten who started the rebellion in the first place?" Gerth asked. "Tol wouldn't have had to rush back to the manor if it wasn't for all the trouble you caused."

Nira tossed her hair, making it flow behind her in a perfect wave. The motion gave her an air of indifference. It was just an act, though. Olivia could somehow sense the other girl's deep regret.

Olivia had put together that Nira had done something to spite Tol, and that it had gained traction in a way Nira never intended.

Olivia didn't know how to go about making Nira feel better. She wasn't even sure she should try. It hadn't escaped Olivia's notice that Nira had done nothing but antagonize Addy at every opportunity. Olivia might feel an inexplicable connection to all of these near-strangers, but her loyalty belonged to Addy first and foremost.

Olivia scrubbed at a stain on the porch, trying not to think about the person to whom the blood had once belonged. She tried not to think about the euphoria on Addy's face when she stabbed her garden shears into one person after another.

Of course, if Addy hadn't killed all those people, Olivia would have stood there with her mouth hanging open until someone bothered to plunge their blue weapon into her heart.

Not only had Olivia been useless, she'd been a liability.

"Tol wasn't being harsh with you because he thinks you're doing anything wrong," Gerth said, like he could read her mind.

To her horror, she realized her eyes were misting up. She wiped furiously at them.

"He's just scared for everyone he's trying to protect," Gerth continued. "And Tol's kind of a control freak." He gave her a friendly pat on the arm. "It's good for our prince to feel a little powerless every now and again. Keeps him on his toes."

Olivia managed something that was partway between a laugh and a sniffle. "I know. I just don't want to be useless."

"You're the savior of our entire race," Erikir said, dropping a wad of motor oil-soaked paper towels into the garbage. "I'd hardly call that useless."

Erikir's eyes were as dark with anger as always, but his voice held just enough gentleness to comfort her.

"Now that we have a second between emergencies," Gerth said, "why don't you tell us what happened when you met the Celestial?"

Everyone looked at her in expectation.

So, Olivia told them everything…or at least, almost everything. She still didn't mention the part about how she'd need to give up her powers at her moment of greatest need. Gerth was the most brilliant person she'd ever met, and Olivia didn't want to clue him into the fact that her life was the price for giving away her magic.

Olivia had made up her mind. There was nothing that would stop her from giving her abilities to the person who truly deserved them. She didn't need anyone else finding out and telling Addy or Tol.

"The Celestial made it seem like I have other abilities besides just telling the future," Olivia said.

Although I have no idea what they are, or how I'm supposed to figure them out.

"She said I needed to fully understand and embrace my strength. Then, I need to choose to give my power away to Addy, just like the Celestial chose to give it to me."

Gerth nodded like it all made perfect sense. Olivia was somewhat relieved to see the puzzled expressions on everyone else's faces.

"And how are you supposed to know when you've reached your full strength?" Nira asked.

"More importantly, how long will it take?" Erikir added.

"One step at a time." Gerth held up his hand like he was a cop directing traffic. He turned his attention on Olivia. "Anything else we need to know?"

A shudder went through her at the memory of those fire balls flying down to consume every major city in the world. She remembered the man hovering in the air next to her, and the way he'd laughed as whole buildings disappeared in a flash of heat and smoke.

Olivia cleared her throat.

The others were silent as she described the half-man, half-god the Celestial had called the Supernal. When she finished, a weighted silence filled the room.

Nira stood with her sponge hovering over a bloodstain. Fred and Aunt Meredith's mouths were open. Gerth was pressing his fist into his temples in fierce concentration, and Erikir…well, Erikir just looked angry.

"How is it possible there was another godly being and we never heard about him before?" Gerth asked.

Olivia assumed the question was rhetorical, since she'd already explained how the Celestial had stripped him of his powers and banished him to the mortal world.

A little shiver went through her at the reminder that this…creature had been set loose on her world.

"We have to find the stone that holds his strength," she said.

She would do anything to make sure her vision of the world burning never became a reality.

"Any idea where to find this stone?" Gerth asked.

"Or where we're supposed to find him?" Fred added.

Olivia shook her head. "I don't even know when this attack is going to take place."

She blew out a frustrated breath. What good were her visions if there was nothing concrete to go with them?

Tol had been right. If she didn't get a handle on these abilities, then she was of no use to anyone. And Olivia wouldn't tolerate being useless.

"Right then. First thing's first."

Gerth plopped down on the floor and crossed his legs like he was getting ready to meditate. He motioned for Olivia to join him.

"Shouldn't we be huntin' down this Supernal?" Fred asked. "Like, right now?"

"Nope," Gerth replied. He narrowed his gaze on Olivia. "You need to learn how to control your visions instead of the other way around."

Olivia sat next to him. Gerth seemed so certain, she didn't have the heart to tell him she had no control over what she saw and when.

"Now what?" she asked after several long moments had passed.

Gerth held out his hands. "I'm no prince, but I'm one of the Chosen. Let's see if you can make the visions come with me as your anchor."

Olivia wished she shared his confidence. She didn't want to make him feel bad, so she took his hand in hers.

Nothing happened.

She squeezed her eyes shut, trying to will whatever was hiding inside her to come out.

Please, she begged it. *Please, please, please.*

Nothing.

She opened her eyes, which were starting to blur from her wasted effort. Was this her destiny…to be useless to all the people who needed her?

"I have an idea," Erikir said.

Tol's angry cousin, whom Addy had threatened to kill more than once since they got to Texas, unstopped the vial hanging around his neck. He swallowed a single, glistening drop of the clear liquid. The golden halo of light around him brightened.

Olivia had seen all of their Hazes flare by now and knew it meant they were accessing their connection to the Source. Still, every time she'd seen it happen before, there had been some kind of emergency. She had never before been able to appreciate the pure magic of the change.

It made them all even more beautiful, even angry Erikir. Maybe even especially Erikir.

He motioned for her to hold out her hand. She did, and Erikir overturned his vial until a single drop of Source had collected on the pad of her fingertip.

A wave of guilt went through her. Erikir's vial was barely half-full, and she knew he couldn't afford to waste a single drop. The thought of one more person needing to drink Addy's blood to get Source made Olivia sick to her stomach.

Gerth's eyebrows pulled down. "She contains the Celestial's power. She shouldn't need to ingest Source to bring it out."

"Maybe not," Erikir replied, "but it might make it easier to draw her abilities to the surface while she's still getting a handle on them."

Still getting a handle on them seemed like a kind way of saying *Has no idea what the hell she's doing.*

Erikir nodded to her, and she put the drop in her mouth the way he'd done.

She expected it to taste the way it looked, thick and syrupy, but the Source didn't taste like anything at all. It somehow had even less taste than water. If it wasn't for the golden light pooling around her, she would have wondered if the drop slid off her finger before she put it in her mouth.

She looked down at herself and sucked in a breath. She was so bright it was making spots dance in her vision. It was like the way Tol had looked on Vitaquias. Gerth and Erikir had to shield their eyes to look at her.

Olivia immediately felt stronger. She could sense…something…inside her. It was like staring into a snow globe that had been shaken up. There was something underneath all that snow, but she couldn't see it clearly enough to make out what it was.

Erikir sat on the floor next to her. He didn't meet her gaze, but at least he didn't flinch away like Tol always did. She took his hands, which were warm and reassuring, and closed her eyes.

Image after image flashed through her mind. They moved too fast for her to get a good look at any of them.

"Focus, Olivia," Gerth said from somewhere far away.

She chose one of the flashing images and reached out for it. Invisible fingers snagged on the corner. The image felt more like smoke than anything solid, and it started to fray as she drew it to the surface.

She tightened her hold on Erikir's hands, letting his strength flow into her. The image solidified.

It was a memory about her, but it belonged to someone else. Two tiny girls were sitting in a bed Olivia recognized. It was the one her younger sister, Rosie, had slept in.

A much younger version of their mother sat against the pillows piled against the headboard. Olivia was nestled against her. She couldn't have been more than four years old. Toddler-Addy was also on the bed, making *vroom vroom* noises as she ran a toy race car up and down their mother's leg.

Their mother was reading *Goodnight Moon*, and with each page flip, little Olivia tried to see how quickly she could spot the hidden rabbit in the picture.

"Sweet Livy," her mother murmured, kissing the top of her head.

The image began to blur and fade.

"No," Olivia whispered.

She tried to drag the vision back, the same way she was desperate to hold her mother again. As soon as she reached for the scene in her mind, the image slipped back into the swirling pool along with all the others.

Desperate to reclaim that piece of the past, she plunged in again. Her mental fingers closed around a vision, but it wasn't the one she'd been hoping for. She could tell even before she looked that this image wasn't a memory. It was blurred at the edges, which she was beginning to learn meant it was a piece of the future.

Current-aged Addy was crouched on a sandy shore, and she was sobbing. She was covered in blood and her clothes were torn, but that wasn't why she was crying.

Olivia's brave, fierce sister was…broken.

Olivia could sense her twin's emotions now as clearly as she could in real life. She'd never known Addy to be in this much pain. Desperate to know what had caused her such anguish, Olivia pulled herself deeper into the image.

The vision fought her, and time slid backward. Olivia saw Addy falling in reverse from the deck of an enormous ship. She saw a blast of light. She heard someone scream Addy's name.

And then time sped forward again. Olivia was inside the image with Addy. She smelled salt in the air and felt wind on her face. And then she was falling. The dark water churned below her, and she braced herself for the impact. At the moment before she hit the water, Olivia was thrust from the vision with such force it propelled her backward.

Someone's arms came around her, keeping her from smacking her head against the floor.

"It's okay," a low voice said. His chest was pressed to her back, and the steady rhythm of his heartbeat brought her back to herself.

She blinked. She was back in her aunt's house, with the smell of wood and leather.

"I'm fine," she gasped, even though she could feel herself shaking.

She was drawing strength from the arms around her. She started at the realization that it was Erikir who was holding her. She'd curled her hands around his forearms to keep him from letting go.

"I'm sorry," she said, quickly letting her hands drop. She scooted away, embarrassed.

When she glanced at Erikir, she saw his Haze had dulled. He sagged from exhaustion.

Aunt Meredith passed Olivia a cold washcloth. Olivia realized she was sweating, even though a cold chill was making goosebumps rise on her arms. She also had a pounding headache. Instead of pressing the washcloth to her own face, she gave it to Erikir. He looked as drawn as she felt.

He nodded in thanks and then pressed it to his eyes, like he was sharing her headache.

"What did you see?" Gerth asked, his eyes bright with interest.

Olivia relayed the condensed version, not wanting to dwell on either the memory of her mother or the one of Addy's heartbreak. She stumbled over her words. She felt as tired as Erikir looked.

"Well, that's a start," Gerth said when she'd finished.

"We need her visions to be more focused if we're ever going to get any kind of useful information out of her," Nira said, tapping a red fingernail on the lacquered top of the coffee table.

"She's a human bein', not some tool," Fred said.

Nira gave him a brief, distasteful glance. Then, she turned her attention back to Olivia.

"Try again," Nira commanded. "We need to find the Supernal before he turns this world into another Vitaquias."

"She can't handle any more right now," Erikir said, his voice thin. "We'll kill her if we push her too far."

Olivia sat there while the others debated her limitations, feeling very much like a broken watch. She didn't like it.

"Give me ten minutes, and then we'll try again," she said, interrupting the argument that was heating up.

"I think you need to get a good night's sleep and then try again in the mornin'," Fred said, still watching her with a worried expression.

"A good meal will fix you up," Aunt Meredith declared. "Come on. Study break time."

CHAPTER 18

OLIVIA

Aunt Meredith herded them into the kitchen and made them sit around the large, circular table while she busied herself at the stove. Fred and Nira helped Aunt Meredith. Gerth scribbled madly on a pad of paper while he muttered under his breath. Olivia and Erikir slumped in their chairs.

Olivia wanted to apologize to him for taking so much of his energy, but she felt too drained to manage even that. She'd never felt so tired in her entire life…not even during harvest season, when she had helped her parents in the corn fields from dawn until dark.

She perked up a little at the smell of peppers and onions sizzling in the huge cast iron skillet Aunt Meredith put on the table. Warm tortillas in a basket came next, followed by bowls of guacamole, queso, and pico de gallo. The smell, and the hissing sound of meat and veggies continuing to cook in the pan, had her practically drooling. She was ravenous.

"Eat up," Aunt Meredith said as she passed around a pitcher of sweet tea. There was so much sugar that Olivia could see the crystals swirling around at the bottom.

Olivia poured herself a tall glass and bit into her first queso-smothered fajita.

"The effects you're feeling are from using Source," Gerth said without looking up from his scribbling.

It was no wonder Erikir was so worn out. Not only had he fought the Forsaken with his Source, he'd given Olivia whatever small amount of energy he had left.

Tol had been right. She needed to figure out how to access this power inside her without relying on others. She hated that she was the reason for those dark shadows under Erikir's eyes.

Olivia still felt tired, but between the fajitas and root beer floats Aunt Meredith made for dessert, she got her second wind. Gerth, Fred, and Nira held up the bulk of the conversation with Aunt Meredith. They told her as much as they could about Vitaquias and the Chosen people without letting her know quite how much danger they were all in.

Some of what they said was new to even Olivia. She soaked up every word, even though she'd have no place among these people as soon as she gave her powers to Addy.

The realization gripped her with an unexpected sadness. That strange sense of rightness she felt around these people was one she had never expected to feel with anyone outside of her own family. She'd known them for little more than a week, but she couldn't imagine saying goodbye to these people forever. She couldn't imagine staying behind while the rest of them departed to another planet.

The point was moot, of course. She wouldn't be staying behind on Earth. She'd be dead.

"Hey, you okay?"

Olivia turned to Erikir, who was looking at her with concern.

She smiled at him. "I'm good."

He frowned. He didn't believe her, but he didn't push her to say more.

After they all helped wash and put away the dishes, they took turns showering. It was barely eight o'clock, but it seemed like Olivia wasn't the only one desperate for sleep.

Once she was clean, she put on the comfy pair of sweats she'd taken from the wardrobe Aunt Meredith filled with new clothes for all of them. She used the hairbrush and toothbrush from the toiletry bag with her name printed across the front in her aunt's handwriting. Since they hadn't had time to pack any of their own clothes or toiletries, Aunt Meredith had gotten enough for all of them to be comfortable while they stayed with her.

Aunt Meredith was so much like Olivia and Addy's mother, both in looks and her caring personality, that sometimes Olivia had to do a double-take when her aunt came into the room. On the one hand, it felt a little like she hadn't completely lost her mom when she was with Aunt Meredith. On the other, her aunt served as a constant reminder of everyone Olivia had lost.

Olivia leaned against the door of the bathroom and tried to breathe.

"You can stop trying to be as gorgeous as me," Nira called from outside the bathroom. "It's never going to happen, and there are other people who want to freshen up."

Sighing, Olivia unlocked the door and slipped out past a pouting Nira.

Needing a distraction from thinking about her family, Olivia wandered out to the bookshelf in the living room. She finger-combed her wet curls while she scanned the titles, looking for something she could snuggle up with before trying to access her powers again.

For as long as she could remember, books had been her only window into a different world. She had a literal different world to think about now, but she missed the characters in her favorite books the way she might miss real people. If she had one of the books she'd read a thousand times, it might make her feel closer to the life she'd had, and the people she'd shared it with before they were stolen from her.

"What are you looking for?"

Olivia jumped. She hadn't noticed Erikir, who was sprawled out on the couch and studying one of Gerth's maps.

"A book," she stammered, caught off guard by his presence.

Erikir smirked, but it wasn't one of his mean smirks. "There seem to be a lot of those on that shelf. Any one in particular?"

"Anything by Jane Austen," she said without thinking. "Or the Brontë sisters."

Erikir's wet hair was twisted into a tight braid. It had never before occurred to Olivia that long hair could make a guy somehow more masculine. On Erikir, though, it did.

His eyes were free of the resentment that usually churned in their depths. She'd never before noticed the perfect shape of his lips, because his mouth was usually turned down in a scowl. She realized she was staring and quickly looked away.

Had he noticed?

"You mean you don't want to read about tractor repair or calving?" Erikir asked, his eyes gleaming in what might have been humor.

Olivia shook her head, smiling in spite of herself. She tried to think of what to say to Erikir, but he had already turned back to his map. Giving up on the bookshelf, Olivia wandered down the hall to Aunt Meredith's study, thinking with little hope there might be some books more to her taste in there…or at least something fiction.

Nira was standing outside the half-open door to the study with her head cocked as she listened to Fred's voice, which was just audible.

"It's not polite to eavesdrop," Olivia told Nira, feeling defensive on Fred's behalf.

"His father is sick?" Nira asked, ignoring Olivia's comment and not seeming in the least bit sorry.

"Your pill case is in the bathroom," Fred's voice said. "Fill it up at the beginning of the week so you don't forget to take any of 'em. Has Mrs. Johnson been comin' by?"

"Mr. Brown has MS," Olivia told Nira, "but Fred doesn't like to talk about it, so don't ask him."

She expected one of Nira's flip remarks, but Nira surprised her.

"My aunts are sick, too." Nira pulled her curtain of hair over her shoulder and frowned at it, like it wasn't as perfect as always.

"I'm so sorry," Olivia said, caught off guard by the other girl's admission.

Nira was wearing a pair of pajamas that swamped her. The clothes made her look young and fragile, as opposed to her usual icy perfection. There was a more human quality about her now. It made Olivia want to give the other girl a hug.

"Don't give me that pitying look, mortal." Nira snapped.

She stalked away, her bare feet slapping against the wood floor.

Fred came out of the study, then. As soon as he saw Olivia, the lines of tension on his face smoothed out. He put an arm around her and kissed the top of her head.

"Us mortals gotta stick together, huh?" He winked at her.

Olivia wrapped her arm around Fred and leaned her head against him.

"That is a pretty girl," Fred commented as they watched Nira disappear around the corner.

Olivia grinned up at him. "Are you trying to tell me you're finally over my sister?"

"Well, let's just say I ain't blind."

CHAPTER 19

TOL

Tol was ready for the nausea and sense of weightlessness this time. He managed to stay on his feet when the portal dumped them onto the driveway. His head hadn't stopped spinning, but he forced his vision to sharpen as he looked at the manor. He braced himself for the sight of flames pouring out of the windows like they'd been the last time he was here.

There were black scorch marks around a few of the windows, but otherwise, the manor looked the way it always did. There were construction crews working outside and the smell of fresh paint filled the air, but that was the only sign anything out of the ordinary had happened here. Tol sighed in relief.

"I think my mode of transportation beats your plane," Addy announced.

"It definitely wins on speed and convenience," he conceded, "but the in-flight service could use some improvement."

Before she could respond with a snappy comment, the manor's front door opened.

"Prince Tolumus?" Henroix, his parents' chief of staff, hurried down the stairs to them. He bowed to Tol and then gave Addy a skeptical look. Tol leveled a stare at the older man, who hesitated for only another moment before bowing to Addy, too.

Tol didn't usually care about formalities, but he'd be damned if he let anyone treat Addy with anything less than utmost respect.

"Where are my parents? Are they alright?" Tol asked, skipping pleasantries.

"Your parents are holding up." Henroix wasn't looking at Tol. His mouth had thinned into a disapproving line as he took in Addy's appearance. "Ms. Deerborn, are you aware that you're covered in blood?"

Addy winced. "I probably should have showered before we came here," she said.

Tol shook his head. Time was a luxury they didn't have.

"We need to meet with my parents straight away," Tol said.

"You want an audience with the king and queen looking like *that*?" Henroix demanded.

"And Gran," Tol added.

When it was clear Tol wasn't budging, Henroix sighed. "Very well. But you're not walking through the manor's halls looking so...disheveled." He sniffed in disapproval.

Tol and Addy exchanged a grin.

Henroix ushered them around the side of the house, making Tol feel a bit like a burglar. Henroix even tried to get them to hunch down when they got to the tall windows, but Tol just rolled his eyes and carried on. Henroix unlocked one of the patio doors off the study and let them inside...after first ensuring the room was empty.

"Try not to touch anything," Henroix told them.

"Would you like to put plastic on my chair before I sit down?" Tol asked.

"He's kidding," Addy informed Henroix, who had perked up at Tol's offer.

Henroix's expression soured.

"Majesty, can I at least bring Ms. Deerborn some fresh clothes?"

"What good will that do when the blood is all over my skin?" Addy asked, looking more amused than annoyed.

"We'll clean up after we meet with my parents," Tol promised, which seemed to appease the older man just a little.

As soon as Henroix left them alone, Tol sat back in his chair and inhaled the familiar scent of old books and furniture polish.

Addy's chair squeaked as she fidgeted. She groaned.

"What's wrong?" Tol asked.

"I just remembered your mom is terrifying."

Tol laughed, but when he realized Addy was genuinely distressed, he squeezed her hand.

"She already thinks I'm a barbarian." Addy scanned the room, like she was considering making a break for it. She pulled away from Tol and got up. "I'm hiding behind the fern. Come get me when she's gone."

"Addy." Tol couldn't help chuckling as he pulled her back down into her chair.

The door to the study opened, and Tol's parents came in. All of Tol's mirth faded in an instant.

He got to his feet.

"Mum." He stepped forward but wasn't sure what to do next.

The last time he'd seen his parents, they had made it clear they didn't support his choice to return to Vitaquias. He had never before disappointed his parents, and knowing he'd done so had been a weight on Tol's heart.

"Tolumus." His mother's gaze softened, and she closed the distance between them to hug him.

He bent down and wrapped his arms around her before stepping back to examine his mother's face. She looked as meticulous as ever in a crisp business suit and with her hair in an elaborate knot. There was something in her eyes that Tol didn't like, though. Her petite frame looked frail in a way it never had before. Her already-thin face seemed hollower, too. She looked haggard.

Guilt closed its fists around Tol's chest and squeezed. He could guess at the strain his parents were under, and it was his fault.

"Mum, what's happened?" he asked.

"Darling, I—" His mother broke off at the sight of Addy. Her gaze moved from Addy's dirty sneakers to the dried blood streaked across her cheeks. His mother's nostrils flared. Tol stiffened.

"You brought Adelyne." His mother raised a single eyebrow, which somehow managed to look insulting.

"Yeah, I brought my fiancé," Tol replied dryly.

"So, it's done, then? She's the Fount now?" Her lips puckered like she'd bitten into a lemon.

Tol raked a hand through his hair. "We're working on it."

His mother's shrewd gaze turned back to him. "Tolumus, we're—"

"—running out of time," Tol finished. "I know."

Addy's face was flushed in embarrassment. Tol stepped away from his mother and went to stand beside Addy.

"I apologize for my appearance, Your Majesty," Addy said in a formal tone she never used. *And was that the hint of an English accent?* "I was occupied with taking out some trash—er, rubbish—and I didn't have time to freshen up before my arrival."

Gods, he loved her.

"The Forsaken attacked us," Tol translated, unable to hold back his amusement.

Before his mother could reply, the study door opened and Gran came in.

Tol froze. He was going to have to tell her about how he's abandoned Walidir on Vitaquias in the middle of a storm he might not have survived.

"Tolumus!" Gran's cane clicked across the wood floor.

Addy's sharp jab in his side had Tol moving forward in spite of the dread tightening his stomach.

"Gran." His throat had gotten too tight for him to manage more than that.

Gran might look frail, but when he bent down so she could kiss his cheek, her grip on his arm was strong.

"I sensed from Walidir that you found him," she said. Her eyes looked huge behind the thick lenses of her spectacles. "You spoke to him?"

"Yes." Tol's voice was barely a whisper.

It was Addy who explained, because shame and regret were eating Tol alive, and he couldn't seem to make the words come out.

Addy had almost reached the end of the story when the study door opened. Tol's father strode in.

"My father's alive?" the king demanded.

Tol and Addy nodded.

"He's living in the ruins of the castle," Tol said, because he refused to accept the very real possibility that his grandfather had died in that storm. "I should have brought him back to you. I'm sorry."

The words felt so inadequate.

He glanced at Gran, preparing himself for her pain and judgment. Tol blinked. Gran was smiling.

"I can feel his presence stronger than ever." She clutched a gnarled hand to her heart.

"I can't believe he's alive," Tol's father murmured.

"Oh, Rolomens. Have you not heard a single word I've said for the last eighteen years?" Gran demanded.

"I heard you, I just didn't believe." Tol's father stroked a hand over his beard.

"Now you know not to doubt your mother," Gran retorted.

She turned her attention back on Tol. "Don't fret. It will take more than a little storm to defeat your grandfather."

It hadn't been a *little storm*.

"Have you…talked to him?" Tol asked. He didn't exactly understand how his grandparents' connection worked, or how it transcended the separation between two worlds.

"Our connection isn't wholly within our control. I haven't heard from him since you showed up."

Tol's lungs constricted.

"Trust me, Tolumus," she said at whatever expression had crossed his face. "We may not have been blood married, but after five-hundred years together, I know your grandfather as well as if we were. He's alive." Getyl went and sat down next to Addy. "Now, tell us everything."

Tol stopped partway through his story when Henroix came in to bring a tray of tea. Then, he had to wait until the tea was poured and Gran drank her first cup.

When he was finished telling his family everything, he slumped back against his chair. He was still reeling from all the strength he'd expended when he Influenced the Forsaken. That, combined with everything else they'd been through, was making him a little delirious.

"How long is it going to take for Olivia to transfer her powers to Adelyne?" his mum asked.

"She's working on it now," Tol replied. "Gerth's helping her, so it won't be long."

Because Gerth had never met a problem he couldn't solve.

"So, you're still determined to go through with this?" his father asked.

Tol stiffened, but before he could speak, Gran said, "Honestly, Rolomens. What did you expect?"

"That my son would remember his duties to his people," his father said under his breath.

Tol's face heated. "I haven't forgotten my duties. If I had, Addy and I would be on holiday right now on some beach without cell service. Well, not a beach," he gave Addy an apologetic grin, "but you know what I mean."

She squeezed his hand under the table. His parents looked unimpressed.

"Tell us what's been happening here," Tol said, getting back to business. "Nira said you didn't distribute the reserves."

"That girl needs to learn some discretion," his mother said, pursing her lips.

"Don't blame Nira for your poor judgment," Gran said amiably.

"And what did you expect us to do?" his father shot back. "Tolumus left us no choice."

Gran turned to Tol. "Your parents determined, against my counsel, not to share the reserves."

"Why?" Tol demanded.

Distributing the reserves would quiet the rebellion long enough for Tol and Addy to blood marry.

"Because the threat from the Forsaken is getting more substantial," the king snapped. "If we gave out the reserves, we'd have nothing left to fight the enemy with."

"Not to mention," his mother added, "we've been preoccupied with putting down rumors about where you've been."

"You didn't tell everyone the truth?" Tol asked.

His father threw up his arms. "You wanted us to tell our subjects you fell in love with the Forsaken general's daughter, and that you were refusing to blood marry the Fount in favor of going to Vitaquias on a suicide quest?"

"It wasn't a suicide quest," Tol pointed out.

"You left us with few options, Tolumus," his mother said.

It was true. He'd put his parents in an impossible position and left them to deal with a mess he'd created.

"I'm here to answer for my choices now," Tol said. "Distribute the reserves. Gather our people. Addy and I will get cleaned up, and then we'll tell them everything."

Tol's father stood up and prowled around the table until he was standing face-to-face with Tol.

"You aren't king yet, Tolumus," he said in a voice that no one else would dare challenge.

"We don't have time for games," Tol replied.

"I agree, which is why I'm going to ask you, *again*, to meet your responsibility to our people and blood marry the Fount."

Tol locked eyes with his father.

"I already told you I would…as soon as Addy is the Fount. We just need a little more time, and giving out the reserves will buy us just that."

His father's chest rose and fell with his contained fury.

"Do you love your people or this girl?" his father asked.

Don't ask me that, Tol silently begged. *Don't ask me to choose.*

"Both," he said. "I love both."

His father shook his head. "It doesn't work that way."

"You love Mum," Tol pointed out.

"Yes, and she understands what you do not…that my priority will always be the survival of our people."

"Your Majesties, we haven't forgotten our promise to you," Addy said.

Tol didn't want to think about the possibility of failure…that he'd have to give up Addy to save his people. That future loomed before him. It came closer with each day.

"Neither have we," Tol's mother said. "While we imagine your intentions are…honorable…we have our doubts about your ability to deliver when the times comes."

"If," Addy corrected. "We haven't failed yet. We'll buy ourselves a little more time with the reserves—"

"Forget the reserves!" Tol's father cut his hand through the air in an angry motion.

"Rolomens, sit down before you have a stroke," Gran commanded.

She glared at all of them until they were seated back around the oak table. Gran gestured for Tol's mother to pour more tea, even though no one else had touched theirs.

Gran seemed unphased by the tension in the room as she sipped her tea and Tol's parents fumed. Tol put his hand on Addy's leg under the table, quieting the nervous tapping of her sneaker.

"Now, then." Gran put down her empty tea cup. "Here's what is going to happen. Tol and Adelyne are obviously in need of a good meal and a night's sleep. Tomorrow, Tol will say what he needs to say to his subjects."

"My subjects," the king corrected.

"Not for long." Gran gave her son's hand a patronizing pat.

The king pointed an accusatory finger at Tol. "You have my permission to address our people, but there will be no mention of the reserves. I forbid it, Tolumus."

Tol bit back a frustrated response. When his father got into this kind of a mood, there was no changing his mind.

"Everything we've done to stave off the rebellion will evaporate the minute he presents *her*," Tol's mother said, barely glancing at Addy.

Tol was about to retort, when he felt Addy's hand close around his. She shook her head. He bit his tongue, although it grated on him to let a slight to Addy go unchallenged.

He satisfied himself with saying, "Our people will accept her as their queen because I have chosen her. Once they get to know her, they'll come to love her as much as I do." He paused. "Well, maybe not as much as I do."

His father sighed in exasperation. His mum looked vaguely ill. Gran was smiling.

"She'll have to sleep in Nira's room, since the guest cottage got the worse end of the fire," the queen said, falling back to logistics.

"Oh, don't be a prude, Starser," Gran said. "Let her stay with Tol."

"Absolutely not." Tol's father looked as scandalized as his mother. "They're not married."

Tol leaned back against his chair, readying himself for a long argument between his parents and Gran. It didn't matter what they decided. Tol had a lifetime's worth of sneaking around the manor, and he had no intention of spending the night apart from Addy. Still, he appreciated Gran coming to their defense.

"They've grown up in a different time in a different world," Gran said. "You wouldn't believe the naughty things young people get up to on the In-ter-net. Besides, the rules of the ritual will keep them from getting too frisky."

Tol groaned. Addy tried to disguise her laugh with a cough.

Gran continued, "Who knows how many days they have left together. Give them this time while they have it."

Tol immediately sobered. He heard Addy's breath hitch.

No one needed to remind him of how fragile his hold on Addy was. Every day, he wondered how many more times he'd be able to kiss her…hold her…look at her….

Tol's father turned to his wife for an answer.

"Fine." Tol's mum crossed her arms. "At least it'll prevent us from having to explain who the bloodstained girl staying in Nira's room is." She turned a hard gaze on the two of them. "I suggest you don't let anyone see you until you're ready to start answering questions. I'll have Henroix bring food and *appropriate* clothes to your room. You can address our people in the morning."

Tol nodded. "Thank you."

Tol's father humphed.

His parents swept out of the room, leaving Tol with the knowledge that, once again, he'd disappointed them. Addy was clenching her fists, looking the way Tol felt. Only Gran seemed at ease.

She poured herself a third cup of tea, sipped, and then said, "Now. Tell me all about my Walidir."

CHAPTER 20

ADDY

Addy kept pace with Tol through the mysteriously-empty hallways as he led her to his room. She suspected the queen had made sure no one else would see the prince and his bloody, barbarian fiancé.

There was a niggling voice in her mind that told her she didn't belong with the Chosen…wasn't one of them. The voice was getting louder every day, it seemed. Addy belonged with Tol. She was certain about that much. But the rest of his people….

Her face heated at the memory of how Tol's parents had looked at her bloody clothes. It wasn't just that she'd showed up at their pristine house looking dirty and bedraggled. It was as bad as holding up a sign that read, *I fight like the Forsaken because I'm one of them.*

Addy's worries quieted when Tol opened the double doors to his room. It was actually more of a suite. She found herself inside a cozy space with two couches, a flat screen TV, and a desk with a sleek-looking laptop. The candle burning on the side table filled the room with a clean, citrus scent.

A curved archway separated the sitting room from a huge bedroom. Everything was cool shades of blue and gray. The curtains over the large window had been drawn aside, displaying a private garden bordered by thick shrubs. She could see a stone patio, complete with a wrought-iron table and two chairs. Little white flowers grew up the sides of a trellis.

"What do you think?" Tol asked.

Addy turned to see he was watching her.

"It'll do." She shrugged, like it wasn't the most beautiful bedroom she'd ever seen in her life.

Tol smirked. "I'm glad you approve."

There was a knock at the door. Henroix, followed by two servants, came in bearing covered silver trays. The smells wafting from them had Addy struggling not to salivate like one of Pavlov's dogs.

"Bathroom's that way if you want to wash up before we eat," Tol said, pointing.

She kicked off her dirty sneakers and walked through the bedroom into the bathroom while Henroix talked to Tol.

Addy just stood in the doorway, taking it in. The walls, floor, and countertops were elegant gray-veined marble. A light fixture that was more chandelier than lamp hung from the ceiling. There were white orchids on both sides of the long counter, and unlike the flowers in her parents' bathroom, these orchids were real. On one side of the bathroom was an enormous jacuzzi-style tub. On the other was the biggest shower Addy had ever seen. There was even a whole separate room within the bathroom for the toilet. There was a bottle of cologne on a glass tray next to one of the *three* sinks. Addy lifted off the top and inhaled the spicy, masculine scent.

Tol.

"Addy, hurry up," Tol called from the other room. "I'm starving to death."

She put the cologne away and stopped gawking. She pulled off her T-shirt and stuffed it in the trash, careful not to let any of the dried blood flake off onto the floor. At least the tank top she was wearing underneath was clean…enough. She washed her hands and arms, and scrubbed at the flecks of blood on her cheeks and neck. When she was more or less free of blood, sweat, and dirt, she dried off with the softest towel she'd ever felt and went out to join Tol.

He was leaning back against the couch, looking completely at ease. When he caught sight of her, he raised his eyebrows and whistled.

Addy laughed.

"What's for dinner?" she asked, feeling flustered at the way Tol was still looking at her.

He finally tore his eyes off her, and they started uncovering trays.

For the first few minutes, their conversation was all about the food. They didn't bother with the china plates stacked on the edge of the coffee table and just dug right in with their forks. There was roasted pheasant in a syrupy pomegranate sauce that somehow managed to be both sour and sweet. Another tray revealed garlic mashed potatoes baked inside a flaky crust of pastry dough. The vegetables were so tender and buttery even her younger, vegetable-hating sisters would have gobbled them down. For dessert, there was sticky toffee pudding. Addy had never had it before, but after her first bite, she tipped her head up to the heavens and demanded to know why her parents had deprived her of something so delicious.

She and Tol chatted about nothing important as they sat curled on the couch together and licked the remnants of sticky toffee pudding from their fingers. There was something so beautifully simple about just eating dinner with Tol. It felt very grown-up and very right.

After they'd put the covers back on the silver trays, Addy nestled into the crook of Tol's arm as they discussed how to broach the next day.

"The Jesuls are playing off everyone's fears of dying to try to take over the monarchy." Tol blew out a frustrated breath. "If we could just give out those reserves, we'd buy ourselves a little more time before full-on anarchy."

"Not to mention saving the people who are hovering on a knife's blade between life and death," Tol added darkly.

Addy felt the oppressive guilt that was weighing Tol down.

This was her fault. If Tol just blood married the one he was supposed to....

No.

Addy cut that thought off right there. They hadn't lost all hope of being together, which meant they needed to find a way to keep his people alive until she could become the Fount.

"Maybe—" she paused, knowing Tol wouldn't like this idea.

"What?" Tol prompted.

"We could use my blood," she said, softening her voice in anticipation of Tol's reaction.

"No." His answer was immediate.

"Why not?" she asked, puzzled. Tol wasn't the stifling, over-protective type. "It's an easy solution."

"You know what my people did to the Source on Vitaquias." Tol looked away from her, like he was ashamed. "I'd rather face my parents' wrath for an eternity than let a single one of my subjects know about the Source in your blood."

"You think they'd rip me limb from limb to suck me dry?" Addy asked. She meant it as a joke, but it came out as more of a question when she saw the genuine worry on Tol's face.

"I think my people's ambition is limitless, and I'm not willing to take the risk that they'll decide your life is worth less than theirs."

Addy didn't have an argument for that.

Tol went to his desk and started drafting his speech for the next day. The thought of standing up there, while an angry mob of Chosen people judged her, sent a thousand moths aflutter inside Addy's stomach. Tol seemed just as edgy as he scribbled out words on thick, expensive-looking paper. He frowned before crumpling up the paper and throwing it into a growing pile on the floor.

After Tol threw out his fifth draft, Addy got up the nerve to ask the question that had been hovering in the back of her mind all day.

"What if your parents are right about me? What if I'll never be able to be a good leader of the Chosen because I'm Forsaken at my core?"

Tol put down his pen and swiveled in his chair to face her.

"You aren't one of them. You're ours. Mine."

"Possessive much?" she asked, a small smile curving her lips in spite of all her worries.

"You gods-damned better believe it."

Tol went back to his speech, seeming even more agitated than he'd been before.

"Forget the speech," Addy told him. "You'll know what to say once you're standing in front of everyone tomorrow."

Tol looked back at his most recent draft, scowled at it, and then pushed back from his desk.

"I guess you're right." He sunk back down onto the couch beside her. He took his phone out of his pocket and looked at the dark screen. "Maybe I'll give Gerth a call. See how much progress they've made with your sister's abilities."

"You and I need to focus on preventing a rebellion here. Livy's working as hard as she can, trust me."

Addy gently removed the phone from his grasp and set it on the coffee table.

"I hope you're right."

Tol got up from the couch on a sigh. He walked into the beautiful bedroom and collapsed back onto the king-sized bed.

He closed his eyes, and Addy thought he might have fallen asleep. She couldn't blame him. Addy felt like ten-pound weights had attached themselves to her eyelids. She tried to comb her fingers through her hair, but the strands were crusted with dried sweat and blood. Grimacing, she headed for the bathroom. She was determined to stay awake long enough to use Tol's magnificent shower.

"What are you up to?" Tol asked, his voice deep and rumbly from sleepiness.

"Shower," Addy replied.

Tol sat up, looking much more awake. His Haze brightened enough to light up the room. "Can I join you?"

Addy laughed, but Tol's *just kidding* didn't come.

"It is a big shower," he reasoned. "It would conserve water and be better for the environment if we shared it."

Addy snorted. "You mean to tell me you're an environmentalist now?"

Tol gave her one of his irresistible smiles. "I can be if it'll get you naked."

Addy's pulse sped up. For the first time, it occurred to her that they were alone with an entire night ahead of them. All thoughts of sleep vanished.

So, why wasn't she pouncing on him right now?

She hated herself for it, but her mind conjured up images of gorgeous Nira giving Tol a lap dance in this very room. Addy had only vague, theoretical ideas about how most of this stuff worked, and she was painfully aware of her ignorance.

Tol was watching her, waiting for some kind of answer. She knew if she said no, he would accept her decision without question. But chickening out just because Tol's ex was a real-live beauty queen seemed stupid.

"What about the rules of the ritual?" she asked.

"Oh, that." Tol gave her a sheepish grin. "I did a little research into the specifics while you were washing up before. You know, just in case it came up."

"Uh-huh." Addy grinned back, feeling some of her tension ease.

Tol continued, "We can't do much, but we can do more than I thought."

"Oh?" Addy raised her eyebrows. "Care to explain?"

Tol gave her a slow, sensuous smile. "I'd rather show you."

He got off the bed and crossed the room to her. As soon as he drew her in for a kiss, all her worries about not measuring up to Nira vanished.

She melted into him. Before her legs failed her altogether, Tol swept her into his arms and carried her across the room. He put her down on the cold marble, breaking their kiss long enough to turn on the shower.

"I've never done this before," Addy told him, her voice coming out high and breathy.

"Neither have I," Tol replied.

"Very funny."

He turned to face her. "I'm not joking."

"But, you and Nira—"

"Never did this." He motioned to the shower.

"Why would—" Addy cut herself off. As steam started to fill the room, she understood.

"It's your arm, isn't it?" she asked.

Tol nodded. "The straps chafe when they're wet, so…yeah."

For Tol, being without his prosthesis was more intimate than sex.

His shyness put her more at ease. Addy raised her arms. Tol immediately took the hint and slid her tank top over her head. Goosebumps prickled her skin from the cool air. Or maybe her reaction was from the way Tol's fingers brushed along her spine as he unhooked her bra.

He worked his way through each article of her clothing slowly, giving her plenty of time to stop him. She didn't.

"Gods, and I thought you were beautiful with clothes," Tol murmured, stepping back to look at her.

It occurred to her that she was standing completely naked in front of a fully-clothed Tol. Her heart was racing, but she couldn't feel self-conscious with the way he was devouring her with his eyes.

She closed the distance between them and unbuttoned his shirt. She was careful with his prosthesis, making sure not to pinch his skin when she undid the clasp on his chest. She took the time to bring his arm into the other room, since she didn't know if the steam from the shower would hurt it, before coming back.

What was left of Tol's clothes were now in a pile on the floor. Addy bit her lip as her heart pounded even faster. She might not have many points of comparison when it came to naked men, but she knew perfection when she saw it.

She stepped closer. They both gasped as their bare skin met. Addy dug her fingers into Tol's soft hair, bringing his mouth to hers.

"My warrior goddess," he said against her lips.

He took her hand and pulled her into the shower with him. The water streaming down his bronze skin made him look like a god himself.

They kissed and touched until Addy forgot about all of the impossible tasks that lay ahead. There wasn't room for anything else except Tol, and the way he filled her heart to bursting.

❋ ❋ ❋

Addy woke from a deep sleep. The warm strength of Tol's body had been wrapped around her, but he was gone now. The space next to her was cold.

"Tol?"

When he didn't answer, she opened her eyes.

It was then that she saw the dark shadow. It had the same feel of the Nyxar, but it was somehow more real…more sentient. Its wraithlike arms were wrapped around Tol. One of its hands was pressed over Tol's mouth, silencing him. The creature was hovering near the ceiling, and it was pulling Tol with it…away from her.

She jumped on top of the mattress and tried to disentangle Tol from the creature. Before she could reach him, the ceiling of Tol's bedroom peeled back, and a black hole opened up in its place. A fierce wind kicked up. The gale pushed Addy away from the black void while drawing the creature and Tol closer.

Addy fought harder. She knew if Tol got sucked into the black hole, she wouldn't be able to follow.

Tol's Haze was dimming, and his olive skin was drained of color. The shadow creature was killing him.

It was dragging Tol farther and farther away from her. The wraith's inky darkness was already spilling into the void.

The creature removed its hand from Tol's mouth. And then it plunged its shadowed hand into Tol's chest.

She screamed.

"Addy."

She tore at the shadow being, but no matter how hard she fought, it only clung tighter…squeezed the life out of Tol faster.

His blood coated her hands.

"Addy!"

She woke as another scream tore free from her lips.

Addy was lying down—not standing on the mattress. There was no shadow creature, and Tol was next to her. Both of their Hazes were lighting up the room. She realized she was clinging to Tol's arm with a death grip that was cutting off his circulation.

"Sorry," Addy gasped. Her throat was raw.

Just a dream. It was just a dream.

Tol winced when she let go of his arm, but the concern in his eyes was all for her.

"What happened?" he asked. "That wasn't your usual dream."

Addy hadn't had her recurring nightmare of drowning…which, as it turned out, wasn't a dream but a memory…since she'd started sharing a bed with Tol. This nightmare was something different.

"I dreamed this monster thing was taking you away." She tried to breathe through the panic that was constricting her lungs. With Tol safe and alive beside her, it all seemed so foolish. But when she remembered the way that creature had plunged its hand into Tol's chest….

She was shaking, but she couldn't stop. Tol wrapped his arm around her.

"It's alright," he murmured. "I'm alright."

Addy nodded, but she couldn't get that image out of her head.

Later, after Tol's breathing had evened back out in sleep, Addy stayed awake. She kept one hand on Tol's chest, feeling the even beat of his heart. The other clutched the garden shears under her pillow.

CHAPTER 21

OLIVIA

Olivia squeezed her eyes shut, ignoring the unpleasant trickle of sweat down her back.

"Tear the book apart, Olivia," Gerth commanded.

She felt his Influence like an invisible hand trying to mold her brain. Talons dug into her thoughts.

She needed him out of her head.

It should be easy. Olivia didn't want to do what he was ordering. She would never destroy a book.

Or would she?

As she met Gerth's unblinking stare, she felt herself lulled by the comforting touch of his hold on her mind. The talons retreated, replaced by a relaxed feeling of protection. She just needed to do what she was told, and then everything would be alright.

"Tear the book apart," Gerth said again.

Suddenly, tearing up the book seemed like the most natural thing to do. Why wouldn't she tear it apart page by page?

"Focus, focus, focus," Gerth chanted. "Push me out of your head."

The magic shields she'd been constructing all morning went up.

She shoved with all of her mental energy.

Olivia's eyes snapped open as Gerth gave a little cry. His nose was bleeding.

"I'm sorry!" Olivia reached out to him.

Gerth grinned, rubbing the back of his hand across his nose.

"Don't apologize. This is progress."

"And raw strength," Nira said, giving Olivia something that might have been a smile. "If I had your power, I'd be bloodying Gerth's nose every day. Tol's too. And Erikir's."

"How about me?" Fred asked.

Nira thought for a moment. "You're tolerable," she decided.

Fred beamed.

"You really are a treasure, Nira," Gerth said. "I can't imagine why Tol picked Addy over you."

"Olivia, be a dear and make Gerth's eyes bleed, will you?" Nira asked, batting her long eyelashes.

Olivia was shaking, and she'd broken out in a cold sweat. And all she'd managed to do was something the Chosen people were able to do from birth. None of them had needed to learn how to resist Influence. She groaned in frustration.

"Don't be scared of what you can do," Gerth said, pinching his nose and tilting his head back to stop the bleeding. "Embrace it."

Embrace your powers. It was what the Celestial had told her she needed to do. It was what she'd been trying to do. She just didn't know how.

"You need to draw out the magic part of you until it's stronger than the mortal part," Gerth continued.

"Okay." Olivia heard the thinness of her own voice.

"Let's get back to trying to find the Supernal, or the stone that contains his power," Gerth told her. "See if you can sort through all those images and find the ones we need."

Easier said than done. She'd been trying to do this very thing all morning.

Olivia still couldn't see the future without Source and physical contact with one of the Chosen. Even then, she didn't get to decide which visions came to her.

"No rest for the weary, Fount," Gerth's cheerful voice interrupted her thoughts. "It's back to the salt mine for you."

"She's looking all sallow." Nira gave Olivia a distasteful look. "I don't want her fainting on me."

"I'll try to faint in the other direction," Olivia told her, channeling some of her twin's ire.

"Let's go again." Gerth settled himself in what Olivia had started calling his evil Buddha pose on the carpet.

Sighing, Olivia dug deep inside herself for the swirling, slippery tendrils of magic. She could see the different strands like colors of a rainbow, but just like a real rainbow in the sky, it only appeared to be within reach. Every time she grabbed for one of the strands, the magic eluded her.

"You can do this," Gerth said. "Concentrate."

His voice faded as she let her mind slip away to that place where the magic became clearer.

Olivia was standing on a ledge…inside her mind. The colorful wisps of magic swam in the darkness below. When she tried to grasp one, it slid through her fingers. It would be there for one tantalizing second, and then gone the next.

Tears of frustration wanted to fall from her eyes, but she was aware of everyone's attention on her, so Olivia held them back.

"She needs to rest," Erikir said, his voice sounding far away.

"We don't have time for her to rest," Gerth replied.

Shut up, she wanted to tell all of them. She almost had one of the slippery strands. If she just reached a little farther—

The ledge in her mind fell away. All of the colorful strands of magic disappeared. Darkness surrounded her as she began to plummet.

Olivia screamed, but the sound caught in her own mind.

Help me! she cried. Again, the words echoed in a place where only she could hear them.

She was falling. There was no bottom…no end

Trapped.

She was caught in her own mind, where power washed over her and passed through her as she fell. And fell.

Terror clawed at her throat and tore into her chest.

Just before the darkness crushed her, Olivia felt arms encircle her, pulling her back from the endless fall. Warmth seeped into her skin and banished the cold panic.

It's okay, a voice—not Olivia's—said into her mind. *You're okay.*

The steady thrum of the speaker's baritone helped ease the rapid stutter of her heart. Relieved tears wet her cheeks. She was no longer lost. She wasn't alone.

A glimmer of light appeared in the darkness.

The glimmer took shape. She saw Erikir, but not the Erikir she was familiar with. This version of him was all light. She couldn't see his eyes. In fact, she wasn't really seeing him at all. She was seeing *into* him.

She saw a lonely boy who grieved for his parents and what might have been. She saw that he'd grown up in his cousin's shadow. She saw his deep love for the Chosen people and a fierce determination to do anything to save them.

The steady warmth anchoring her was ripped away. The shock of it pulled Olivia out of the place she'd been and back into Aunt Meredith's living room. She sucked in a breath, trying to get her bearings.

"What the hells was that?"

Erikir was on his feet, his chest heaving. Fury blazed in his eyes. It wasn't his usual irritation at everyone and everything—this was a deeper anger that bordered on hurt. Maybe even betrayal.

"I'm sorry," Olivia said, trying to hear her own voice above the pounding of her head. "I didn't mean to. I didn't realize—"

"What happened?" Gerth asked.

Erikir didn't even glance at him. His hateful gaze was burning a hole through Olivia.

"You had no right." He spit out each word.

Olivia flinched away from his fury. "I'm sorry," she said again.

"Don't yell at her," Fred growled.

"Yeah, give the mortal a break," Nira said.

"What happened?" Gerth asked again.

The screen door banged. Aunt Meredith came in, whistling.

"I'm off to the grocery store for provisions," she announced, oblivious to the tension in the room. "Any special requests?"

"I'll come." Erikir got up without looking at any of them. He was halfway to the door when he turned back. "Go dig around in someone else's brain. I'm done."

Olivia shook her head. She hadn't intentionally gone rifling through Erikir's private thoughts. It had just happened. She didn't know how she'd done it.

"You saw into Erikir's thoughts?" Gerth asked, seeming more intrigued than disturbed.

"No wonder you look so upset," Nira said. "Erikir's head is the last place I'd want to see inside."

Olivia was sure Erikir wouldn't appreciate it if she told the others they'd pegged Erikir all wrong.

"I think I should practice alone for a while," she said, hearing the defeat in her own voice. "I don't want to hurt anyone else."

Nira let out a heavy sigh. "And you were just starting to get less squirrely about your abilities. Now, this is going to take forever."

"Here." Fred held out his hand to Olivia. "You can use me as your anchor. I don't mind if you see my thoughts."

"It won't work with you, stupid," Nira told Fred as she ran her fingers through her glossy hair. "You've got no connection to the Source."

"I ain't stupid," Fred retorted, his face reddening with indignation. "And maybe Liv just needs someone who isn't yelling at her and pushing her to her breaking point every second of the day."

"Oh, I'm sorry." Nira put a hand over her heart. "It's not like our entire race's survival depends on her or anything."

Olivia took advantage of the momentary respite their argument offered. She nestled deeper into the soft leather of the couch.

Just one minute, she thought as she closed her eyes. *Then, I'll try again.*

✳ ✳ ✳

When Olivia opened her eyes, she was lying on the couch underneath a soft blanket. It had been mid-afternoon the last time she'd been awake.

165

Now, it was dark outside. A single lamp had been left on. Fred was passed out on the other couch, snoring softly.

Guilt filled Olivia. She had only meant to rest for a few minutes. How had she managed to sleep for so long? Why hadn't anyone woken her?

Every day that passed brought her new friends' people closer to death. Every day brought her own world closer to annihilation.

Olivia was the one who was supposed stop it all.

If she could figure out how to use these abilities inside her instead of letting them run wild inside her head.

But instead of trying to master her abilities…instead of being useful…she'd slept the day away.

Olivia sat up. Her eyes were immediately drawn to the book resting on the coffee table right in front of her. It was a brand-new copy of *Pride and Prejudice*.

For several seconds, she just stared.

She covered her face with her hands, making sure the silent tears streaming down her cheeks didn't fall onto the book and warp the pages. She tried to stop—she didn't even know why she was crying—but the tears kept coming.

Before she woke Fred with her sniffling, she tiptoed to the front door and eased it open. Olivia sunk down onto the porch steps and hugged the book to her chest as she cried.

She had never felt so lost and alone. She had never felt so out of control. So many people were depending on her, and she didn't know how to do what they were asking.

Mostly, she cried for her lost family.

She missed working side-by-side with her dad in the corn fields and grooming Jenny, their old cow, with Rosie and Stacy. She missed bouncing Baby Lucy in her lap until she got the hiccups from giggling so hard. She missed shucking corn while her mom quizzed her about history dates or Spanish subjunctives. She missed the room she shared with Addy, where they laughed and gossiped until they fell asleep.

"Olivia?"

She squeaked and whirled around. Erikir was sitting on the swing on the other side of the porch.

"I didn't mean to startle you. I can leave you alone—"

"No, it's alright." Olivia quickly wiped her eyes.

Had he heard her crying?

It was a stupid thought. How could he *not* have heard her?

The floorboards creaked as he crossed the porch and came to sit next to her.

"Do you want to talk about it?" he asked in a low voice.

Olivia shook her head, not trusting herself to say anything for fear she'd burst into tears again.

Erikir just nodded in acceptance. For several minutes, they both stared out into the black nothingness beyond the porch.

She was still clutching *Pride and Prejudice* to her chest, and she relaxed her grip before she bent the book.

"I have you to thank for this, don't I?" she asked, holding out the book.

She glanced over in time to see his curt nod. His attention was tilted up at the stars, so she couldn't read the expression on his face.

"How did you know it's my favorite?" she asked.

Erikir shrugged a shoulder. "You seem like a romantic, so I thought it would be up your alley."

His voice was carefully neutral when he said it, so Olivia couldn't tell if he was making fun of her or not.

"You have no idea what this means to me," she told him, feeling awkward and exposed at the admission.

He gave her a small smile. "Don't tell me you're one of those people who thinks the concept of the blood marriage is romantic, too."

"Certainly not with Tol," she blurted out.

Erikir laughed. Olivia realized it was the first time she'd heard the sound from him.

"Aside from that part," Olivia continued, "I haven't thought about it."

There was no point. As soon as she did what she'd set out to do, Addy would be the only one getting blood married.

"Most people are afraid of giving someone else that much insight into their mind," Erikir said. "When you're blood married, you can't hide anything from the other person. Fears, insecurities, desires…they're all right there. There are no secrets in a blood marriage."

"I can imagine how that might scare a lot of people off," Olivia replied. She didn't know how she'd feel about someone being able to see her every thought and feeling. The idea was unnerving.

"I can see the appeal," Erikir said. "Might be nice to know there was someone who would always have your back."

Olivia thought again about the loneliness she'd glimpsed when she saw into Erikir's mind.

Addy and Fred would always have her back, but Olivia knew that wasn't the kind of loyalty Erikir was referring to. It was the all-encompassing, eternal kind of love that Olivia hadn't really believed existed outside of books…until she saw Addy and Tol.

They were silent for another minute before Erikir said, "I shouldn't have yelled at you the way I did earlier. I was caught off guard, but it's no excuse. I'm sorry."

Olivia hadn't been expecting an apology.

"I'm the one who should be sorry," she said, stumbling over her words a little. "I would never intentionally intrude on your thoughts."

"I know." Erikir turned to face her.

Olivia was momentarily taken aback. The anger that always lived in his eyes and twisted his mouth was gone. Without the ugly shield of those emotions, it was impossible to ignore how handsome he was.

Even though he shared many of the same features as his cousin, he looked nothing like Tol. Erikir was slight, like Olivia. His face was angular, and the hollows of his face brought his cheekbones into stark relief.

He had the nicest eyebrows of any guy she'd ever seen. It was a strange feature to notice, and yet, she had to stop herself from reaching out to run her finger across them. There was the barest hint of a shadow on his chin and upper lip, which struck Olivia as intensely masculine.

She realized she was staring and quickly looked away.

"I saw things about you, too, you know."

His words lurched her out of her embarrassment.

"What?"

Erikir shrugged. "I guess whatever you did opened up a connection that went both ways. I didn't see anything I hadn't already guessed."

Olivia swallowed. She forced herself to ask, although she wasn't sure she wanted to know.

"What did you see?"

"Kindness. Determination to make your sister happy. Desire to save a race of people whose existence you only just discovered. And you think it's a mistake that you're the Fount."

"Wow." She let out a shaky laugh. "Good thing I wasn't already self-conscious or anything."

"You're wrong, you know," Erikir said. "The Celestial didn't make a mistake with you."

Olivia shook her head. "Addy is meant to be a queen. I'm just…." She searched for the right explanation.

It wasn't that she thought less of herself than she thought of her sister. It was just that they had different strengths. Addy's would make her a great ruler of a powerful people. Olivia belonged on her family's farm. Her kingdom was meant to be a house full of a laughing, loving family. Her subjects would be the stray animals that wandered onto their property and became part of the family.

At least, that had been her dream before everything changed.

Now, she'd dedicate whatever time she had left to giving her sister the gift of eternal happiness. It would be enough.

She tried not to think about the permanence of death…that endless expanse of black nothingness. She imagined it would be something like falling off the ledge in her mind, except when she died, no one would be there to yank her back out.

Olivia shivered.

"Your sister might be able to kill the Forsaken, but it'll take more than brawn to rule a people like the Chosen."

"Addy isn't just—"

"There's something that's been bothering me," Erikir said, cutting her off. "Everything to do with the Fount's magic is about sacrifice. The Celestial had to sacrifice all of her strength for our people to have a second chance. The blood marriage that will reunite us with our immortality requires the sacrifice of two people's individual freedom." Erikir's gaze held hers, and Olivia found she could barely breathe. "But you never mentioned what price you'd need to pay to give up the power that's now a part of you."

The darkness might have masked whatever expression was on her face, but it did nothing to hide her shocked gasp.

"I—I don't know—"

"It's your life, isn't it?"

Olivia considered lying, but she'd never been a good liar, and she knew Erikir would see straight through her.

"Don't tell anyone," she begged. "If Addy and Tol find out, they'll try to stop me."

Erikir drove his fist into the wooden railing hard enough that she felt the vibrations in the step beneath her. "What in the two hells makes you think their happiness is worth more than your life?!"

Olivia didn't understand his fury.

"Because she's my sister," Olivia said simply.

Erikir made a sound of disgust as he got to his feet. He stomped across the porch, yanked the door open, and slammed it shut behind him.

Olivia sat on the porch steps, clutching her book and wondering what had just happened.

CHAPTER 22

TOL

It was still dark when Tol woke. Addy had finally fallen asleep, and she'd draped herself around him. He remembered the panicked look in her eyes when she woke up from her nightmare, and her death grip as she'd screamed his name. He nuzzled against her neck and breathed her in. Her usual piña colada scent had been replaced by the smell of his own shampoo.

She sighed in contentment when he kissed her neck.

How many more times would he wake up next to her?

His heart gave a painful lurch in his chest.

He and Addy had vowed that if the reserves were depleted and they hadn't found a way to be together, he would fulfill his duty to his people with Olivia.

The thought made him as sick as it had in the moment when he realized Olivia, and not Addy, was the Fount.

It wouldn't just be about blood marrying Olivia, either. In order for the bond to work without killing both of them, he'd have to find a way to destroy the love he still felt for Addy.

The blood marriage was a complete uniting of body and spirit, and if one of the parties was less than fully committed, it would be like an open, festering wound on both of their hearts. Olivia would know his misery, and those feelings would become hers a thousand-fold. Eventually, the pain of it would kill both of them.

The last thing Olivia deserved was to die because of him.

Olivia was a good person. She deserved better than to be eternally bound to a man who didn't want her. If it came down to it, it would be up to Tol to guard her life and heart in the same way she protected his.

He just didn't know how he was supposed to let Addy go.

Tol gently untangled himself from Addy and got out of bed. As he strapped on his prosthesis, he looked down and saw Addy was gripping her garden shears with the hand that hadn't been wrapped around him. He considered taking them away from her so she didn't hurt herself while she slept. Knowing Addy, it was more likely he'd get his face sliced open if he tried.

He went into the other room and paced around. He took another few unsuccessful shots at his speech. Then, he paced some more.

Each time he crossed the room, he glanced at the digital clock on his desk. As he watched the seconds and minutes slide away, he knew time was the one thing he didn't have.

✳ ✳ ✳

Addy's low heels clicked against the marble along with Tol's own steps. He was wearing a suit, and Addy had on a dress and blazer that had clearly been selected by his mum. She was even wearing clip-on pearl earrings. The outfit looked good on her—everything looked good on Addy—but Tol could tell she was uncomfortable in the clothes.

When the servant who brought her outfit suggested dying her hair *a tasteful shade of brown,* Tol had ordered the woman to get the hells out in a voice he usually reserved for Erikir.

Tol didn't appreciate his mother's attempts to mold and bend Addy into the kind of queen his people expected. He understood his mum was doing it to protect him and his throne, but Tol had no intention of trying to change anything about Addy. She would rule beside him as herself, and their people would come to respect her for it.

When Tol noticed Addy patting her thigh, he looked down and noticed the garden shear-shaped bulge in her skirt. He chuckled to himself. He should have known that, even as his mother tried to turn Addy into one of them, she'd find a way to still be herself.

Tol could sense his people's unrest in the quiet halls, which were usually bustling with activity and voices. It was only when he felt Addy's hand slip into his that he realized he'd gone rigid with tension. He forced himself to relax.

At least a hundred chairs had been set up in the middle of the clifftop garden, and every one of them was already occupied. Tol heard Addy's soft intake of breath, and he squeezed her hand as he led her to the podium at the front.

"We've got this," he whispered, not wanting Addy to know he felt as nervous as she looked.

Every pair of eyes was glued to them.

Tol unfolded the most recent version of his speech and smoothed the papers on the podium. He adjusted the microphone and then raised his eyes to stare out at their waiting audience.

Some of his people's faces were full of hope. Others looked impatient to hear what Tol would say. On a few, he saw distrust.

Tol glanced down at the words he'd written that morning. Making a decision, he crumpled up the papers and stuffed them into his pocket. He lifted his chin and faced his people.

He knew what he needed to say.

❋ ❋ ❋

ADDY

Addy had never before felt so…scrutinized.

She patted the outline of her garden shears beneath her skirt as she tried not to fidget. She'd felt a little badly about cutting into the lining of such an expensive suit to create a makeshift pouch, but it had been the only way for her to bring her shears without carrying them openly.

Leaving them behind hadn't even been a consideration.

She raised a self-conscious hand to her ears, checking to make sure her earrings hadn't fallen off. They were clip-ons, since Addy had never had any interest in poking holes through her ears, but the pearls were real. She smoothed her hair, hoping it would be enough to tame the flyaways.

Tol was the one giving the speech, but Addy was nervous enough for both of them. When she glanced at him, she was a little peeved to see that he looked as cool as a cucumber. He wasn't even bothering with the speech he'd written. It wasn't until she put a hand on his back that she felt how every one of his muscles was tensed.

Tol's parents and Getyl were sitting in the first row of chairs, looking regal and terrifying. Right then, Addy would have taken on a thousand armed Forsaken rather than try to hold Queen Starser's disapproving gaze.

Tol's mother really was the scariest woman Addy had ever met. She could give Addy's own birth mother a run for her money….

"Good morning," Tol said into the microphone attached to the podium. "Thank you for coming."

His voice was warm, relaxed, and full of confident power. He looked every bit the king he would soon be. Addy, on the other hand, had never felt like more of an imposter.

In this sea of bronze skin and black hair, she had never been so acutely aware of her red hair, pasty skin, and green eyes.

Tol continued, "I know rumors have been abounding, and for reasons beyond their control, my parents have been unable to tell you about where I've been. I'm here today to explain myself to all of you."

Tol was still speaking, but Addy's attention caught on two people sitting in the back of the crowd. They weren't paying any attention to Tol. They were huddled together and whispering.

Did these people have no manners?

If she didn't think it would distract Tol, she'd go over there and *make* them be polite.

"Our people's history is full of mistakes and missteps, but we have always been united. We have never been violent toward our own." He raised his chin and stared into the crowd. "Until now."

Addy looked back at the rude couple to judge their reactions. She blinked. They were gone. Their chairs were empty, and Addy saw no sign of them.

Where did they go?

They had probably just gone somewhere where they could complain without getting shushed. Still, Addy couldn't ignore the unease prickling along her spine.

"…and I'm going to ask you to lend me your patience a little longer," Tol was saying.

Addy shifted her attention away from the two empty seats.

In a strong voice that was devoid of apology or hesitation, Tol explained to his people that, on his quest to find the Fount, he'd found the only woman with whom he wanted to share a throne.

Addy moved close enough to Tol that their shoulders brushed. It was probably a terrible breach of etiquette and the British equivalent of public indecency, but she didn't care.

Tol briefly described her history growing up with a mortal family. He didn't lie, but he didn't mention the Forsaken part of her background. Addy was grateful. With her Haze hidden inside her, she looked mortal to anyone who hadn't seen the Forsaken general for themselves, which was everyone in this crowd except for Tol's family. Besides, she didn't think she could handle all of Tol's people looking at her the way his parents were.

There were muffled exclamations and disbelieving whispers when Tol described their trip to Vitaquias. He talked about his meeting with the Celestial, skipping over the multiple times they'd all almost died.

Addy could see the awe on his people's faces. Some of their mouths were even hanging open. All of them were riveted to his speech.

Addy tried to pay attention to his words, which were beautiful. Something felt wrong, though. She couldn't quite put her finger on it.

"I know everyone is scared we'll never get home," Tol said. "I'm asking you to trust that I will not break my vow to protect you. I swear I will bring you back to Vitaquias and restore your immortality. But to be the king you all deserve, I'm asking you to give me a little more time to make Adelyne my queen."

The crowds' murmurs went from shocked and awed to angry.

"And what are you giving us in return for our patience?" someone shouted from the crowd.

Addy couldn't see who had spoken, but she heard the challenge. She heard the betrayal.

"I'm so glad you asked," Tol replied. His smile and posture were easy. He looked completely relaxed. "My family and I have decided to distribute the Source reserves to all of you."

Sound erupted. It was a good thing, too, because the noise overrode her own shocked gasp.

Addy distinctly remembered Tol's father forbidding Tol from giving out the reserves. He'd even used that word…*forbid.*

A fierce and silent argument raged between Tol's gran and parents. The king, his face an alarming shade of red, shook off Getyl's gnarled hand on his jacket sleeve. He got to his feet and strode to the podium.

Addy could feel the man's fury radiating off him. She took an unconscious step closer to Tol and away from the king.

"What in the two hells do you think you're doing?" the king hissed at Tol.

"Guards," Tol said in a cool, commanding voice. "Bring the reserves."

Cheers erupted. Some of the people were on their feet, shouting Tol's name. Others were weeping openly.

The guards turned their heads from Tol to the king, an uncertain look in their eyes.

The king's face was now the color of a ripe plum.

Addy finally understood what Tol had done. If the king undermined Tol now, it would show all of their people that the royal family was divided. It would make them look weak.

Now that the announcement had been made, the king couldn't go back on Tol's promise unless he wanted complete anarchy on his hands. The king was stuck, and he and Tol both knew it.

Bloody brilliant, as Gerth would have said.

As though he could read her thoughts, Tol tipped his head and winked at her. Addy couldn't stop herself from grinning.

The king gave the waiting guards a terse nod, and they hurried off to carry out Tol's orders.

"Do you have any idea what you've done?" the king asked in a furious whisper.

"Yeah," Tol replied, meeting his father's stare. "I just bought us six more months before the elders start dying."

"One month," the king snapped.

More cheers came from the crowd as two guards strode back up the path. One of them held a lockbox, which Addy assumed contained the extra vials of Source.

"What?" Tol demanded. "Where's the rest?"

"Gone," the king replied tersely. "Between searching for the Fount, saving two vials' worth for the blood marriage, and fighting off the Forsaken."

Tol met Addy's horrified gaze with one of his own.

The two guards stopped beside the podium, bowed to Tol and the king, and opened the lockbox. The vials inside looked so small…so insubstantial.

Addy massaged the place above her collarbone that was growing tighter by the minute.

One month.

The people were still applauding and shouting their thanks as the formed an orderly line…*queued*, as Tol would say. Some of them looked like they'd rather push and shove. Addy couldn't blame them. After all, some of their vials had mere drops left. She supposed their Britishness kept them polite even in the face of more Source.

As Queen Starser loved to remind Addy, the Chosen weren't barbarians. *Like her*, was the part Tol's mom didn't say out loud…because she didn't need to.

"Here," Tol said, handing Addy the box full of vials. "You do the honors. Twenty drops for each."

Tol's mouth was pressed in a tight line, and she could feel his worry humming through him. She knew the same thoughts that were circling around in her mind were also in his.

Before, their deadline had been an abstraction. Now, there could be no more debating…no convincing themselves that they could squeeze out more time from some hidden corner.

One month was all they had left.

Getyl hobbled up to the podium and nudged Tol aside. He adjusted the microphone so it was low enough for his grandmother.

"I would also like to say a few words," she said.

Her voice was as strong and clear as Tol's had been. The crowd quieted down enough to hear her words.

"There are some who might argue my grandson's pursuit to spend eternity with the one he loves is selfish." Getyl glared at the king, who had one foot poised in the air like he was ready to come and wrestle the microphone away from her. "I say it's the mark of a great leader. The prince knows what—and specifically whom—he needs to be his best self."

While Getyl spoke, Addy went down the line of people, putting twenty drops of Source into each waiting vial. They each thanked her. Some talked about how the gods would bless her and Tol's union. Some were even crying as they watched the droplets slide down into their vials. Viola and Marise, the two women who had helped get Addy ready for her first dinner at the manor, kissed her on both cheeks as tears streamed unabashedly down their faces.

Addy saw the elderly Chosen leaning on their canes as they waited on line for their twenty measly drops of Source. She looked into their rheumy eyes and wrinkled faces and knew every minute that prolonged their suffering was her fault.

If it wasn't for her, these people would already be back on Vitaquias. They'd all be healthy again, and their biggest problem would be deciding where to build their new manor.

Tol's parents had been right when they called her selfish. If she just let go of Tol…if she let him do what he was meant to…none of these people's lives would be in danger.

"Forever live Prince Tolumus and Princess Adelyne," Getyl said. "Forever live the king and queen."

"Forever live the Magnantius family, our eternal sovereigns!" the crowd chanted.

That's when Addy felt it. The prickling unease that had been there, persistent and annoying, turned into something she recognized. She felt a whisper of her people's power.

Normally, when a Forsaken was around, she had no problem sensing them. It was as easy as picking out a person standing on a nearby bench and shouting his lungs out. This felt different. It wasn't until she saw the faint blue glow out of the corner of her eye that she understood.

The Forsaken weren't here, but one of their weapons was.

CHAPTER 23

TOL

Tol sat between his parents as Gran addressed the crowd of Chosen who had lined up to accept their allotment of Source. He was too stunned to feel the panic he knew would come later. All of the elation he'd felt at outwitting his father—at giving his people what they so desperately needed—was gone.

He'd known there had been increasing conflict with pockets of the Forsaken, who were trying to discover the location of his family's manor. His parents just hadn't told him how much Source had been needed for those skirmishes. They wouldn't have wanted anyone to know, since it would have strengthened the Jesuls and made his family look weaker.

Tol had thought that distributing the reserves would buy them another six months. But now….

Addy smiled and talked with each person as she dropped the Source into their vials. Her demeanor was enough to convince anyone that she had been preparing for this position for her entire life.

"What in all the worlds were you thinking?" Tol's mother hissed.

Tol pulled his attention away from Addy and focused on his mum.

"Why didn't you tell me the other five months' worth of reserves were gone?" he countered.

"It shouldn't have even been relevant," Tol's father snapped from his other side, still in a whisper so as not to draw any attention. "If you had just blood married the Fount—"

"Lower your voice," Tol's mum whispered.

Tol's parents turned an accusing stare on Addy, like she was to blame for whatever run-ins they'd had with the enemy.

The king leaned closer as he said, "Now, because of what you've done, we'll have nothing to use against the Forsaken the next time they threaten us."

Guilt and worry gnawed at Tol's insides. There was no argument he could make to that. He was gambling everything on the desperate hope that Olivia would transfer her powers to Addy before the month ran out.

"And what happens when our people discover their future queen is the Forsaken general's daughter?" Tol's mum asked.

That was something Tol had privately wrestled with—whether or not to tell his people who Addy was. In the end, he'd decided not to say anything…for now, at least.

"Addy is Sue and Gary Deerborn's daughter," Tol replied. "She grew up as a mortal. It's the only life she knew until she was eighteen, and that's the only history that matters."

"Forever live Prince Tolumus and Princess Adelyne," Gran said, smiling down at him. Forever live the king and queen."

Tol nodded his head to Gran, wanting her to know how much her words meant to him, even as his thoughts continued to spin.

"Forever live the Magnantius family, our eternal sovereigns!" the crowd chanted.

After another hard look at Tol, his mother rose and went to the podium to address the crowd. The king stayed where he was, stewing about Tol's latest betrayal.

Tol looked for Addy. A minute ago, she had been distributing the Source. Now, she was nowhere to be seen. Tol stood up. He saw a puzzled-looking elder clutching the reserve vials in his palms.

Tol caught sight of Addy. Her Haze lit up her entire body as she sprinted across the lawn. She leapt over one chair and plowed right through another. Tol winced.

What in the two hells was she doing?

Before he could take a step in her direction, Addy pounced. She flew through the air and tackled…Lord Jesul.

Addy had the man pinned beneath her in two seconds flat.

Oh gods. Addy was punching the man in the face.

"Addy, stop!" Tol called, running for them.

Other people were yelling now, too. Tol stopped in his tracks when he saw Addy yank the unconscious Lord Jesul to his feet. Beneath him, wedged into the grass from the weight of their bodies, was a glowing blue Viking-style sword.

As soon as their weight was no longer holding the weapon down, it shot straight up into the air and disappeared into the foggy English sky.

Tol didn't understand. He grasped for his vial of Source, looking around for the Forsaken. He only saw his own people.

"Tol, move!" Addy shrieked.

He threw himself to the ground, just as something blue whistled over his head. He rolled onto his back in time to see the sword spin around to come hurtling back toward him.

Addy dove, grabbing the sword out of the air. She wrestled it down the same way she had Lord Jesul. She hit the ground and rolled, hugging the sword to her chest. The weapon quivered and pulsed in her arms.

A muffled chatter was coming from the weapon as it fought against Addy. Tol watched, helpless and furious, as the sword shredded Addy's sleeves. There were streaks of blood on her bare arms. Tol wanted to kill someone for every drop of her blood that was being spilled, but aside from the sword, there was no enemy. Jesul was just regaining consciousness and surrounded by three guards.

Addy pinned the sword to the ground with her knees. She raised her garden shears, which looked as harmless as a pair of safety scissors compared to the sword.

She slammed the point of the shears into the sword's blade. The larger weapon shattered. Shards of metal sprayed outward. And then, the sword was gone.

"Addy—" Tol began, but she had already disappeared again.

Her red-gold hair had come loose, and it streamed behind her like a banner. She crossed the garden so fast she was a blur. She jumped on top of a row of chairs, racing across the backs of them like she was a gymnast on the high beam.

That's when Tol saw Lady Jesul. She was hidden behind a hydrangea bush on the far edge of the garden. It was only the blue glow that gave her away.

Too late, Olivia's vision came back to him.

There was a woman, and a glowing blue axe was heading straight toward her….

Lady Jesul released the double-bladed axe in her hands. The weapon sliced through the bush and arced into the air. Addy skidded to a stop, halfway between Tol and Lady Jesul, and then doubled back. Everyone looked up.

Tol lost sight of the axe in the clouds' brightness. A whistling sound announced the weapon's return.

It shot through the air, gaining momentum with each passing second.

Addy landed right in front of Tol and his mum. She knocked the queen onto the ground and then leapt. She struck out with her garden shears. There was a harsh clang as the two weapons collided. Then, the axe was flying back the way it had come. It moved too fast to track.

There was a wet thud as the axe struck flesh. Tol recoiled as Lady Jesul fell through the cloven hydrangea bush. She collapsed face-first, further embedding the axe's blade in her face.

Lord Jesul's agonized scream cut through the stunned silence.

For several long moments, no one else moved or even seemed to breathe.

"Are you alright, your Majesty?" Addy asked, smoothing her skirt with one hand and offering the other to Tol's mum.

Addy looked around, and Tol saw the moment she realized every pair of eyes was on her. For a moment, she looked terrified. Then, Addy stood to her full height and said, "Let that be a lesson to anyone who tries to mess with my family."

CHAPTER 24

ADDY

Everyone was staring at Addy. And then, as the shock started to wear off, people began to mutter.

An old man, who only a few minutes earlier had told her he would give his life to serve her, stood up. He pointed his cane at Addy and bellowed, "Forsaken!"

He wasn't the only one. His cry had been taken up by others. All around, people's Hazes were flaring brighter as they consumed drops of newly-acquired-thanks-to-Addy Source.

Addy was too shocked and dismayed to do anything except stand there. Tol reacted faster. He pushed Addy behind him, using his body to block hers in case anyone tried to Influence her. Tol's gran was next. She was only four feet to Addy's six, but she stood on Addy's left, protecting her from anyone who might try to come at her from the side.

Tol's mother stood on Addy's right, and the king stood behind her.

"Close your eyes, Adelyne," Getyl commanded.

Addy did as she was told. She'd been under Influence once, and she had no desire to ever repeat the experience.

"Let it be known that an attack on my son's fiancé is an attack on the entire Magnantius family," the king's voice called, somehow rising above the crowd's angry cacophony.

"You didn't tell us she was Forsaken," someone nearby snarled.

Addy flinched, but she didn't open her eyes.

"She's a hero," Getyl replied, her own voice as loud and clear as the king's had been.

"She may have been born Forsaken, but she's no more one of them than I am," Tol said.

"She sure fights like them," someone in the crowd retorted.

"And if she didn't, my wife would be dead," the king replied. "Where is your gratitude? Your loyalty?"

"Kill the Forsaken! Kill the Forsaken!"

One voice turned into two…turned into ten. Pretty soon, it seemed like everyone in the crowd was calling for her death. Addy cracked her eyes open. Her mouth went dry.

They were a tiny island surrounded by a furious mob.

"Kill the Forsaken! Kill the Forsaken!"

Tol's parents' voices were lost in the chant. Addy didn't know what to do. She looked to Tol. He was on the phone, of all things.

When she heard him shout, "Get Olivia," she understood.

Addy caught a glimpse of her sister's tired face on the screen for a fraction of a second. Then, Tol turned back to snap at someone in the crowd who was getting close enough to touch.

Someone else reached over Getyl's head, trying to brush Addy's bare skin. Addy twisted to the side, but she forgot to look away. She met the woman's stare.

Addy felt the padding go up in her mind. The angry voices of the crowd dulled to a meaningless drone in the background. All of her worries slid away as she stared into the brown eyes fixed on hers.

The Chosen woman opened her mouth to speak. Addy eagerly awaited whatever command might come out. But before she could utter a word, the woman was blasted into the air.

The Influence was ripped away. Addy would have collapsed if Getyl and the queen weren't wedged close enough on either side to keep her vertical.

The crowd was mid-chant when their voices cut off all at once. The Chosen woman who had been Influencing Addy was still hovering in the air, her frumpy skirt flapping in the wind. Addy caught sight of some serious granny panties. Tol flicked his hand, and the woman flew twenty feet away from them. She plopped onto the grass in a graceless heap.

"Tolumus," his mother gasped.

The king and queen were staring at Tol like they'd never truly seen their son before this moment.

Tol's Haze was so bright Addy was seeing stars just from glancing at him. He was holding his phone, and Addy could see Livy, her eyes squeezed shut, on the screen. No one else would notice that, though. Tol was so bright the crowd probably couldn't see anything except his golden outline.

"I am the Chosen prince," Tol said. Even his voice sounded inhumanly strong. It carried like he was speaking into a megaphone. "The Celestial's magic runs in my veins. I am your future king and the most powerful of the Chosen."

The crowd was staring at Tol in awe. The ones who had gotten close were stumbling backward as they blinked and shielded their eyes.

"Are there any who wish to challenge me?"

Hushed murmurs ran through the crowd, but Addy could tell they weren't angry anymore. They were enthralled by Tol's display of power.

There was movement as the people at the front of the crowd dropped to one knee and lowered their heads. The rest of the Chosen quickly followed suit. Within seconds, Addy and Tol's family were the only ones still standing.

Tol held out a hand. Addy stepped out from behind him to take it.

They stood side-by-side as they faced all of the kneeling subjects.

"I present to you Adelyne Deerborn," Tol said to the enraptured crowd, "my future wife and queen of the Chosen."

CHAPTER 25

TOL

When the mob started taking on a life of its own, Tol had known he had only one choice. He'd hoped that if he heard Olivia's voice and saw her face, he'd be able to tap into their shared power.

He'd known that, if his desperate plan worked, his display would intoxicate the power-starved Chosen. He'd been right. The crowd had gone from shouting for Addy's blood to demanding to know what else Tol would be capable of once he completed the blood marriage.

The scholars' questions were making Tol more uncomfortable by the minute. They wanted to know the limits of his strength, and how their own abilities might be enhanced once Tol became king.

He had expected this reaction, and it was why he wouldn't have shown off his power if he'd had any other choice. But it had been the only way to get the crowd to back down.

"Do it again, Prince Tolumus," one of his subjects pleaded.

"Tol needs to sit down," Addy said testily.

"The gods' magic is stronger in you than any we've ever seen," one of the scholars said. "Please, do it again."

Addy wrapped one arm around Tol's waist and tried to steer him back toward the manor. The crowd swarmed around them. Unless Addy started waving around her garden shears, they weren't going anywhere.

"Your Highness, if we could just take a sample of your blood and run a few tests before you depart—"

"Now I get why you didn't want to tell them about my blood," Addy muttered under her breath.

Tol gave her a curt nod. Even after everything that had happened…after everything his people had done…they hadn't learned the concept of moderation. They still hungered for more.

And was he really any different?

The decision to borrow from Olivia's strength had come much too easily. He had wanted to feel that power again. He'd wanted to feel the prickle of his left arm and possess the strength to Influence every one of his subjects.

He had reined in his desire and done the bare minimum to have the intended effect, but it was more of an effort than he wanted to admit. When it was over, it was harder for Tol to separate himself from that borrowed power than it had been the last time. Tol knew if he relied on the magic enough, he'd reach a point when he couldn't disassociate at all.

Then, the Celestial's warning and his deepest fears would come true.

He would lead his people and his world to a ruin from which they could never recover.

"Tolumus, perhaps it would be prudent to do a few tests," his father said. "I'm sure we'd all like to know what you're capable of."

"It'll help the scholars begin planning for the reconstruction of Vitaquias," his mother agreed. "Think of how much you'll be able to accomplish once the Source is restored and the gods are guiding your hand."

"Adelyne," Getyl muttered low enough that only they could hear. "Do whatever you need to do to get my grandson out of here before he's eaten alive."

Tol's eyelids were growing heavy. He could tell he wasn't far from unconsciousness. He saw a flash of blue light through his slitted eyes, but it wasn't the blue of Forsaken weapons. The talons of blue light were coming from the stones on Addy's ring.

There were more appreciative murmurs from the crowd. They didn't know about Addy's ring, and they probably thought it was more of his inexplicable power that was generating the portal.

Tol felt the sucking of the vortex. For once, he didn't hesitate to let it sweep him away.

✳ ✳ ✳

The portal spit them up onto Meredith's front lawn. Tol considered just going to sleep right there. He was pretty sure he was lying on top of a fire ant hill, but he was too tired to care.

"You okay?" Addy asked.

Tol just grunted, because he was too exhausted to manage actual words.

"Me too," she replied, flopping down onto the ground beside him and using his stomach as a pillow.

Tol knew he should be happy. After what he and Addy had done, no one would challenge his parents' reign. There would be no rebellion or anarchy. The Chosen would all be too busy planning for how to best make use of Tol's unrivaled power.

Of course, Addy was the only one who knew the magic wasn't just Tol's. It had been his in combination with the Fount's.

Tol had done what he'd set out to do, but he didn't feel any relief. The reserves they'd distributed would barely be enough to keep his people alive for an extra month. The guards were left with nothing to defend his people. If the Forsaken attacked, there wouldn't be enough Source to protect the manor. Whether his people were killed by the Forsaken, or they used all of their Source and then succumbed to Source-starvation, the outcome would be the same.

And now, his people thought Tol had the gods' magic running endlessly through his veins. They would expect miracles from him…ones he had no ability to perform. His own ambition was an elixir that would quickly turn to poison if he drank too much. He had promised the Celestial he would conquer this weakness on his own, and he would.

Right now, though, he just wanted to fall asleep surrounded by Addy's warmth.

"Mate, get up." Gerth's face loomed over him.

"Why?" Tol squinted against the harsh Texas sun.

"First, because there are ants all over you. Second, because there's trouble in town."

"Trouble?" He sat up so fast his head spun.

Gerth nodded. "Olivia might have caused a *tiny* earthquake yesterday, and the neighbors have their knickers all in a bunch. Not to mention, they're starting to get wise that we might have had something to do with dearly departed Anthony Fowler going missing.

"Meredith and Freddo have been trying to talk them down, but these farmers are a suspicious lot. One of them is threatening to go to the papers."

Tol rubbed his eyes. It seemed like a small thing in comparison to their other problems, but they couldn't risk gaining the attention of mortals. Tol hated to waste so much as a drop of Source on the townies, but if they didn't listen to Fred and Meredith, then he'd have to. Keeping the mortals ignorant about the fact that there were *aliens* on their planet was safer for everyone.

Besides, if the Forsaken got word of suspicious magic activity at the site of the portal, Tol would have bigger problems to deal with.

"Okay." Tol inwardly groaned at the thought of getting to his feet. Even the diabolical ants that were feasting on his back and arm weren't enough to make him want to move.

Tol caught sight of Erikir striding across the lawn toward them. *Wonderful.*

Tol blinked as his cousin came to stand beside Gerth. Something looked wrong with Erikir, but Tol couldn't place it because a combination of nausea from the portal and Source-exhaustion had him seeing triple of everything.

"Why don't you let us take care of the townies so you and Addy can rest?" Erikir suggested.

There was something wrong with Erikir's voice, too. Tol squinted at his cousin, trying to focus. That's when it came to him.

"You're not being sarcastic," Tol said. It came out as an accusation, but in all fairness, nothing was more suspicious than Erikir behaving like a genuinely nice human being.

And that was another thing…Erikir didn't have his usual nasty smirk on his face. It was unsettling.

"I would have taken care of it without you, but Gerth didn't want to start Influencing mortals without your permission." Erikir shrugged, like he wasn't bothered by the idea of needing Tol's permission.

"Are you feeling alright, Erikir?" Addy asked.

"Yes, why?" Erikir's eyebrows drew together in puzzlement. Tol couldn't tell if it was real or feigned.

"No reason," she murmured, giving Tol a *What the hells?* look.

"We'll take care of the mortals," Gerth said, "and then I want to know what happened at the manor."

"Yessir," Tol replied before falling back onto the grass.

"Forsaken," Addy said, grabbing Tol's arm. "I feel one. Here."

Tol was on his feet and prying open his vial before his body could protest.

Addy already had her garden shears out.

"Get back to the house and watch the others," Addy told Gerth and Erikir. Tol took a second drop of Source, shook himself, and nodded to Addy that he was ready.

She prowled forward and ducked down behind one of the Forsaken jeeps still parked on the lawn from the last attack. Tol crouched down next to her, looking for a dust trail on the road to announce their enemy's arrival.

He was still staring at the road when he realized Addy wasn't next to him anymore. Anxiety spiking, he looked around until he spotted her. She was racing across the lawn. She somehow managed to look both graceful and deadly as she ran.

Tol didn't even see the other bloke until Addy threw him to the ground. Addy raised her garden shears, but instead of the spray of blood Tol was expecting, the Forsaken man lifted his own weapons. In each hand, he held a half-moon blade that glowed Forsaken-blue. The blades looked wickedly sharp. With the way his hands curled around the center grips, the weapons almost seemed like extensions of his hands.

Their blades tangled together.

In an instant, Tol's exhaustion was gone. He ran for them. His only thought was of Addy.

She had the soldier in a headlock, but the man was bucking and twisting in her arms. He slashed out with his blades, getting within centimeters of Addy's skin.

The closer Tol got, the heavier his legs became. Tol fell to the ground. His legs refused to work anymore.

Every time he tried to get closer, Tol felt like he was being propelled backward by some invisible force. His head started to pound. His throat filled with bile.

What was wrong with him?

Out of the corner of his blurred vision, Tol saw the others emptying out of the house. Relief swept through him. Addy needed help, and try as he might, he was being worse than useless.

Gerth got to them first. He reached out for the Forsaken man's flailing arm, but before their skin could connect, Gerth was flung backward.

Nothing had touched him, and yet he actually sailed through the air. He landed halfway across the lawn. Nira didn't even get that far. She doubled over and threw up. Erikir made it almost all the way to Tol before he stumbled and went down on his knees. Olivia, who was right behind Erikir, tried to pull him to his feet. Her face was tinged green. A few more seconds had her throwing up next to Nira.

Was it some kind of poison?

Tol tried to warn Addy, but his throat wasn't working.

Gods, everything hurt.

Seconds before he passed out, he saw Fred jam the nail gun into the back of the Forsaken man's head.

"Freeze, you filthy Forsaken," Fred snarled, "or I'll blow your head off."

The Forsaken man couldn't see that it was a nail gun instead of a real one pressed to the back of his skull. It wouldn't have mattered either way, since the Forsaken were immune to mortal weapons. Still, the man stopped struggling and dropped his half-moon blades. They hit the ground with a dull thud.

"Wait," the soldier choked, raising his hands. "I'm not here to hurt you."

"Yeah, that's what the other ones said," Addy snapped, tightening her hold on the Forsaken man. "They're all dead now."

Another wave of dizziness passed through Tol.

"Kill him, Addy," Tol said, blinking against the darkness that was sliding across his vision.

"No, wait!" the man writhed in Addy's grip. "I have to talk to you. It's about the Supernal."

CHAPTER 26

ADDY

*I*t's about the Supernal.

Addy was usually more of a *kill first, ask questions later* kind of girl. But at the mention of the psycho half-god who was out to destroy Earth, Addy's garden shears stopped halfway to the man's throat.

"Should we tie him up?" Fred asked, still holding the nail gun against the back of the Forsaken soldier's head.

"Just let me think for a minute," Addy replied.

There was something about this Forsaken…something that drew Addy to him in a way she couldn't explain.

She peered more closely at the man. He looked like most Forsaken with his light skin, blonde hair, and gray eyes. His head was shaved in a military cut, and he had a close-trimmed beard. He was half a foot taller than Addy and buff, even by Forsaken standards.

He looked about the same age as the rest of them, or maybe a couple of years older. Normally, that didn't mean anything for the people from Vitaquias. The vial hanging around his neck was empty, though, which meant he was the age he appeared.

There was nothing about his physical appearance to explain the intense draw Addy felt to him. The guy was good-looking enough, but physical attraction didn't have anything to do with the way she felt. It was something else…something she couldn't put her finger on.

Addy didn't understand. The beast inside her that usually awakened at the first hint of violence was curled up and asleep. In fact, if her anger really had been a vicious animal, it would be purring right now.

"I need to talk to you about the Supernal," the man said again.

He spoke with a light accent—Russian, maybe, although Addy wasn't familiar enough with languages to be sure.

Everything about him spoke of militaristic seriousness, but when Addy looked into his gray eyes, she caught the hint of emotion.

Anger? Or maybe disappointment? She couldn't tell.

"Give me your word you'll hear me out, and I'll put the stone away."

"What stone," Addy began, trailing off at the sight of the man's left fist, which she only now realized was closed around something.

The stone.

It couldn't be *the stone*, could it?

If it was, then the object they desperately needed to find had just walked right onto their front lawn.

The man uncurled his fingers.

Addy's garden shears fell out of her hand. They hit the ground in front of her, but she made no move to pick them up. She was mesmerized by the stone resting on the man's palm. The sight of it filled her with so much wonder and longing she could hardly breathe. It was like she'd been searching for something her whole life, and she'd finally found it. She wasn't sure if she wanted to laugh or cry.

The stone itself wasn't much to look at. It was obsidian, like any one of a thousand rocks she'd seen littered across Vitaquias. For all Addy knew, it could have come from Earth. It was that indistinct. The stone was smooth and oval and fit neatly onto the man's palm. Aside from the magical blue halo pulsing around it, there was nothing special about it.

So, why did looking at it make Addy feel like she'd come home?

The cobra inside her uncurled…not in anger, but in longing. The stone's magic calmed and called to it.

"Jeez, Ads."

She tore her gaze away from the stone to look at Fred, whose mouth was hanging open.

"What?"

He gestured with the hand that wasn't holding the nail gun. "You're glowing."

Addy frowned. Mortals couldn't see Haze.

Addy looked down at herself and sucked in a breath. Her Haze was brighter than she'd ever seen it. It looked as bright as Tol's and Livy's had been on Vitaquias. Except, her Haze wasn't its usual gold color. It had turned blue.

Blue…like the Forsaken's weapons….

"You can see my Haze?" Addy asked Fred.

"You're blue," he replied, his voice full of awe and maybe even fear.

Addy looked down at the incriminating light surrounding her and fought the urge to hide behind Fred. *Why couldn't her Haze just behave normally, like everyone else's?*

"I've never seen the stone affect anyone like that before." The man's serious frown turned into a puzzled expression.

"Ads, something's wrong with Tol."

Addy whipped around. Tol wasn't standing behind her like she'd thought. He was on the ground…unconscious.

"Tol!"

She rushed to his side. He was breathing, but his face felt clammy.

Was this what happened when someone used too much Source without resting?

"Nira," she began, looking around for the only one of them who had medical training.

Addy's frantic gaze found the other girl, who was dry-heaving on the grass. Gerth was doing the same. Erikir was holding up Livy, who was also passed out.

"What did you do to them?" Addy shrieked, grabbing the Forsaken man by his collar and shaking him.

Fred, who was kicking the Forsaken man's half-moon blades farther out of the warrior's reach, looked as healthy as Addy felt.

"It's not what you think—"

"What did you do?!" Addy wrapped her hand around the man's throat and slammed him to the ground.

She eased up her grip just a little when she realized he wouldn't be able to answer her if she crushed his windpipe.

"The Supernal's magic," the Forsaken man gasped. "It doesn't like the Chosen."

It doesn't like the Chosen? What was that supposed to mean?

"So when I kill you, will they be alright?" Addy dug the point of her garden shears into the man's neck.

"Just wait. Please. I need your help."

"Whatever you're doing to all of them, make it stop," Addy commanded.

"I will," the guy said, his Adam's apple scraping against the blade of Addy's shears. "If you give me your word you'll hear me out."

Addy and Fred exchanged a look.

"You have my word," Addy told the soldier. "Now, fix them."

He nodded and then dug a hand into his pocket.

"Slowly," Fred growled.

"I'm just reaching for this." The man held up a small metal box. "It's made out of lead, and once I put the stone inside, its power won't affect the Chosen."

"If you're trying to pull one over on us, I'll shoot you where you stand," Fred warned.

To his credit, Fred sounded more like someone you wouldn't want to mess with than the teddy bear he was. If Addy wasn't so worried about everyone passed out on the lawn, her buttons would be bursting with pride in her best friend.

There was a soft click as the man closed the stone inside its lead box.

"What just happened?"

Relief filled Addy at the sound of Tol's voice. She looked back to see him standing. Erikir was helping Livy up, and Nira and Gerth were getting to their feet.

Addy turned back to the Forsaken man. "Explain."

"My name's Jaxon, and I'm the keeper of the Supernal's magic."

Jaxon.

"You're the one who sent all those others to attack us."

He shook his head, and that look came back into his eyes. This time, Addy recognized it for what it was. *Disgust.*

"They didn't come to attack you," Jaxon said. "They came to ask for your help. And you murdered them."

Addy opened and closed her mouth.

That one Forsaken had said something about needing her help. At the time, she'd been too consumed by her furious need to protect her family to give a second thought to the man's words. People who knew they were about to die said all kinds of things…didn't they?

"I miscalculated," Jaxon continued. "I thought you would listen. I didn't realize how deeply you'd been poisoned against your own people." His gray eyes turned stormy before he looked away from Addy and toward the rest of their group.

"Addy?" Tol was moving toward her, his gait unsteady. A sheen of sweat coated his brow.

"Just a second." Addy put up a hand to stop him before he swallowed a drop of Source.

"Tell me about this stone," she ordered Jaxon.

"If you try anything funny, I'm going to blow your brains out," Fred told him.

"I know it's a nail gun," Jaxon replied without a trace of humor. "And mortal weapons can't hurt me. But like I said before, I'm not here to hurt you."

"You mean there's nothing I could do to you?" Fred looked crestfallen.

"What are you doing here?" Addy asked Jaxon, trying to steer the conversation back on point.

"I'm here because General Bloodsong is hunting me, and I didn't know who else to turn to." Jaxon swallowed, his gaze going from the lead box still clutched in his palm to Addy. "And because the Supernal's powers led me here."

CHAPTER 27

ADDY

They all tramped into the air-conditioned kitchen, which smelled like fresh-out-of-the-oven sugar cookies and heaven.

"Who's your handsome new friend?" Aunt Meredith asked, slinging a dish cloth over her shoulder.

"Um, this is Jaxon," Addy said. "He just dropped by to—"

"Tell us some stuff," Fred supplied.

"Well, ya'll better sit down," Aunt Meredith said, going into the living room to grab another chair.

"First, do we need to be worried about a thousand of your nearest and dearest coming after you?" Gerth asked Jaxon, glancing out the window.

Jaxon shook his head. "Not for the moment. I was careful to make sure no one followed me." He gave Aunt Meredith a solemn nod when she put a sweating glass of lemonade in front of him.

"What did you mean the Supernal's power led you to Addy?" Tol demanded.

Jaxon was unnervingly calm, given that he was surrounded by enemies and was supposedly being hunted by the Forsaken general.

"I can't explain how the stone led me here," Jaxon said. "It just did."

"Like the blood on her bracelet?" Fred asked Gerth.

Gerth *hmmmd* in consideration. Addy was feeling like more of a freak show by the second.

"I think I've seen him in a vision," Livy said, squinting at Jaxon. "He's important."

"Murder us in our sleep important, or help us defeat the Supernal important?" Gerth asked.

"The second one…I think."

Addy was having trouble listening to her friends interrogate Jaxon. She squirmed and twisted her hands together. She wanted to reach out and grab the lead box in Jaxon's pocket. She wanted to see the stone. She wanted to hold it.

Addy could still sense the stone, but it felt far away. It was like she was going through some kind of withdrawal.

The blue glow of Addy's Haze had retreated back inside her. She felt emptier, but she was also relieved. She'd been self-conscious with that blue light all around her, like the stone was calling her out for being a fraud among her Chosen companions.

Knowing how much the stone repulsed Tol and Livy, Addy's inexplicable urge made her feel dirty.

"Can't you leave that stone somewhere else so it's less nauseating?" Nira complained.

"The only reason you're still conscious right now is because the box dampens its power," Jaxon said. "And no, I can't leave it somewhere else."

Jaxon took the box out of his pocket, and to Addy's simultaneous shock and distress, threw it across the room.

The box got as far as the fireplace in the living room before it stopped in mid-air. It hovered for an instant and then zoomed back to Jaxon.

"It won't leave me," Jaxon explained.

"Well, it's killing my appetite," Nira huffed.

"More for me," Fred said, plucking another cookie off the plate and taking a huge bite.

Nira gave him a death stare.

"Does the stone work like one of your weapons?" Gerth asked, nodding at the half-moon blades, which were propped against the wall where Jaxon couldn't reach them.

"Only the Supernal can wield the powers it contains," Jaxon said. "I'm just its keeper."

"Start at the beginning and tell us everything." Gerth leaned back in his chair and licked powdered sugar off his fingers. "We promise not to kill you until you've finished."

Tol gave a grudging nod of assent.

Jaxon sat forward, his serious gaze meeting each of theirs in turn. "There is a small group of Forsaken who never wanted war between the Forsaken and Chosen. My father was their leader, for a time.

"When Vitaquias fell into ruin, the Celestial entrusted my father with the stone containing the Supernal's powers." He paused, and Addy caught a hint of emotion from the stoic Forsaken. "My father…didn't make it. My mother took the stone and, when I was sixteen, gave it to me. I've been its keeper since."

"It was a good strategy for the Celestial to give the stone to one of the Forsaken," Gerth said in appreciation. "The Supernal would have never expected it."

Jaxon nodded. "The Supernal assumes one of the Chosen has it. He's been…aggressively searching."

Addy looked at Tol. "All these extra Forsaken attacks," she said, putting it together. "Are they because the Forsaken think one of the Chosen has the stone?"

Jaxon nodded again. "My family hid the secret well." He lowered his head. "That is, until recently."

He looked as worn out as Addy was. She didn't want to feel anything for this Forsaken man, but she couldn't help but pity him for whatever he'd been through.

"Explain," Gerth said.

"General Bloodsong began suspecting I was the stone's keeper, so she had me under surveillance," Jaxon said. "I guess she didn't want to tell the Supernal anything until she had proof."

The general knew Jaxon had the stone? Addy exchanged a worried look with Tol and Livy.

"I'd heard the rumors about the general's daughter who had allied herself with the Chosen. I sent people I trusted to speak with you instead of coming myself, since I was being watched."

Jaxon gave Addy that disgusted look again.

"You killed good men and women," he said in a low voice. "They would have been powerful allies."

Addy felt a cold knot of guilt expand in her stomach. She had never before regretted killing her enemies. They were a threat to her or her loved ones, and thus, they needed to die. But if what Jaxon was saying was true…if those Forsaken had come here for Addy's help….

You've murdered your own, that Forsaken had said. At the time, those words had meant nothing to Addy. Now, she couldn't shake them.

"The stone has the ability to make itself invisible, which it did whenever the general's men searched me," Jaxon continued. "But she knew I had it. About a week ago, she called my bluff and arrested me. She told the Supernal she knew the identity of the stone's keeper."

Jaxon let out a breath. "I had no choice. If the Supernal came anywhere near me, he'd be able to sense the stone. So, I fought off my guards and ran."

"But now they all know you have it," Gerth said.

Jaxon nodded. "General Bloodsong is looking for me. I don't need to tell you that her resources are vast. I won't be able to stay hidden for long."

Addy felt her anger stir back to life at the mention of the general.

The general. That was the only way Addy could think of the woman, because *mother* made her want to throw up. Or slice something apart with her shears.

"Tell us about the Supernal," Gerth said. "Weaknesses, abilities, where we can find him." He ticked off the points on his powdered sugar-covered fingers.

"He has no real power without the stone," Jaxon replied. "Aside from that, all I know is that he and the general have been meeting. They've come to some kind of arrangement, but I don't know what."

Aunt Meredith's low whistle broke the heavy silence filling the room. "This sounds like a two-cookie kind of day," she said, sliding another cookie in front of Jaxon, even though he hadn't touched his first.

He gave Aunt Meredith another nod of thanks.

Jaxon might look like he was their age, but he was so serious that he seemed much older. If it wasn't for his empty vial, Addy would have been sure he was.

"The Supernal will do anything to get his powers back," Jaxon said. "He's weak now, but the general and all her guards are searching for me. I can't outrun them forever."

"Your life is in danger because you didn't give up the stone," Gerth said.

Addy was surprised to hear sympathy in Gerth's voice. She wasn't the only one who had noticed.

"He's still one of *them*." Nira glared at Jaxon. "You don't need to feel sorry for him."

"I'm not sure you were listening." Gerth turned to Nira. "He sacrificed everything for the sake of keeping our people and the mortals safe. He's a hero."

Color spread down Jaxon's neck, but his features remained impassive.

Because of the choices he'd made, Jaxon was now a man without a people.

"The Supernal wants to use that magic to kill all the mortals and Chosen," Livy said, her voice barely more than a whisper. "I've seen it."

Jaxon nodded. "The Forsaken desire a world to call their own, where they are the ones in control rather than the abandoned race."

"You keep talking about the Forsaken like you aren't one of them," Tol said.

"I am Forsaken, but I don't wish for dominion or bloodshed. It's why the Celestial entrusted the stone to my family." Jaxon straightened in his chair. "We've been waiting for someone who could lead us against General Bloodsong and help us end millennia of war."

That accusing look returned to his eyes as he pinned Addy with his gaze.

"I thought we were waiting for you," Jaxon told her. "I was mistaken."

Addy's heart stalled. "You thought I would lead the Forsaken against the general?"

"Not all of them," Jaxon replied. "Just the ones like me, who think there might be a way for Forsaken and Chosen to live side by side without trying to annihilate each other. But you killed the ones I sent to talk with you."

Addy was having trouble getting enough air into her lungs. She'd killed people who wanted peace with the Chosen. They would have helped her take down the Supernal and make sure Livy's horrible visions never came true.

I didn't know, she wanted to say, but she knew it would do no good. Those men and women were dead. Nothing Addy did or said would bring them back.

"Now, we're an even smaller minority than we were before," Jaxon continued.

"Why me?" Addy asked, because she didn't know how to make sense of any of the other thoughts swirling through her head.

"You're Lezha Bloodsong's daughter, but your loyalties are to the mortals and the Chosen. You're the only one with the motivation and strength to unseat her from power."

Addy was speechless. She had every intention of murdering the general for what had been done to Addy's family, but she wasn't just going to take the general's place.

"Being queen of the Chosen isn't a part-time job," Tol said to Jaxon in a cold, deadly voice. "You'll have to find someone else to lead your crusade."

Jaxon didn't falter under Tol's stare.

"I've never seen this stone react to anyone the way it did to you," he told Addy. "If you were looking for proof of whether you're one of us, this stone has answered it."

"She's one of *us*," Tol snarled.

"If that was true, then I wouldn't have been able to sense a connection to her," Jaxon replied evenly. "And the stone would have sickened her the way it did the rest of you."

"You've always been blind when it comes to Addy," Erikir accused Tol.

"It's not blindness," Tol said without taking his eyes off Jaxon. "It's the truth."

Jaxon looked right at Addy. "You're Forsaken, no matter what you'd rather convince yourself. Look at your Haze."

They all did. No one needed to ask him what his point was. Even though it was no longer blue, the stone's presence was making her golden Haze brighter than she'd ever seen it. Addy was luminescent.

Addy wanted to argue against everything Jaxon was saying. She wanted to prove that she belonged with Tol and Livy. At the same time, she could feel the way her insides burned with need for that stone.

There was something desperately wrong with her. The fact that Jaxon was here proved it. Tol was too stubborn and too in love to see it, but Addy could feel it.

"You are the only one with the strength to unite the Forsaken who oppose General Bloodsong's violence," Jaxon told her. "Those of us who are still alive are scattered around the globe." He gave Addy another seething look full of judgment. "For obvious reasons, we cannot come forward. But if we were united under the leadership of someone strong enough to take down the general, it would change everything."

"I can't help you," Addy said. Even as the words left her mouth, she felt their wrongness. "I'm sorry."

Jaxon's gaze seared into hers. "Then, you're condemning the mortals and Chosen. Once the Supernal kills me and regains his power, there will be no hope for the rest of you."

CHAPTER 28

OLIVIA

Everyone was talking at once. Well, everyone except Olivia. She was still feeling a little sick from the stone, but more than that, a sense of anxiety was growing inside her by the minute.

"Let's slow down for a second," Gerth said, holding up a hand. "Step one is destroying the Supernal's magic. Uniting the Forsaken under new leadership is step twenty-five."

"I've tried to destroy the stone," Jaxon said. "It's impossible."

"The Fount will be able to destroy it once we kill the Supernal," Tol said.

Olivia started when she realized everyone was looking at her. She still wasn't quite used to the title of *Fount*.

She coughed on a sip of lemonade, which had begun tasting sour. The thought of going anywhere near that stone, even to destroy it, made her want to curl into a ball.

At Jaxon's look of confusion, Gerth gave the Forsaken man a condensed explanation of Olivia's role in saving the Chosen people and restoring their world. Hearing about everything she was supposed to accomplish spoken out loud made Olivia even more anxious than she already was.

"She'll need to be at her full strength before she attempts it," Erikir said, looking concerned. "Otherwise, it'll kill her."

If Olivia didn't already know that her death was inevitable, those words would have frozen her blood. Now, they barely made an impact.

She would do as much as she could to help the people and world she loved before she was gone.

"You won't have to do it alone," Tol told Olivia, giving her a small smile. "I'll help you."

Olivia nodded her thanks. She knew how uncomfortable their connection made him feel…not that she was any happier about being telepathically linked with her sister's fiancé.

"I'll do my best," she said. "But like Tol said, we'll have to kill the Supernal first."

Part of Olivia was appalled by the fact that she was so casually talking about orchestrating someone's murder. The other part of her would gladly kill anyone who was a threat to her people.

Her people. She still didn't understand this sense of ownership she had over the Chosen—most of whom she'd never met. All she knew was that she felt it deep inside her.

"How are *we* supposed to kill something that's half-god?" Nira demanded.

"First, we need to find him," Gerth pointed out.

"Well, what do we do with the barbarian in the meantime?" Nira gave Jaxon a cold look. "He'll probably stab us in the back the first chance he gets."

"If I wanted to kill you, I'd already have done it," Jaxon said, his flat tone sending a shiver down Olivia's spine.

"Not so fast, buddy," Addy said, easing some of the tension. "Don't forget about me."

Jaxon turned his hard, gray eyes on her. "You're powerful but untrained. I could have taken you."

Addy, who always had a comeback on the tip of her tongue, actually stuttered. Olivia didn't think she'd ever seen her sister tongue-tied.

"I could teach how to fight," Jaxon told her.

"Addy doesn't need your help," Tol said in that voice that made Olivia vaguely uneasy.

"Unless you want to become a live punching bag," Fred added, glaring at Jaxon with distrust. "Ads could use one of those."

Tol and Fred exchanged a look of manly solidarity. It was amusing, especially since the two of them had hated each other mere seconds before Jaxon showed up.

Olivia noticed that, even though her sister's face was red with indignation, Addy hadn't rejected Jaxon's offer.

"Jaxon knows the most about the Supernal, so he and I will work on a plan to catch this being at unawares," Gerth said, ending the argument before it could get too heated.

Gerth got up from the table, his Chief Strategist hat firmly in place. "Tol and Addy, go to sleep before you're completely useless to us."

"I'll set my booby traps back up in case more people come after us," Fred said, picking up his nail gun and heading for the door. Gerth nodded in approval before turning to point a finger at Olivia. "You keep working on your magic. The sooner you're strong enough to destroy the stone, the sooner we'll eliminate the biggest threat in two worlds." He turned to Erikir. "Stand by in case she needs to borrow any of your strength."

Erikir gave him a short nod.

Gerth said, "Meredith, Nira, and I will do damage control with the townies before they start crying alien to the local papers." After a short pause, he added, "We'll bring Jaxon with us so we can keep an eye on him."

Olivia was a little dizzy from the whirlwind of Gerth's orders, but the others seemed used to the way his brain always fired on all burners.

They were all starting to disperse, when Aunt Meredith stopped them.

"Alright, who's bleeding all over my floor?" she asked.

"I believe it's me," Jaxon said. Everything he said came out formal and polite. Maybe it was his Russian accent, or just the fact that everything about him seemed built for intense focus.

"I believe those scissors got my arm."

"Scissors?!" Addy demanded.

Olivia stifled a gasp when Jaxon held up his arm. There was a deep gash across his forearm.

Addy crossed her arms and huffed. "I guess that just goes to show I'm not *that* much of a weakling."

"I didn't call you weak." Jaxon pressed the dish towel Aunt Meredith gave him over his arm, while Nira rummaged through the medical supplies she'd organized on the kitchen counter.

Olivia had to hide a smile. Nira might hate the Forsaken and pretend like she didn't care, but Olivia wasn't fooled. Nira had a strong need to help anyone who was hurt.

Earlier, Olivia had seen a glimpse into Nira's mind the same way she had into Erikir's. She saw Nira's two aunts, who were suffering because of a lack of Source, and how gently Nira cared for them. Nira's helplessness over their condition had been the reason behind her choice to go to med school.

Nira was the youngest-ever graduate from Cambridge's medical school and was about to start her surgical residency. She didn't care about that, though. She only saw the diminishing health of the two remaining members of her family, and hated that there was nothing she could do to help them.

Nira, her eyes narrowed in confusion, stomped back over to the table.

"Who stole the syringe and pain meds?" she demanded.

"No one's been stealing your medical supplies," Tol said in a tired voice.

"Maybe you misplaced them," Erikir suggested.

"Oh yeah, now I remember." Nira snapped her fingers. "I was taking a walk with the bulls, and I brought some anesthetics just in case any of them were feeling bad. I must have left the meds out in the field. Oops."

"There aren't any bulls on this ranch," Fred informed her.

Olivia thought it was either very brave or very stupid of him to bait Nira with the mood she was in.

Nira hissed at Fred like she was some kind of a snake. She bandaged up Jaxon and then grabbed a key to one of the Forsaken jeeps.

"Where are you going?" Gerth asked.

"I don't want to be without any of my supplies with you idiots around," she replied in a haughty tone. "With the rate things are going, I'll have to do brain surgery on someone before bedtime. By the way." She backtracked and stomped up to Addy. "I need a refill." She held up her nearly-empty vial.

Olivia saw the way Tol's jaw tightened as Addy pricked her wrist with her shears and let the drops fall into Nira's vial. Tol didn't say anything, but it was obvious he wanted to.

"You too?" Addy asked Gerth, once Nira's vial was full.

"May as well," Gerth said, sliding an uncertain look at Tol before unstopping his own vial. "I have to admit, it's convenient being able to fill up whenever we run low. Takes the pressure off."

He wilted a little under the glare Tol gave him.

Olivia felt torn as she watched Addy's blood trickling down into the empty vials. On the one hand, she hated to see her sister spill even a drop of blood. On the other, Gerth and Nira would be completely vulnerable without it.

"What about you?" Addy asked Jaxon, giving a pointed look at his empty vial.

"Addy's blood has Source in it," Gerth explained at Jaxon's confused and slightly repulsed expression. "We're not just getting freaky with her blood or anything."

"I'm good," Jaxon said. "I don't drink the blood of my own people."

"Wise choice," Tol murmured. He grabbed a bandage out of the first aid kit and started wrapping it around Addy's wrist before she could give her blood out to anyone else.

Nira pulled a prescription pad out of her tiny purse and swung the jeep's keys around her finger. Even that motion conveyed her irritation.

"We're going to deal with the townies now," Gerth said, as he, Jaxon, and Aunt Meredith headed for the door. "Can't you get the meds after?"

"I'll meet you," Nira said. "Just text me an address."

"Is your phone encrypted?" Gerth asked.

Nira rolled her eyes and gave Gerth a *duh* look.

"While you're in town, pick up some rope in case we need to tie the Forsaken up at night," Erikir told Nira.

"And we're running low on mini marshmallows," Gerth added.

Nira gave both of them the finger before slamming the screen door behind her.

* * *

A pleasant breeze was coming across the porch, so Olivia took her copy of *Pride and Prejudice* and settled herself on the swing. She didn't really think having the book in her lap helped her reach her power, but feeling its solidness in her hands comforted her when she started slipping down that rabbit hole of magic.

She could call up the Celestial's power now without much difficulty, and she got flashes of both the past and future whenever she concentrated on a particular person. It was progress, but it wasn't enough. She could sense that she was only scratching the surface of her abilities.

Olivia had always considered herself a model student, but that had been back when her mother was assigning her physics equations and poetry analyses. There was no textbook or practice test when it came to the Celestial's magic. And if she had thought getting accepted into Cornell was high stakes….

It was only a matter of time before the Supernal tracked down Jaxon. Addy had told her about the one month's supply of Source reserves that was the only thing keeping Tol's people alive. Olivia thought of the storm that had been tearing Vitaquias to shreds.

There were a dozen different timers racing down to zero. And all of their successes hinged on her.

Olivia let out a steadying breath. She settled herself on the swing, leaned back, and closed her eyes. She walked to the ledge that hovered in her mind and peeked over. She saw the swirling, rainbow-y wisps of magic, and beyond them, an endless black abyss. She leaned over and reached for a thread of magic.

The one she wanted separated itself from all the others and lifted up on an invisible breeze, delivering itself into her waiting hands.

She saw the Supernal laughing. She saw the world burning.

It was the same scene she'd witnessed when she had her first vision in the Celestial's cave. The images were clearer now, and she understood the reason was because this particular future was approaching.

The vision floated away. Olivia opened her eyes. She was shivering, and her fingers had gone bloodless from how hard she was gripping the book in her lap. When the screen door creaked open, she jumped.

"Anything new?" Erikir asked, as he stepped out onto the porch.

She shook her head.

"What good are my visions if I can't figure out how to prevent them from coming true?" she grumbled.

Thinking about how changeable the future was made her brain feel like it might explode.

"You'll figure it out." The swing jostled as Erikir sat beside her. "Just give yourself time."

Time. It was the one ingredient there was never enough of.

She groaned in frustration.

"This might help," Erikir said, dropping a bar of chocolate on her lap.

Erikir had been doing little things like this for her for the past two days. Sugar helped banish the terrible cold that filled her after she'd been using her powers. It was a kindness she hadn't expected after she accidentally invaded his mind.

"I'm going to gain a thousand pounds if I keep using magic," she said as she peeled back the wrapper and broke off one of the squares.

Erikir shrugged. "You'd still be beautiful."

She stopped with the square of chocolate halfway to her mouth.

Olivia wasn't sure how she should respond. Erikir was looking out at the grazing cattle, so she couldn't see his face. When he turned back, his expression was guarded.

"Well, I guess I should get back to it," Olivia said. "No rest for the weary, right?" She laughed a little.

Something about Erikir's silence was making her feel the need to fill up all the air.

He probably thought she was being ridiculous.

"I could lend you some of my strength," Erikir offered.

"No thank you," Olivia replied, maybe a little too quickly.

"You're exhausted," he said gruffly. "Let me help."

"I don't know what'll happen," Olivia whispered as he took her hand in his. "I might see things you don't want me to."

Her breath caught when, instead of just holding her hand loosely in his, he threaded their fingers together. She hadn't realized how icy cold her skin was until it was flooded with warmth from Erikir.

"It's okay," he said. "I trust you."

When she dared to glance up at his face, she saw the truth in his eyes. It banished the rest of the cold inside her.

She closed her eyes and let the Celestial's power wash over her.

Not the Celestial's. Her *power.*

This time, she didn't need to reach for the magic. It came to her. It swallowed her up into its colorful depths.

She saw the huge ship she recognized from her past visions. It towered above her, like she was in the water and staring up at it. She heard the Supernal laugh.

She saw Addy, covered in blood and sobbing on the sandy shore.

Addy was hunched over a lifeless body.

Was the body Olivia's?

Was she witnessing the moments after she sacrificed her own life to make Addy the Fount?

Olivia leaned in farther, needing to look, but at the same time, terrified to see.

She knew the moment she leaned too far. She started to fall.

Olivia let out a silent scream. Colors and darkness flushed past her at lightning speed. She thrust out her hands, desperate for something to grab onto…something to stop this endless fall.

There was nothing—no handholds to slow her descent. The power was limitless, but she couldn't grab onto any of it. She fell. Faster and faster. There was no end. She'd fall forever….

"I've got you."

A voice in her head broke through the panic.

"Olivia, I've got you. Come back."

She was shaking, but that voice in her ear pulled her back onto the ledge, back above the swirling magic below.

She opened her eyes.

"I've got you," Erikir said in her ear.

Olivia realized she had her face pressed into his neck. She was shaking so hard her teeth were chattering. Erikir had one arm around her back, holding her against him. The other was brushing strands of hair from her sweat- and tear-stained face.

She concentrated on his voice until the blackness was gone, and all that remained was her reality.

She had almost been sucked into a pit of magic so limitless she couldn't begin to comprehend it. If Erikir hadn't been here, she might have fallen forever.

But Erikir was here.

She met his gaze and realized their faces were only inches away from each other.

"Are you—" Erikir swallowed. "Are you alright?"

The screen door banged, and they both jumped. She shifted back onto her side of the bench. Erikir stood up so fast the chains holding the bench to the ceiling rattled.

"Hey, Liv." Fred gave Erikir a suspicious look.

Erikir muttered something too quiet to make out, and went inside.

Fred, who was completely oblivious to what had just happened…whatever had just happened…came to sit down next to Olivia.

"Liv, I'm worried about Meredith and the others," he said. "They've been gone for two hours."

"Oh." Olivia shook her head, trying to push away the sensation of a hundred wings fluttering around in her stomach. "Well, there are plenty of cars. Should we go after them?"

Olivia didn't think there was any trouble the townspeople could throw at Aunt Meredith, Gerth, Nira, and Jaxon that they couldn't handle.

"I already tried going after them." Fred's gentle face was creased with worry. "I didn't see any sign of the jeeps they were driving, and no one in town remembered seeing them." Fred hooked his thumbs through the beltloops of his jeans.

"Okay." Olivia sat back against the swing and closed her eyes. "Let me see if I can find them."

Olivia hadn't used her powers this way before, but she knew all of their mental imprints. She didn't see any reason why it wouldn't work. She was careful not to go too deep for fear she'd be sucked down into the depths for good this time, but she didn't need to go far. The colorful threads of magic hovered within her reach the moment she closed her eyes. One of the strands separated itself and unraveled in front of her, displaying…Aunt Meredith.

The jeep she was driving was bumping along on an unpaved country road that wasn't one of the ones that led into town. Gerth was sitting beside her in the passenger seat. The image was sharp in the way Olivia had come to recognize as a vision from the past.

Where are you? Olivia thought, stepping back within the confines of her vision, looking for a street sign or some kind of landmark. There was a long row of dilapidated orange sheds, and an old silo that looked like it had been abandoned for years. She remembered seeing that silo on their way from the airport.

She opened her eyes.

"Do you know where they are?" Fred asked. His leg was bouncing in his growing anxiety.

"Yes."

After the wave of dizziness passed, Olivia got to her feet.

"I'll just tell Addy where we're going, and then I'll meet you out front," she told Fred.

Addy and Tol's bedroom door was closed and no sound came from inside. Olivia didn't want to wake them, so she decided she'd just leave a note.

She went into her aunt's study, looking for sticky notes and a pen. Before she reached the desk, her gaze caught on a framed photo of her family that had been taken last summer. Olivia looked at her parents' and sisters' smiling faces. She wondered how everything had changed in such a short time.

Movement outside the window drew her attention away from the photo. Erikir was on his cell phone, and he was pacing back and forth. He kept glancing around as though to make sure he was alone. Olivia could tell from his expression that he was angry.

Olivia inched closer, staying against the wall where she wouldn't be seen.

"I'll get him there," Erikir's muffled voice came from the other side of the window. "You just make sure you're alone."

Erikir listened. Whatever the person said made him frown.

"If I see anyone but you, I'll leave," Erikir warned.

He nodded at whatever the person on the other end was saying. He glanced at the window.

Olivia flattened herself against the wall. Guilt filled her at the realization that she'd been eavesdropping. Her cheeks flushed with shame as she hurried out of the study.

CHAPTER 29

OLIVIA

T ake a left," Olivia told Fred as he steered Aunt Meredith's old pickup truck around a pothole. They were approaching the row of orange sheds.

Fred put on the truck's blinker, even though they were the only ones on the road. Halfway through the turn, he slammed on the brakes. Olivia jerked forward. The seatbelt hit her chest with so much force it knocked the breath out of her. Before she could ask Fred what had gotten into him, he was jamming his foot down on the accelerator.

"I said left," Olivia gasped as the jeep swung right.

Fred didn't say anything. There was a look of deep concentration on his face as he pushed the needle on the speedometer higher. The truck shuddered in protest, and an unhealthy-sounding vibration began in the dash.

"What's that?" Olivia asked, noticing smoke in the distance.

"Trouble," Fred replied.

He thumped his fist on the steering wheel and shouted at the truck to go faster. Olivia hung on and kept silent, not wanting to distract Fred at this speed.

A few more seconds brought them close enough to see through the smoke. She recognized the jeep as the one Nira had taken earlier to go to the pharmacy.

The jeep was upside down, and it was engulfed in flames.

"Stay in the car," Fred yelled to her. He jumped out of the truck and ran for the jeep.

Olivia hurried after him. By the time she caught up, Fred was already lying on his stomach beside the driver's window.

"Turn your head," Fred called to Nira.

There was the sound of breaking glass, and then Fred was reaching in through the window.

Olivia smelled gasoline. She looked down to see the fluid dripping out of the jeep.

She didn't need her premonitions to know the jeep was going to explode.

"Fred," she began.

"Liv, get back in the truck!" he shouted.

"Leave me." Nira's hoarse voice came from the broken window. "Get the Fount out of here."

"Not a chance," Fred grunted as he wrestled with something inside the car.

"She's caught in the seatbelt," Fred called. "I need a knife…scissors…something!"

Olivia raced back to the truck.

She opened the glove box first, which was empty aside from the car registration and a bunch of other useless papers. There was nothing in the backseat aside from a crumpled box of tissues and a melted granola bar. She jumped out of the truck and ran around the back.

Come on, come on, come on. She ripped off the tarp covering the truck bed.

There was a pile of bailing twine, loose hay, and—there! Wire cutters. She grabbed them and dashed back to the burning jeep.

The fire's heat was suffocating. Olivia got down on her stomach and slithered closer to the shattered window to pass Fred the wire cutters.

"The Fount can't die," Nira shrieked, her broken voice barely audible over the crackling flames.

"I ain't leavin' you!" Fred shot back.

Sweat streamed down Olivia's face, and all she was doing was watching helplessly as Fred worked the wire cutters through the seatbelt.

Fred wrestled Nira free from the jeep's wreckage and gathered her into his arms. Olivia sprinted for the pickup and wrenched the passenger door open for Fred. Then, she ran around to the driver's side.

Fred threw Nira into truck and then climbed in after her. Olivia didn't even wait for him to shut the door before she hit the gas.

Tires screeched and a cloud of dust momentarily blinded her as the truck picked up speed.

They made it to the other end of the road before the jeep exploded. Olivia felt the blast of heat as red and orange flames burst into the sky. The flames were replaced by a giant cloud of ink-black smoke.

Olivia hunched down in her seat on instinct, but she didn't stop driving until she was sure they were far enough away.

Fred was holding a hysterical Nira. She was saying something over and over again, but she was crying so hard Olivia couldn't understand her words.

As her sobs grew less forceful, the words Nira kept repeating became audible.

"You came for me. You came for me. You came."

"Of course, we came," Fred replied.

Nira's pain, loneliness, and gratitude slammed into Olivia. She hurriedly drew up the mental shields Gerth had helped her construct, but not before she saw the truth inside Nira's head. All her life, Nira had been the one to take care of others. It never occurred to her that there might be someone willing to do the same for her.

Olivia realized that Nira might not have been pining over Tol, so much as craving the kind of unconditional love Tol and Addy shared. Nira wanted someone who cared enough to do anything for her. Like crawl into a car that might explode at any moment.

Nira was explaining through sobs and gasps how she'd taken a wrong turn on her way to meet Gerth and Aunt Meredith. A huge delivery truck had driven her off the road. The jeep had gone into a ditch and flipped. She'd been stuck, helplessly waiting for the jeep to blow up.

Fred tore off part of his shirt, which he was using to bandage a nasty-looking cut on Nira's palm. Adrenaline was pumping through Olivia at a thousand miles an hour, but Fred's hands and voice were steady as he bandaged and comforted Nira.

Olivia was reminded of a couple of years ago, when one of Mr. Brown's dairy cows was giving birth. There was a bad snow storm, and the vet wasn't able to get to the farm.

Mr. Brown was having a flare-up of his MS, and so it had been up to Fred to deliver the calf. Addy, who had been at the Browns' house at the time, called Olivia to bring over every clean towel they had.

When Olivia arrived, Mr. Brown and Addy had been nervous wrecks. Fred, who was the one doing all the real work, was as steady and level-headed as he always was. Two hours later, Fred delivered the calve without incident.

Olivia remembered the calm, gentle way Fred had treated the calf and its mother. She'd been amazed by the way he reacted in the midst of a crisis.

It was the same when he'd rescued Nira from that burning car.

Nira's voice was a whisper when she said, "I didn't think anyone cared enough to notice I was gone."

"I care," Fred said, holding her closer. "*We* care."

"Thank you." Nira wrapped her arms around Fred's neck and cried. "Thank you."

* * *

Olivia was still shaking from their near-miss with the exploding jeep when they arrived at the old silo. She counted thirteen Texas farmers surrounding Aunt Meredith, Gerth, and Jaxon.

The conversation didn't look friendly.

"Stay with Nira," Olivia told Fred.

He looked like he wanted to argue, but Nira was still bleeding and crying. So, he gave her a short nod.

"Be careful," he told her. "Yell if you need me."

Olivia jumped out of the truck. She tried to keep her footsteps steady as she crunched across the dusty, shriveled grass. She didn't want to spook any of the farmers, all of whom were holding rifles.

"Sullivan, be reasonable," Aunt Meredith was saying when Olivia got close enough to hear. "How on God's green earth could we have caused an *earthquake*?"

One of the other men strode up to Aunt Meredith until they were almost nose-to-nose.

"How do you explain this endin' up on your property?"

Olivia didn't at first understand why the man was holding up an old boot in Aunt Meredith's face. The man's next words made her go still.

"We know ya'll are behind Anthony Fowler's disappearance."

Olivia's heart went into her throat.

"I think this is all just a big misunderstanding," Gerth said, his tone light and friendly.

Olivia noticed that he had one hand wrapped around his vial, with his finger poised over the stopper.

"We've just been visiting with Addy and Livy's aunt," Gerth continued. "And now you're accusing us of making earthquakes and disappearing people?" He chuckled. "Sounds like something you'd see on the telly."

"We ain't talkin' to you, Brit!"

"Okay, it's clear this conversation isn't going anywhere," Gerth said, unstopping his vial.

"What the fuck are you doin'?" the farmer demanded.

"I'll thank you to watch your language in front of my guests, Sullivan," Aunt Meredith said in a voice that no sane person would ignore.

Sullivan, apparently, was not sane.

He cocked his gun and aimed it at Jaxon.

"Tell us the truth or we'll blow his head off," Sullivan warned.

Jaxon stepped forward until the muzzle was digging into his chest. He didn't say anything, but it was almost scarier that way. Olivia saw the man at the other end of the rifle waver, uncertain.

"Really, Sullivan," Aunt Meredith said, her own voice getting higher with her growing anxiety. "This isn't the Wild West. I'm filing a police report as soon as we get home."

"Do it," Sullivan growled. "Then *I'll* file a report 'bout how you murdered poor Tony."

While the men were focused on Aunt Meredith and Jaxon, Gerth swallowed a drop of Addy's blood from his vial. His lips were bright red as his Haze flared.

"Pardon me," Gerth said, catching the eye of one farmer, and then another.

Both men's eyes glazed over as they fell under Gerth's Influence. They turned their guns on the other farmers.

"Go away," one of the men under Influence told the others. "Leave these people alone."

He moved forward, his stride jerky.

"Oh my Lord, they're doin' somethin' to 'em!" one of the other farmers shouted.

Aunt Meredith and Jaxon used the opportunity to move in on the farmers. Aunt Meredith came up behind one of the men, grabbed his gun right out of his hands, and smacked it over the top of his head. The man went down.

Jaxon took down another with a single punch. A third man's eyes glazed over.

"They'll kill us all!" one of the farmers shouted.

A deafening crack split the air. Aunt Meredith screamed.

Olivia watched the bullet hit Jaxon's muscled shoulder, stall for a moment, and then bounce right off. The pellet fell harmlessly to the ground.

"Devils," one of the farmers whispered.

"Aliens," another croaked.

"Run!" shouted a third.

"We can't let them get away," Gerth said. "If they go to the media…if the mortals find out about us…."

He didn't have to finish the thought. Olivia understood what kind of chaos would ensue if it ever came out that mind-controllers and super-human warriors were loose on Earth.

Aunt Meredith, Jaxon, and the three Influenced men went after the fleeing farmers.

Gerth's cheeks were red, and he was huffing with the effort it was taking for him to maintain his Influence.

Olivia went to stand beside him. Without saying a word, she took his hand. Immediately, she felt power wash over her.

"Atta girl, Livy," Gerth said.

She closed her eyes. She saw the farmers' minds. They looked like dim globes hovering over the fleeing men's bodies. Gerth's energy didn't enhance her abilities like Erikir or Tol's, but it was enough to let her grab hold of the ten minds that weren't yet under Influence.

You didn't see anything unusual here, she thought to the men. *We're not responsible for what happened to Anthony Fowler, and—*

Olivia's breath wheezed out. The farmers' minds slipped out of her mental grasp.

"Livy?" Gerth asked. He said something else, but she didn't hear the words.

The dusty road and old silo disappeared from her vision.

She found herself sitting at a dimly-lit bar. A neon sign over the liquor shelf read "Fisherman's *Wart.*" A martini was in front of Olivia. The TV overhead had a baseball game in progress. The San Francisco Giants were playing the LA Dodgers.

Olivia looked into the mirror behind the bar, only to find it wasn't her face staring back. It was his…the same man she'd watch destroy countless cities on Earth.

The Supernal.

Olivia fell backward on a gasp. She caught herself before she hit the ground, and when she righted herself, she was back on the dusty Texas road. The farmers were all getting in their cars and driving away. Olivia didn't give them another thought.

"LA Dodgers and San Francisco Giants," Olivia said, breathless.

"What?" Gerth looked at her like she'd lost her mind.

"They're baseball teams," Aunt Meredith explained.

"When are they playing?" Olivia asked.

"Why is this even relevant?" Jaxon countered.

"When are they playing?!"

Gerth, catching on that there was a reason why she needed to know, pulled out his phone and started to type.

"Looks like they're playing at 2:45 California time on the eighteenth." Gerth looked up from his phone. "That's in three days."

"Why you asking, pumpkin?" Aunt Meredith asked.

Olivia felt a grin stretch across her face.

"At 2:45 on the eighteenth, I know exactly where the Supernal is going to be."

CHAPTER 30

ADDY

Addy was sweating everywhere. There was a shallow cut across her calf from one of Jaxon's half-moon blades.

And she was having a blast.

"Too slow!" She grabbed Jaxon's forearm and flipped his entire body over hers.

"Stop holding back," he replied, leaping back to his feet in a single motion. "And I'll give you a real fight."

He wasn't even out of breath.

"I wouldn't want to hurt you again," she taunted, hoping to annoy him enough that he'd slip up.

That's how good he was. Addy was sinking to petty insults, and Jaxon didn't even have the good graces to be distracted by them. The guy was cool as a cucumber, while Addy was sweating like a pig.

Before she knew what was happening, Jaxon hooked his foot around her ankle. Addy *oofed* as her butt hit the ground.

"Stop holding back," he told her again. "You're Forsaken. Fight like one."

Addy felt a moment's hesitation. Then, the angry cobra she kept locked inside her stirred awake.

No, she thought, trying to push it back down where it wouldn't hurt anyone.

Jaxon tackled her.

They rolled over the ground, fighting for control.

Jaxon was bigger, and he'd been right about Addy being untrained. Compared to Jaxon, every one of her strikes seemed bumbling and sloppy. He was winning. She could feel her sweat-slicked palms refusing to obey simple commands as Jaxon's choke hold tightened. She felt the cool metal of his half-moon blade graze her cheek.

"Stop holding back," he said again.

Addy tried to shake her head…tried to tell him what would happen if she unleashed that beast inside her.

You're Forsaken. Fight like one.

She wasn't one of them. She didn't want to be.

Her vision was going spotty from lack of oxygen. Jaxon tightened his hold.

Would he really kill her? Addy hadn't thought so, but she couldn't breathe….

She couldn't die. Not here…not now. She had things to do.

The cobra sprang to life. It rose up, fangs extended. Everything she'd fought so hard to control flooded out of her.

Addy's Haze flared.

She wasn't even aware of what was happening until, a few seconds later, Jaxon was pinned beneath her and gasping a single word.

"Mercy."

She released her hold and flopped down onto the ground beside him.

Every other time that beast inside her had come to life, it had taken everything Addy had to shove it back down, and the only way she'd managed it was *after* she'd killed every one of her enemies.

Jaxon was very much alive, and it had been easy to stop fighting. She had wanted to stop, so she'd stopped. So simple…and yet, it was everything.

Addy realized that tight knot of anger she always carried wasn't gone, but it had shrunk. It didn't take up all the empty places inside her. Instead, it was just one of many parts of her. It was there to be used when it was needed and forgotten about when it wasn't.

"I don't understand," she whispered.

Jaxon got to his feet.

"You've been rejecting your nature and suppressing your abilities," he said. "Your magic has been fighting back."

Addy shook her head, still overwhelmed that she hadn't killed him in her usual angry rage.

So, you're saying if I accept that I'm Forsaken," Addy swallowed, "I'll stop feeling this…rage?"

Jaxon leveled a stare at her. "I'm saying you need to stop trying to be what the Chosen want you to be. I'm saying you need to accept that you're Forsaken."

It couldn't be as simple as Jaxon was trying to make it.

Could it?

"You're the one who's meant to lead our people," he said. "To pretend otherwise is to lie to yourself."

She didn't know what to say.

"The stone recognized you, and I know you felt something for it, too," Jaxon persisted.

The stone.

"I'm not like you," Addy said. The words sounded hollow and empty.

Jaxon didn't reply. He pulled the box out of his pocket and opened it.

Addy felt her heart swell in her chest. Her Haze turned from gold to blue, matching the color radiating from the stone.

"If you were like all of your friends, you'd be emptying your guts right now," Jaxon said.

Addy didn't notice she was reaching for the stone until her fingers had almost connected with the glowing blue surface.

No, no, no.

Her reaction to this stone was all wrong. Addy didn't belong with the ones who had murdered so many of Tol's people. She didn't belong with the woman who had almost drowned her and was responsible for her real family's deaths.

And yet, Addy remembered the way Tol's people had looked at her after she stopped those Forsaken weapons. She heard their shouts.

Kill the Forsaken.

It hadn't mattered that she had just saved their queen's life. She was still the enemy.

"It won't bite," Jaxon told her, nodding at the stone. "It calls to you because its power is part of your essence. It's part of us."

The screen door banged. Addy yanked her hand back, like she was doing something illicit, as Gerth came out onto the porch. Jaxon put the stone back in its box. Addy tried to ignore the sense of loss she felt once it was out of sight.

"Addy, Jaxon," Gerth called. "Go get cleaned up. Family dinner in an hour, and we've got a lot to discuss."

"What are we discussing?" Jaxon asked, his intense gaze still fixed on Addy.

"How we're going to kill the Supernal in two-and-a-half days."

✳ ✳ ✳

After her shower, Addy wandered into Aunt Meredith's bedroom. She found Livy passed out on top of the covers. Livy was hugging a copy of *Pride and Prejudice*—her favorite—to her heart.

Addy was surprised Aunt Meredith had the book, since Jane Austen didn't really seem like their aunt's style.

For a woman accustomed to living alone with her cows, Aunt Meredith had taken to all the people, violence, and magic now filling her house without batting an eye. Whenever any of them tried to apologize for the maps strewn over every available surface, or the blood and oil streaks permanently embedded in the wood floors, Aunt Meredith had just waved them off and said *What's mine is ya'lls.*

Even now that Aunt Meredith knew the truth about everything, she didn't look at Addy or Livy any differently. To Aunt Meredith, they were still just her nieces.

Addy loved her all the more for it.

Addy climbed onto the bed and nestled against her sister. It was just like when they lived on the farm…back when their whole family was alive, and they'd been Firecracker Addy and Sweet Livy instead of the Forsaken general's daughter and the Fount.

Livy made a sleepy sound and turned over to face Addy. They wound their arms around each other.

"How are you?" Addy whispered.

Livy blinked and smiled. The bruise-like circles under her eyes made Addy's gut twist. Livy was pushing herself to the breaking point, and she was doing it all for Addy.

Livy hadn't asked for any of this, and yet she hadn't uttered a single complaint. She'd fallen into Addy's pack of other-worldly friends without so much as a peep of protest, and she'd taken all of the strange and terrifying events of the last few weeks in stride.

"I wish this wasn't all falling on you," Addy told her twin.

Livy squeezed Addy tighter. "I'm actually grateful there's an important reason for everything I'm doing. It helps with the guilt."

Addy narrowed her eyes. "What could you possibly have to be guilty about?"

Livy bit her lip. After a short silence, she said, "Sometimes, when I'm practicing with my magic or talking to…one of the Chosen," she glanced away as a flush crept up her neck, "I forget about Mom and Dad and our sisters."

Livy winced at the admission.

"It feels kind of like we've abandoned them," Addy said.

"That's right!" Livy's soft curls tumbled around her shoulders as she nodded. "I feel like I'm being disloyal to them, or not honoring their memory."

They lay in silence for several minutes.

"I feel more like a Forsaken than a Deerborn," Addy blurted out.

She hadn't realized how true the sentiment was until this moment. Now that she'd said the words, she couldn't reel them back.

Addy let out a humorless laugh. "You and Tol can barely stand to be in the same room as Jaxon. Meanwhile, I'm drawn to that stupid Supernal's power like a moth to the fire."

"Oh Addy." Livy kissed her forehead. "You are who you are. I'd love you even if you had lizard blood in your veins, and so would Tol."

Addy managed a real laugh this time. She stuck out her tongue and hissed in her best lizard impression.

"You know what I mean." Livy swatted her.

"I know." Addy squeezed her twin. "Thanks."

Livy leaned her head in and whispered, "Have you noticed that Jaxon is kind of cute?"

Addy pffed. "Cute? He's too big to be cute. I'd say he tips right into hotness territory."

Livy giggled. "I *know*. And with that accent—"

"He's just so serious." Addy tried to mimic Jaxon's stoic expression, which got another laugh out of Livy.

"I saw how much fun you were having during your practice fight earlier," Livy said. "Tol better watch out or he might have some competition."

"No chance."

Addy cringed at the way her voice came out dreamy and girly. Still, she couldn't help the smile that spread over her face at the thought of Tol. *Her Tol.*

"Jaxon is all yours," Addy told her twin.

"Hm, tempting." Livy tilted her head, pretending to consider it. "He's not really my type, though."

"Yeah, you're probably right. He seems like he goes to bed with his blades rather than *The Canterbury Tales*."

Livy did her best impression of a glare. It was sweet.

"Love you, sis," Addy said.

"Love you more," Livy replied.

CHAPTER 31

ADDY

Aunt Meredith had outdone herself. Dishes of food covered the whole surface of the picnic table. Everyone loaded up their paper plates and spread out on the ground.

Aunt Meredith had made her *Texas famous* pulled pork. The smoky, tangy smell curled up from the meat and perfumed the air. Nira had been horrified by the idea of piling the messy, barbecue sauce-drenched pork onto slabs of bread and eating it with her hands, which further endeared Addy to the meal. There was also potato and macaroni salad, baked beans, fried pickles, and thick slices of watermelon.

The conversations were as loud and varied as any dinner at Deerborn Family Farm had ever been. This new family Addy had somehow accumulated would never replace the one she'd lost, but as she stared around at the people sprawled out on the lawn, a soft warmth filled her chest.

She noticed, with an equal mixture of amusement and irritation, that Nira was flirting with Fred. The two of them had been thick as thieves ever since Fred pulled her out of a burning car.

Like he wouldn't have done that for any poor schmuck.

Now, Nira was tossing her long hair and *accidentally* brushing her hand against his leg. When Fred dropped his fork on the grass, Nira leaned over to pick it up for him. Addy was honestly worried Nira's boobs would fall right out of her *very* low-scoop tank top.

Fred didn't seem to mind. He was trying so hard not to stare that Addy thought he would burst a blood vessel.

Addy wanted to tell beauty queen piranha to leave her best friend alone, but she knew Fred could take care of himself. Even surrounded by people with magical abilities, Fred had held his own. Besides, Addy wasn't exactly sorry that Nira had stopped constantly reminding everyone that she had slept with Tol.

The sight of Nira and Fred together wasn't the only surprising sight. Livy and Erikir were deep in conversation, and Livy seemed to actually be enjoying herself.

He leaned in to hear whatever Livy was saying, and—*be still her heart*—Erikir smiled. Addy couldn't hear their exact words, but she could tell from the jubilant expression on her twin's face that they were talking about books.

Addy nestled against Tol while Aunt Meredith peppered him with questions about his family and world.

"What I don't understand is how you can have a seven-hundred-year-old grandmother when you're only eighteen," Aunt Meredith said, biting into a slice of watermelon.

"Children are extremely rare among our kind," Tol replied patiently, even though he'd already answered about a thousand of Aunt Meredith's questions.

"And downright impossible in the mortal world," Gerth added. "The scholars can't figure out why."

"The Forsaken haven't had problems reproducing in the mortal world," Jaxon said. He inclined his head at Addy. "If you were hoping for children, you'd have more luck with a Forsaken."

"Addy's taken," Tol snapped.

Jaxon's pale cheeks flushed. "I didn't mean it the way you're thinking."

"Yeah, right." Tol rolled his eyes. "Don't tell me you haven't thought about it."

"Mate," Gerth said out of the corner of his mouth.

"I might not be able to kill you *yet*, but if you come on to my fiancé—"

"*Mate*," Gerth hissed.

"I'm not interested in her like that because I'm not…." Jaxon squirmed, and it occurred to Addy that it was the first time she'd seen him at a loss for words. "I'm not interested in any woman like that."

Oh.

Gerth smacked a hand to his forehead. "I tried to tell you."

Now, it was Tol's turn to be embarrassed. "Oh, sorry." He cleared his throat. "I guess I overreacted, then."

Tol looked at Addy, but she just shook her head and gave him an *I can't help you* shrug.

Jaxon lifted a shoulder. "It's not something the Forsaken are against, but I don't usually talk about it with people I've just met."

"Understood." Tol rubbed at his left shoulder in the way he did when he was uncomfortable or stressed.

"Our people are less tolerant of different preferences," Gerth explained to no one in particular. "Mostly because there are so few children as it is."

"It's one of the Chosen's most antiquated beliefs," Tol said. He frowned. "I guess the Forsaken are more progressive than we are in that regard."

Addy knew what it cost Tol to admit the Forsaken were better than the Chosen in any way. She snuggled closer to him.

Gerth was staring at Tol with a strange intensity. "Are you saying you wouldn't exile someone for being gay?"

"The Chosen do that?" Addy asked, horrified.

Tol winced. "Not anymore, but previous monarchs did." He put an arm around Addy before turning to Gerth. "I'd have to be a special kind of hypocrite if I judged any of my subjects for who they chose to love."

Before Gerth could reply, another voice joined the conversation.

"There's another way the Forsaken are more progressive than the Chosen." Erikir spoke loud enough for everyone to hear.

Without waiting for a response, he continued, "The Forsaken understand that power needs to be earned rather than inherited."

His comment was met with a chorus of reactions and insults—most of the latter coming from Addy. Erikir seemed immune to all of them, until Livy gave him a disappointed look before turning away. The slight wasn't anything compared to what Addy had just said, and yet that one little look made Erikir shrink in on himself.

Another point for Team Deerborn, Addy thought with satisfaction. Her sister might not have Addy's firecracker temper, but she had her own ways of getting things done.

"Alright," Gerth announced. "Time to talk strategy." He rubbed his hands together. "We have the stone that contains the Supernal's magic. He wants what we have. And in three days, he's going to be at a bar in San Francisco called 'Fisherman's Wart'."

"Maybe we can find a way to take him and the general out in one fell swoop," Addy said, liking the sound of it. Regardless of her new, confusing feelings of kinship toward the Forsaken, she hadn't changed her mind about the general. Addy was going to kill the woman responsible for her real family's deaths.

"We can't let either the general or the Supernal find out what we're up to," Gerth said, stroking his chin in thought.

"Even with this advantage, the Supernal won't be easy to kill," Jaxon warned.

Gerth turned to Jaxon. "What can the Supernal do without his stone?"

Jaxon lifted a shoulder. "No one knows exactly, but there are rumors. I'd guess he's still an excellent fighter."

Gerth nodded, his thoughtful frown in place.

"I need quiet to work out the logistics," he announced.

Everyone else shut up. Gerth muttered and cursed to himself.

"Is he having a fit or something?" Jaxon asked after several minutes had passed.

"It's his process," Tol explained.

Since the revelation of Jaxon's sexuality, Tol had stopped being openly hostile. Addy was glad for it. Even without the added benefit of the stone in his pocket, Addy liked Jaxon.

"I think I've got a plan," Gerth announced. "But I need more time to work out the details. We'll commence Plan Supernal Assassination in the morning."

"We should take turns keeping watch tonight in case any of the Forsaken catch up with us," Jaxon said. "I was careful coming here, but the general is determined to find me."

Gerth looked affronted, and Addy realized it was because Jaxon had thought of something Gerth hadn't.

Gerth's irritation quickly shifted to grudging respect, and he nodded in agreement.

"Ya'll just let me know what I can do to help," Aunt Meredith said. Her expression darkened. "*After* I deal with those imbecile farmers who tried to threaten my guests."

"I imagine they're scared enough that they won't try anything else," Gerth said. "Not to mention, their brains are probably still mottled from Influence."

"They better hope for their own sakes that they don't try to mess with my people again," Aunt Meredith huffed.

"We can't tell you how much we appreciate your hospitality," Tol said in that voice that made it impossible to forget he was a future king. "But," he glanced at Addy before continuing, "it'll be safer for you if you stay here. There will be no reason for the Forsaken to come after you once we're gone."

"Once we've killed the bad guys, we'll come back and get you," Addy promised.

Aunt Meredith pursed her lips. "I understand I'm a liability, what with my bullets bouncing off people's chests." She narrowed her gaze on Addy and Livy. "But do you have any idea what your mother would say to me if she knew I was letting you run around killing people?"

Addy winced.

Aunt Meredith let out a heavy sigh. "Then again, if I could tell your mom ya'll were out saving the world, she'd ask me what else I could expect from her Firecracker Addy and Sweet Livy."

Aunt Meredith leaned in and kissed Addy's forehead. She looked from Addy to Livy. "Just make sure you come home to me." She glanced around the circle. "All of you."

CHAPTER 32

OLIVIA

Olivia and Erikir relieved Addy and Tol from their watch at midnight. When Erikir had suggested being watch partners, she'd felt like the most handsome boy at prom had just asked her to dance.

Of course, Olivia hadn't been to prom, since she and her siblings had been homeschooled. And of course, she and Erikir weren't dancing. They were peering into the dark for any sign of the people who wanted to kill them.

Nonetheless, she felt content just sitting next to him. Erikir was so different when it was just the two of them.

Olivia would have been angry with Erikir for his cruel remark to Tol at dinner, but she understood the reason behind his taunts. He resented Tol's position—not because Erikir desired power or authority, but because he loved his people so deeply. He truly believed he would be a better king of the Chosen.

Erikir hid his devotion to his people behind a shield of insults and bad temper. Olivia wished he would let the others see him the way she did.

She leaned back against the bench, listening to the gentle creak of the chains.

Olivia had made more progress with her abilities today. She'd pulled herself in and out of visions without needing to draw strength from any of the Chosen. She had also managed to Influence Gerth, even though she hated the thought of controlling someone else's mind. Doing it to those farmers who had wanted to hurt her aunt and friends was one thing. Controlling Gerth's mind was another.

She had felt awful and dirty afterward, even though all she'd compelled him to do was the Macarena. She'd been the only one who was upset. Everyone else had celebrated it as a major achievement. The only other person who could Influence the Chosen was Tol, and even he didn't have that ability outside of Vitaquias.

She was getting stronger. The bottomless well of her power still frightened her, but it was less terrifying now that she could pull herself back onto that safe ledge without anyone else's help.

Olivia listened to the gentle music of the wind chimes. She rested her back against the blanket draped over the bench and let her eyes fall closed.

She jolted up when she realized she'd been dozing.

"I'm sorry," she said, shaking her head to clear away the cobwebs. "Some poor watchwoman I'm making."

"I would have woken you if any Forsaken were about to attack," Erikir assured her, his lips twitching upward.

Olivia was mesmerized by the way the golden light from his Haze reflected in his dark eyes.

The wind kicked up, making her hair whip across her face. While she gathered her loose curls, Erikir leaned closer to pull the blanket over her shoulders.

Her thanks died on her lips when she realized how close they were. He seemed to realize it at the same moment. They froze.

"Olivia," he whispered. "I   " he swallowed.

She wasn't sure if she read the emotion in his eyes or if it was her magic, but she sensed Erikir's uncertainty and self-doubt.

His lips didn't move, but she heard his voice in her head.

She's too good for me.

The thought angered Olivia. Startled by her own boldness, she leaned forward and pressed her lips to his

Erikir hesitated for only a moment. Then, he wrapped his arms around her and pulled her against him.

Erikir held her gently, not like she was fragile, but like she was precious. Olivia felt her magic stir at her heightened emotions, but she pushed it back down. She didn't want to look into Erikir's mind or see some glimmer of his future. She just wanted to kiss him.

"I guess we're both bad watchpeople," Erikir said when they separated.

They were both breathing hard, and their arms were still wound around each other. Erikir smiled. Olivia realized she'd never seen him happy. If he'd been handsome before, it was nothing compared to what he looked like now.

And she'd been the one to make him feel this way.

The realization had her smiling too. She was still smiling when she leaned in for another kiss.

CHAPTER 33

TOL

Tol was seriously going to punch his cousin in the face…that was, if he could find the useless git.

Everyone else was ready to go, but Erikir had announced he was *going for a short drive*. That had been almost an hour ago, and now, they had to go searching for him instead of beginning the first phase of Gerth's plan. Their flight to San Francisco was in two hours. They needed to get moving.

Addy didn't sense any Forsaken nearby, which meant Erikir hadn't been kidnapped. If it hadn't been for Olivia's insistence that they wait for him, Tol would have left the prick behind, although he would have felt badly leaving Addy's aunt with his company.

Tol called Erikir again, resisting the urge to throw his phone across the room when his cousin didn't pick up.

Tol's irritation cut off as his vision blurred. He grabbed onto the back of a chair to keep himself standing as Olivia's fear and worry entered his mind.

It took him several seconds to bring the room back into focus.

"What happened?" Tol asked, his brain still fuzzy from the shockwaves of magical energy.

Addy had her arm around Olivia, who looked as drawn as Tol felt.

"I saw the Forsaken attacking the Chosen manor," Olivia said, her voice heavy with exhaustion.

He jerked up.

"There's still time," Olivia hurried to say. "At least, it hasn't happened yet. I can tell when a vision is past or future, and this one's future."

"Can you tell how far in the future?" Gerth asked.

Olivia shook her head. "There wasn't anything to tell me the exact time." Her worried gaze flicked to Tol. "I saw at least a hundred armed Forsaken, and the general was the one leading them to your house."

And now, with all of the Source reserves Tol had given out, his parents' guards would have nothing extra to defend themselves against the Forsaken who were coming for his people. He'd put a temporary hold on the rebellion that threatened his parents' reign, and in doing so, he'd left his people vulnerable. If the Chosen fought the Forsaken, their Source would drain faster. If they didn't fight, the Forsaken would kill them.

"Calm down, mate," Gerth said, reading Tol's mind. "Once we get the Supernal and general out of the picture, the Forsaken will be too wrapped up in their own problems to worry about attacking the manor."

Tol nodded, even though Gerth's words did little to ease the knot of panic in his chest.

"I could use my ring to portal all of the Chosen somewhere else," Addy offered.

Tol considered that. Stay and defend, or run and hope they weren't chased?

"No," he said finally. "They're as likely to be attacked wherever we try to hide them, and the manor is safer than anywhere else we could find right now."

Tol started to pace. His people were in danger, and he wasn't with them. It was his job to protect them, and instead, he had abandoned his flock to be devoured by the wolves.

Everything was just moving too slowly. And it was all out of his control.

Tol's phone buzzed.

"Where in the two hells are you?" he growled as soon as the call connected.

"I need to talk to you. Alone." Erikir didn't bother to acknowledge the fact that he'd already delayed them an hour. "Just start driving into town and you'll find me about ten miles out."

"Are you joking?" Tol demanded. "You do remember we had things to do today, right?"

"Tol, please. It's important."

Tol was immediately suspicious. Erikir had never before asked for a heart-to-heart, and he definitely never said *please*.

"Is there a problem?" Tol asked.

"No. Just come. As fast as you can."

Tol rolled his eyes skyward. "I'll be there in ten minutes. If you don't have a good explanation for holding everyone up, I'm going to rip your head off."

"Just you," Erikir said, ignoring Tol's threat. "Don't bring anyone else."

Tol ended the call.

"I'm going to get Erikir." He grabbed the keys to one of the jeeps off the counter.

"I'm coming with you," Addy said.

"Erikir insisted I come alone, but—" Tol shrugged. "I'm not feeling particularly accommodating at the moment." Tol tossed Addy the keys, knowing she'd want to drive.

Olivia put out a hand to stop them, her brow furrowed. "If Erikir said you should come alone, then shouldn't you do as he asked?"

"I don't trust that weasel as far as I can throw him," Addy said, cracking her knuckles. "Actually, scratch that. I could throw him much farther than I could trust him."

Tol agreed.

"I trust him." Olivia didn't raise her voice, but there was something unyielding in it.

"Is this some kind of Fount premonition thing?" Tol asked.

"No, it's a human decency thing," Olivia shot back. There was an edge to her voice Tol had never heard before. She was normally so even-tempered.

Tol looked at Addy.

"If you say so, sis," Addy said with a shrug.

"I trust him," Olivia said again.

Addy gave Tol back the keys. "If you're not back in half an hour, I'm coming after you."

Tol gave her a quick kiss. To Gerth, he said, "Keep your phone on in case I need backup."

Since he was driving one of the Forsaken's jeeps and not Meredith's truck, Tol floored the gas and didn't bother to avoid potholes.

When he saw the other Forsaken jeep, with Erikir leaning against the open door, Tol pulled over.

Did the sodding idiot run out of gas?

Tol parked behind the other vehicle and got out.

"Thanks for coming," Erikir said, seeming unaware of the fact that Tol was ready to wring his cousin's neck.

"Get in." Tol gestured to his still-running jeep. "We can just leave the other one."

Erikir was holding one of his hands behind his back as he approached. "We need to talk."

"We'll talk in the bloody car. Now get in!"

"She's almost here." Erikir glanced over his shoulder as he came to stand beside Tol.

"Who's—" Tol saw a cloud of dust at the end of the road. A warning shivered down his spine, and he was reaching for his Source before he even thought about what he was doing.

"Can't let you do that, mate," Erikir said.

Something stung the side of Tol's neck. He flinched and pressed a hand to the sharp pain. Instead of a wasp or one of the other Texas insects he'd been expecting, he drew away…a needle and syringe.

"Erikir…what?"

Tol took a step and stumbled. He sagged against the side of the jeep.

"I borrowed some of Nira's drugs," Erikir explained, as cool as if he was talking about what he'd eaten for breakfast.

Tol remembered Nira saying the pain medicines had gone missing.

"You bastard—" Tol reached for Erikir, but his cousin easily stepped out of his way.

Tol's limbs were heavy. His brain felt like it was stuffed full of cotton. His tongue was thick in his mouth.

Tol reached for his Source, but his right arm was clumsy, and his prosthesis had become nothing more than dead weight.

"Why?" The word came out sounding strange, as Tol tried to navigate his newly-swollen tongue.

"You left me no choice. I realized you'd never stop putting Addy ahead of your own people. You're going to get everyone killed." Erikir folded his arms. "Our people deserve a prince who prioritizes their survival over his own selfish desires."

"Let me guess," Tol said, forcing out the words even though his mouth had become a desert. "Our people need a prince like you?"

"I don't want you to die, but it's the only way to save our people." Erikir looked at the approaching dust cloud.

I don't want you to die....

If it weren't for these gods-damned drugs, Tol would turn Erikir into a mindless zombie. He couldn't get to his Source, though, and his brain was moving slower by the second. He remembered his phone in his back pocket and reached for it.

He missed. He tried again and somehow managed to get the phone in his right hand. It felt slippery. Or maybe it was his hand that was slippery.

The phone fell onto the ground. He bent to retrieve it, ignoring the waves of dizziness crashing over him.

As Tol's useless body fought its growing weakness, Erikir strode over and stomped on the phone. The metal and plastic crunched.

"You'll pay for this," Tol promised his cousin.

The words didn't sound as threatening as he'd meant them.

He knew he should be angrier, but the cotton in his brain was dampening his emotions. He wanted to fight. He wanted to kill. But his body wouldn't obey even the simplest command.

"Once you're dead, I'll be the prince," Erikir said. "I'll be able to finish the blood marriage and bring our people home."

Tol tried to respond, but the words were too big for him to manage in his foggy state.

"It didn't need to be like this." Erikir looked at Tol with a combination of regret and anger, like it was Tol's fault that Erikir had to murder him. "If I'd been prince from the start, I would have blood married the Fount the moment I found her, even if she was some troll." His expression hardened. "But, as it turns out, she's anything but a troll. You're so blind you can't even see perfection when she's staring you in the face."

Tol blinked against the harsh sunlight, noticing that the cloud of dust had turned into a Hummer painted in army camouflage.

"You called…Forsaken?"

"I called the Forsaken general," Erikir corrected. "The idea came to me after the Forsaken attacked us. When I escorted that one off the property, I Influenced her to deliver a message to the general. It didn't take long for the general and I to reach an agreement."

"General killed your father," Tol slurred.

Why would Erikir make a deal with his own father's murderer?

"That's right. I hate the general more than anyone in two worlds, and guess what, Tol? I'm putting aside my own selfish needs to do something bigger for my people." Erikir's lip curled in disgust as he regarded Tol. "I reached a peace agreement with the general, and you're the price she demanded for sealing our bargain.

Desperation pulsed alongside Tol's fury. He had to stop this before the general got here.

Move, he begged his useless limbs.

It was no use. He may as well have been cemented in place.

"I'll do anything for my people, even if that means making an agreement with my enemy." Erikir met Tol's foggy gaze. "And that's the difference between us, cousin."

"She'll kill you," Tol managed to say.

Erikir shook his head. "I told her if anyone came except her, our deal would be off."

Tol could see in his cousin's eyes how much Erikir wanted to take control of the general's mind and avenge his father's murder.

That's when the part Tol hadn't understood made sense. "You're…gonna make…look like the general killed me." Every word was an effort.

Erikir nodded. "I'm going to tell everyone the general attacked us. I'll say she killed you, and I barely escaped. None of our people will be able to blame me for your death, and they'll know I was the one to force the general into a peace agreement." A victorious expression lit Erikir's face.

You really planned this whole thing out, didn't you? Tol thought bitterly. *Except….*

"She'll never keep…peace," Tol slurred.

"She will. I've promised to give her Addy in exchange." Erikir scowled. "Why everyone wants Addy so badly, I'll never understand."

The idea of Erikir using Addy as a negotiation strategy was enough to make Tol's legs work. Somehow, he managed to get his right hand around Erikir's throat. His cousin's eyes bulged in surprise before he threw up an elbow.

It was enough to loosen Tol's flimsy grip.

"Kill me then, coward," Tol ordered his cousin. "Look me in the eye."

Erikir glanced away from him, and Tol saw his guilt and a flash of uncertainty.

The Hummer stopped right in the middle of the road. The door opened, and General Lezha Bloodsong stepped out. Her boots thudded against the pavement as she took even, unhurried steps to them.

"I brought the prince as a show of good faith," Erikir told the general, shoving Tol forward a step.

Tol shook with fury and hatred, or maybe it was just some effect of the drugs coursing through his system.

"Where is my daughter?" the general demanded.

"I will bring her to you after I'm king and the official peace treaty is in place," Erikir replied.

Tol tried to shout. He tried to move. Both were impossible.

The general let out a mirthless laugh.

"There will never be peace between our people, *boy*."

Erikir opened and closed his fists at his sides. A muscle in his jaw twitched.

"Then, you've left me with no choice," Erikir replied. He swallowed the drop of Source poised on the tip of his finger.

Tol expected the general to turn away and shield her eyes. She didn't. She continued to stare straight at Erikir.

Something was wrong. Even in Tol's barely-there state, it was obvious. The general wasn't under Erikir's Influence.

Erikir's expression faltered. The general raised her right hand, and a ring on her index finger caught the light. A large red stone pulsed with light in the same way Addy's did right before she created a portal.

"What the hells?" Erikir demanded.

"It was a gift," the general said softly, her expression inscrutable. "It contains a piece of the gods' power, and it protects me from any attack from the Chosen."

Erikir's face paled.

Tol was in no position to do anything at this point. He couldn't even move his lips enough to speak. He fought against the unnatural exhaustion that was trying to drag him under.

He couldn't pass out.

Addy said she'd come after him in half an hour. He had no idea how long it'd been, but if he could just hang on…keep them here a little longer….

"I remember the look on your father's face before I killed him," the general said, leering down at Erikir. "It was much the same as the one on yours now."

Tol saw Erikir's expression transform from fury to panic. The general was safe from Influence, and Tol was paralyzed. Erikir was facing the strongest of the Forsaken without his only weapon.

Tol saw the moment his cousin realized they were both going to die. The Chosen people would be bereft of any legitimate heir to the throne. They would be doomed.

Way to go, Cuz.

Tol knew he should feel…something, but it was taking every ounce of his concentration just to stay awake.

"You'll never find Addy without me," Erikir said, full of desperation. "Kill my cousin and agree not to attack my people, and I'll bring your daughter to you."

"I don't need your help to find her," General Bloodsong said. "She is going to come to me."

"But our agreement—"

The general gave Erikir a pitiless smile. "This princeling is far more valuable to me alive than dead. I imagine there's nothing the Chosen king and queen won't do to keep their son alive."

Even as thoughts of murder and destruction went through Tol's mind, he felt his legs give way. A dark veil was being drawn over his eyes. He blinked, desperate to stay conscious.

"Run, little Magnantius," the general told Erikir in a soft, mocking voice. "Tell your people how you've betrayed them. And tell my daughter what has happened to her prince."

Erikir looked from the general to Tol. His gaze filled with fear.

Erikir ran.

The general straightened. She watched Erikir scramble into his jeep and tear down the road. Then, she looked at Tol.

Tol's body was lifted off the ground. His world went dark.

CHAPTER 34

OLIVIA

Olivia blinked up at Addy and Aunt Meredith, who were hovering over her. She felt…fuzzy. Olivia had never been drunk before, but she imagined it would feel something like this. Her limbs were heavy, and she was seeing double of everything.

"What happened?" Addy asked, pressing the back of her hand to Olivia's forehead, checking for a fever.

Olivia didn't feel feverish.

"I'm not sure." She shook her head.

The strange feeling was beginning to pass. Olivia stood up, leaning against her twin as another wave of dizziness turned her vision dark.

"Was it a vision?" Fred asked.

Olivia frowned, trying to remember. Something had happened. *Why was her brain moving so slowly?*

"Here, love bug." Aunt Meredith gave Olivia a glass of iced tea.

Olivia accepted it gratefully. It felt like her tongue had swollen until it barely fit in her mouth.

"Better?" Addy asked, still watching in concern as Olivia sipped her tea and tried not to drop the glass. Her fingers felt rubbery.

Olivia nodded.

"Then, I'm going after Tol," Addy said. "I don't have a good feeling about this."

"His phone is dead." Gerth came in from the other room, frowning.

Tires ground to a halt outside. A few seconds later, the front door slammed, and Erikir ran in. His shirt was plastered to his body, and perspiration dripped from his face. There was something in his eyes that Olivia had never seen before. It pulled her out of the fog she'd sunken into.

"Where's Tol?" Addy demanded, looking past him to the empty front yard.

Erikir ignored her. All of his attention was on Olivia.

"I'm so sorry," he said, his voice cracking. "I—I'm so sorry."

"Where's Tol?" Addy grabbed Erikir's shirt and shook him.

Erikir was still looking at Olivia when he said, "The general has him."

"What?!" Addy had her garden shears at Erikir's throat before anyone else could blink.

"Addy, wait." Gerth motioned to Jaxon to pull Addy away before she hurt Erikir. "What happened?"

Olivia couldn't move. She gaped at Erikir.

"I thought I was saving our people." His eyes pleaded with Olivia to understand.

She didn't.

Addy was writhing against Jaxon, who was using every ounce of his strength to keep her from killing Erikir. Olivia should have been horrified by the bloody gashes Addy's garden shears and nails were making in Jaxon's arms. Instead, she was trying to process the meaning of Erikir's apology and that look in his eyes.

Olivia stood frozen in place while Erikir explained the agreement he'd made with the general, how he'd drugged Tol, and how it had all gone wrong.

Addy was screaming and fighting against Jaxon like a wildcat. Fred had joined Jaxon, and it was still taking all of their combined strength to restrain her.

Olivia hardly noticed. Tol had gone to meet Erikir alone because she had told him to. She'd told him to trust Erikir. She was the reason why Tol was in enemy hands. If he died, it would be her fault.

"How could you?"

The words came out sounding like her mouth was stuffed full of cotton. She understood now what she was feeling. The drugs in Tol's system were somehow affecting her, too.

"Olivia, I'm sorry," Erikir said again.

"I told Tol to trust you." Her chest felt like it was compressing. "I trusted you."

He reached for her, but she backed away. She was sick at the thought of touching him. She was sick with the thought that she'd let him touch her last night, and that she'd been wanting it to happen again.

I trusted you.

"How could you?" she demanded. "He's your cousin."

"I thought I was doing the right thing for my people."

"You betrayed your people." Olivia's heart was throbbing against her ribs. It felt like it might pound right out of her chest. "You betrayed your family."

You betrayed me.

Olivia's whole body was shaking with hurt and anger.

"Forgive me. Please." Erikir's downcast eyes moved up to Olivia's face before lowering to the floor again.

"Never." She kept backing away from Erikir. "What you did is unforgivable."

She'd told the others to trust him. And now, Tol was in trouble. He might even be dying.

"Olivia, please—"

"Get away from me," she gasped. "I don't want anything to do with you ever again."

"Tell us where to find him," Gerth said, raising his voice over Addy's frantic shouts.

"I—I have no idea," Erikir said. "The general was supposed to kill him."

Addy smashed the back of her head into Jaxon's face. Jaxon cried out and let go. Addy flew across the room so fast she was a blur. She slammed Erikir against the wall of bookshelves. Books topped onto and around them, but Addy didn't even notice. She dug the blades of her shears against Erikir's throat. Blood was already soaking the collar of his shirt.

She wasn't the sister Olivia knew. The look in Addy's eyes was unfamiliar. Feral.

"I was wrong," Erikir said, his voice choked from the blades pressed against his neck. He turned his head, making the blood flow faster. "Tell Tol—"

Addy drew back her garden shears. Olivia knew her sister was about to kill him.

People were shouting, but Olivia's world narrowed to Erikir and Addy. She had less than a second to make her decision. She didn't have time to close her eyes and reach for the swirling threads of magic inside her. She reacted on instinct and thrust up her hands.

CHAPTER 35

ADDY

One second, Addy was about to kill the rat who betrayed Tol. The next, she was blasted across the room. Her back hit the far wall, and she barely managed to stay on her feet.

She was stunned into forgetting about killing Erikir…at least until she figured out what had just happened.

Livy still had her arms outstretched. Her Haze was blazing. But the part that caught Addy's attention…that part that filled her with dread…was Livy's eyes. Her twin's sweet, chocolate-brown doll's eyes had vanished. In their place were swirling pools of silver light.

When Addy tried to move forward, an invisible air current kept her in place.

Rage, confusion, and desperation pulsed through Addy.

"Let me go," she told her sister. "Livy—"

"I'm sorry, Addy, but I won't let you."

Even Livy's voice sounded different. She didn't raise her voice, but it carried and echoed in a room that didn't normally echo.

Addy could hardly process what was happening. Livy had never so much as argued with her, and she'd just *thrown* Addy across the room. *With her mind.*

"Killing people in self-defense is one thing," Livy said, her eyes still those eerie silver pools, "but he is Chosen and one of mine to protect."

He isn't mine, Addy thought, furious. *I'm Forsaken, and he's the enemy.*

The thought passed through her mind before she had time to process it.

"We'll deal with the little prick later," Gerth said. "Right now, we need to track the general down and get our boy back." He reached through the air barrier, which apparently only restricted Addy's movements, and grabbed Addy's upper arm.

"Can you sense the Forsaken?" Gerth asked.

The general had Tol. Where would she bring him? What would she do to him?

"Addy, can you sense any Forsaken?" Gerth asked again.

Addy swallowed, trying to get a handle on her panic.

"No," she said. "I can't feel them at all."

"What about you?" Nira asked Jaxon.

Jaxon shook his head. "I don't know any Forsaken besides Addy who have that ability. I can't sense my own kind any more than you can."

There wasn't time to process that strange piece of knowledge.

"If Addy can't sense them, it must mean they're already too far away," Nira said, her eyes wide with worry.

Addy was hyperventilating. Her mind filled with rivers of Erikir's blood. She felt it coating her hands. She smelled its coppery heat.

"Adelyne Deerborn, get a hold of yourself," Gerth ordered in a stern voice. "Tol needs you. Don't go falling apart on us."

Gerth was right. Addy took a deep breath and then pointed her garden shears at Erikir. She didn't say a word. She didn't have to. Her promise was clear.

"Okay," Gerth said. "Erikir, tell me everything you know about the general's plans. We need to catch up before her trail goes cold."

Gerth's voice was steady, but Addy saw the way his hands shook. Addy knew he was as much a brother to Tol as Livy was a sister to her. If they didn't get Tol back, Gerth would help Addy kill Erikir.

Not that she'd need help.

"The general came in a car and met me ten miles down the road, since I thought it would be far enough that Addy wouldn't be able to sense her." Erikir swallowed. "I have no idea where she came from or where she was going."

Addy was going to kill him. She was going to rip his head right off his body. She was going to—

"The general has a ring that protects her from Influence," Erikir continued. "I barely escaped."

Hatred constricted Addy's lungs until she couldn't breathe. She stayed where she was, because Gerth was right. There would be time for revenge later. Right now, all that mattered was getting Tol back.

Addy grabbed the keys to the Hummer and headed for the door.

"Addy, wait a second," Gerth said. "We need to think this through."

"I'm going to see if I can pick up the general's trail where she met Erikir."

If she didn't do something, she'd lose her mind.

"I think I might have a better idea."

Addy whirled on her twin, who was standing in the middle of the kitchen with her eyes closed.

"What?" Addy demanded. "Livy, what?"

"I think…."

Addy jangled the keys. She didn't have patience to spare on the best of days, and right now….

Livy's eyes snapped open.

"I can sense Tol."

CHAPTER 36

TOL

A fierce crack reverberated through Tol's skull, jolting him awake. *Two hells.*

It felt like a mallet crashing across his cheek. He forced his eyes open and caught a flash of red hair and green eyes…two traits that usually filled him with love. There was a whoosh, and then the general's palm slammed his head back into the wall.

Stars exploded at the corner of his vision.

"Wake up, Prince Tolumus."

That cold, merciless voice made Tol's skin crawl.

"General Bloodsong," Tol said, his voice sounding strange and a little slurred. "Not exactly the face I was hoping to wake up to."

Erikir's drugs hadn't done anything to Tol's memory, so he knew why he was here. He just had no idea where he was, how he'd gotten here, or how much time had passed.

His pulse quickened at the memory of Erikir luring him out to that abandoned stretch of road and handing him over to the Forsaken general.

Focus, he told himself.

"Where am I?" he asked in his most commanding voice.

A small, amused smile crossed the general's lips.

"You may be used to people following your every whim, but around here, I give the orders."

Tol's cheek felt like it was on fire.

He glanced around at his surroundings. He was in a small room with two Forsaken guards posted at the door. The air smelled like metal, cheap cleaner, and more distantly, cafeteria food.

Tol shifted and heard the clank of chains. His wrists were handcuffed in front of him. His legs were shackled, too. He reached for his vial of Source on instinct.

It was gone.

Tol felt the first icy tendrils of fear, although he made sure the emotion didn't show on his face. The general could probably sense weakness like a shark could smell blood in the water.

Tol curled his lips in distaste. "I'm not sure I'd be bragging about being in charge of this place."

Smack.

If it hadn't been for the chains holding him upright, Tol would be sprawled across the ground.

He focused on keeping his breathing even. He might be helpless, but he wouldn't let the general see him react to the pain.

"You are here for two reasons," the general said, as calmly as if they were making civil conversation. "The first is to facilitate a conversation between myself and King Rolomens, and the second is to reunite me with my daughter."

"Good luck with either of those," Tol scoffed.

The general jerked her hand up, and Tol flinched before he could stop himself. A smile crept across General Bloodsong's face. It was a twisted mockery of Addy's beautiful smile.

Tol had never felt such loathing.

"I would also like you to help explain a small mystery." The general's voice was soft, almost gentle. It put Tol on his guard more than her vicious slaps. "Six months ago, one of your people fell into my hands."

Tol stiffened. He knew the general was referring to Jariath. He was one of the Chosen guards, who had been captured by the Forsaken when he got close to discovering the general's hideout. The Forsaken had tortured the man and then left his mutilated body in Rio de Janeiro.

Tol's parents had never found out what secrets Jariath had revealed before his death.

The general casually adjusted the ring on her index finger…the one that had prevented Erikir's Influence from touching her mind. Tol was sure she hadn't had it in Alaska.

"I will commend the Chosen for one thing," the general said, still playing with her ring as she studied Tol. "You might be laughably weak in a fair fight, but if your friend was any indication, your people have quite the tolerance for pain."

Tol forced back his reaction. He wouldn't give the general the satisfaction of seeing his rage. He wouldn't give the general anything.

"My interrogators discovered that you were searching for a mortal girl," the general continued. "She was apparently very special, but your guard regrettably died before he could tell us why."

Tol forced a blank expression on his face. He didn't want the general to know she'd just divulged something important. Until this moment, Tol hadn't been sure how much the general knew about the Fount. Now, he had his answer.

The general didn't know anything. That was how he was going to keep it.

"People say lots of things when they're being tortured," Tol said with a careless shrug. "What would I have wanted with a mortal?"

It wasn't easy to hold the general's stare, but Tol refused to blink first. The general studied him for any sign of deception.

Time to pivot, as Gerth would say.

"You know," Tol said, leaning back against the wall and making a show of getting more comfortable, "if you were hoping for an invitation to Addy's and my wedding, I'm afraid you're going to have to try a little harder."

The general took another step closer. She reached up her hand, but instead of striking him again, she grabbed hold of his left shoulder. She dug her fingers under his prosthesis, clawing at the place that always caused him pain.

Tol clenched his jaw until he thought it might break.

When the general released him, her fingertips were bloody. Tol reeled back, gasping. He couldn't keep his eyes from watering.

"You're the reason why my daughter thinks her family is the enemy and her enemy is her family," the general said.

Tol thought about the way Addy had been smiling after she'd sparred with Jaxon. He remembered the way she'd literally lit up at the sight of the Supernal's stone. Even now, he remembered Jaxon saying his people would follow her as their leader. After he'd said that, there had been a moment when Addy had looked…intrigued.

"Killing Addy's *real* parents made you her enemy," Tol said, raising his voice over the uncertainty echoing in his own mind.

The general's steely gaze sharpened. Tol knew he'd angered her.

Good.

"Whatever lies you've been whispering in her ear will fall apart as soon as I get her back," she hissed.

"My fiancé isn't the type of person who can be manipulated," Tol said, noticing the redness appearing on the general's pale cheeks. He decided to press his luck. "But I think you already know that about her, don't you? If memory serves, the last time you were alone with your own daughter, she tried to kill you."

Tol pasted a smirk on his face while he studied the general, reading her expression as her calm deteriorated.

"It's a disgrace," the general snapped. "I won't allow my daughter's Forsaken blood to be tainted by yours."

Tol sensed another crack in the general's composure. He lowered his voice, like he was sharing a secret with the general.

"Frankly, I'm not sure my parents are thrilled about their grandchildren having Forsaken blood, but what are you gonna do?" Tol shrugged.

He didn't even see the general's fist flying at his face until his head was cracking back against the wall. For a second, he saw only blackness before his sight returned.

"My daughter will leave you as soon as she tires of your weakness." The general stared at Tol's prosthetic arm with open disgust.

Tol forced a smile onto his lips. "If you thought I was weak, you wouldn't have taken away my Source and chained me up."

The general lifted a shoulder. "I'm cautious."

Tol sighed and looked around, as though he had somewhere more important to be. "I don't mean to be rude, but…actually, change that." Tol gave her a hard stare. "I do mean to be rude. So, why don't you get the fu—"

"Sergeant Sentano," General Bloodsong barked.

The door to Tol's small room opened, and a Forsaken man strode in. He was so huge, he dwarfed Tol and the general. Tol readied himself for the giant warrior to begin raining blows down on him. Instead, the man handed the general a laptop before saluting and marching out of the room.

"Now, I don't suppose you want to tell me where your parents are keeping their extra Source and save me a phone call?" the general asked Tol.

Tol gave the general's nearly-empty necklace a pointed stare. "Feeling a little vulnerable?"

The general's steely gaze met Tol's. "Your people have always thought you were superior, but that's about to change. There are other powers in play that you can't begin to imagine."

"Like the Supernal?" Tol asked, feeling a moment's satisfaction at the look of surprise on the general's face.

"Yeah, we know about him," Tol continued. "He's not much good without his full abilities, though, is he?"

"He'll have his powers returned," the general said, her composure back in place. "I've discovered the stone's keeper, and now, it's just a matter of finding him. And to do that, I need more Source."

Tol's mind raced as he tried to stay one step ahead in this mental chess game. He didn't know whether it would be advantageous or harmful to tell the general his friends had Jaxon. He decided it would be better not to draw any extra attention to him.

Gods, he needed Gerth in his head right now.

"My parents will never give you our Source."

Even if we had any to spare.

"Oh, I'm sure your parents will produce their supply with the right amount of pressure."

Tol felt his anxiety spiking, even though he forced his expression to remain placid.

The general spun the laptop around so Tol could see she had pulled up Skype. Tol glanced at the number already typed in and waiting to be called. His heart stopped.

His father's private cell phone number was staring him in the face. He had no idea how the general had gotten it. At least the phone was encrypted, so the Forsaken wouldn't be able to trace the phone's location.

"Another parting gift from Jariath," the general explained in answer to Tol's unasked question. "Do you know he actually had *King Rolomens* as the contact name?" She smirked.

"Leave my parents out of this," Tol said, hearing the fear in his own voice.

Olivia's latest vision came back to him.

There were at least a hundred armed Forsaken, and the general was the one leading them to your house, she'd said.

Was the general going to try to use Tol to discover the location of his family's manor? The barbarians could beat him to death before he'd say a word that would endanger his people.

The general tapped the green icon, and a dial tone came through the laptop's speakers.

The screen flickered, and Tol's face appeared on the webcam. Horror flooded his system as he realized what the general was doing. Just as the call connected, Tol thrust his chained wrists at the computer, trying to knock it from the general's hands.

"Who is this?"

Tol's father's voice filled the small room as the laptop went flying. The general reached out and caught it before it hit the ground and cracked.

She gave Tol a look that promised retribution before turning her attention on the screen. She kept the screen facing her. Tol's pulse raced as he tried to think of what to do. If only he had a drop of Source. If only he had a fraction of the power that had existed in his veins on Vitaquias without Source….

Maybe there was another way.

He forced down his panic, blocking out his father's angry voice. He turned so he was facing the wall. It would only buy him a few seconds before the Forsaken forced him around, but he needed a chance to think of something. He closed his eyes.

Olivia, he thought. *Are you there?*

She appeared at the far end of a dark tunnel. Her light was weak, and Tol knew a vast distance separated them.

Tol?

Olivia's voice came inside his head.

I need help.

Tol was forced out of that place inside his mind when something hard cracked against his spine.

"Pay attention," one of the Forsaken standing behind him ordered.

"King Rolomens. I am requesting a small trade," the general said, while Tol tried to breathe through the pain. "Every drop of Source your people possess. In exchange for your son's life."

No.

Olivia, Tol thought desperately.

He couldn't get back to that place in his mind. Too much else was happening.

"You will pay for making idle threats against my family, Lezha," Tol's father said.

"There is nothing idle about this threat, Rolomens," the general replied, her voice like a sliver of glass.

Tol felt hands grabbing his arm and the back of his neck. They forced him to turn around.

He fought against them, but his physical strength was no match for the Forsaken. They wrenched his right arm behind his back and locked his head in place by gripping the back of his neck.

There was nothing Tol could do, nowhere he could go. The general spun the computer around so it would capture Tol's face.

"Say hello to your father, Prince Tolumus."

CHAPTER 37

ADDY

Addy drove like a she was a champion race car driver in the Daytona 500. Except her adrenaline had been replaced with anxiety. And no matter how fast she drove, it wasn't nearly fast enough.

Normally, hurtling down the road at a hundred miles an hour would make her feel like she was at least doing something. But now that she had the ability to create a portal to anywhere in a matter of seconds, driving didn't have the same appeal. Especially not when Tol's life was at stake.

It was late morning on the eighteenth, which meant they wouldn't make it to the San Francisco bar where the Supernal would be this afternoon. Addy had expected an argument about whether to go after Tol or the Supernal, but no one had questioned her decision. Jaxon had seemed like he wanted to argue, but he'd taken one look at Addy's face and kept his mouth shut.

Addy couldn't bring herself to care about the Supernal or anything else right now. All that mattered was rescuing Tol.

Livy had the vaguest sense of the path Tol had traveled, but she couldn't get a clear enough image to see where he was now. Without a specific location, Addy had nowhere to create a portal to. So, here they were, racing through Corpus Christi toward the Gulf of Mexico.

"Get off here," Livy said.

There was screeching, both from tires on the asphalt and Nira in the backseat, as Addy cut the wheel. She didn't slow down.

"Have you talked to Tol again?" Addy couldn't help asking.

Livy shook her head, keeping her eyes closed. A sheen of sweat covered her brow, and her face was drained of color. "He's conscious, but I think he's…busy."

Busy? What did that mean? Was the general threatening him? Hurting him?

"Olivia, you need to rest," Erikir said.

They were the first words he'd spoken since Livy stopped Addy from killing him. They'd brought the traitor because no one wanted to let him out of their sight, and because Addy was looking forward to murdering him after they'd rescued Tol. It was obvious from the mournful expression on the weasel's face that he didn't have any more plans to betray them.

"Shut up," everyone except Livy snarled.

Livy was concentrating again and didn't seem to hear anything that was going on around her.

"She'll burn herself out if she keeps pushing herself like this," Erikir said.

"Don't pretend to care about my sister," Addy snapped.

"It's touching how concerned you are," Gerth added, "but did it ever occur to you what would happen to Olivia if the general made good on her promise and killed Tol?"

Killed Tol.

Just hearing those two words together were enough to drive Addy insane.

"They may not be blood married," Gerth continued, "but the Celestial's power connects them. I imagine if Tol died, so would Olivia."

Addy's breathing turned to short gasps.

"I didn't think—" Erikir began.

"No, you didn't," Gerth retorted.

"Faster, you hunk of metal," Addy yelled at the Hummer.

She was grateful beyond words for the connection between Livy and Tol. If it wasn't there, she'd be driving around with no destination. Still, all of this would be so much easier if Addy was the one connected to Tol on a telepathic level. She should be. She *would* be, just as soon as Livy was strong enough to make Addy the Fount.

They were driving over a causeway now, and there was water on both sides. Addy gripped the steering wheel and stared straight ahead. Normally, she'd be shaking and hyperventilating by now, but she kept a tight leash on her fear. Even her lifelong terror of drowning was no match for her desperation to rescue Tol. She'd swim down to the bottom of the ocean if that's what it took to get him back.

"He's on a boat," Livy said. "Moving away from land."

"Head toward the marina," Jaxon told Addy.

They had debated whether or not to bring Jaxon, since it was a risk to have him anywhere near the Forsaken. In the end, Jaxon had been the one to suggest using himself as a distraction while they rescued Tol. Addy didn't fully understand why Jaxon would put himself at risk for all of them, but she was grateful nonetheless.

Right now, Addy couldn't even think about the Supernal or the mortal world going up in flames. She couldn't think about anything except Tol.

Addy drove right onto the pier. She slammed on the brakes, and they all got out of the Hummer.

"Hey, you can't park here," someone yelled.

"Tow it!" Addy shouted.

She sprinted toward a sleek speedboat bobbing in the water.

Addy reached the end of the pier and looked down at the water. The murky shallows quickly turned blue-black, hinting at their endless depths. She felt her breathing sharpen.

"It's okay, Addy," Livy said. She took Addy's hand and squeezed.

Addy sucked in a ragged breath.

For Tol. Do it for Tol.

She jumped off the dock and into the boat, gritting her teeth as the flimsy thing rocked back and forth.

For Tol. For Tol.

Fred was already bent under the steering wheel and pulling wires out from behind the key ignition. He twisted a red and blue wire together, and then touched the open wires against a third. The boat thrummed to life beneath them.

"How did you do that?" Nira asked, sounding more impressed than Addy had ever heard her.

"I just—"

Fred's explanation was lost as Addy pushed the throttle.

"Hold on!" she yelled.

Fred whooped as the boat shot through the water.

"Slow down!" Nira called.

Addy glanced back at the other girl, smiled, and then pushed the throttle up as far as it would go.

They were going so fast the boat skimmed over the water. The bow was tilted up, and the salty mist sprayed across her face.

Addy wasn't scared. She was driving too fast to be scared. It was like all those times when she and Fred had raced their parents' trucks down abandoned roads late at night…except this was so much better. She laughed. The wind tore the sound away as they cut through the waves.

Get your affairs in order, Lezha Bloodsong. I'm coming for you.

Addy saw something massive appear in the distance at the same time Gerth shouted, "Is that where we're going?"

Livy gave them a thumbs-up with one hand as she hung onto the side of the boat with the other. Addy craned her neck to get a better look as their boat continued to race forward.

It was still far in the distance, but there was no mistaking their destination. It was an aircraft carrier.

CHAPTER 38

OLIVIA

Something was happening to Olivia. She'd been digging deeper and pushing farther into her abyss of magic to find Tol. She'd ignored barriers and ledges that had frightened her before. She hadn't asked for anyone's help. She hadn't needed it.

Olivia knew if she couldn't find Tol, no one could.

She hadn't needed Erikir's embrace or gifts of chocolate or betrayal. She'd needed only her connection with Tol and the power inside her.

Instead of drawing her into a vortex of power that would swallow her forever, Olivia found a sense of balance she'd never felt before. Raw strength roiled under her skin.

She was on the brink of some kind of tipping point.

She could sense she was approaching the moment when she would be able to access the full extent of her abilities. And that meant she was approaching the moment when she'd choose to give her powers to Addy.

Olivia wasn't afraid…not really. She was as determined as ever to end Addy and Tol's nightmare and give them the power to save the Chosen. That was the part she focused on. She tried not to think about the price she was going to pay to make it happen.

Olivia loved her life, but she loved her sister more.

The closer they got to the aircraft carrier, the more certain she became that something was wrong. Olivia could sense Tol's anger and desperation growing stronger by the minute. Whatever was going on with him, there was no time to waste. She didn't need to tell Addy that, though. If her sister pushed the boat any faster, Olivia was afraid they'd all be sucked off from the sheer force of the wind.

Addy slowed when they neared a party boat, which was anchored a short distance from the aircraft carrier. Music blasted from the boat's speakers, and there were whoops and cheers as bikini-clad women jumped off the side. It seemed inconceivable that people could be doing things like drinking beer and floating on inflatable lounge chairs, when their entire world was on the brink of destruction.

Olivia stared up at the aircraft carrier in front of them.

This was it. This was the boat from all of her visions. She had seen Addy falling from this monstrous ship.

"Addy—" she began.

Her head snapped back. A blinding pain ripped through her skull.

"Olivia?"

She heard Erikir's anxious voice, but for several seconds, she couldn't see. Then, someone punched her in the face again. And again.

"Livy!" Addy called.

Olivia tried to sit down, but she missed the seat and collapsed on the floor of the boat. Her sight flickered, and she saw Tol. He was on the ground beside her. Blood was streaming down his face. He was shouting at a computer, but Olivia couldn't make out his words. The fist came flying at her—his—face again, and she was thrust back onto her own boat.

"Livy, what's happening?" Addy demanded, her eyes wide with worry.

Gasping, Olivia raised her hands to her face. The sticky blood she'd been expecting to feel wasn't there. Neither was the swelling. But her head pounded and she felt sick to her stomach.

She looked at Addy. She didn't want to tell her sister, but she knew she couldn't lie.

"I think the general's beating Tol."

The look in Addy's eyes was pure violence. It was the same expression Addy had worn when the Forsaken attacked Aunt Meredith's house, and again when Erikir told them about what he'd done.

Olivia loved everything about her sister…except for that look. It was wild and terrible and full of malice.

"Don't freak out, Ads," Fred said, reaching out as if to pat her back before thinking better of it. "We need a plan."

"Then, think of one fast," Addy said through gritted teeth.

"On it." Gerth put a fist to his temple and cursed under his breath in the way he did when his mind was going a thousand miles an hour.

"How in the two hells are we supposed to get on that ship without anyone seeing us?" Nira demanded.

"There could be hundreds of Forsaken and thousands of mortals on board," Jaxon said. "If we wait until night—"

"No," Addy said. "We're getting Tol out now."

"I agree." Gerth put up a placating hand. "But it's not like we can just climb on board."

"You said the general wanted Addy, right?" Jaxon asked Erikir.

Erikir nodded.

Olivia looked away from Erikir before he tried to catch her eye. Right now, all her focus needed to be on Tol. She couldn't let herself look at Erikir. She couldn't think about how he'd duped her. She wouldn't.

"The other option is for Addy to go on board first," Jaxon said reluctantly.

When they all just stared at him, he continued.

"No one will hurt her, since she's General Bloodsong's daughter. The rest of us can climb up while Addy keeps everyone on deck busy."

"That's good thinking," Gerth said, nodding along with Jaxon's every word. "Once we're on board, we can split up. Livy can bring some of us to get Tol out, and the rest can help Addy distract the Forsaken."

"Works for me." Addy felt her back pocket, where Olivia could see the outline of her garden shears through the denim. "See you soon."

Before Olivia could ask what Addy was doing, she saw her twin jump into the water.

"You don't know how to swim," Olivia gasped. Her sister's paralyzing fear of the water had made swim lessons impossible growing up.

"All Forsaken know how to swim," Jaxon said at the same moment that Addy said, "I do now."

Olivia didn't have time to fully appreciate her sister's own power or the amount of love that had gotten Addy into the ocean without having a panic attack.

"I think we should leave Fred and Jaxon on the boat," Nira said, her brow furrowed in worry. "We can't afford to let the Forsaken get anywhere near the Supernal's powers, and Fred is—"

"I ain't weak or useless." Fred crossed his arms and glared. "The last time everyone got locked in a Forsaken prison, I was the one who got us out."

"I agree about Jaxon," Gerth said.

Jaxon's serious gaze met Gerth's for several heartbeats. They seemed to have some kind of silent exchange before Jaxon nodded.

"It's safer if the Forsaken don't know I'm here," he conceded, although Olivia could tell he hated the idea of being left behind. "I can stay on the other side of the party boat, where none of the Forsaken will be able to see me.

"We'll be back for you as soon as we have Tol," Gerth told Jaxon. To Addy, who was treading water next to the boat, he said, "As soon as you're on board, we'll come over."

"Be careful," Olivia added, even though she knew it was a stupid thing to say. Addy was swimming to an aircraft carrier filled with thousands of enemies.

What she really wanted to say was *don't go!*

Olivia hadn't stopped thinking about that sandy shore and Addy's gut-wrenching sobs from her vision. That moment was connected with this ship. If Olivia's suspicions were accurate, it meant that she didn't have much time left.

CHAPTER 39

TOL

Tol's head jerked back as the Forsaken man struck his jaw. He heard his mother's screams coming from the computer, and that was enough for him to keep his hold on reality.

"Mum, hang up the phone." His words were a little garbled from the blood and swelling.

His parents were crumbling at the sight of their son being bloodied at the hands of their worst enemy.

"They aren't going to kill me." He winced as a fist came at his stomach. *Not yet, anyway.*

"Hang up," he gasped. "Don't give her anything."

Her. General Lezha Bloodsong.

"Have you changed your mind about the Source?" the general asked, her tone placid.

"I told you," the king said in a desperate voice. "We used all of the reserves. Our people have twenty drops apiece. There isn't any more."

The general nodded at the Forsaken soldier standing in front of Tol.

This time, the man didn't hit Tol. He grabbed Tol's throat and started to squeeze.

Tol felt the instinctive panic that came with losing one's oxygen supply. He forgot how useless it was to struggle against these warriors. He flailed, even though the Forsaken man's grip never faltered. Tol's sight began to dim.

"We don't have any more Source, but I'll give you something else." Tol's father's words ran together in his haste. "I'll give you something better. I'll tell you about the Celestial's Fount."

"The Celestial's Fount? I haven't heard of such a thing." The general's gaze slid to Tol. "Does this have anything to do with the mortal girl you were searching for?"

"Yes." The king's voice cracked. "I'll tell you everything about her. Just let our son go."

The grip on Tol's throat eased, and with it, the meaning behind those words made it into his oxygen-starved brain.

"No." The word rasped from Tol's throat.

Tol choked and leaked blood onto the soldiers' polished boots as his parents told the general about Olivia and her power.

"Mum, stop!"

Tol shouted himself hoarse, but it didn't do any good. His parents spoke until every secret about the Fount was laid out at the general's feet. He saw the general's green eyes brighten. He saw the cogs turn in her head.

"General Bloodsong."

A different Forsaken was standing in the doorway, his gaze fixed on the general as he held a salute.

"Speak," the general barked.

"Your daughter is here."

Tol saw a glimmer of emotion on the general's face before she replaced it with a mask of indifference. Tol felt the stutter of his own heart.

Addy was here.

The general slammed the laptop closed and passed it to one of the men whose fists were covered in Tol's blood. "Get a team together. The Supernal will want this Fount to be ready and waiting as soon as his powers are returned."

"No." Tol was desperate. "My mum's lying. There's no way back to Vitaquias. There's no such thing as the Fount."

The general turned toward the Forsaken soldier still standing in the doorway without so much as acknowledging anything Tol had just said. "Where is my daughter?"

"She's on the upper deck, ma'am. She insists you speak with her alone. She says she has…demands." The Forsaken man winced, like he was expecting a blow.

If Tol wasn't so panicked by what his parents had just revealed, he would have smiled at that. Only Addy would face a whole army of Forsaken and have the gall to make demands.

The general spun on her heel and marched down the passageway.

Tol had to get out of here…wherever *here* was. Now.

He forced all of those thoughts aside. It was the first time in what felt like hours that he was left alone. He'd be able to panic later. Right now, he needed to concentrate.

Tol turned his attention inward, searching for that mental connection he shared with Olivia.

Are you there?

He felt her presence immediately. She was close enough that he could reach out one of his lightning-bright hands and touch her.

Hold on, Tol. We're coming for you, Olivia's voice replied in his mind.

No. He didn't try to hide his frantic thoughts. *The Forsaken know about you. You have to get as far away from here as you can.*

Olivia sent him something that felt like a wave of calm. Tol tried to shove it aside, but the cloud enveloped his mind. His worry slipped away.

This place is crawling with Forsaken, he told her. *You better have a plan.*

He felt, rather than saw, Olivia's smile.

Trust me, we do.

CHAPTER 40

ADDY

Why hello, Mommy Dearest," Addy said. She gave the general her best impression of a crocodile smile.

This woman had imprisoned Tol. She was torturing him. Addy was going to kill the bitch.

"Daughter, we need to talk," the general replied. She moved slowly, like she expected Addy to bolt.

Oh, I'm not going anywhere, she thought.

"I'm feeling a little squirrely with all of your people running around. Tell them to go inside, and then we'll talk."

Addy was expecting some kind of negotiation, but the general gave the order. Within seconds, the upper deck was cleared.

The aircraft carrier had looked massive from afar, but now that she was here, it felt even larger. She was almost dizzy with its sheer magnitude. Several small planes were parked on top, and with the whole deck empty of people, it looked more like a floating metal island than a ship.

The acrid scent of fuel and hum of various engines surrounded her. She should have been freezing with the way the wind passed through her sodden clothes, but her veins were full of molten fury. Her biggest challenge would be not killing the general the first chance she got.

"Keep your hands where I can see them," Addy said as the general approached. "And don't even think about taking any Source."

Addy's fighting skills had improved thanks to Jaxon, but she didn't want to take her chances with the general hopped up on Source.

Addy waited until the general was only steps away. Then, Addy shoved her. She took advantage of the general's imbalance and brought her garden shears to the woman's neck.

"I don't want to hurt you," the general said. Her voice was steady despite the weapon at her throat.

Too bad the feeling isn't mutual, Mommy Dearest.

"Where's Tol?" Addy demanded.

The general's muscles were relaxed, and she seemed in no hurry to get away.

"If you harm me, my soldiers will ensure you never see that boy again," the general warned.

"Oh, I'll get him back," Addy promised. "The only question is will it be before or after I kill every single person on this ship?"

"Daughter, listen to me—"

"I am *not* your daughter," Addy snapped. "I had parents…a family. They're dead because of you."

Addy's hand jerked, and a trickle of blood zig-zagged down the general's neck.

"They stole you from me." The general's nostrils flared. "For eighteen years, I searched the mortal world for you. My lieutenants were convinced you'd died in the portal. But I felt you." The general raised a hand and pressed it over her heart.

"Are you really trying to get sympathy from me?" Addy was incredulous.

"You were barely a week old when the Chosen forced us all to flee from Vitaquias," the general continued, unbothered by Addy's scorn or the shears pressed to her neck. "I was still suffering from blood and Source loss from your birth."

There was frustration in the general's voice, but her face revealed no emotion.

This sob story could just be a ploy to distract or manipulate her, but Addy didn't think so. The general prided herself on her strength. She wouldn't fabricate weakness where it hadn't existed.

Addy didn't want to have anything in common with this monster of a woman. She didn't want to feel anything except loathing for the general.

Sue and Gary Deerborn. Stacy. Rosie. Lucy.

Addy said the names of her dead family in her mind. She pictured their smiling faces.

She remembered finding them on the kitchen floor, their clothes soaking up the blood that had drained from their bodies.

They had been killed because the general was searching for Addy.

The general's steady gaze met Addy's. "The Celestial made sure the Chosen accessed the portal first. I was trying to help the rest of our people escape."

"How touching," Addy deadpanned.

"I did everything I could to protect you. You were the one good thing to come out of a nightmare."

A glimmer of emotion flashed through the general's eyes. Addy searched for something to say that would keep the woman preoccupied until her friends snuck on board.

"You mean the ruin of Vitaquias?" Addy asked, even though she could somehow sense that wasn't what her mother was talking about.

"No." The general lifted her chin, but she kept her gaze fixed straight ahead rather than turning to look at Addy. "I didn't intend to become pregnant."

Addy spoke around the inexplicable lump that had formed in her throat, wondering why she cared. "I get it. One too many drops of Source, a candlelit dinner, and nine months later, a Forsaken baby comes along…."

"No, Adelyne."

It was the first time Addy could remember the general using her name, and for some reason, it stopped her next sarcastic comment before it tumbled out.

The general took a deep breath. Addy felt the woman's throat press up against the point of Addy's shears, but the general didn't even seem to notice.

"Your conception was not…consensual."

Addy almost lost her hold on the shears.

She couldn't form words. When she'd first learned the general was her birth mother, Addy had asked who her father was. The general said he wasn't in the picture, and Addy had been so determined to distance herself from the general and the rest of the Forsaken that she'd never given another thought to who her father might be.

Was he still alive?

Addy gagged on the acid that was rising in her throat.

To think someone had forced her mother…that Addy was the product of rape….

Addy looked at the most fearsome warrior in a race of warriors. She couldn't imagine a man strong enough to force this woman to do anything.

"Who?" Addy choked on the word. "Who is the father?"

She couldn't bring herself to say *my* father. It was too horrible to contemplate.

The general shook her head. "That is a secret I intend to take to my grave."

Addy was shaking her head. "How?"

The general's lip quirked in a mockery of a smile. "Let's just say I'll always be weak against this particular man."

Addy felt her lungs compressing. It was bad enough when she'd discovered she was the daughter of a murderer. But to be the daughter of a rapist….

Addy Deerborn. She was Addy Deerborn, the daughter of two corn farmers who had loved each other and wanted her.

Except, she wasn't.

As Addy looked at the general, she tried to ignore the sympathy worming its way inside her heart. The general hadn't just needed to survive the destruction on Vitaquias. She'd been trying to save her newborn daughter and an entire race of people who had no one else to fight for them.

"I don't want your pity," the general said in a harsh tone. "I only want you to understand the choice I've made."

"Choice?" Addy asked. "What choice?"

Addy's heart and mind were racing. She needed her sister. She needed Tol. Once she had them at her side, everything would start making sense again.

"I am going to find the stone's keeper so the Supernal can become the force of power and destruction he was made to be," the general said. "Then, he will return our strength and immortality. We will never be weak or vulnerable to the Chosen people's greed again."

"Sounds like an epic plan," Addy mocked. "If only you knew where that magical stone was hiding."

The general's eyes—the ones Addy shared—hardened.

"You know where the stone is."

"You betcha." Addy gave her mother a sly grin. "And let me just tell you that you will *never* find it."

Addy had to stop herself from glancing in the direction of the party boat, which was within view of the aircraft carrier. Her hands had started to sweat.

Come on, Livy!

Once the rest of the group arrived, they'd free Tol, and then Addy would kill the general like she'd planned.

"Don't make the mistake of underestimating me, daughter," the general said in an icy calm.

"Don't *you* make the mistake of underestimating *me*." Addy tightened her grip on her garden shears.

Addy caught movement out of the corner of her eye.

Finally.

Fred, followed by Gerth and Livy, had just reached the top deck. Addy pivoted, using the shears at her mother's—the general's—neck to keep her facing in the other direction. Nira and Erikir popped their heads up next, and Addy gestured to all of them to hide on the far side of the giant radar tower. Livy and Gerth went one way. Everyone else went another.

Addy waited until they were all out of sight before she said, "Bring your soldiers up here. I want to get a good look at the people you think I belong to."

Addy's heart stalled while she waited to see if her mother would give the order. She did.

"You must put away your weapon," the general said.

Addy didn't move. Army boots pounded up metal ladders from the lower decks.

"You are either with me or against me," the general said. "Decide quickly. I will not be made to appear weak in front of my own people."

The first soldiers emerged on deck.

Before Addy knew what was happening, the general's elbow was in her ribs. Addy twisted to protect herself from another blow, but she wasn't fast enough. Her mother's forearm crashed into her wrist. Even without Source, the general was stronger…faster…better.

Addy let out a choked breath as her garden shears went skittering across the deck. Addy struck out with her fists, but the general wound an arm around Addy, locking her body in place.

Don't panic, she told herself.

As soon as the general lowered her guard, Addy would be able to repay the favor. She and Jaxon had practiced for this. She had a whole arsenal of new moves she hadn't had the last time she and the general met. She forced herself to relax in her mother's iron grip.

As each military-clad, inhumanly muscled Forsaken came onto the flight deck, Addy's heart sank a little more. There were so many of them.

"Take a look around you, Daughter. These are the survivors. They are the future…a future I want you to share."

Addy felt something spike in her chest, like a shot of adrenaline, at being surrounded by so many of the Forsaken. With the exception of Jaxon, she'd never been around Forsaken without trying to kill them.

She was unprepared for the sense of rightness she felt in their presence. The beast insider her was awake, but it wasn't howling at her to fight and kill. It was…content.

"So, what do you think?" the general asked in her ear.

"I think," Addy replied in the same whisper, "that I'd rather take my chances with the Chosen."

The general turned to look at Addy, loosening her hold just a fraction. It was enough.

"Now!" Addy yelled at the top of her voice.

She thrust her head back, smashing her skull into the general's face. Fred, Nira, and Erikir leapt out of their hiding places.

Chaos erupted.

CHAPTER 41

OLIVIA

Olivia and Gerth were in an airplane hangar…on a boat. Gerth could barely hold back his excitement. Olivia could tell it was only his worry for Tol that had him walking through the hangar without stopping to study its every feature.

Olivia wouldn't have minded a leisurely tour of a ship that was large enough to hold airplanes in its belly…if Tol's life and the fate of Earth weren't hanging in the balance.

Olivia heard footsteps.

They crouched behind one of the planes moments before a dozen Forsaken strode past them.

"Close one," Gerth whispered.

They stayed in place while twenty more of the brutal warriors passed, their expressions so blank it made Olivia shiver. Each of them reminded her of the ones who had captured her and murdered her family.

Were her family's killers on this ship now?

"Hey." Gerth nudged her with his shoulder. "We've got this."

She gave him a shaky nod as she let out the breath she'd been holding. They had a job to do, and she couldn't afford to let her emotions go flying in a thousand different directions. She needed to keep her mind empty of everything except for her connection with Tol.

Now that they were in such close proximity, Olivia didn't even need to close her eyes. Tol was right there in her mind. She could sense his thoughts as clearly as if he were standing right beside her.

Tol didn't know where he was on the ship. He'd sent her a telepathic image of the tiny room where he was chained. Olivia saw the two Forsaken standing guard by the door, but that didn't help narrow down Tol's location. He could be anywhere on this ship. Olivia followed the thread connecting their minds, letting it tell her whether they were getting closer or farther.

It was like playing the least fun game of Hot and Cold.

The guards had eased up on their beating, but every few minutes, one of them would slam their fist into Tol's face or stomach. Olivia felt every blow like she was the one being struck. At one point, all of the air rushed out of her lungs. Her legs gave out, and she would have cracked her head on a pipe if Gerth hadn't grabbed her.

Hang on, Tol.

They were so close. She could feel it. Just as they rounded another corner, her connection to Tol snuffed out. Olivia panicked.

"Gerth, I can't—"

Did they kill him? No….

"What is it?" Gerth whispered, grabbing her arm when she didn't immediately respond.

A shuddering breath. A whisper in her mind.

Olivia's knees went weak with relief. *Not dead.*

"I think Tol's unconscious." She chewed on her bottom lip in worry. "I can't feel him well enough to find him."

Gerth's face paled, but Olivia saw him bury his own panic so he could think.

"You said we were close, right?" Gerth looked down at the blueprints he'd downloaded on his phone. "And we've already searched all the passages around here."

He looked up at Olivia. There was a knowing twinkle in his eye. "I think we're on the wrong level."

Voices and stomping boots announced they were about to have company, and they were standing right in the middle of a narrow corridor with nowhere to hide.

"Head for the lift," Gerth whispered. "I'll get rid of them."

"The what?"

"Elevator. Whatever." Gerth rolled his eyes as he slipped a drop of Addy's blood between his lips. His Haze brightened, and then he was gone.

Olivia crept forward in the direction Gerth had indicated. She rounded the corner and found a bank of elevators.

She was too worried about who might come out of the elevator when it stopped on their level to really appreciate the fact that she was on a boat that was big enough for elevators.

She pressed against the wall and tried to make herself as small as possible when the doors opened. No one came out, but footsteps pounded against the corridor where Olivia had just been. Someone was heading her way.

Gerth, or one of the Forsaken?

Olivia's heart was in her throat.

"What are you waiting for?" Gerth demanded, skidding around the corner and into the elevator. "Let's go."

When the elevator—*lift*—doors opened back up, they found themselves in a mess hall…filled with people.

Soldiers were sitting at tables and milling around with plates of food in their hands. The hum of conversation cut off as everyone in the room caught sight of Olivia and Gerth.

Too late, it occurred to Olivia that they should have found some army fatigues to steal so they'd blend in.

"Mortals," Gerth said, already unstopping his vial of Source and measuring out another drop of blood.

"Let me help." Olivia eyed the roomful of people.

"You're going to need your strength for more important things." Gerth swallowed the drop. "Go find our boy. I'll catch up with you in a bit."

He addressed his next words to the crowd of soldiers in the mess hall, who were looking from Olivia and Gerth to each other as they tried to figure out what to do. "Alright. Which one of you is in charge?"

Gerth didn't have the power to Influence this many people. The few soldiers sitting nearest to Gerth locked their gazes on his, but the rest seemed as confused as ever. Some of them were reaching for their weapons.

Olivia moved to Gerth's side.

"What are you doing?" he hissed.

"What does it look like?" she replied. "You can't handle all of them on your own."

Gerth hesitated, but they both knew she was right.

She closed her eyes. Olivia felt for the filaments of magic inside her, which were no longer buried in a bottomless, black ocean. Instead, they floated on top. She plucked the strand she needed. She saw all of the mortals' consciousnesses hovering above them like a candle's flame. In comparison, her mind was an inferno.

Her light moved over to make room for another, which was just as blinding.

Tol.

"I found him," Olivia gasped.

Tol was no more than a hundred feet to her left.

"Go. Livy, go!"

She turned and began to run. She kept all of her attention on her bond with Tol. She couldn't risk losing sight of him again…not now, when they were so close.

She barreled around the corner and ricocheted off something solid.

Not something, Olivia realized. *Someone.*

Her hold on her power faltered as she stared up at the immovable body before her. Her gaze met the gray, pitiless eyes of one of the Forsaken. And not just any Forsaken. He was one of the warriors who had stormed into her house and slaughtered her family before her eyes. He'd been the one to kill Stacy and Rosie. Olivia would never forget the way he'd smiled as he broke their necks.

"Never thought I'd see you again."

The man gave her that same smile…the one she'd seen a hundred times in her nightmares.

He raised a butcher knife. *Was it the same one that had been used to kill her parents?* Its metal blade gleamed in the light of her Haze.

Olivia screamed.

CHAPTER 42

TOL

Tol's eyes flew open as Olivia's scream echoed in his own mind…and down the nearest corridor. She was here. And she was in trouble.

His two Forsaken guards, who had been amusing themselves by using Tol as their personal punching bag, stopped hitting him. One of them stayed inside the room, while the other ran down the hall.

Tol fought against his chains. The Forsaken slammed him back against the wall.

His back hit the unforgiving metal hard enough that he should have slumped to the ground, especially in his weakened state. He stayed standing, though, and that's when he felt it.

Power.

His Haze wasn't any brighter than usual, but when he turned his attention to that place inside his mind, he saw Olivia burning like a live, golden flame. And he saw her terror.

It wasn't his strength he was sensing. It was hers. Her magic boiled and churned, like it was about to spill over. There was so much of it. Tol reached inside his mind, expecting the power to be just beyond his reach. It wasn't.

He dipped his hand in, pulling out fistfuls of magic. It soaked into his veins and crowded his mind until there wasn't room for anything else. He was overwhelmed by all the power.

Olivia screamed again. Tol didn't think about what he was doing. He let her strength combine with his own. Then, without so much as raising a finger, he broke the shackles binding his wrists.

Tol heard the metallic snap, which was followed by a weightlessness around his right wrist.

"What the hells?" the Forsaken demanded.

Tol opened his eyes. He didn't have to move a muscle to fling the Forsaken man across the room. The man hit the wall with a sickening thud. The force of it was stronger than any blow Tol had been dealt. The warrior slid to the ground and didn't move again.

Tol didn't give his captor another thought as he focused his attention on the chains around his ankles. This time, instead of tearing the metal apart, the power inside him gathered itself into tiny atoms of golden light. The light particles rearranged themselves until they resembled the shape of a key. The key fitted itself into the lock on his left ankle and turned. The cuff sprung open.

Tol kicked the shackles away and ran toward Olivia.

He saw the butcher knife in his mind before he rounded the corner. He raised his hand, and the Forsaken man's arm stopped mid-swing.

The image, which existed only in his mind as a swirl of darkness and golden light, became a reality as soon as Tol entered the next corridor. Olivia was ducking out from underneath the Forsaken soldier's arm, which was still frozen in mid-air.

"You okay?" Tol asked. He grabbed Olivia and pulled her away from the Forsaken in case the man regained control over his limbs.

"He's the one," Olivia said. Her lips were white, and she was shaking so badly her teeth were chattering. "Stacy and Rosie."

Tol knew those names, but it was the image in Olivia's mind—now in his mind—that showed him how the warrior had killed those two girls.

Tol had seen their small bodies on the linoleum floor himself. Their necks had been broken. They had died trying to shield their youngest sister, who was killed last. Her throat had been sliced open.

If Addy was here now, she would have grabbed the man's weapon and carved out his heart while he was still frozen in place. But Addy wasn't here. Olivia was.

Tol didn't have to ask if she wanted to kill the man herself. Olivia didn't have that kind of violence inside her.

He did.

"Kill yourself," Tol commanded the Forsaken soldier. Then, at the memory of Addy and Olivia's younger sisters lying in a pool of blood, he amended his command. "Slowly."

Tol pushed Olivia down the corridor in front of him, blocking her view of the act that sent a spray of blood splattering across the walls.

He followed Olivia until they reached a mess hall, which was filled with people. He glanced around and saw Gerth, who had two Forsaken standing in front of him. They were shielding him from at least a hundred mortal soldiers. The mortals were shouting and brandishing their weapons.

Gerth's Haze was dim, and Tol could see the sweat gathering on his best mate's forehead.

Tol saw the minds of every mortal in the room.

Weak, his magic thought.

Tol hadn't felt this much power since he was on Vitaquias. The more he drew, the stronger he became.

With a mental nudge, Tol sent the mortals who were about to reach Gerth sliding back across the floor. They would have gone farther and more violently, but Olivia pulled on the threads of Tol's magic, tempering the force of his will.

Innocent, her anxious voice said into his mind.

While Tol's magic was like a bulldozer, Olivia manipulated her power the way a musician played her instrument. She wove filaments of magic in and around the mortals, until they were sitting complacently at their tables and smiling as though nothing were amiss. Not a drop of blood had been spilled, and not a single one of the mortals glanced their way.

"Mate!" Gerth, shaking off his exhaustion, gave Tol a back-slapping hug. "You look terrible."

Tol grinned, feeling more like himself as the magic in Olivia's blood quieted.

"Where's Addy?" he asked.

"Up top." Gerth motioned for them to follow him. "Come on."

CHAPTER 43

OLIVIA

Olivia was still marveling over the fact that she had found Tol— and that they were in one piece—when she stepped onto the flight deck.

An arcing torrent of water almost shot her right off the side of the ship. "Sorry!" Fred's voice called from nearby.

Olivia exchanged a look with her companions, and then she peeked out while keeping her body safely behind the wall of the elevator.

A surprised laugh escaped her. Fred, holding a massive fire hose, was blasting Forsaken right off the deck before they even had a chance to use their glowing blue weapons.

"Come on," Gerth said, running into the fray. Tol was right behind him.

Nearby, Nira was standing with her arms crossed while two Forsaken defended her. The men were clearly under her Influence, since they were battling their own people. Erikir was Influencing three Forsaken who were fighting alongside Nira's.

Olivia's heart flew into her throat at the sight of Addy, her shears meeting the general's knife blow for blow. Their weapons moved so fast Olivia's eyes couldn't keep track of them.

For a moment, she didn't know what to do. There were Forsaken everywhere, and more were flooding onto the deck with each passing second. Their Hazes all surged as they consumed drops of Source.

Olivia imagined a single punch from one of them would be enough to crush her skull.

She stopped gawking at the pandemonium when she caught sight of a Forsaken nocking an arrow in his bow. He was aiming for Fred.

Olivia shouted a warning, but Fred probably couldn't hear anything over the rush of the water shooting from his hose. She raised her hands and felt the corresponding surge of power. Just before the soldier released the arrow, he jerked his arm up and shot his weapon straight into the sky.

The Forsaken warrior looked at Olivia. With a feral cry, he raced for her.

Olivia didn't think. She drew on the magic she knew was inside her and thrust the man back. The cyclone of wind that had emerged from her own mind was now dragging the Forsaken higher into the air.

Olivia let the gust of wind die. The man dropped onto the unforgiving deck head-first. His skull shattered. Blood and brains leaked across the ground.

Olivia gagged.

She hadn't meant to kill him. She'd only meant to stop him….

Her breathing turned shallow and rapid. She couldn't get enough air.

I didn't mean it. I didn't—

"Olivia."

Strong, familiar arms came around her…arms she shouldn't still be craving after what he'd done. Erikir's heart beat against her back. His lips were at her ear.

"Calm down."

There was no kindness in the command, and it oddly comforted her.

"I killed that man," she began.

Erikir spun her around to face him. They clung to each other in spite of the chaos surrounding them.

"Yes." He pulled her closer until all she could see—all she could feel—was him. "And if you hadn't, he would have killed you."

Olivia knew it was the truth, but it didn't make her feel any better. She wasn't a killer. She was just—

"Fight with me." Erikir's breath was warm against her cheek. "Your people need you."

His words spoke to some deep yearning inside her. It wasn't wholly hers, but at the same time, wasn't *not* hers. He was right. These were her people, and they were surrounded and outnumbered.

Her magic could save them.

Erikir dropped his arms from around her. She let out a shuddering breath and gave him a grim nod. Together, they turned back to the Forsaken.

So many. There were so many Forsaken, and only seven of them.

Tol's frustration was like a pulsing ache in her own skull. He wanted…needed…to get to Addy, but there were too many soldiers in his way. Olivia turned in time to see Nira go down on her knees. Fred saw too, and he tried to turn the force of his hose on the Forsaken swarming around her. But at that moment, the jettison of water coming from his hose slowed to a trickle.

Fred threw the hose down on the ground and raced for Nira. He was weaponless. Nira's Haze had become so dull it was barely visible.

"Olivia."

Erikir's voice cut through the panic and fury swirling through her thoughts.

"I've got you."

She closed her eyes, knowing Erikir would make sure nothing happened to her body while her mind was elsewhere. She reached for her magic.

She opened her eyes and was almost blinded. A jagged line of pure white light was ricocheting through the ranks of the Forsaken. It severed the Forsaken's bodies in half. It moved so fast, they didn't seem to realize anything had happened. Some of them even raised their weapons and stepped forward. And then they disappeared into puffs of blue smoke.

Panicked screams filled the air.

"Holy shite!" Gerth shouted as the light weaved around him and Fred before slicing through the Forsaken they'd been fighting.

The Forsaken tried to run…tried to fight…but they were no match for this weapon.

Olivia could do nothing but watch as, one by one, the Forsaken transformed from flesh and bone into smoke. There were so many swirling wisps of blue that the air was clouded with it. Olivia couldn't even see through the blue fog to Tol and Addy on the other side of the deck.

She had done this. She knew it, and yet, she couldn't quite process the magnitude of destruction. She watched the white bolt of light pass from enemy to enemy in a removed kind of way…like it hadn't already killed dozens of people…like she wasn't the one responsible for their deaths.

Olivia! Tol's voice screamed in her mind.

It took her less than a second to process the source of Tol's panic. The bolt of white light was shooting across the deck, and it was headed for Addy and the general.

Olivia didn't understand exactly how it worked, but she knew the magical, deadly bolt was targeting the Forsaken.

Addy was Forsaken.

Closing her eyes and forcing herself to focus, Olivia reached out her mental hand for Tol. He grabbed it with enough force that he would have broken bones if he was holding her physical hand.

Olivia saw the bolt splinter into a million harmless particles of light that scattered on the wind. She staggered backward from the effort, ignoring the surge of exhaustion. Her only thought was of her sister.

Before, there'd been a hundred Forsaken between them. Now, all that remained of the deadly warriors was a dusting of blue ash on the ground.

The general was on her knees on the other side of the deck. Addy was standing behind her, and it looked like she was tying the general's wrists behind her back. There was a handful of other Forsaken in similar positions. Tol had Influenced them into throwing their weapons over the side and kneeling on the ground with their hands locked behind their heads.

The mortals were running back down into the belly of the ship. Their expressions ranged from confused, to disbelieving, to terrified. Olivia and Tol would have their work cut out for them with Influencing all of the mortals to make sure they didn't remember what happened here. But that was a problem for later. For now, they had done what they'd come here to do. They were all safe, and the general was their prisoner.

They were all safe.

Olivia turned, searching for Erikir before she was even conscious of doing so. His eyes were already on her. Olivia felt confused, uncertain, and a little sick.

If it hadn't been for Erikir's betrayal, they wouldn't be here. Tol's face wouldn't be a bloody mess. The rest of them would be safe and far away from here.

And yet, if it hadn't been for all of this, Olivia would still be grasping at tiny wisps of her power. Between finding Tol and fighting the Forsaken, she had reached farther inside herself than she ever would have otherwise. She still hadn't accessed enough strength to give her powers to Addy, but she was almost there.

CHAPTER 44

ADDY

Addy left the general and the other handful of Forsaken who were still alive. She gathered up their Source necklaces, figuring Tol and the others would be due for a refill. Then, she raced across the deck to Tol. She threw herself into his arms.

"Addy." He pulled her against him, his black velvet voice vibrating against her neck. "My warrior goddess."

"My Tol." She pushed back his hair and examined his black eye, swollen jaw, and split lip.

Addy's mother would pay for this. So would Erikir. So would every Forsaken still living.

"Addy." Tol's voice was full of wonder. "You're on a boat right now."

It took her a second to catch his point. As soon as she did, she grinned. "Turns out I really like speedboats. Also, you were here." She shrugged like it was no big deal, even though they both knew it was. "Guess the combination of the two just shocked the fear right out of me."

Tol lifted her off the ground and spun her in a circle. "You can be honest. It was really the speedboat that got you over your fear, wasn't it?"

"Obviously." She wrapped her arms around the back of his neck and leaned in.

"Absolutely not!" Gerth had a hand on each of them and was pushing them apart.

"Gerth," Addy complained.

"Do you not see that his mouth is covered in blood?"

Tol's face paled. He stepped back so fast Addy lost her balance. "Gods, I completely forgot."

"What?" Addy asked, not understanding.

"If you were to get even a drop of my blood inside your body before the ritual, you could never blood marry," Tol said.

Addy's eyes widened at the horrible thought.

"It's like a contaminant that makes it impossible for the blood marriage to take," Gerth explained. "You can touch him, you just can't ingest his blood before the ritual."

Addy linked her arms behind her back and took another few steps away from Tol. No way was she taking that kind of risk…especially now, when they were so close.

"Listen, the general knows about Olivia," Tol said.

"Shite." Gerth looked as worried as Tol.

Icy tendrils crawled down Addy's spine. It shouldn't matter; Addy's mother was tied up and weaponless. And yet, Addy hated the idea of the Forsaken general knowing anything about Livy.

"What do we want to do about them?" Gerth nodded his head in the direction of the few Forsaken who were still alive.

"We'll kill them as soon as they tell us everything they know about the Supernal," Tol said. His expression darkened.

Addy knew what he was thinking. 2:45pm had come and gone, which meant they no longer knew where the Supernal was going to be. If anyone knew where to find him, it was the Forsaken.

"Does anyone need immediate medical attention?" Nira asked, coming over to join them.

Of all of them, Nira was the only one who wasn't covered in blood, blue smoke residue, or some combination. She looked like she'd just stepped out from the page of a magazine. Addy kind of wanted to strangle her.

Except, Addy had seen the way Nira fought side-by-side with Fred. She couldn't help but appreciate Evil Beauty Queen for that, if for nothing else. While Nira examined Tol's wounds, Addy went to her sister.

She crushed Livy into a hug. "Thank you for finding Tol," she said, ignoring the small ache that came with admitting she hadn't been able to do it herself.

"I've almost reached my full power," Livy said, her eyes shining. "It'll be soon. I can feel it."

Addy's heart soared. She felt the weight in her chest ease. *Soon.* And then, the next time Tol needed her, she wouldn't be helpless.

Soon, Tol would be really and truly be hers. They'd save his people before their Source ran out. Maybe they could get married on Vitaquias so Tol's grandfather could be there….

"Thank you," she told Livy again, knowing her sister would understand all the things words couldn't even begin to say.

"I love you," Livy said.

"Love you more." Addy gave her twin one more squeeze for good measure.

"Can I drown Erikir now?" Addy asked Tol. "Or chop him into tiny pieces and then toss him over the side?"

Either way was good by Addy…just as long as he could never hurt Tol again.

Erikir wilted under everyone's unforgiving gazes, but he didn't say anything. There was nothing for him to say.

"We'll deal with him later," Tol said, giving his cousin a murderous look.

Addy heaved a dramatic sigh. She didn't like to wait on these kinds of things, but she was too relieved to have Tol back to be worried about much else…even this weasel's betrayal.

"Right now, I need to call my parents before they lose their minds," Tol said. "Then, we'll interrogate the Forsaken and figure out where the Supernal is hiding." He looked around. "Where's Jaxon?"

"On the other side of that party boat." Addy pointed.

Tol blew out a breath. "You mean the one that's full of mortals who are filming us?"

They all looked over the side of the aircraft carrier. Gerth and Addy cursed.

"It's fine." Tol wrapped his arms around Addy and pulled her against him. "Olivia and I can Influence them when we go pick Jaxon up."

After Tol called his hysterical parents and explained that he was fine, they made their way across the deck to the general. Addy's mother watched their approach with an unreadable expression on her face. Her eye was swollen from where Addy had gotten in a solid punch, and blood was still trickling from the shallow cuts along her neck from the shears' blades.

Still, Addy didn't feel the sense of victory she knew she should.

Seeing her mother like this, bleeding and on her knees, filled Addy with an odd sense of pity. She didn't want to feel the emotion for the woman who had murdered her real family, but she did.

You birth wasn't consensual.

Addy wanted to scream until those ugly words disappeared.

"The general's ring protects her from Influence," Tol said. "I already tried pulling it off, but it's bound to her like yours. So, unless you want to cut her finger off, you might need to do the persuading for this interrogation."

Addy glanced down at the ruby stone on the general's index finger. She hadn't even noticed it before with everything else that was happening.

"A ring that protects her from Influence?" Addy asked. Erikir had said something like that earlier, but Addy had been too frantic about getting to Tol to give it a second thought.

"Yeah. Right before I passed out, I heard her tell Erikir it has the gods' magic. I'm guessing the Supernal gave it to her, just like the Celestial gave us yours."

Addy didn't have a chance to respond. The sound of a helicopter in the distance was getting louder. Addy squinted.

"Is it just me, or is that helicopter heading straight for us?" Gerth asked.

The general, whose expression had been blank when all of her soldiers were killed by a beam of light, and who hadn't so much as blinked when Addy held a blade to her throat, wasn't calm anymore. As she stared at the approaching chopper, her pale face went white as a ghost. Even her lips were bloodless. Addy knew the look in her mother's eyes, because it was the way she knew she looked when she awoke from her drowning nightmare. It was terror.

"Adelyne." The general's voice came out strangled. "You have to get off this ship. Now!"

CHAPTER 45

ADDY

He wasn't supposed to come here." The general's pitiless veneer had been replaced by panic.

"Who is it?" Addy asked.

"You can't let him see you. You have to go, now!" The general was beside herself. It was unnerving to see someone who was always so in control to be so…not.

Addy stared at her mother, uncomprehending. Their little group had just killed a hundred Forsaken. They'd deal with whoever came out of that helicopter the same way.

Wind whipped Addy's hair as the hovering chopper started to lower itself to the deck of the aircraft carrier.

The general was shouting for Addy to get out…to hide. Whatever else she was saying was torn away by the helicopter's rotor.

"Source up, everyone," Gerth said. "I have a feeling we're gonna need it."

The helicopter settled on the deck, its blades whipping the air into a frenzy. Addy felt a strange dread as she caught sight of people moving around inside. The door opened.

Instead of the giant Forsaken soldiers with glowing blue weapons she'd been expecting, a single man climbed out of the chopper.

His foot reached for the ground. He was wearing sandals with socks. *Classy.*

The man fell gracelessly when the ground was farther away than he had expected. He scrambled to his feet, but he was facing away from them, so Addy could only see his back. He was on the taller end of average, maybe an even six feet. He was certainly no taller than Addy. He had thinning gray hair and wore a wrinkled white button-down that had come loose from his baggy corduroy pants. *Who wore corduroy in the summer?*

"He's just a mortal," Erikir said.

It was true; the man had no Haze. For the life of her, Addy couldn't understand her mother's panic.

Maybe she was afraid of someone who was still inside the chopper.

The man started to turn, but the general leapt to her feet. The motion drew his attention away from Addy. The general's lips were moving, but the man wasn't paying attention to her. He put up a hand, and the general cut herself off mid-sentence.

While the man's attention was elsewhere, the general turned to Addy and gave her a final pleading look. "Go," she mouthed.

Addy craned her neck to get a better look at the mortal, but the man's back was to her.

He couldn't be…. No.

Addy's father had to be a hulking brute of a Forsaken. Whoever this mortal with corduroy pants and socks with his sandals was, he wasn't someone capable of forcing the Forsaken general to do anything.

The man strode to the edge of the ship and peered out over the water.

"What's he looking at?" Addy asked, even though a terrible suspicion had taken hold.

There was only one object of interest within view of the deck.

The man pointed. The general stared out over the water. Addy leaned over the railing to see what had caught their attention. She almost didn't want to. She didn't want to confirm her suspicion.

There it was. The speedboat. It was barely visible from the deck of their aircraft carrier. Most of it was concealed behind the party boat, but the bow was just peeking out.

Jaxon.

"Guys, we've got a serious problem," Fred said.

"On it," Addy replied. She had her garden shears out and ready, and she was striding toward the man when he slapped the general across the face.

Addy went rigid, too stunned to react. The general's arms were tied behind her back, but her legs were free. She could fight back, but she wasn't even trying.

The general lowered her head. If Addy didn't know better, she would think the general was apologizing.

Oh, hell no.

Addy took off for the man. Her blood pounded a furious rhythm in her chest. She was forced to come to a stop when the helicopter started to lift back off the ground, leaving the man behind. The wind from the blades pushed Addy back several steps.

"Oh gods," Gerth said, coming up behind Addy.

Addy whipped her head around.

She temporarily forgot about the man as a new horror unfolded before her eyes. The helicopter was heading straight for the speedboat, which was slicing through the water.

When the chopper reached the boat, the door opened. A rope was lowered. Two Forsaken shimmied down the rope. Addy could see the blue glow of their weapons reflecting in the harsh sunlight.

Addy saw Jaxon dive over the side. The men clinging to the rope jumped, using their momentum to close the distance.

The Forsaken came at Jaxon from both sides. Addy saw the spray of water and glow of blue Forsaken weapons as they fought. All the while, the helicopter hovered directly over them.

Long minutes passed.

Addy and the others watched in muted horror as the helicopter lifted the rope that held three people. Jaxon was dangling from the one-handed grip of one of the Forsaken. Jaxon wasn't moving, which meant he was unconscious…or worse.

Addy cursed.

"How did they figure out Jaxon was there?" Nira asked.

"What do we do?" Fred asked in a nervous voice.

"Tol—" Gerth's voice cracked.

"I can fix this," Tol said.

He held out his hand to Livy. She took it, and Addy had to watch as their Hazes brightened in tandem. She swallowed.

"*Look.*" Fred pointed.

The man standing in front of the general was pinwheeling his arms. It started out as a slow rotation, getting faster and faster. A cloud of blue smoke began to rise.

"What is that?" Addy asked, desperate for someone to refute the insane suspicion that was growing in her mind.

"Um, Tol." Gerth tapped him on the shoulder. "I think we've got another problem."

Tol opened his eyes, breaking his connection with Livy.

The blue smoke was swirling and billowing. The man's arms moved faster, and as they did, the smoke began to form into shapes. *Human shapes.*

"No freaking way," Nira whispered.

Addy would have been convinced she was seeing things if it wasn't for the expressions plastered on her friends' faces.

The smoke thickened and solidified. The man's arms were moving so fast now they were a blur. A group of Forsaken…people who had died by Addy's own shears…morphed into existence. They stepped out of the smoke, as alive as they had been before she killed them.

They weren't ghosts or phantoms. They were real.

Everywhere Addy looked, more Forsaken were stepping out of clouds of blue smoke. She watched as two smoke halves of a body fused, and then the smoke transformed into flesh and bone. The newly-remade Forsaken rolled his shoulders. He reached out a hand and caught the blue smoke sword that was heading his way. As soon as the smoke touched his flesh, it turned solid.

What the—

All around them, the dead were coming back to life.

"Holy shite," Nira whispered, summing things up.

"This is bad," Fred added.

Even though the air was warm, Addy had started shivering.

More than a hundred newly-remade Forsaken were now standing on the ship's deck. Their expressions weren't friendly.

The man's pinwheeling arms slowed. As they did, he turned to face them.

Livy's gasp confirmed what had become obvious to all of them.

This man was the Supernal.

The helicopter lowered itself to the deck. With everything else that had happened, Addy had forgotten all about Jaxon. The pilot cut the engine, and the whirring rotor slowed.

The chopper's door opened. One of the Forsaken dragged Jaxon onto the ship's deck. He twitched when he hit the ground, which meant that at least he was alive, but his eyes stayed closed. Addy took one step toward them and stopped.

The man—no, the Supernal—had grasped the general's shoulders. He was shaking her until her head flopped around like a bobblehead. The general wasn't fighting back. Even though she was taller than the Supernal, she looked so small to Addy in that moment.

"Hey, why don't you pick on someone who isn't all tied up?" Addy called.

The Supernal started to turn toward her, but the general shoved her shoulder into his arm to keep his attention on her.

"Who's behind me?" The cool, deep voice sent a shiver of dread through Addy. "What are you trying to hide from me, Lezha?"

"Nothing, my Lord," the general said.

He turned. Blue light erupted all around Addy.

Tol, who was standing shoulder-to-shoulder with her, jerked away like she'd burned him.

Addy looked down at the blue light streaming from her skin. It was brighter than any Haze, and the wrong color, besides. It was like she *was* one of the Forsaken's weapons.

She'd reacted this way once before, only it hadn't been so strong. It had been when she first came into contact with Jaxon's stone.

The stone…which contained the Supernal's powers….

The man strode toward Addy, pushing past the general when she tried to waylay him again.

"My, isn't this a surprise." The Supernal looked from Addy to the general, noting their unquestionable resemblance.

"Addy, what the hells?" Tol whispered.

"Lezha, your memory must be failing." The Supernal turned to smile at Addy's mother. "You neglected to mention we had a child."

CHAPTER 46

TOL

The Supernal was here. So was Jaxon, who possessed the stone that contained all of the Supernal's powers. So were a hundred Forsaken who had been dead a few minutes ago.

And the Supernal was Addy's father.

Tol was moving before he'd even fully processed the meaning of it all. He had to kill this man…this being.

"Get Jaxon and Livy out of here!" he shouted to Addy.

If the Supernal was reunited with his powers, he'd have the strength to destroy two worlds.

Jaxon was bleeding and unconscious on the deck. His half-moon blades hovered over his head, zipping out of the way of anyone else who came near them. A wall of non-dead Forsaken stood in front of him.

Light was spilling from Addy's ring, and the first beams of the portal were swirling into a lasso of magical energy.

Good, Tol thought.

The general, whose hands were no longer bound behind her back, appeared beside Addy. She brought a long metal bar down, which Addy barely managed to block before it cracked against her ribcage. The light of the portal winked out.

"What are you doing?" Addy cried.

Tol heard the general say something about Jaxon, the stone, and making her choice for the good of the Forsaken.

Tol made himself to look away from Addy as the general forced her backward. Addy could take care of herself. Right now, he had a job to do. He needed to deal with the Supernal.

He turned his attention inward on the bond connecting him to Olivia. A surge of power went through him at the strength she leant him. He used it to tackle the Supernal.

It wasn't graceful, but he got the man pinned beneath him. It was easier than he thought it'd be. He gripped the Supernal's throat and began to squeeze, infusing his hold with magical strength.

That was when Tol felt a searing pain in his right hand. It spread to his knees and every other part of him that was touching the Supernal.

A shout tore free from Tol's throat. Smoke was rising around him. Not a magical kind…the kind that came from something that was on fire.

He was on fire.

"What the hells are you doing to me?!"

His flesh made a hideous sound as he tore it off the Supernal. Tol roared as pain ripped through him. His whole body began to convulse. Even his prosthesis was melting and warping everywhere it came into contact with the Supernal.

The Supernal wheezed out a laugh at Tol. "The Celestial's power is strong in you."

That's when Tol understood. His reaction to the Supernal was a variation of what had happened to him when he got too close to the stone Jaxon held. It was the opposite of Tol's magic in every way. It was poison to him.

He reached for the Supernal with invisible fingers of Influence. He pulled more energy from Olivia as he tried to control the Supernal's mind.

The Supernal's features tightened. Sweat broke out on his face.

He's fighting me, Tol realized.

Tol felt the pressure in his mind. He'd never experienced anything like it before. It felt like his brain was swelling until it might burst.

Not happening, barbarian, Tol thought with a new kind of desperation.

Tol bit out a curse as he tightened his mental grip on the Supernal. Tol's hold was fraying. One by one, the invisible fingers he had latched onto the Supernal's mind were torn away.

Pain ripped through Tol's skull.

Black spots gathered at the corners of his vision. Tol was weakening, and the Supernal was growing stronger.

"Ah," the Supernal said. "My power is here."

Jaxon's stone, Tol's pain-fogged brain registered. He saw a pulse of blue light coming from the stone that was no longer in its lead box. An unconscious Jaxon was clutching it in his fist as a Forsaken soldier tried to pry it loose.

Nausea roiled in Tol's gut as the wrongness of the stone's power sunk into him like a fast-acting poison.

Don't pass out, he ordered himself.

He needed—

Addy. Where was Addy?

He glanced up, only to see her locked in combat with the general. The hundreds of Forsaken the Supernal had somehow brought back to life were pushing Tol's friends closer and closer to the ship's railing.

Anger, and a sense of injustice, surged through Tol along with the sickness. His friends' Hazes were dull. The weaker his people became, the stronger the Forsaken grew.

"They wait only for my order," the Supernal taunted Tol. "Shall I tell them to put your little friends out of their misery?"

Tol couldn't speak. He fell to his hands and knees and retched. The stone's power was burning him from the inside out. His blood had turned molten. His every breath felt like he was inhaling pure fire.

"Your sorry race will soon cease to exist," the Supernal gloated. "I don't even need to fight you. I must simply sit here and watch my magic burn you alive."

No, Tol thought desperately. He wasn't just going to dissolve here while the Supernal taunted him. *He had to do something.*

"As soon as you're dead, I'll reclaim the strength that was stolen from me," the Supernal continued. "I'll be the most powerful being in the worlds. The mortals will become my slaves, and I will destroy what's left of the Chosen with little more than a thought."

Get up. Get up, get up.

Tol's muscles screamed. His head was about to burst. His lungs were on fire.

The Supernal bared his teeth at Tol. "The Celestial will fade into nothingness, along with the broken world where she lives."

Not if I can help it.

Tol rallied himself. He drew in a short gasp of pure fire. He focused his mind and channeled his concentration. He closed his eyes, letting the Supernal think he was giving up.

Olivia, he thought.

Almost immediately, her mental presence shone like a light through the darkness in his mind.

Tol? What do we do?

He smiled. *Let's kill the bastard.*

CHAPTER 47

ADDY

Addy slashed her garden shears at her mother, hearing the clang as they came up against the metal bar the general was using as a weapon.

"You foolish girl." The general's eyes were bright, like she was holding back tears.

The thought of the general crying was almost as incomprehensible to Addy as the knowledge that her father was somewhere between an immortal and a god.

Addy and the general's strikes were sluggish, but it wasn't for the same reason why the Chosen were flagging. Addy and her mother were hesitant to attack each other. They also both had their attention on the Supernal, who was fighting Tol.

"How could you?" Addy demanded, parrying another strike. "I was going to get Jaxon and the stone out of here. Because of you, this…thing…will have the power to destroy everyone."

"I made a choice." The general stepped out of the way of Addy's half-hearted blow.

"The Chosen are the only ones who have any Source left. Our people would have been doomed. Now, with the Supernal returning to full strength, at least the Forsaken will survive."

"But if the Supernal is the one who…raped you," Addy said, almost choking on the words, "how could you want to help him?"

The general lowered her weapon. Addy could have sent the general over the side of the ship with a single good kick, but she didn't move. She had to know. She had to understand.

"Our people could either die a slow death in the Chosens' shadow, or we could regain our immortality and become the ruling power of all the races. I chose to ensure our people's survival."

Addy wanted to scream at her mother. At the same time, she couldn't deny the selfless bravery of such a choice. The general was willing to live in her own personal hell for the sake of her people's survival.

"Now that he knows about you, he'll expect you to rule with us," the general said, her voice sounding defeated.

"He can expect all he wants," Addy said in disgust, hating the sight of this fearless, strong woman in so much pain.

An idea occurred to Addy.

"Help us destroy him," Addy said. "We can make a deal for going back to Vitaquias together. I'll be queen of the Chosen, and we can come up with an agreement to share the world and Source."

The idea was so good, Addy couldn't believe she hadn't thought of it sooner.

Instead of jumping at an offer that avoided empowering the devil who had raped her, the general shook her head.

"The Chosen people would succumb to their limitless thirst for more, and then we'd be right back where we started," she said.

Addy opened her mouth to argue.

"Tell me that isn't your blood filling the Chosens' vials," the general challenged, pointing at Nira and Gerth. Their lips were bloodstained.

"They're my friends," Addy said, wondering why it sounded weak.

"Tell me every one of the Chosen wouldn't bleed you dry if they knew what your blood contains."

Kill the Forsaken. Kill the Forsaken. The screams of Tol's people echoed in her ears.

Addy shook her head. The general was playing mind games with her. She and Tol would be in charge of the Chosen people, and things would be different.

"The Chosen turn everything they touch to ruin," the general continued. "I saw the Nyxar released on Vitaquias. That shadow creature exists because the Chosen destroyed the balance of our world."

Addy was angry now. Her mother was trying to confuse and manipulate her.

"Did you know the Celestial allowed the Supernal to return to Vitaquias after millennia of banishment?" the general asked.

The change of subject threw Addy.

Before she could reply, the general continued, "The Celestial hoped it would be enough to undo all the destruction the Chosen had wrought. That was when I first met the Supernal."

Addy's stomach clenched, and she found she couldn't hold the general's eye. She felt disgusted and helpless. She hated it.

"Let's just say he took a liking to me. And I discovered that even the strongest of immortals is powerless when it comes to the whims and desires of a being that is more god than human."

"I'm sorry," Addy mumbled. The words felt all wrong, but she had no idea what else to say.

What else *could* she say?

"I know you believe me cruel for forcing you to drink from the Source. All I knew was that I never wanted you to be as vulnerable as I'd been."

Addy felt herself nodding as the knot in her throat tried to untangle itself.

In spite of what she'd been through, the general had done everything she could to protect her child and her people. It didn't undo the atrocities she'd done to Addy's family and so many of the Chosen. But Addy was coming to understand the general in a way she never expected to.

"It is my responsibility to ensure the Forsaken survive," the general said. "Everything I do is for them."

It was no less than Addy would do for the people she loved.

"I've made my choice, and soon, you'll have to make yours," the general continued. "You cannot be both Forsaken and Chosen."

"I've already made my choice," Addy said with more confidence than she felt. She thought about Tol's parents, and the way they had looked at her when she showed up at the manor in bloody clothes. She thought about the crowd of Chosen chorusing for her death after they discovered who…what…she really was.

"I choose Tol and Livy," Addy said. Those words, at least, felt right and true. "I choose Aunt Meredith and Fred and Gerth."

Addy shook her head. She'd wasted enough time. Right now, what mattered was getting Jaxon and the stone out of here. And then they needed to kill the Supernal. Everything else could be dealt with later.

She closed her left fist, imagining the sandy shore next to the pier. That would be a good enough starting place. They could figure out where to go from there.

The magic in her ring stirred.

Addy cried out as a blinding pain ripped through her left hand.

The general lowered her metal bar.

"Choices, Adelyne," the general said.

Rage filled Addy. She lunged at her mother, tackling her. They both hit the deck. Another scream was wrenched out of Addy as her left hand slammed against the hard surface. Her broken fingers throbbed.

The general struck Addy's head with a glancing blow that had her seeing stars.

"Stay down," the general commanded before getting to her feet.

Addy drove her shears into her mother's leg. The blades lodged in the back of the general's right knee with enough force Addy knew they had found the bone.

The general howled. Tears streamed down her pale cheeks.

Addy yanked the shears back out and left her mother hunched over her bleeding leg. She turned her attention back to her ring.

"Come on," she begged it.

Her left hand had gone numb. Without it, she couldn't feel the power in her ring. Addy tried to pull the ring off her finger and switch it to her other hand.

Come on. Come on. Come on.

Tears and sweat poured down her face. It was no use. Her finger was broken and swollen. The ring wasn't budging.

Addy tore her attention away from her ring at the sound of Tol's shout. He was on the other side of the deck, having some kind of mental battle with the Supernal. It wasn't clear which of them was winning. Blood was trickling out of Tol's nose and ears.

The Forsaken had Jaxon. They seemed to be trying to pry the stone loose from the death grip he was maintaining even in unconsciousness. They were dragging his body closer to the Supernal. Livy and the others were trying to stop them, but they were outnumbered. And the stone that was giving Addy strength was weakening them.

Addy gave her mother a kick in the ribs.

"*You* stay down," she told the general.

She ran to Tol.

"Tol, protect Jaxon," she gasped. "I'll take care of this piece of garbage myself."

As soon as Tol backed away from the Supernal, his Haze grew brighter. But the distance seemed to also strengthen the Supernal. The Supernal leapt to his feet in a single, fluid movement.

The Supernal dodged to avoid Addy's shears. The two of them circled each other.

"Do you know how many generations I've had to hone my skills as a warrior?" the Supernal asked. "I may not have been able to access my full power, but I am—and always have been—the Supernal."

Addy feinted to the left and drove her shears to the right. The Supernal avoided the blow before she could do more than slash a line through his shirt.

She tried again. Effortlessly, the Supernal spun away from her shears.

Addy let out a frustrated huff. The Supernal was toying with her.

She didn't like being toyed with.

"I expect more from my only offspring," he taunted.

"I am not your anything," Addy spat. "You are nothing to me except a target."

The Supernal smiled. *Leered* might have been a better word. As he did, he seemed to grow bigger.

"Show me you're worthy of the blood running through your veins, and I'll let you lead my people in Lezha's stead."

"Thanks, but no thanks." Addy's chest was heaving, but she kept her attention locked on her opponent. She remembered every move Jaxon had showed her. She planned to use all of them on this despicable being.

The Supernal reached behind him and tore away a piece of the ship's railing. Metal groaned and broke free as easily as she might rip up a clump of grass. The Supernal swung his new weapon. Addy's whole body vibrated as their two weapons clashed.

Holy shit, this guy was strong.

"Tell me, what special abilities have you enjoyed from the godly blood running through your veins?" the Supernal asked as they circled each other.

Special abilities? Addy immediately thought about the way a drop of her blood on a bracelet had allowed Fred to track her across continents.

She remembered Jaxon saying normal Forsaken couldn't sense each other the way she could. She hadn't known the reason for that particular ability, but now, she understood.

The Supernal thrust his pole at Addy with so much force it took all of her strength to block it.

"I don't have any special abilities."

Addy smiled as her shears raked across the Supernal's leg. "I guess without my friend's stone, you're just another average fighter."

She yawned to hammer in the point.

The Supernal's face reddened, even though the effort of their fight hadn't seemed to even wind him.

Egotistical prick.

Addy was gathering herself to pounce, when the Supernal grew before her eyes. The blue light surrounding him became brighter, eclipsing her own Haze.

There was nothing human-looking about him, now. He was pushing seven feet in height, and his muscles had bulked up to match. The gray had faded from his hair, which was now gold and shiny. His eyes were the least human part of him. They were reptilian. Each had a jagged black pupil that looked like a lightning bolt, and the rest of the iris was pure gold.

"Ahh." The Supernal looked down at the blue light surrounding him. "It's beginning."

CHAPTER 48

OLIVIA

Olivia thought she was getting the hang of all of this. Jaxon's stone had made her feel weak before, but she'd found that with a force of will, she could block out its magical vibrations. Now, she felt like she could do anything.

She and Tol stood back-to-back, and the physical contact made both of them stronger. Half of her existed in that shadow realm in her mind. The other half of her was fighting in the physical world. There were more than a hundred Forsaken. They were all trying to reach Jaxon and pry the stone loose from his grip.

Oh no, you don't, Olivia thought with renewed determination.

Olivia's Influence was keeping all of them away from Jaxon. For now. Even with all of the strength coursing through her, it wouldn't be enough to hold them off forever.

Tol's attention was focused on the general, who was lashing out at him with her weapon. One of her legs was bleeding, but it didn't seem to be slowing her down. With the ring on her finger that prevented Influence, Tol was at a serious disadvantage. He was holding his own, but like Olivia, his strength wouldn't last forever.

Olivia could see their fight in her mind, which was weird since it was going on in real life behind her back. Tol was slowing the general's strikes with his mind, but she was still strong. It was taking all of Tol's concentration to keep her away from Jaxon. Without Influence, he was devoid of his greatest weapon.

While she was controlling a hundred Forsaken, Olivia was also trying to slow the Supernal's transformation. She could sense the power flowing from the stone to the being who was locked in combat with Addy. Olivia was diverting as much of her magical energy to helping her twin as she could. She was managing to build a kind of invisible barrier between him and the stone. It seemed to slow down the transfer of power from the stone to the Supernal, but it wasn't enough.

Sweat ran down her back. With her attention split in so many different directions, it was only a matter of time before Olivia's strength fractured.

Nira, Erikir, and Fred were standing protectively around Jaxon. Gerth was crouched by Jaxon's side. He was shaking him, trying to get the unconscious man up.

"We need Addy's portal," Gerth called. "It's the only way to get him out of here."

Addy was busy, and Olivia wasn't going to risk breaking her sister's concentration.

"There might be another way," Fred said.

Olivia used her Influence to shift the Forsaken around on the deck so they'd be out of Fred's path. She almost lost her hold on their minds when she realized where Fred was heading.

The helicopter.

What are you doing? she thought, but her concentration was too preoccupied for her to say the words out loud.

"What in the two hells are you up to?" Nira called.

"What does it look like?" he replied. "I'm getting us a ride outta here."

"Do you even know how to fly a helicopter?" Gerth demanded.

"It's a machine," came Fred's huffed reply. "How complicated could it be?"

"Judging from how you can't even seem to figure out how to get inside, I'd say pretty complicated," Nira said in an airy tone.

Fred finally managed to get the door open and swing himself inside. He turned to grin down at Nira.

"Focus, Freddo," Gerth grumbled. "Nira, why don't you make yourself useful and pull up some flight manuals?"

"You people are insane," Nira replied, but her long nails were already clicking away on her phone.

Their conversation faded as a surge of magic raced through Olivia. She wasn't sure if it was her proximity to Tol, or if it was because she was using so much of her power. Either way, Olivia felt as close to invincible as she ever had in her life.

She looked at the Forsaken, who were straining against the mental hold Olivia had on them.

I'm sorry, she thought, feeling a wave of guilt. But it was the Supernal's people or hers. There was no contest.

Olivia swept her arm to the side. With the motion, Forsaken flew off the deck.

I'm so, so sorry.

Another wave of her arm sent more over the side. Their surprised, panicked shouts echoed around in her mind.

"Hells, yeah!" Gerth shouted, pumping his fist into the air.

For Addy. For the Chosen.

Another swipe of her arm. More Forsaken disappeared. In a matter of seconds, she'd cleared every one of the Forsaken except for the Supernal and general from the deck of the ship. The general's ring protected her, and the Supernal's stone protected him. She couldn't defeat them as easily as she had the rest of her enemies. She'd just have to find another way to bring them down.

Strength hummed in her veins. At that moment, something inside Olivia broke.

The dam, or floodgate, or whatever it was that was holding back the full extent of her power, fell away. A tidal wave of strength coursed through her.

That's when she knew. She knew the full strength of the Celestial was inside her. It wasn't just accessible to her…it was a part of her. The back of her neck prickled in understanding.

No barriers remained. Olivia felt drunk as power poured into her and filled every empty space inside her. It was all around her, because it was her.

She was no longer the vessel that possessed the Celestial's magic. She *was* the Celestial's magic.

My power, she thought. *My strength. Mine.*

She felt Tol stagger under the weight of all that power leaking into the telepathic connection between them. Then, he absorbed it, and the magic became a part of him, too. He gathered a handful of the power and thrust it at the general. All it took was one shove from Tol's mind, and the general collapsed on the deck. Her chest still rose and fell, but her muscles were relaxed in unconsciousness.

It was that easy.

"Addy will want to kill the general," Tol said, motioning toward the woman's still figure.

Yes, she would.

The only remaining task was to kill the Supernal so they could destroy his power.

"He's mine!" Addy yelled as Olivia moved forward to help her. "I'm killing him myself."

Olivia was about to protest, but one glance told her that her sister had the Supernal under control. Addy swung her shears, knocking a metal pole out of the Supernal's hands. It clattered to the deck. Addy kicked it over the side.

Addy still had her garden shears, and the Supernal was unarmed. And Olivia had accessed the Celestial's full strength.

She'd done it.

She had accepted and embraced her magic. She no longer felt any fear about what would happen if she stepped off that ledge in her own mind. The ledge no longer existed. She and the Celestial's powers were one and the same.

The air crackled with her unspent magical energy. Even the stone in Jaxon's closed fist dimmed. The Supernal's light faded. Olivia and Tol's Hazes burned brighter. Liquid strength flowed through her. All she had to do was wait for that moment of greatest need.

The thought sobered her.

When the time came, she would be ready. She would make the choice that would give Addy and Tol an eternity of happiness.

Would her death be quick? Would it hurt?

Would she be able to say goodbye?

Olivia thought of her vision of Addy, crouching on that sandy shore as her heart shattered.

What could Olivia say to Addy to make the loss hurt less? Would she have time to say anything to Erikir? Would she even want to say anything to him?

"Olivia."

Like he'd sensed her thoughts, Erikir's voice came out as little more than a ragged whisper. She turned to see that he had sunk onto his knees. He'd used so much Source to fight the Forsaken that the exhaustion was pulling him into unconsciousness.

Olivia didn't think. She took his hands in both of hers, infusing him with all of the strength that had been leached out of him.

Olivia felt a spark at the contact. It had nothing to do with magic, and everything to do with the attraction she couldn't help but still feel for him.

At her touch, color returned to Erikir's skin. His eyes brightened along with his Haze. His hands tightened on hers.

"Please don't do this," he begged, his voice stronger than it had been a moment ago.

I have to do this, she thought, filled with a quiet certainty.

He pulled her closer. She could have pushed him away, but she didn't.

He reached up to brush his fingertips over her cheek. Olivia leaned into his touch before she was even aware of doing so.

In spite of everything he'd done, in spite of her anger toward him that felt like live coals in her chest, she craved his touch. She didn't understand how she could want to be near someone who had done what Erikir did. And yet, her impulse to touch him had her fisting her hands to keep them from doing just that.

"I've seen goodness in you that I didn't think could exist in any world," Erikir whispered, their faces so close she felt the warmth of his breath against her cheek. "When I look at you, I know I'm seeing the future Chosen queen."

"No." Olivia pulled back. "I'm just a vessel…a place holder. As soon as the moment comes, I'm going to give the magic to Addy."

"You can't," Erikir said, real fear showing in his eyes. "Our people need you. I—"

He cut himself off, and Olivia felt her cheeks heat as she realized what he was about to say.

"I care for you," he amended. "Please think about this. Please—"

"Cousin."

They broke apart, and whatever Erikir was about to say died as Tol came to stand over Erikir.

Tol's bloody face was grim. He looked huge compared to Erikir, and Olivia had the insane urge to push Erikir behind her.

Then, she remembered what Erikir had done…that every drop of blood on Tol's face was Erikir's fault.

She stayed where she was.

"Once Addy finishes with the Supernal, I'm going to let her dispense your judgement and punishment." Tol's smile hardened as Erikir's face blanched. "But while our future queen is occupied, I'm going to speak on her behalf and tell you to get your gods-damned hands off her sister."

Tol might be his future king, but Erikir didn't cower under the glare that would bring anyone else to their knees.

"Do what you will, *Cousin*," Erikir spat, his voice full of disgust. "Anyone who is willing to let Olivia die is no sovereign of mine."

"Erikir," Olivia gasped.

Tol turned his hard gaze onto her. "What's he talking about?" he asked, his voice holding all the authority of a soon-to-be king.

"Gun!"

They all turned at the sound of Addy's voice. Olivia was so relieved for an excuse to avoid answering Tol, that she didn't at first comprehend the meaning of the word Addy had shouted.

"Gun. Everyone down!"

This time, the words penetrated.

"What kind of a coward uses a gun?" Nira asked, her voice full of scorn.

They were the only words Nira got out before Fred tackled her, using his own body to shield hers.

But the gun wasn't pointed at Nira. The weapon was easy to spot, because it was glowing blue. Blue like the Supernal's power and Jaxon's stone.

Olivia had just enough time to process the direction of the gun's aim, and the fact that Erikir was no longer beside her, before the gun went off. The sound exploded in her ears.

CHAPTER 49

OLIVIA

No! It was the only conscious thought in Olivia's mind.

She saw the Supernal aim the gun at Jaxon. She saw Erikir dive into the bullet's path. She heard the explosion of the weapon.

Olivia's frantic heartbeat crashed in her ears as she tried to make sense of what was happening. Everything around her looked slightly blurred, even the people. As she watched, she realized everyone was still in motion, but it was unnatural…slow to the point of impossibility.

That's when she saw the bullet. The deadly piece of metal, its surface glinting in the sunlight and tinged blue from the Supernal's magic, was moving through the air at a snail's pace. The people surrounding Olivia were moving even slower. Addy seemed to be opening her mouth to shout, but she was moving so slowly she may as well have been frozen in place.

Erikir was diving at the same, barely-visible speed that made it look like he wasn't moving at all. He was protecting Jaxon's body with his own.

Olivia followed the path between the bullet and Erikir. It was heading straight for his chest.

She stepped forward, expecting it to feel like she was trying to walk through quicksand. It didn't. Whatever slow motion strangle-hold had taken over the others didn't affect her. She moved at the same speed she always did.

She went straight for the bullet, having the idea to simply push it off course so it flew harmlessly over the side of the ship. She reached out to do just that, when she felt a warning ripple across her mind. She hesitated with her finger outstretched.

The bullet was in no danger of connecting with anyone for at least a few minutes, so she left it while she tried to make sense of the voice in her head telling her not to touch it.

She moved closer to Erikir. Jaxon, who was right behind him, had regained consciousness and was in the process of getting to his feet. Olivia reached out and, sensing no warning from her magic, wrapped her hand around Erikir's. His fingers were cold, but as soon as her skin connected with his, they began to warm. She felt his pulse in his wrist where it hadn't been moments ago. He inhaled and looked at her without moving his head. His body remained contorted in mid-air in an unnatural pose.

You stopped time. Erikir's voice spoke inside Olivia's head. She could hear his awe, even though his expression hadn't changed.

Some part of Olivia knew that was what she'd done, but hearing Erikir say the words made it real in a way it hadn't been before.

It's okay, he told her. *Olivia, it's okay.*

It was only when she felt his somber acceptance that she began to comprehend what Erikir had already figured out.

It couldn't be. It wasn't possible.

All the puzzle pieces began to fall into place. She understood the warning from her power. She realized what it would mean if she moved the bullet onto a different path.

The Celestial had told her she'd have to choose to relinquish her abilities at her moment of greatest need. Olivia had assumed that meant a moment when her own life would be at risk.

But she had been wrong.

This wasn't what she'd been expecting. It wasn't what she'd planned for.

Disconcerted waves of power were flowing through her mind. The magic was agitated…churning around and around as though it knew it was about to be displaced.

"The moment of greatest need," Olivia said out loud. She understood the horrible truth, but she still didn't want to accept it.

This. This was her moment of greatest need.

The Celestial said she would know when it had come, and she did. It had just never occurred to Olivia that her moment of greatest need would come on someone else's behalf rather than her own.

No. No, no, no.

If she chose to give her powers to Addy, it wouldn't be her own life she'd be sacrificing. It would be Erikir's.

Olivia had the ability to move the bullet out of his path, but she'd need to use the Celestial's power to do so. If she saved Erikir, she would lose her one and only chance to give her magic to Addy. Addy and Tol could never be together. Olivia would be the Fount for eternity.

She wanted to shout her feelings of injustice at the top of her lungs. She wanted to rage at the Celestial, to demand to know why she'd been tricked. But of course, there was no one to yell at. Everyone was frozen in place on this ship.

No one could tell her what to do. No one could help her.

Desperation had her turning back to Erikir. He was visible inside her own mind, like he was standing in front of her.

It's okay, Erikir said again, his dark eyes fixed on her. *I'm glad it's me and not you. I can live with that.* His lip turned up in a sardonic smile. *Well, figuratively speaking, of course.*

"How can you be joking at a time like this?" Olivia demanded as her throat threatened to squeeze shut.

Erikir's physical body twitched. His expression clouded over. Olivia had the sense that he was trying to come to her before remembering his body was frozen in place.

It's better this way, he insisted. *You're the most amazing woman in the worlds, and you deserve happiness. I hope you find it.*

Olivia was crying, but she couldn't make herself stop. It was so unfair.

How was she supposed to make this choice?

Trading her own life for Addy's happiness was an exchange she was willing to make. It was one she had the *right* to make.

Do it, Erikir said. *I only ever wanted to save my people. I thought I was doing the right thing when I almost got Tol killed, but it was the closest the Chosen ever came to losing any hope of surviving.* He held her gaze. *This is my chance for redemption. Let me have it.*

Olivia was shaking her head back and forth, but she couldn't manage a single word.

The bullet quivered, and then its speed increased. As Olivia's distress grew, her hold on the power that was keeping everything in place weakened. The bullet was already more than halfway to Erikir.

This is the only way, Erikir insisted. *If you don't let me die, Addy and Tol will never be able to blood marry. You'll have to be his queen.* Erikir's eyes were full of emotion when he said, *I don't think I could stand that.*

It'd be better than you being dead. Olivia would have shouted if tears weren't clogging her throat.

Her magic was becoming more erratic. Out of the corner of her eye, Olivia saw the Supernal's arm move. It was only a slight motion, but the air rippled. Olivia knew she had only seconds left to make her decision.

Whoever you choose to love, tell him if he doesn't treat you right, I'll haunt him from my grave. Erikir gave her a sad smile.

Her magic wavered again. The bullet jumped forward. With a sob, Olivia let go of Erikir's hand. Sweat streamed down her forehead as she clung to the magic that was slipping through her fingers like water.

She glanced at Addy, who was frozen with her hand outstretched. With the angle of her body, it looked like she was reaching for Tol.

Tol was held in place too, but as Olivia looked closer, she realized he wasn't as motionless as everyone else. She sucked in a gasp at the sight of him. The blood vessels in his eyes had burst. A vein was throbbing in his temple, and a muscle twitched in his jaw.

Tol was conscious, at least in the part of his mind that linked him to Olivia. He was screaming inside his own mind, but Olivia couldn't make out the individual words. It was like her connection with Erikir had somehow blocked off Tol.

The bullet was no more than a foot from Erikir. He kept his gaze steady as he looked at Olivia.

Olivia reached out.

"I'm sorry," she whispered.

The bullet was hot on her fingertips as she pushed it a few inches to the left.

And then her magic exploded.

CHAPTER 50

ADDY

Addy launched herself at the Supernal and wrestled the gun away. She threw it over the side of the ship before turning back to Jaxon, who was falling backward with Erikir on top of him. Somehow, the Supernal had missed.

Addy didn't have time for relief. She tackled the Supernal.

She had him in a headlock when an explosion of light erupted from the other side of the deck. Addy looked up to see silver flames pouring from Livy. They weren't hurting her. It was like they were a part of her.

"What have you done?"

Tol's voice, full of despair, cut right through to Addy's soul. But he wasn't looking at her. He was looking at Livy.

Addy turned back to the Supernal. Something was happening to him. His blue light was flickering, and he was cringing like he was in pain. A burst of silver light from the other end of the ship made the Supernal cry out.

Addy had no idea what was happening, but she wasn't going to give up this advantage while she had it. The Supernal was still writhing and muttering something about the Celestial.

Addy knelt until she was directly in front of the Supernal.

"This is for what you did to my mother," Addy hissed.

She took his head in her hands. The motion was agony for her broken left hand, but she ground her teeth together and tightened her hold. With a vicious twist, she snapped the Supernal's neck. She dropped him to the ground and raced across the deck.

A torrent of heat hit Addy's face before she reached her twin.

"What's happening?" Addy yelled.

Livy was wreathed in silver flames. Addy wanted to reach out, but instinct told her that if she touched her sister, her skin would be incinerated from the heat. Her only consolation was that the silver fire didn't seem to be hurting Livy.

"Addy, I'm so sorry," Livy said. The tears rolling down her cheeks were silver from the light swirling around her.

Tol was beside her. His Haze was as bright as it had been on Vitaquias, but it was nothing compared to what was going on with Livy.

"What have you done?" Tol groaned.

Addy opened her mouth, but whatever she might have said was silenced as the helicopter whirred to life. Fred was sitting in the pilot's seat with a headset slung around his neck. Nira was sitting in the other seat. Gerth was leaning out of the open door.

Jaxon and Erikir were both getting to their feet, looking dazed.

Addy glanced back at the Supernal's body, and then she did a double-take. He wasn't lying on the ground where Addy had left him.

Addy had broken his neck. She'd felt the bones come apart. She'd heard them pop. She'd felt the Supernal go limp.

And yet, the sight before her was no illusion. The Supernal was on his feet, limping toward them. His head was lilting at an unnatural angle, but he was very much alive.

"Silly offspring," the Supernal called. "It'll take more than a broken neck to kill me."

"We need to get Jaxon out of here," Addy yelled to no one in particular.

Terror held her in an icy grip as she watched the formerly-dead Supernal head for them. Livy and Tol stepped forward together, their moves identical and synchronized in a way that tore at Addy's heart, despite the danger they all now faced.

So much was happening that Addy didn't at first understand the prickle of unease traveling down her spine. She glanced around.

Where was the general?

The Supernal was almost to them. Addy drew her garden shears, but before she could go to finish him off, the Supernal was blasted off his feet.

Tol and Livy raised their arms in a coordinated movement. The Supernal was thrown across the deck. Neither of them had touched him, and yet, it was obvious they had thrown the Supernal with the power of their minds.

Jaxon reached up his hand, and Gerth and Nira pulled him into the helicopter.

That's when Addy saw the general.

The woman sprung out from behind one of the planes on the other side of the deck. She ran for the helicopter.

Addy tried to warn her friends. Between the chopper's engine and whirring blades, there was no chance anyone could hear her.

Tol and Livy were busy with the Supernal, who was trying to fight his way back to their side of the ship. The three of them were straining against each other. Whatever they were doing, it was taking all of their energy.

Addy sprinted across the deck, but she knew she wouldn't make it in time. The general was almost to the chopper. Even with her wounded leg, she was fast.

Addy flexed her left hand, wincing at the waves of fire that shot through her broken fingers.

Come on, she pleaded with her ring.

The stones flickered, but it hurt too much to close her hand into a fist, and she didn't know how else to activate the magic.

The chopper lifted off the ship's deck. A new fear took hold of Addy as the flying contraption lurched and almost crashed into the radar tower.

Addy knew for a fact that Fred had no idea how to fly a helicopter. She watched in muted horror as the helicopter corrected itself and started to rise again. The general leapt into the air. She caught the landing skids like she was Tom Cruise in *Mission Impossible*. She dangled for a few seconds before hauling herself up.

The helicopter tilted. Addy wasn't sure if it was from the general's weight or because Fred was the one flying it. Addy's horror only grew when the general reached up and yanked open the door. Like a gymnast, she swung herself inside.

The glare on the windows made it impossible for Addy to see what was happening. The chopper was hovering fifty-or-so feet above the side of the ship. Addy sprinted for them. She didn't know how she was going to help, but she wanted to be ready in case she could.

The helicopter jerked. Someone shouted. Two figures tumbled out of the open door. Addy had just enough time to comprehend the two people were Jaxon and the general.

No normal human could survive the fall. But Jaxon and the general weren't normal humans.

They crashed to the deck in a tangle of limbs and weapons. Neither of them took time to recover before they were scrabbling again. The general struck her fist across Jaxon's face. While he was stunned, she got up and limped out of his reach.

Ignoring the general, Addy went to Jaxon.

"Addy, we can't hold the Supernal much longer," Tol yelled. "Get the stone out of here!"

The stone.

Jaxon reached into his pocket. Addy saw the horrible realization on his face before he said, "It's gone."

They all looked at the general. Her expression was grim as she held up the glowing blue stone.

"No!"

Addy and Jaxon both lunged.

Jaxon plowed into the general as the stone left her fingers.

Addy could do nothing but watch as the stone curved up into the air. It moved so fast Addy lost sight of it in the sunlight and Livy's impossibly-bright Haze.

The Supernal's hand shot up as he caught the stone.

Addy watched as the Supernal's closed fist began to glow blue.

A tremendous crack sent the enormous ship rocking beneath her. The first shockwave was followed by another. The ground underfoot began to shake.

Addy looked down.

The ship's deck was breaking apart.

CHAPTER 51

TOL

Defeat crashed over Tol.

It's over.

As Tol watched the blue light travel from the Supernal's fist to the rest of his body, that was the only thought he could process. The rest…the horror of what Olivia had done…was secondary to this.

Cracks shivered down the steel beneath their feet like it was nothing more than plywood. The ship shuddered and lurched. Tol knew it was a matter of minutes before it started taking on water…if it wasn't already. Tol could hear the distant screams of the mortals as they jumped from the lower decks and attempted to swim for safety.

The Supernal tossed the stone onto the deck of the ship. It no longer glowed blue. It was black and lifeless.

Because its power now resided within the Supernal.

"Two-thousand years I've waited for this!" The Supernal's roar made a steel cable snap apart and burst through the flight deck. If Tol had been a meter to the left, it would have impaled him.

"Finally. This world is mine. Mine!"

The Supernal's laughter was like the sound of shattering glass.

Tol was exhausted. He was bloody. And he was furious.

They'd done everything they could to keep the Supernal from reclaiming his power. He'd done everything he could to make Addy the Fount. Neither one of those plans had worked out.

Everything was going to shite.

No, he told himself. He could salvage this disaster. He *would* salvage it.

On the other side of the deck, Addy and Jaxon were fighting the general, who seemed to have also grown stronger. Her limp was gone. The blood streaming from her temple and leg had disappeared.

Tol delved into that endless reservoir of power that Olivia had unearthed. It didn't belong to him—not yet—but he could sense its vastness and borrow strength from it.

He and Olivia met in that mental space he hated and resented, because it should be a place that belonged to him and Addy.

Except now, because of what Olivia had done, he was going to lose Addy.

Not now, he told himself.

Tol and Olivia struck out at the Supernal with invisible hands. The Supernal roared as a jagged slice opened across his chest. Instead of blood, thick, oily Source poured out.

The Supernal hissed. He was looking less and less human with each passing second. He had grown to the point that he was easily twice the size of even the largest Forsaken. The sight of his physical body expanding wasn't half as terrible as the way his strength grew with each passing second.

There was a burst of heat, and then electricity was crackling on the Supernal's open palm.

The Supernal threw the jagged splinters of electricity at Tol. Tol dove to the side, but the electricity changed course and came after him.

Another section of the deck peeled back. A jagged edge of the metal bit into Tol's calf as he tried to avoid the crackling shards of lightning.

It was Olivia who lassoed the ball of electricity and yanked it back. She hurled it into the Supernal's chest, where it sizzled and burned into the being's flesh. The Supernal's back bowed. His blue Haze flickered.

The Supernal roared, and the electricity vanished. The gaping wound that was spilling Source began to close up. The Supernal wasn't whole, though. He was weaker than he'd been.

This was their chance.

Hit him with everything you've got, Tol thought.

Tol felt Olivia's strain. He felt his own mind shrieking in protest. Blood and Source pulsed through his brain, blocking out every other sense. There was nothing else except for them and the Supernal. Power crackled between them.

With each burst of magic, the ground beneath their feet grew less stable, but the Supernal also became weaker. Little by little, they were wearing him down.

And yet, every blow to the Supernal took something away from them, too. Tol could feel their strength depleting. Their strikes became less powerful. They were reaching their combined limit.

"Hey, asshole. Why don't you give someone else a chance?"

Addy. She threw a sheet of metal like a Frisbee, which sliced a line across the Supernal's throat. Source gushed from the wound.

Tol went down on his knees, gulping in magic-heated air. The general was down. There was a deep slash across her stomach that Tol was pretty sure she wasn't recovering from any time soon.

And now, Addy was here. The Supernal didn't stand a chance.

"You reek of the Chosen," the Supernal said, turning his attention on Addy.

"Thank you," Addy replied, throwing another chunk of metal at the Supernal, "but it's a little late for flattery."

Tol couldn't help but grin before pulling himself back inside his mind. He gathered his strength, letting it intertwine with Olivia's until they had a tight knot of magic held between their minds.

This was it. Together, they were strong enough to rid the worlds of this evil.

Tol poured more and more of himself into the ball of magical energy in his mind until he had nothing left to give. Olivia was doing the same. He knew it would be enough to bring the Supernal down. It would have to be.

They held the growing ball of power between them. It was as hot as lava and as vast as a mountain. Half of it was linked to Olivia, and the other half to Tol. They'd have to release it at the same moment, otherwise it would fall apart.

Addy was keeping the Supernal busy. She threw things as she taunted him, giving Tol and Olivia the time they needed. She was leading the Supernal away from them.

The Supernal was leaking Source, and he was slowly shrinking back to the size he'd been as a mortal.

"You're stronger than I guessed." The Supernal exhaled noisily as Addy sliced his cheek with her garden shears. More Source spilled out. "I suppose I shouldn't be surprised, since you are mine more than any other Forsaken."

Tol blocked out the Supernal's words before he had to deal with who—what—that thing was to Addy. He'd be able to process all of that later. Right now, he had one job. He couldn't fail.

Tol drained every last ounce of his strength into the weapon he and Olivia had created. His knees started to buckle, but he clung to his half of the magic.

The power was unstable. It shivered and shuddered as Tol and Olivia worked to pull it free from their own minds and turn it into something tangible. Neither of them had anything left for a second attempt.

He wasn't going to let their weapon fail. He wouldn't fail his people.

ADDY

Addy and the Supernal circled each other. She really didn't appreciate having a nigh-invincible enemy.

If the Supernal snapped her neck, she wasn't going to recover. That put her at a serious disadvantage against her opponent.

But as she continued to mark the Supernal with her garden shears, Addy realized he was weakening. Slowly, but surely.

It occurred to her that the Source was the Supernal's lifeblood. If she drained enough of it, she'd kill him. It was just like spilling any other enemy's blood.

That was her theory, anyway.

Every ounce of pain she caused the Supernal…every drop of Source…was a victory. She wanted to make this creature scream. She wanted to make him bleed.

Addy wouldn't stop until the Supernal was broken. She wouldn't stop until he'd gotten what he deserved.

That thought was enough to keep Addy fighting long after her energy was spent.

Tol and Livy were working up to something big. She wasn't exactly sure what, since they were both just standing motionless with their eyes glazed over, but she could feel the growing intensity of their power.

"Perhaps you have too much of your mother's will in you to be useful to me, after all," the Supernal mused, blocking Addy's next strike with a wall of blue flame. When Addy got close enough to cut him, the flames burned her.

Addy staggered back. Pain welled inside her, but it was nothing compared to her fury. The beast inside her was awake. And it was hungry.

"If you ever harnessed that strength, you might be a real challenge to me," the Supernal said. "And since you insist on opposing me, I'll have to destroy you."

"You're welcome to try." Addy circled around for yet another attempt.

A somewhat regretful look passed over the Supernal's glowing blue face. "As you wish, my child."

Addy gagged on those words, *my child*, coming from his mouth.

"I'm nothing to you," she spat. "*You* are nothing. You're just a dried up wanna-be." She sneered up at the creature. "You're pathetic."

A jagged bolt of electricity burst onto the Supernal's raised palm. Addy felt the incredible amount of strength that was needed to create it. It felt like she was in a pressurized container, and someone was ratcheting up the crank. Her ears popped.

The crackle and heat of the Supernal's magic kept her from getting any closer. Addy hadn't realized until this moment how much he had been holding back.

For the first time since this fight began, Addy felt afraid.

Addy curled her left hand. Her broken fingers thrummed with pain. She could almost sense the magic in her ring again. Maybe she could somehow create a portal to attack him from behind while he was still doing whatever he was doing.

The Supernal might be unlike any enemy she'd ever faced, but Addy had never lost a fight.

She wasn't going to start now.

Addy glanced up from her ring, which was glowing but hadn't yet produced the smoke that came with the portal's formation. She took an involuntary step back when she saw the Supernal had a full lightning bolt clutched in his hand. It crackled and glowed white-blue. There was so much power in the air that Addy couldn't breathe.

She could sense the Supernal was pouring every ounce of his strength into this lightning bolt.

Addy started to back away. There was nothing else she could do. Not even her garden shears, which had never failed her before, could help her now.

She kept moving until her heel came up against the beam that marked the edge of the ship. There was nowhere else for her to go.

"Goodbye, first descendant," the Supernal called to her. His voice echoed like he was speaking into a megaphone. "It is time for you to die."

TOL

Tol was concentrating so hard on his half of the magical weapon that the Supernal's words didn't at first register in his mind.

"And since you insist on opposing me, I'll have to destroy you."

Tol's attention jerked to the outside world. He felt the ball of power wobble dangerously in his mental grasp. He saw the Supernal, who was holding a bolt of blue lightning in both of his hands. Electricity passed up and down the bolt and into the Supernal's skin, but he didn't seem to notice. The whole of his attention was focused on the tiny woman still backing away from him.

Addy.

"Goodbye, first descendant."

The lightning bolt crackled.

"It is time for you to die."

Time slowed for Tol. It wasn't like before, when Olivia magically froze all of them.

It was the kind of slowing when a pinnacle moment had come. Tol's mind cleared. He saw the choice before him. He and Olivia were ready to strike. If they coordinated and put the whole of themselves into the effort, they could kill the Supernal. But they wouldn't be able to do it before the Supernal killed Addy.

Olivia was so intent on picking up the slack from Tol's diverted attention that she wasn't aware of anything else. She didn't know what was going on between Addy and the Supernal.

The Supernal raised the lightning bolt over his head. He aimed, like he was readying a spear, only an infinitely more dangerous one.

Tol's mind was made up.

He released his hold on the magic, feeling it splinter and shatter in his mind. It didn't matter anymore.

He ran.

The Supernal released the lightning bolt. Tol threw Addy to the side, out of the lightning's path. Tol recovered his balance and turned to face the Supernal.

The jagged end of the lightning bolt pierced his chest.

The pain was indescribable. And then, there was nothing.

✳ ✳ ✳

Tol knew he was abandoning people who needed him. He also knew he'd made the only decision he could ever make. In the end, it had been all about love.

Addy.

She was his last thought as darkness closed around him. He fell.

CHAPTER 52

OLIVIA

One moment, Olivia was holding up her half of a magical energy that would destroy the greatest threat to her people. The next moment, she was holding the ragged edges of what amounted to a pile of nothing.

Tol had just abandoned her. And they'd been so close.

Olivia drew herself out of the deep concentration she'd needed to keep hold of the power. That's when she heard Addy scream.

It was a sound unlike any Olivia had ever heard. It was the kind of scream that would haunt her dreams for an eternity.

Olivia saw the lightning bolt strike Tol's heart. She felt the impact of it in her own mind. The pain was so horrible she felt like she was dying, too.

It wasn't just the physical agony that was tearing her apart.

The part of her mind where she had become accustomed to sensing Tol's consciousness was gone.

Tol's body fell backward, but Olivia could sense his mind was already lost. The beams at the ship's edge weren't enough to stop his momentum.

He disappeared over the side of the ship.

Addy's ring flashed. Wisps of blue smoke curled around her as she dove off the ship.

Icicles were stabbing through Olivia's brain, and she could barely keep her vision from flickering out. She pulled the fragmented shards of her power back to her. Desperate. Dying.

She couldn't stop time…she was too far gone for that. But she slowed it.

Olivia forced her legs to move. She jumped over cracks in the ship's deck. There was a terrible groaning as the ship stretched, and the deck bowed under her. The helicopter hovering just overhead made a strange sound as the blades turned in slow motion.

Olivia ran to the side of the ship and looked over. She saw Addy falling at an exaggeratedly slow speed as her hands stretched out for Tol's lifeless body. The smoking wisps were starting to form a portal, but it wouldn't be complete before they hit the water.

From this height, the water would give them as much cushion as concrete.

Olivia infused the portal with every ounce of her remaining power. She made it speed up to double time, and then triple. A void opened up. Olivia's sight wavered, but she held on. She had failed her sister in every other way. She wouldn't fail in this.

Olivia teetered on the edge of unconsciousness, but she pressed on until the portal was complete. She used the last of her strength to return time to its normal speed.

And then, she let the darkness take her.

CHAPTER 53

ERIKIR

Erikir felt how much power was in the bolt of lightning that struck Tol's heart. He knew if the Chosen prince wasn't already dead, he would be soon. That meant that Erikir was now the only legitimate heir to the Magnantius throne.

The thought didn't bring him pleasure, as it once would have. Instead, it filled him with terror.

Tol and Olivia's telepathic connection had grown infinitely stronger since she accepted the Celestial's powers and chose to remain the Fount. What would Tol's death do to her?

His people needed her. *He* needed her.

Where was Olivia?

His heart went into his throat when he saw her limp body wedged against the ship's railing. If the deck tilted any more, she would be tossed right over the side.

There was a flash of blue. Erikir saw the Supernal, weakened from his attack on Tol, crawl to the general's unmoving body. The Supernal wrapped an arm around her waist. His fading blue light wavered. Then, both of them just…disappeared. There was no blue smoke to indicate they had been killed. They were just gone.

Erikir didn't give them another thought. He scrambled, climbed, fell, and got back up again as he crossed the deck to Olivia.

Please. Please. Please.

The gods had never cared about what Erikir wanted or needed. But he'd never wanted or needed anything as badly as this.

Please let her be alright. Let her live.

Olivia's head lolled to the side. Erikir couldn't tell if she was breathing.

He couldn't afford to lose himself to panic right now. All that mattered was getting her off this ship. He had to save her.

Hang on, Olivia.

He gathered her into his arms and staggered to his feet. She felt so light. So fragile.

Erikir's heart tripped and stumbled over itself.

What was left of the vessel's stern tipped up even higher. Erikir caught sight of the churning waves below. A whirlpool had formed from the part of the ship that was already submerged. It was trying to suction down the rest.

The chopper hovered just overhead. Jaxon was lowering a heavy metal chain out the open door until it dangled above Erikir. The ship lurched. Erikir was thrown forward. His arms were around Olivia, so he had no way to break their fall.

His foot caught on the railing at the last second. The toe of his sneaker was all that kept him and Olivia from being thrown into the swirling, frothing water far below. A ragged breath stuttered out of him. Even the smallest movement might be enough to send them plummeting to their deaths.

Something hard tapped Erikir's head. He glanced up to see the end of the chain dangling above him.

Erikir took one hand off Olivia to grab hold of the chain. He could barely grasp it in his sweating palm, let alone pull both of them up with it.

Erikir wound the chain around himself in a way he hoped would hold his weight when his grip faltered.

The ship continued to shimmy and heave. The giant radar tower started to fall. It was coming straight for them, and it was too enormous to avoid.

Erikir grasped the chain with one hand and wrapped the other around Olivia's waist. Then, trusting in the Forsaken man on the other end…and the mortal in the pilot's seat…he jumped over the side of the ship.

He heard the crash of the radar tower as it bowled over the deck's cracked remains.

Erikir tightened his hold on Olivia. He felt a moment of weightlessness before the chain went taut. The ship fell away below them.

Then, they were flying.

THE END

* * *

Because reviews are so important for a book to be successful, please consider leaving a brief review on your favorite retailer if you enjoyed *The Forsaken's Choice*. Many thanks!

* * *

Sign up for Stephanie Fazio's e-Newsletter to learn about upcoming books at:
https://StephanieFazio.com/subscribe/

Acknowledgements

I absolutely loved writing this series, and all of the incredible people on my team made the entire process such a pleasure.

To my editor, Ellen Schaeffer. Thank you for being amazing!

To Keith Tarrier, for making such gorgeous covers that continue to exceed all expectations. Thank you also to Bob Brodsky, Rhoda Schneider, and the rest of my ARC team. Your advice, support, and encouragement are invaluable.

To Mom and Dad, for your endless support and advice (even when I think I don't want it). Thanks for always believing in me.

Thanks to Two Steps From Hell and Thomas Bergersen for your fantastic music. This book would never have been finished without you.

To my fantastic readers. Thanks for making what I do matter!

And to Andrew. For being my very own prince charming.

About the Author:

Stephanie Fazio is a fantasy author. She grew up in Syracuse, New York, and prior to writing full time, she worked in the fields of journalism, secondary education, and higher education. She has an undergraduate degree in English from Colgate University and a Master's degree in Reading, Writing, and Literacy from the University of Pennsylvania. Stephanie lives in Austin with her husband and crazy rescue dog. When she isn't writing, she's getting lost in parks, hosting taco nights, or ironically and miserably losing at word games, but having fun while she does it.

Connect with Stephanie Fazio:

Visit her Website: https://www.StephanieFazio.com
Sign up for her newsletter: https://StephanieFazio.com/subscribe/

Discover other books by Stephanie Fazio

Bisecter Series

StephanieFazio.com

www.ingramcontent.com/pod-product-compliance
Lightning Source LLC
Chambersburg PA
CBHW051628180726
48284CB00006B/1645